'A good novel about that extraordinary person, the ordinary soldier . . . always readable and often moving' Monica Dickens

The Eighth Champion of Christendom is the first in a trilogy of novels about World War II, originally published in 1945 to remarkable critical acclaim.

Each title carries the distinction – rare in any novels of World War II or any other war – of being written almost 'contemporaneously with the action. All convey the immediacy of journalism as well as the more profound qualities the reviews proclaim.

'A good story told with considerable gusto' *The Sunday Times*

The Eighth Champion of Christendom

Edith Pargeter

HEADLINE

Copyright © 1945 by Edith Pargeter

First published in 1945
by William Heinemann Ltd

First published in paperback in 1990
by HEADLINE BOOK PUBLISHING PLC

ISBN 0 7472 3290 3

Printed and bound in Great Britain by
Collins, Glasgow

HEADLINE BOOK PUBLISHING PLC
Headline House
79 Great Titchfield Street
London W1P 7FN

"Besides, it's so obvious that someone has to do something about it, however inexpertly. So back we come to the charge again, without even the stimulus of self-admiration to buoy us up. We despise our own muddled efforts, but we go on making them.

"Once, when I was very young, I believed in all the traditional English virtues. But now I've lost all the legends long ago, and being a champion of Christendom without them is a dreary business."

"SHE GOES TO WAR"

CONTENTS

PART ONE

ENGLAND, 1939

"Of late years the English have given up
the practice of starting wars; but they
have usually finished them."
CASSANDRA: *The English at War*.

I

WHEN the night fell on September 1st, 1939, that was more
than an ordinary falling. The shape of the world had
changed since morning, and the shape of the approaching night
was not after the fashion of the other nights of that summer. It
was stiller and more ponderous, more like the clenching of a
hand than the folding of a tired wing. It came down upon the
world after the harvest heat as the lid of a coffin closes. It
was a symbolic twilight, not the twilight of gods, but the twilight of men. It found and fed upon the little hopes of little
people, and showed them that present peace was a mirage, and
future existence a matter of precarious chance, that Warsaw
burned and Danzig was a shambles, and the colours of fire and
blood in the sunset over London had become omens of a .like
vulnerability. They listened to the news bulletins in cottages
and canteens and flats and pubs, and heard how Polish working men and women, not unlike themselves, were being machine-
gunned in their own fields and streets. They said it was a
damned shame, but feeling as yet little of the shame and nothing
of the damnation.

And while the twilight of liberty fell, the small details of life
went on, unrealising. Children came home to bed from the
apple-harvesting, and buses brought back from overtime cargoes
of clay-smeared colliers, and women hung over backyard fences
gossiping with their neighbours; and all was as before in a
world in which all was changing and passing away. Out of the
general obscurity neither saviours nor destroyers had yet
emerged, and the protagonists of this black crusade were still
unsifted, small from great. The formidable mould of the future
shrouded both devils and archangels, so that they went about
unfashioned and unrecognisable among their fellow-men. At this
time Vidkun Quisling was still an unimportant Norwegian
politician, Wavell a scarcely-known name, Charles de Gaulle

1

one of a hundred French generals, and undistinguishable, except by a handful of experts, from the ninety and nine. And at this time Jim Benison was still under-foreman of a road gang, and played dominoes every Friday evening in the snuggery of the "Clay Pigeon" at Morwen Hoe on the Sheel, in the county of Midshire, in the heart of England.

2

They always had the nine o'clock news bulletin on in the bar at the "Clay Pigeon", but it wasn't always possible to hear it from the snuggery. They didn't always want to hear it; the old men could be solemn over that sort of thing in the bar if they wanted to, but the young men liked to shut themselves in and be cosy over something less tedious. But to-night Clye got up and opened the door, and Delia, moving about with glasses, trod soft and steadily, and the burden of the news came in. Jim was listening with one ear, and for the dividing of his mind had played his double-five before he was aware of it, and given away an eight and his last chance of the club handicap. Lamenting the mischief, but abstractedly, he missed something of the first day's fighting in Poland.

Delia said: "Ssh!" and Clye said: "Shut up, will you!" And he shut up, and listened the bulletin out. It was pretty dirty. Fancy, after all that pretence of good intentions, crashing over the frontier of a peaceful country on the dot of the hour, like that, to a deliberate plan. What sort of people were they? He'd never wondered much about foreigners; he supposed they were different from English people, but he found it odd that they should not, after all, behave in much the same way. It didn't occur to him to try and imagine how it must feel to be invaded like that, without any warning, just tanks boring their way suddenly ahead into England with guns blazing away at everybody and everything. But that was daft; they couldn't do it with England even if they wanted to; as why should they, for there was nothing they and England had to fight about, such as this here free city, this Danzig they were squabbling about with Poland. But they couldn't do it, anyhow, not with England. There was water all round England.

"It's a damn' shame," said Delia, grinding her high heel into the rug and swirling her short skirt with a scented breeze as she turned to pick up the tray. "It hadn't ought to be

2

allowed, that's what I say. They ought to stop it. All this fighting and killing people! Why don't they give the man what he wants, for goodness sake, and keep him quiet?"

"Because he wants the earth," said Clye grimly, "and if he had it, he still wouldn't be satisfied. He'd start having blasted territorial claims on heaven and hell."

But Clye had a bee in his bonnet, as everybody knew, and talked about nationalisation on a Socialist plan, and would have liked the Reds to win in Spain; so you couldn't expect him to see anything reasonable or good on the other side. Nobody minded him. He was all right. But people in Morwen Hoe didn't go cracked about ideas, and were suspicious of those who did. What difference was there between one fanaticism and the next?

"Anyhow we tried it long enough, didn't we?" said Tommy Goolden, rolling a cigarette. "It didn't work. Seems to me we'll have to try the other tack this time."

"Don't seem in any hurry about it," said Clye. "Not a word said yet about declaring war."

Jim hadn't thought about that. It surely wasn't a thing to go into in a hurry. It was a bit of a shock to realise that it might involve England at all. Why should it? He couldn't quite see. It was hard luck on the Poles, of course, but at that distance how could you be sure that they weren't partly responsible for the whole business? And anyhow, it was all about a town miles away on the Baltic, nowhere near England or anything English. Not that a chap wanted particularly to steer clear of other people's troubles, but he couldn't feel very strongly about an issue so distant and so imperfectly understood.

Having no opinion, or none clear enough to be voiced, he said nothing. Somebody else would take Clye on; somebody always did. Jim emptied his pint, and let Tommy fill it up again, and was silent, watching the stirring of the smoke cruise back and forth in the upper air as the door opened and closed, and the circle of faces sharp-boned in the steep descending light, and Delia's rolled curls, coloured like sheaves of ripe red wheat, dancing in time to her springing step as she came and went with her tray and her smiles and her illuminating beauty. Her walk made of the red quarries of the bar floor an expanse of strong, deep turf, and she passed him in a gust of carnation-scented air.

"What, just for a tuppenny-ha'penny town nobody's ever

3

heard of?" Sam Reddin said, and laughed. "You can't tell me the government are such bloody fools as to go to war for that."

"Can't tell you nothing, anyhow," said Clye sourly. "You know it backwards."

And that was true enough, however many bees Clye had in his bonnet. Sam Reddin was in the know about everything, according to his own tale; and the more pints he put away, the further did his influence stretch, till by the end of the evening it would have been as much as the Prime Minister's job was worth to declare war without first consulting Sam. Jim, who kept his own mouth shut even upon what he thought, much more upon what he knew, had always a lingering desire to close Reddin's for him. Some day he'd do it, too, if the beggar didn't keep his hands off Delia. Every time she set down the pint pot refilled in front of him, he had to be squeezing her elbow, or touching the soft underneath of her arm as she withdrew it, or somehow being intimate with her. The devil of it was that she didn't seem to see anything offensive in these gestures. They had fallen out over it more than once, and she had told him impatiently not to be daft, that Reddin was all right, that she liked him, that anyhow Jim Benison wasn't her proprietor, and she'd look after her own affairs, thank you very much. The trouble, of course, was that Reddin was good-looking, for all his slicked-back hair and smart-aleck ways; whereas Jim could hardly find himself better than tolerable even when dressed up for church, with his new dark-grey suit and wash-leather gloves. Besides, women went for that self-confident line of talk of his, took him at his own valuation. And yet sometimes Delia Hall had made it pretty plain that she found Jim Benison good enough company.

"Look at it this way," said Reddin, stubbing his finger down upon the table with great finality. "If we do go to war, how're we going to set about it? How're we going to *get* any troops into Poland? There isn't no way in by land, there's Germany and neutral countries in between whichever road you try. And there ain't no way in by sea except through the Baltic. And I s'pose Germany's going to let us run troop transports through there twice a week? I tell you, it can't be done. We'd be crazy if we joined in. It wouldn't do them any good, and it might be the finish of us."

"Who said anything about sending troops to Poland? Germany's got a frontier this side as well, hasn't she?"

4

"Yes, with a bloody great line of fortifications all the way down it."

"Ugh!" said Clye disgustedly, "they wouldn't need them if all the British Army was your sort. A boy with an airgun would be enough."

"Now, look here, Jerry Clye, I'm takin' none o' that talk from you——" And Reddin was on his feet, a big man, and years younger than Clye; ready, thought Jim, to fight to the death as long as there was no prospect of anybody getting hurt.

"What y' goin' to do about it?" asked Clye, coming joyously to his.

Into this promising quarrel Delia sailed grandly, curls and skirts flying. She put a hand on Reddin's shoulder and a hand on Clye's, and had them back in their chairs again in a minute; her tongue, at once vitriolic and persuasive, going nineteen to the dozen.

"Now, then! Now, then! I'm surprised, grown men being so childish. Why, if either of you had the wits you were born with, you'd be able to find something better to do than squabble at a time like this."

They took it like lambs; they were all under Delia's thumb. She came over to where Jim was sitting, and drew a chair close to his. "Like a couple of damn'-fool kids! I've got no patience with 'em!" Her shoulders lifted and shook. "If it was me, I'd let 'em knock each other's blocks off, but Joe, he doesn't like to see 'em falling out." She leaned her elbows upon the table, and looked at him long and steadily with her dark blue eyes. "Jim, d'you reckon we *shall* go to war?"

"I wish I knew!" he said cheerfully.

"I don't know as I ever thought about it much before. I mean you *don't*, do you? War, and that! I mean, it doesn't seem to be anything to do with people like us. But Mr. Clye was saying we've given these Poles guarantees, or something. He says we can't do other than join in now."

"That's what I was thinking," said Tommy Goolden, gazing into his empty pint pot. "We *did* give 'em guarantees. If we hadn't, I daresay they'd have fought just the same, but you can't be sure, they might have given in. So that way, if you see what I mean, we're partly responsible. I don't see how we can back out now. You can't go back on what you've said." And he said this with satisfaction, so that Jim, who believed he knew his Tommy through and through, was moved to take a long and critical look at him, and wonder why he should

5

sound so pleased about it. A nice lad, full of the devil till he married the Johnson girl at twenty-one, and then she had him where she wanted him, and pretty soon quietened him down; and the baby had finished the job, turning him into a staid young father who only popped in at the "Clay Pigeon" once or twice a week, and usually left well before closing time. Not much of the devil left in him these days, but somewhere a spark of perversity survived, it seemed. "I tell you what!" he said abruptly. "If we do join in, I'm off."

Delia's big eyes opened to their widest. "Well, I never expected to hear you say a thing like that! And you a family man!"

"There's family men in Poland, too, seems to me. Them Czechs, too, they've got wives and children same as the rest of us. I shouldn't be easy if this all went over and me not in it." He sounded a shade puzzled himself about this, but quite decided. He reached for the white china ash-tray and helped himself to a match, and lit his cigarette with the vehement deliberation which Nance seemed to have put into him in place of the old craziness. "I'm bloody fed up with Hitler, anyway."

The faint blue curls of smoke laced the room, dimming the corners of reality. The world, the known world, the granite world which sat squarely in the middle of small human discords and knew no change—that world itself was dissolving in the dusk outside the curtained cosy windows and the cigarette-fug within. There was going to be war. No doubt but Tommy Goolden was right, for all the complex arguments Reddin was still producing against the probability, over in his corner. Jim didn't know much about war. He'd never thought much about it. The last one had been before his time, or at least he'd been born towards the end of it, too late to notice even the dark-green blinds and the ration cards. He associated it with "Tipperary" and khaki, and mud, from the one or two films he'd seen about it; but mostly he'd avoided it, because the films were inclined to be soppy, and the books dry, and any-how he always suspected they were trying to work on him. He objected to having his withers wrung; objected, anyhow, to these clever beggars thinking they could play on him like Charlie Kunz played on a piano. He tried to think what it would be like, this thing Tommy wanted to be in; but the prospect before his mind's eye remained uncompromisingly blank. Anyhow, the "England, home and beauty" line was played out this time. This was all on behalf of Poland. And yet, suppose there hadn't been water all round Britain? Supposing it had been over our borders that the heavy tanks had come nosing, early this very morning? What about England, home and beauty then? Delia's beauty—that big, golden, vigorous loveliness. What about Tommy's Nance, and Clye's Mary, and any of the girls he'd squired around here and there to dances and socials? That red-headed sister of Ben Jones's, and Jane Hayden, and young Imogen Threlfall——

"Well, this won't get the baby washed," remarked Delia with a short sigh. "Time's getting on, boys; are you going to have another one?"

"My shout!" said Jim. "What'll it be, Tommy?"

"Same again. And then I'd better be shoving along, I think."

"The missus'll be fretting," said Delia with a sudden glowing, teasing smile, as she gathered three tankards in one hand. "I'd better rush this order." She went off singing; she hadn't much of a voice, but it was sweet enough, and she had a way of tossing her head as she burst into song, like a fine, high-spirited pony. When she went out the room always seemed smaller and emptier and not quite so cosy.

It wasn't so bad, when you came to think of it, to have a missus waiting at home. Who wouldn't quit the snuggery a little ahead of closing time, if somebody like Delia was sitting by the fire at home? He'd thought about asking her, some time; but there was no hurry; they got along all right as they were, and if she walked out with the landlord's son and he took Imogen Threlfall to the pictures—well, as things were, no one was hurt. There were a lot of things to be thought about before you did so final a thing as getting married. And Jim Benison was a cautious man.

Tommy emptied his tankard and rose. "Well, I'm off. Be seeing you around to-morrow? I'm working till five."

"I was thinking I'd do a bit at the First Aid Post, or something. But I'll be in here some time before Joe closes."

"O.K., we'll play off that game I've been owing you." He waved a hand airily from the door. "See you be good, now."

A gush of sweet twilit air came in through the doorway, across the smoky, half-past-nine fug of the bar, with its accumulated scent of cigarettes and beer and old aromatic woodwork. Joe Goodwin was playing darts with three of his regulars, and Mrs. Joe, with her ample person spread along the edge of the bar, was bossing the general conversation and the game just as she bossed the two maids and the daily woman and all their activities at the "Clay Pigeon". How could poor old Joe get his finishing double with her directing operations in that robust man's voice of hers? He couldn't; he didn't. He put his partner in the madhouse, and that was that, because the air-raid warden was never known to throw for double-top and miss. It was all over bar the shouting, and the drinks, the last of the evening, were on Joe.

"You don't see what I'm getting at!" Sam Reddin's fine bass swelled suddenly into a wave which swamped the lesser noises in the room as it swamped the chapel choir on Sunday mornings. "Now look here! This here pint-pot's England, see, and this here ash-tray's Poland. Now here's how the coastline goes, look you, down here, and all this in between's Germany. Now, with this here Maginot Line along here—so——"

"Stick your mucky finger in your own beer," said Clye, and removed his glass from reach just in time.

"Sorry, I'm sure—my mistake. Well, here you are, then." He drew complicated outlines studded with domino forts and block-houses. The air-raid warden came to his shoulder, grinning, and egged him on to elaborate what was already an eccentric relief map occupying the greater part of the table. "Now, you reckon the Siegfried Line could be turned, up here in the north. All right, how're you going to do it? Go on, let's see you do it. You can't. Nobody can. That's a perishing deadlock, they can't get through to the French, and the French can't get through to them."

"Maginot Line's dryin' up," said the air-raid warden helpfully. "Better have another pint, Sam."

A moistened finger restored the defences of France. The argument went on and on, backwards and forwards over the fortunes of war which had not yet even begun; while somewhere along the road to Cracow a thousand miles away, the war which had begun pursued its methodical course unmindful of them and all their theories: Jim lost the train of sound in a vague, pervading murmur made up of seven or eight conversations, the treble of the piano in the bar, the thump of darts going home as Joe Goodwin and Bert Parkes played round the clock, and the rustling of leaves outside the orange-curtained windows. A pleasant, peaceful, occupied noise like the gossip of a lime tree full of bees.

"Well," said Delia, from the outermost edge of his drowse, "I never thought I'd see you nodding off to sleep with best part of a pint of beer in your hand. Look at you! You'll be pouring it over your shirt in a minute."

"Not me! I can drink beer in my sleep without spilling it."
He looked at her, standing there with her hands on her hips and her extravagantly shod feet wide apart, in an attitude which would have been unlovely in anyone smaller or less self-possessed than she; and she knew that she was being admired, knew she deserved admiration, and smiled at him accordingly. "Coming on the river to-morrow afternoon? We could go down to Beckett's Cove and take our tea."

"Thought you were going to do a bit at the First Aid Post!" she said, still with that conquering smile.

"Ah, it won't come to anything. Don't let's waste a fine day. How about it, Delia?"

She laughed, seeing him yawn even in this eager moment. "Go on home, you big kid, you, and get some sleep. You can't keep your eyes open."

"Not me, not until you say it's a date."

"At this rate," she said, "you won't be awake enough to know me when you see me. Well, all right, then, but if it rains, it's off. Where'll I see you?"

"By the ferry, three o'clock sharp. O.K.?"

"O.K., but you got to get me back by six, remember." The abrupt voice of Mrs. Goodwin called her from the bar, and she fled, leaving behind her on the air a waft of carnation scent and the warm memory of an intimate smile.

Jim finished his beer in a haze of contentment. It wasn't as if he wouldn't have filled sandbags dutifully enough, yes, all afternoon and all evening too, if there'd been any need. But it wouldn't happen. They'd see in a day or two. It would all blow over, like it had always done before, without any fireworks. Bad luck on Poland, he supposed, but after all he knew next to nothing about the quarrel, or who was in the right and who in the wrong, and it hadn't really got anything to *do* with him. Why should he miss a good September afternoon on the river with Delia, just because a lot of old women had got the wind up? No, not on your life. Time enough for needless worry when you're old. Time enough——

"Time, gents, time, please! Ten o'clock just striking. Drink up! Time!"

The road from the "Clay Pigeon" ran down through a corner of the village, and on into the main road, which even at night was dusty with cars; but Jim never went home that way. There was a lane turning aside from Goodwin's, along the lilac hedge of the vicarage garden and past the fish-and-chip shop, where a faded sign slung on the hingeless gate proclaimed inaccurately: "Hot Peas To-night". From this lane a field path wandered away through a meadow and an oat-field, slanting down and down towards the silver and green Sheel coiled among its pollard willows. Beyond the river, the rolling land went up in a patchwork of coloured crops, wheat and barley and potato, greenish-fawn of stubble and crimson of beet; and beyond that again the folded hills, dark blue and hazy with mist, lay down together and slept. Always, when Jim came to the rim of this painted bowl by daylight, he had to pause and sit down on the lopsided stile for a moment, and take in the whole of it in silence, much as an ear of wheat takes in the sun. He did not know he was looking at England. He did not consider for a moment that he was in love with her. The Sheel valley was to him a nice-looking bit of country, not bad to work in, better to play in. Sitting there with his heels hooked on the bottom bar of the stile, and a straw between his teeth, he drew from the serenity of it vague, contented thoughts. It might not be such a bad life, after all, the land. Sometimes it dawned on a chap that there was something to it. Fancy being able to point to your own wheat, with ears among it standing six feet high. Fancy turning up your own soil, heavy and clean along the ploughshare, behind big ebony horses like Fred Blossom's. Jim knew more about tractors than horses, but he got on with them fine in casual field friendships, and he was dead sure he could work with them as deftly as most men. In the enthusiasm of the moment, he had often wished he had taken to the land. On winter mornings he was not so sure.

But to-night the sun was long gone, it was already more than half dark. All the browns were umber, all the greens olive, all the blues ultramarine. The distant hills hugged one another under a blanket of haze, but the upper air was clear with that dazzling clarity which seems to utter a note of thin and far-off music, like a smitten glass; a note of stillness, and tension, and change. The first trumpet of winter was in it, with summer not yet gone. The first foreboding of frost was in it, with the high green of the leaves scarcely soiled, and frost a month away.

Jim drew in with the chilling air that promise and that threat. He thought of the sharp nights ahead, and the game preserves round Sheel Park, and the new places he had selected last year for this year's snares. Better be having a walk round that way pretty soon. Maybe take the dog on Sunday. The little whippet bitch knew enough to keep close to his heels by daylight, and act as if she didn't know what a rabbit was, unless he set her on. Deeper than the sea, she was. Sharper-witted by far than that lurcher of Bob Freebourne's that got shot last year, and he was a good dog in his day. Should be plenty of sport this season, thought Jim, with an extra keeper on the place as well as Brady. He didn't like his fun made too easy.

Halfway down the meadow, the hedge on his right hand gave place to the lichen stones of the churchyard wall, with bushes and yews leaning over, and the squat shape of the church tower, almost as old as the Conquest, looked out from the nest of trees down the darkening valley. A girl was sitting on the wall, drumming with the trodden heels of her sand-shoes against the green seams of sand and moss where once mortar had been. A Sealyham sat in the crook of her arm, where she had lifted him, and nuzzled her neck and chin with a wet and whiskery nose.

"Hullo, goblin!" said Jim.

"Hullo, ghost!" she said.

She was eighteen, really, but she didn't look it, except perhaps on Sundays, when she was all dressed up for church. All the rest of the week she wore no hat on her short dark hair, and no stockings on her brown, bramble-marked legs. She was small, dark by nature and darker with sunburn, and her eyes, which should have been black as sloes, broke all the rules by being an exceedingly deep and brilliant blue. She was in many ways a very deceptive person. She could pass for slim, but she wasn't, she was on the plump side, if anything; he had had her in his arms more than once, and he knew. She could make you think her demure and shy, but she wasn't, she was the most incalculable little vixen who ever ran wild in the woods of Sheel. She could seem trusting and biddable, but she wasn't, she was the last word in perversity. Once, long ago, when he was eleven and she was five, he had been blessed with the task of seeing her safely to school and back twice a day, so no one could tell him anything about managing Imogen. She had broken away, and he had chased her, she had dawdled and he had dragged her, she had sat down under the hedge and

11

refused to move, and he had smacked her, and she, more often than not, had bitten or pinched him in return. Sometimes she had even sworn at him with her full, fawn's lips, surprising oaths picked up goodness knew where. But all, apparently, by way of passing the time and beguiling the journey, for he had never known her to cry, and always in the end she had voluntarily taken his hand and ended the walk cheerfully enough and at his pace, bearing no malice and expecting him to bear none. Now that she was eighteen he had reminded her, sometimes, of those days, teasing her with tales of her dubious promise at five years old. But Imogen was never drawn; she smiled and seemed to listen, but there was never anything in her face to show that she remembered or believed that she had been that aggravating little person.

"Have a dewberry!" she invited, spreading her linen skirt, which was half-full, and smeared with stains. The shape of her mouth was distorted with juice-marks, and the tips of her fingers were purple. The Sealyham yawned, and rubbed his eyes against her sleeve. "All from inside the wall here," she said. "Why go further!"

Jim left the path, and came, through stubble that crunched and young new grasses that hissed, to the wall beside her. Leaning upon it, he was nearly as tall as she, their eyes were almost on a level. He ate dewberries, thoughtfully, turning them in his fingers to make doubly sure they were clear of grubs.

"What are you doing out so late? Little girls should be in bed by this time."

"Teach your grandmother!" she said, but without indignation, as if he was only allowed by a generous fiction to make believe that he had known her at an age other than eighteen.

Leaning against her brown, scarred knee, he said thoughtfully: "I haven't seen you for a long time. Where've you been hiding?"

"Nowhere. You haven't looked for me, that's all. Been too busy with that Delia Hall, I expect, to notice anyone else." She said this with a sister's disdain, rather than a sweetheart's chagrin, though she had been, after her fashion, a sweetheart of his for three years, almost ever since she had left school. "What's the attraction?" she asked, licking juicy fingers. "Free beer? I can't think of anything else it can be."

He laughed and agreed. After all, he was not tied to Delia's red-gold hair. They understood each other perfectly.

"I'm sorry," said Imogen, regarding him suddenly with the

full blazing blue of her disconcerting eyes, "we don't sell beer. But we could do you a very nice line in graves."

She said that sort of thing without thinking, but thought wouldn't have stopped her. A queer kid she was, perhaps through being raised in the churchyard, so to speak, for the verger's cottage was tucked under the lee of the church, and all the windows on one side of it looked out among the graves. She had made use of the place as a playground all her life, and it was hardly surprising that she could feel no proper awe of it now.

"I ought to go in," she said, swinging one leg over the wall. "I only came out to give Jiggs a bit of a breather, really. He hasn't had his run this afternoon. I've been making black-out curtains all day."

"Poor old Jiggs!" The Sealyham, hearing his name, flapped his moist tongue abstractedly in the direction of Jim's face. "Couldn't you leave off for half an hour to give him his run?"

"I could have, but I don't like leaving things half-done. Besides, there's going to be a lot of jobs wanting doing, if it happens. I think it will happen, don't you?" She gathered the folds of her skirt in one hand, and eased herself down from the wall into the long grass on the other side. "There's another lot of gas masks to be fitted together, and they're getting some special ones for babies now. We've got to do the black-out curtains for the First Aid Post, too, some time. What are you going to do?"

"I don't know. It hasn't happened yet." He wondered what she expected him to say to a point-blank question like that. But then, she always supposed that other people would choose their courses at a glance, as she chose hers. "I'm waiting to see what does turn up, before I go jumping ahead. As likely as not it'll all be over in a few days, and no harm done."

"What a hope!" she said, definite as ever.

"Why should I do anything about it, anyhow? It's nothing to do with me. I'm here to be told what to do. That's what I pay the government for, isn't it?"

Imogen said, quite simply: "You're an awful liar, Jim Benison. You know jolly well you don't mean a word of that. You're just like the rest, you like to have your own way and pretend it's all from a sense of duty. Just like Dad. He says he's going."

"Going?" said Jim blankly. "Going where?"

"Going. Joining up. Going wherever they do go—wherever they send him, I suppose." She took fire at his incredulous smile, and demanded sharply: "Well, what's so funny about that?"

"Nothing. Only—well, damn it, it hasn't even happened yet, and there's a lot of fellows ready and willing to go, without men of your dad's age jumping to get ahead of them. He must be nearer fifty than forty."

"Well, that's not exactly decrepit," she flashed. The blue of her eyes assailing him was like the blue of lance-heads in the dusk. "He'll be a sight more use than you and your sort," she said provocatively. "He's been a soldier, and knows about guns and tanks and things, and he's a jolly good shot. And anyhow, he has got enough gumption to keep himself clean and tidy without a woman to do it for him—and that's more than you have. Where would you be without your mother to sew buttons on for you, and wash your shirts, and boil your shaving-water? I bet she even cleans your shoes."

Fading into the dark, she laughed, a neat, derisive sound. Jim was the more nettled because his mother, as it happened, did clean his shoes. It wasn't as if he wanted her to, or asked her to. She just did it, and that was that; but he was damned if Imogen Threlfall should toss the chance truth at him over the churchyard wall and get away with it.

"You little devil!" he said, and was over the wall and after her so quickly that fleet as she was, and bewilderingly as the delighted Sealyham danced between them, she had no chance to elude him. Under the beeches, in the narrow paths between the graves, his arms took her and lifted her bodily about in mid-air, so that she came breast to breast with him, her hands braced to thrust him away. Out of the crumpled linen skirt the dewberries spilled between them into the grass. She laughed, soundlessly but for the quickening of her breath, and twisted this way and that in his arms until he turned her shoulders squarely back against the beech-trunk, and pinned her there by the arms, leaning upon her so that she could not even trample his toes with her small, soft-shod feet, or lift her knee into his stomach. The darkness under the leaves was olive-green; her face glowed in it, star-like, and her eyes were alert and wild with mischief. If he so much as shifted his hold of her she would be away. He knew her tricks; there was no end to them.

"Now, then!" he said, watching her warily. The rustling of

the leaves grew quiet as they were still. "Now, what have you got to say for yourself?"

"Now, look here, Jim Benison . . ."

He was looking; closely, and closer, so that the lines of her face faded into a dim, unfocused light, and her wide eyes dilated into blue worlds, and her mouth, shaken with laughter and temper, was of the colour and texture of poppies in full bloom. She grew very quiet, without quite knowing why. She knew he was going to kiss her, and she could have stopped him if she had liked, but she simply waited for the moment with a sort of bemused curiosity. So he kissed her without hindrance.

He had never done it before; he wondered what had impelled him to do it now. She was growing up, certainly. Some day some fellow would court her in earnest, but not Jim Benison. Not that she'd do anything but laugh at him if he did. And yet that momentary lingering softness of her mouth, quite still and easy under his, had a pleasantly disturbing quality. She wouldn't have taken it like that if he'd been anyone else, not she; she'd have had his ears off. He supposed Jim Benison didn't matter to her one way or the other. So there was no harm done.

"Well, I hope you're satisfied, you big ape," she said, shaking back her hair. "Now take your hands off me. I'm going in."

But he didn't take his hands off her. He stood there holding her by the wrists, and watching her intently, as if something about her bothered him, worried at his memory and yet stopped short of recollection. "What are you going to do if your dad goes? You can't stop here by yourself."

"I don't want to. I'm going to my Uncle Jack's, at Caldington, and getting a job."

"You mean you're closing the cottage altogether?"

"I mean if he does go, we shall sell up and go for good. What's there to come back for, anyhow?"

"Not much, I suppose," he allowed dubiously. "Just that folks around here all know you, and you've got friends here——"

For he didn't want her to go. The shuddering of the earthquake of change was suddenly perceptible under his feet. Ten minutes ago he hadn't believed in the war, but now he felt the gestures of its hands, casual and uncaring, brushing away like cobwebs the detail of his life. Not for long would it be nothing to do with him.

15

"Most of them will be gone, too," she said, and it was rather as if she had added: "You with the rest."

"Well, I hope you'll get on all right," he said, "but maybe it won't happen, you know, after all. Nothing's come of it so far."

But that was an old argument, and getting threadbare from repetition by now, so that even as he held it up he could see through it. Logic was all very well; nothing had happened yet. But the thing was already there, ominous in the gathering night over the Sheel valley, shaking the ground underfoot, making the immemorial Midland earth insecure, removing neighbour from neighbour and friend from friend. He wanted things to remain the same, he wanted the people he had known all his life to remain stable in their places; but they would go, too, and he with the rest. To-night he could kiss Imogen under the churchyard beeches among the graves, and to-morrow Delia under the shimmering long shade of the backwater willows; but in due time he would be uprooted and swept away with the rest.

"We might hear something definite to-morrow," said Imogen. "I don't honestly want to go, Jim, but after all, nothing will be the same if it does happen, so it doesn't seem to matter if I'm here or in Caldington, does it? Look, I've got to go in now—I'm getting cold."

He took his hands from her slowly. "Good-night, kid. See you on Sunday?"

"I don't know. I might not be out." She receded from him slowly into the darkness across the churchyard, where the invisible cottage was. "Good-night, Jim!" said her voice, floating back very still and small; and she whistled the dog, and she was gone.

He went on down the field towards home, very slowly in the enfolding night. The wave had gone by him, it seemed, and smitten the old man, for to him forty-five was old; it was time to turn and look again at the world, at things as they were and things as they ought to be; and above all at what one ought to do, at what one would have to do. He was twenty-four; this was supposed to be a young man's world, wasn't it?

4

On the morning of Sunday, September the third, he awoke to the insistent and raucous trumpeting of his mother's bantam cock in the yard outside his window; he cursed it drowsily, withdrew his head still further beneath the sheets, and went to sleep again until Sue, the whippet bitch, came scrabbling and bounding onto his chest and nibbling at his hair. Mrs. Benison had already made three attempts to awaken him, but Sue's methods were more successful. He abandoned reluctantly the last shadow of a dream undefined but pleasant, through which Delia floated with bouquets of crystal beer-mugs in her hands, and opened his eyes upon the full daylight of a fine morning, clear, mild and radiant with a pale, hardy sun. He lay watching the apple branches swaying lightly across the white space of the window, and he was filled with a consciousness of well-being which came to him only on Sunday mornings in early autumn. He fended Sue off from his face, and sat up, and seeing how the sun made golden even the roof of the old shed where he kept his bicycle, he was no longer tempted to go to sleep again.

His mother, who had lived with men all her life, brothers and husband and son, had long ago given up expecting rhyme or reason in anything they did, and was consequently never put out of her placid stride by any inconsistencies in those from whom she looked for nothing but inconsistency. A husband in a temper and a son in a hurry were all in the day's work to her. Though Jim, having stayed in bed until a quarter to ten, was disposed rather to blame her for the waste of a good two hours of his day, and though his father was busily coddling a cold he had brought upon himself by going coatless against her advice, she moved between them smiling and undisturbed, supplying their needs and demands with the efficient calm of a nurse ministering to the helpless.

"Where's my paper?" demanded Jim, looking round for the usual accompaniment of his Sunday breakfast.

"Folded up by your plate—the last place you'd ever think of looking for it. And don't get too deep in it, either; I want these things off the table. They've been there an hour and a half already."

"Well, you should wake me up properly, and you wouldn't have breakfast lasting half the day," he said ungraciously.

"I like that. Three times I came up and shook you; *and* you woke up, too—unless you asked me the time in your sleep. Come on, now, get on with your breakfast, while it's eatable."

"The tea's cold," he grumbled next, from behind the pages of the *People*.

17

"Don't exaggerate. It's not as hot as it was half an hour ago, but cold it is not. And I'm not going to make a fresh pot at this hour of the day, so don't you think it."

He stopped listening before the end of this sentence, the exchange being more or less a matter of routine. The news pages he passed by with scarcely a glance; the sports page was his breakfast reading; it went better than anything else with bacon and eggs, besides being the only part of the news in which he was normally interested. Sue sat beside him as he ate, and pawed and sang to him; it was not her intention that he should be allowed to forget the purpose for which she had got him out of bed.

After breakfast there was another scurry before they finally got away. Shaving was always a business, not to be carried through in a hurry; and after that there was the right tie to be found and adjusted, and other equally vital details to be taken care of. Sunday was a day for looking one's best in Morwen Hoe. Everyone who had a dog would be out walking this morning; every girl who had a boy, every boy who had a girl, would be out walking this afternoon; every family that had new clothes or visitors would be out walking after church or chapel this evening. It was a grand routine, not to be varied except for rain or snow; and Jim, who during the week was perfectly willing to be nondescript, conformed to the accepted local rule as if by a natural instinct. Besides, he might be passing Rose Hazlitt's mother's, and Rose was very good-looking.

"Where's my shoes?" he demanded from half inside the shoe-cupboard, on top of which the wireless half-heartedly uttered uninspiring music.

"By the hearth, standing waiting for you to put 'em on, same as they always are."

He turned and looked, and it was exactly where they were. She had cleaned them, of course, polished them until the toes glowed. That struck a chord from Friday night, the dusk under the trees, and the long, gracious descent of the valley before him, and the minx Imogen laughing as she taunted him; "She even cleans your shoes!" Queer that a laugh should be the only sombre thing in that gay morning.

He put on his shoes, Sue dancing frenziedly between him and the open door. For her barking he did not hear the voice that announced the Prime Minister, and only snatches of the Prime Minister himself. But something of gravity came in, and the conviction of strangeness with it. It was a September morning, bright, brisk, kind, and yet the world suddenly reeled and turned upside-down.

"*What* was that he said?"

"How can I hear with that little devil barking her head off? Something about a state of war—'evil things we shall be fighting against'——"

"That means we've declared war. Did you hear that, Dad? We've declared war!"

" 'Bout time, too," said his father roundly. "Folks were beginning to wonder if they meant to."

But it was easy for him; he was old, he didn't have to turn round and look at the thing and find it the only thing in the world. His very self would endure, and would not be changed. The responsibility was not his, the terror was not his; if there should be a vision, the vision would not be his, and that was gain as well as loss. To be an old man at war, with the weight of life behind you, and very little need left to do anything about anything—that was an easy thing. But to have the whole of life ahead of you, and the world reeling under your feet, and the sky bowing over your head; and to feel fallen upon your sole self the onus of keeping the one secure and the other suspended—that was not so easy. He didn't think of it like that. He thought: "I'll have to make up my mind what to do. It's up to me to do something now." Nothing clearer, nothing more complex than that.

He took the lead from its hook on the door, and went out slowly, and left them to listen in peace to the end of what the Prime Minister had to say. He had heard, imperfectly but unmistakably, all he needed to hear. It had happened. He went in a dream, with fixed eyes, seeing the clear morning through a mist of his own mind, a chaotic mist, full of movement but without form. The future was curiously blank, but only as the curtain is blank before the beginning of a play. A tragedy, perhaps; but that kind of tragedy is hard to visualise as it is easy to foretell, and has life and colour as well as darkness and death. He knew very little of what he was to live through, nothing of what was to happen to his mind, before the fogs cleared again. But he knew that something had begun, that though he might not die, he would be changed; and he knew, though not in those nor in any words, that at twenty-four it was impossible to wish to turn back or aside from whatever was ahead, or even to look away or close one's eyes in going through it, but only to face one way, and that way squarely forward.

He walked away from the cottages of Lamb Lane, up into the soft-turfed hills above the village, where the larks soared in choirs, and the rabbits drove Sue frantic with joy. To-day she could get him to take no interest in the white-scutted meat which teased her senses at every turn; he would not say the word she awaited, and tell her to go after her wits; so she ran beside him and flashed round him, and remained unseen and unsatisfied. He was thinking of very different things.

It was strangely peaceful up there. The air was still, and very clear, so that the sky became, as he looked up into it, unimaginably lofty. He wondered what he was going to do. It was all very well being in a reserved occupation, and of use to the country, and so on, but there was no glamour in road-surfacing. It wasn't exactly a uniform that he wanted; he didn't go much for that sort of thing. But you'd feel much more in it if you joined up. It would be something different, and the upheaval in the world cried out for an answering violence of change in the little things which make up life. Throw away all the stray bits of the past together, and reach for something new; because the whole thing's so new it terrifies and fascinates you. You don't think it can happen; it's one of the things that doesn't happen; but it's happening now—yes, beginning from now. And you want to do something that marches step by step with it, something as new and vital, something of equal stature. Besides, though you can't very well admit it, you want to fight for your country in any cause she may have decided is good enough for her.

All this is at the back of the mind. At the front is a sort of hesitation, like a timid bather poking his toes into cold seas; because, after all, it's a bit of a plunge, and you may be throwing away all sorts of comforts and securities, and all the claims your people have on you, too. And nobody wants to go and fight and get hurt, anyway; it isn't the sort of thing you do without thinking twice. Not unless you're a ruddy hero. But if the country's in a spot you can't sit back and look on— not if you're even half a man. If England's in trouble, so must you be. No use keeping your fingers out of the fire and hoping to hold on to what you have; because if the country goes, everything goes. You still don't profess to know what it's all about, but you know it's going to be a life and death business. You're going to be needed; you'll feel both mean and cheated if you stay at home. That's what you know.

In this storm of mind, he wandered into the edge of Morwen Hoe, and looked thoughtfully along the village street all demure with Sunday, and saw Tommy Goolden coming along at a purposeful pace. There was one who knew where he was going, wife or no wife. And Jim Benison was a single man.

He stepped aside a pace or two in the direction of the "Fox and Hounds", changed his mind, and came back to meet Tommy Goolden. He said: "Hullo, Tommy!" and Tommy said: "Hullo, Jim!" and they fell into step together, not talking any more.

5

It was the end of September, and the world had changed. Lwów and Cracow were in ruins, and the Germans were in Warsaw; and yet Morwen Hoe and its sister villages and its county town had never heard so much as a siren sounded in earnest. But one night the first siren of the war wailed from the police-station and settled like a cold hand upon the comfortable village quietness of heart; and though nothing happened on that occasion, yet suddenly the war was real, and monstrous, and present, to be accepted, to be overcome.

It happened just after midnight. The sound split Jim's sleep like an axe splitting wood, and he sat up in bed with a jerk, to find his mother tapping on the door and calling softly: "Jim, wake up. There's an air-raid; they'll be wanting you up there." In the very same tones she might have used had Tommy and Tommy's spaniel called for him to go for a walk some Sunday morning, and found him still in bed.

He answered her sleepily, struggling into his clothes in the dark. "All right, I'm awake. What are you going to do?"

"Go back to bed, I suppose. Nothing else special for me to do, is there?"

"You ought to go down in the cellar, Mum. Anything might happen, you know, now they've started."

"I'm going in no cellar," she said firmly, "until the bombs start falling, and even then I'm not so sure. I like to be above-ground until I *am* dead." And back to bed she went, and there was no time to argue with her. Anything could happen at any moment, and he was wanted at the First Aid Post.

The sirens were still shrieking as he let himself out by the back door, and ran hell-for-leather up Lamb Lane towards the warehouse behind the Talbot, where the casualty services had established themselves. It was a clear night, but dark, and there were searchlights; and besides the banshee wail of alarms, there was another sound, somewhere in the upper air, faint, persistent, directionless, the pulsing hum of aircraft. But nothing to see, nothing at all except a flood of light from an open bedroom window at "Fir Cottage", where Mrs. Linnet, with her hair standing upright with curl-papers and fright, leaned out inanely beseeching Jim's passing footsteps to reassure her that everything was all right.

"Sure it's all right!" he called, still running. "But if you don't close that dam' window and pull the blind down, you'll have the whole German Air Force over here." And she disappeared and so did the light, so quickly that it seemed she was not past reason. Silly fool, he thought indignantly, she was only concerned for herself, and to hell with the rest; yes, and there were plenty more like her. He did them less than justice, of course; this was the very first air-raid warning they had ever heard, and their reactions were necessarily slow. Afterwards they became adept in this as in other accomplishments.

He was not first at the Post. Clye was there, and Joe Goodwin was there, and Peel, and half a dozen more, all sitting round the little oil-stove, smoking and talking and mustering their ambulance kit in readiness for a call. And Mary Clye was there, bustling about with kettles of hot water; and Imogen Threlfall was there, too, filling water-bottles. He didn't know her at first; he took her for a boy, for she was wearing corduroy trousers and a thick brown sweater, and her short hair was pushed back anyhow in a couple of kirbi-grips, and kept falling in elf-locks over her face. When she saw him she flushed, and went on very quickly with what she was doing. He wondered what was the matter with her, but that was no time to ask.

"Nice night for a raid," he said, hanging up his cap and reaching for the tin hat and civilian service mask which hung on his peg. They were rarities both as yet, only the older members had them, and they were prized and jealously guarded.

"Now don't get rushing round looking busy," exhorted Joe Goodwin. "We've got everything all ready for action, and young Billy Banks sitting over the telephone, so there's nothing left for you to do. Quit rushing up and down making a draught down my neck, and sit in and light up." He pushed his own chair back to make room. "How's it looking outside? Anything doing?"

"Not a thing. You can hear 'em, but that's all. More than enough for some folks, though. They've lost their wits already." He recounted the Linnet incident.

"Ay, I've seen a few like that myself, on my way down. The High Street was like pre-war. Everybody just threw the windows open and leaned out to have a look at what was going on."

"Give 'em time," said Clye. "They'll learn."

"Warden's having a lively time, anyhow. Think they'll be likely to drop anything here, Joe?"

"Shouldn't think so, meself. More likely just cruising over here looking for the town—or maybe the electric plant up the valley. There's nothing here they'd want. Never can tell, though, they might get playful and send us a souvenir just from lightness of heart. Best to act as if we expected it."

So they acted as if they expected it. They sat over their equipment, listening to the silences and the faint recurring drone, waiting for the first concussion; but it did not come. The night went by them slowly. They talked about the war. What else was there to talk about? They started a darts match, and played it out, and still nothing happened. And Imogen Threlfall, squatting over the electric ring in its dark corner, made strong tea, and brought them mugs of it, boiling hot and sweet, russet with tinned milk.

Jim went over and sat beside her on the narrow bench against the darkened window. She gave him a half-hearted smile, and looked away again, and went on sipping her tea.

"Hullo, you!" he said.

"Hullo, Jim."

"You're not very talkative to-night," he said rallyingly. "What's up?"

"Oh, nothing special. I'm just tired, that's all."

"You needn't have come down, surely—all that way by yourself in the dark. I'm surprised your dad let you."

"Let me?" she said, giving him a sudden sidelong flare of her lashes. "I don't wait for people to *let* me do things these days, Jim Benison."

"Oh, all right, don't get on your high horse with me, young Threlfall—not at this hour in the morning." He reached for the big earthenware teapot and refilled his cup. "I suppose you'll have heard I'm going?"

The dark head nodded, shaking another tangle of crisp hair out of the nearer kirbi-grip over her face.

"On Monday, I have to report."

23

"Oh! Where?"

"A camp in Warwickshire. Ecclesham, it's called. Seems daft, when it's the Midshires I'm joining. Tommy Goolden goes the same day, so anyhow we shall have company by the way. What's doing with you, Jenny? I heard your dad was going soon."

She nodded again. "I'm going to Caldington, to my Uncle Jack. But we're keeping the house on here; it's ours, so we can keep it empty if we like. Or we might let it furnished—some of these people who're rushing to get out of the town might like it here."

"I won't see you when I come on leave," said Jim.

"Much you care!" she said with a short laugh, and turned her shoulder squarely on him, and buried her nose in her cup.

"All right, Miss Threlfall, if that's how you're feeling to-night I'll leave you to it." And he rose, and made to walk away from her, but she turned quickly and caught him by the wrist, shaking hot tea over her hand.

"Sit down, and don't act that way, Jim, you big halfwit. As if you have to take any notice of me. Anyway, it's true. Much you *do* care whether you see me or not, or you'd have come up to the house before now, and Jane Hayden wouldn't have had to tell me about you passing your medical and getting your calling-up papers, and everything." She met his surprised stare with a smouldering sullenness which flamed suddenly into high defiance, though her voice remained quiet as always. "Yes, I do care, see. I don't like hearing about you second-hand from people you haven't known above five minutes."

"You don't think she got it straight from me, do you?" said Jim, humouring her.

"No, most likely Delia Hall told her. She's the only one who knows much about you and your doings, these days." He hoped she couldn't guess how probably right she was about that; but the odds were that she could, for she was quick on the uptake, and knew him inconveniently well. So he ignored the immediate point, and sat squarely down beside her again, and said firmly: "Now look here! You know perfectly well that I wouldn't have gone away from here without seeing you and telling you all about it. And you know that I never told Jane Hayden, nor anyone else around the village, ahead of you. You know as well as I do she doesn't matter a curse, so don't go working up a temperament about it. It doesn't suit you."

24

"Oh well," said Imogen, scrubbing splinters out of the bare floor with the toe of her shoe, "what does it matter, anyway? You're going just the same." She was quiet a moment, acutely aware of his eyes upon her boyishness, in concern and curiosity; she didn't like being studied so intently, not even by Jim—no, especially by Jim. He'd known her all her life. Why did he suddenly have to look at her as if she might any moment turn into quite a new person? Almost as if she already had. She was the same Imogen, corduroys or no corduroys.

"Well," she said, turning to him abruptly, "I hope the light's good enough for you? Would you like me to move under the lamp?"

"I've never seen you in those things before," he said defensively.

"I had them made so I could get dressed quick if—well, if we had to come down here at night. I know they make me look broad in the beam, but they're for use, not beauty. You don't have to stare at 'em, do you?"

"You look O.K. to me," said Jim.

"Well, I look pretty awful to me, but it won't have to matter." She sank her chin into her hands, and sat gazing at the rim of her cup as if the significance of the world was drawn into its curve. He wondered why she looked so much older; her face had hardened and assumed form and character, and her mouth was a firmer, thinner line, indrawn at the corners, uncompromising. "How long do you suppose it will last, Jim?" she asked. "As long as the last?"

"Good Lord, no, it can't. You'll see. It'll all be over in a few months, most people think. A year at the outside." But he didn't begin to explain how or why it would end within the year, because a kid like Imogen could hardly be expected to follow the workings of high strategy, or understand the marvels of static defence as exemplified in the Maginot Line. "You needn't think you'll be getting rid of me indefinitely, young Imogen. I'll be back in civvies before you know where you are."

"You'd better marry Delia Hall quickly, then, if you really want her," retorted Imogen. "It's only the thought of the uniform that's keeping her hanging round your neck."

Jim said: "You little hell-cat!" and half meant it. And then Imogen laughed, brief and hard, with distinct pleasure in having stung him. "Well, think it out. You never were quite so much her number one boy-friend before, were you? She liked Sam Reddin well enough until she came to the conclusion he'd never get into battle-dress. When you're all back in civvies you'll have lost your pull, so don't kid yourself you won't."

"I'm not going to fall out with you," said Jim, recovering his good humour. "It's too early in the morning. But watch out for yourself when next I come down the fields, my girl."

"It'll have to be soon," she said. "You're going on Monday."

Then there was a silence, and out of it the terrifying sound of aircraft engines blossomed again, slowly, thrumming leisurely overhead, still directionless, still undecided. It swelled, and drew them all into a single tension threaded upon the sound of it. Jim felt Imogen grow tense against him, draw closer and lift her hand to his sleeve; but her face changed very little; only the lines along cheekbone and jaw seemed to tighten and blanch with the pressure of skin upon bone. His own scalp pricked, and the beat of his heart quickened. This was the beginning of what was to come. Whether it stayed now or passed, whether they were drawn suddenly into action or whether they had wasted their time, this was the first of reality, the first edge of the shadow under which England was to live, the end of the beginning.

The sound persisted for a long time, throbbing overhead in slow, considering circles, and the strain of concentration upon it tightened within them all like the winding of a spring, tugging them to their feet, fixing their senses in a kind of hypnosis. Jim put his arm around Imogen's shoulders. He was not aware of it, nor for the moment aware in any personal way of her; but he felt her small body suddenly pressed closer to his side, and looking down, met her eyes which were fixed upon him with a look he had certainly never seen before, in Imogen's or any other eyes. He was so used to thinking of her as a little girl that it was something of a shock to find himself casually embracing a woman; but that quiet, intent face, with wide eyes steadily and startlingly blue, and full mouth set like stone, belonged to no child. Her mind was shut and locked behind those eyes. Her thoughts were her own, hidden and deliberate, withheld even from him; she had never before cared how much of her Jim Benison knew.

He wondered, suddenly anxious, what she was thinking. Was she frightened? Very likely; who wasn't? But certainly not more frightened than the rest. Was she excited? Very likely, too, for Imogen wouldn't by her very nature react in noisy ways. He supposed she had been brought up short against this first presence of the enemy, as they all had; but if that was what ailed her, why did she, in the moment of her earliest realisation of danger, stare so unwaveringly into his face? At one time she might have looked at him for reassurance, but this wasn't that kind of look.

He stood there puzzling over her, clutching at the elusive and embarrassing significance of that regard, and quite unaware that the pulsing disturbance overhead had faded and passed, and at his back Joe Goodwin and Clye and the rest were all coming out of their trance. He had forgotten them altogether for the moment. All he wanted was to know what was going on behind the metamorphosis of Imogen's face.

He might even have found out, if the "All Clear" had not soared just then out of the silence. But more probably she would have continued to baffle him. He was not very good at that sort of thing.

6

As soon as he was fairly in it—and it took no more than a week of Ecclesham to make him part of the khaki landscape—all the darkness and turmoil which had made the threshold sombre, disappeared utterly, as if he had stepped out from an unlit room into the open air. The ground was firm again under his feet, and the sky secure over him, just by reason of his having put on battle-dress and picked up a rifle. Most of England was feeling the same reaction just then. The horror and the uncertainty were over, and the plunge taken; and instead of the expected chaos they found everything as before, England unmoved, the stars firm in their station, the sun not retarded nor hastened in its rising and setting. And their spirits rose in a great wave of relief, and joy, and vigour; and Jim's with them. That period was the nearest England came to hysteria, and the nearest Jim Benison came to complacence.

It was as if he had used up all his thought, and all the necessity for thinking, in the single decision to join up. There was no longer any need to ponder the future, or wonder what he was going to do; he had done that once for all. Now all he had to do was settle into the place he had made his own, obey orders, and leave the thinking to someone else. So he had energy and to spare, and according to those who were in authority over him he showed considerable aptitude for his new life.

It was so much easier than he had expected it to be, that he took to it as women take to mirrors, first with eagerness and curiosity, then with devotion. He was adaptable, though it was a quality he'd never had occasion to use until then; he was quick at picking things up, at least where his interest was caught, and he felt no insidious individualistic urge to query the rightness and reason of any command which might be given him; so his N.C.O.s approved of him, and his officers considered him a good type of man—willing, conscientious, giving no trouble. It never occurred to Jim that they had any opinion of him at all.

Drill was easy enough, fatigues were all in the day's work, rifle practice was a joy. He was not used to the type of gun he found himself handling, but being already a fair shot he soon got the hang of it; besides, there were scores who had never touched a rifle before, so there was scope for a hedgeside shot to shine more brightly than he had ever expected. And Jim shone, and was not displeased with his radiance.

So as time went on, and the war which had sprung out on England like a wild beast turned out to be a very tame beast after all, it all turned into a kind of game, played for the fun of it. He worked less hours than he had worked since he was fifteen; he was comfortable, fed and diverted, for at heart it came easy to him to be satisfied with things; while he had very little money he found he needed little; and life was easy and full of companionable people like Tommy, and Alec Ross, and Scotty Walsh and a hundred more; and above all, in the midst of innumerable happenings, nothing, nothing had happened. Fearful tales had been told of the next war—of this war—tales of cities bombed to pieces from the air, of invasion, and rapine, and slaughter. But England was as she had always been, France was untouched, the sun shone on them both, the rain fell on them both, and the season wandered onward into full winter, and all was as before. A pricked bubble, this war scare. There was nothing to it, nothing at all. The efficiency, the power of Germany dwindled into insignificance. Wait till we get at 'em. When we're ready we'll move, and you'll see what their rickety old Luftwaffe's worth, and their tin-pot panzers, and their regimented demi-gods. We'll eat 'em alive. It'll all be over by the summer at latest.

The 4th Midshires, marching light-heartedly along frosty Warwickshire lanes, sang to the young December morning their latest and most inspired profession of faith:

"We're going to hang out the washing on the Siegfried Line,
Have you any dirty *wash*ing, mother dear——"

Early on Christmas Eve it snowed a little, not enough to cover the ground properly, but almost enough for the illusion of whiteness which Christmas needed; and having snowed, it froze; and having frozen, it crystallized into a silver stillness, wonderful, brittle and enchanted, without wind to shake it, and resentful of sound.

She had made an excuse to slip out of the bar for a moment, and stolen out to the garden gate to watch for him coming along the lane. She was there when he came, leaning over the gate in the glittering dark, watching her own tinsel breath dissolve away into the quietness. And he came softly, stealing along close to the hedge, and had her by the shoulders before she knew, and kissed her clean through her gasping, startled laughter, a sudden, hard, elated kiss, not too well-judged, but very sure of itself. He knew his Delia. All this had happened before, though not in a December frost. There was no new quality in kissing Delia; only the continued adventure of rediscovering the old: her warmth, and her acceptance, and the unshaken generosity with which she took and returned his touch. Surprise in her was no more than skin-deep. She was incapable of being surprised by caresses.

"Jim, you fool!" she said with her first quick-recovered breath. "Not here in the lane! My goodness, anybody might come along!" It was not in her nature, certainly not in her mood, to care how many thousands came, but one says these things. "Oh, Jim, I been looking for you all evening. When d'you get in?"

"Not above three-quarters of an hour ago. Hours late, we were. I got thinking I was going to spend Christmas on the railway. Gosh, kid, if you knew how I've been aching to see you!" And he held her by the shoulders across the gate, and she felt his eyes straining after her in the dark. Not for nothing had she spent half an hour on the arranging of these showering, shining curls, and broken early into the new rouge she had intended keeping for the New Year dance. She shone, even in the dark.

"Better come inside, then," she said, "and then you can have a good look at me. I'll have to do a bit of work between-whiles, but I'll be around." But he knew she was in no hurry to go back to the bar, any more than he was.

"No, wait a bit. Don't go in yet. You're not cold, are you?

Here, put my greatcoat round you." Big as she was, it swallowed her whole. She leaned upon the gate with her chin tucked into his khaki collar, and laughed for sheer pleasure, because she liked him to be bigger than she was, because it filled her with satisfaction—no with exultation—to be paraded like a trophy on his arm through the length and breadth of Morwen Hoe and beyond—but how far beyond she was careful not to look.

"There, how's that? Good fit, isn't it? Warmer?"

"I'm fine. But look Jim, I've got work to do. If I stick around here playing with you, I'll get thrown out on my ear. They're busy inside. You may not have heard, but it's Christmas Eve with us."

"All the more reason you should stay right here with me. Christmas comforts for the troops come first, my girl."

"But the trade——" protested Delia, laughing.

"To hell with the trade! You're coming out of it, anyhow, just as soon as I can get you out. It never was any place for you—serving beer to a lot of silly apes like Sam Reddin, and having them treat you like a chorus girl, pawing you about and calling you Delia——"

"What do you call me?" she asked indignantly, though her indignation was no more than a ripple upon the ocean of her pleasure in being so coveted. "And who's pawing me about now, I'd like to know? Jim Benison, you have the nerve of the devil!"

"Come off it!" he said, his voice suddenly low and urgent in the great quietness. "You know darn well this is different." And she knew indeed that it was, but not how different.

"You're pretty sure of yourself, aren't you?" she said in a soft, purring voice he had heard only once before, once at Ecclesham, that time she had come down for the week-end—under the rustling brown lilac-trees at the foot of the garden at Mrs. Britten's, with the drift of November rain filming their eyes, and his coat about them both. But now the velvet tone of it was clearer and wonderfully intimate in the crystal air of the night, so that he caught every inflection, and knew he had her. She wouldn't back out. She was for him. "I might have something to say to that. Never thought of that, did you?"

"Right enough you'll have something to say." He put his hand under her chin and turned her face up to him, not gently. "You'll say 'Amen', and like it."

It was she who began that kiss, deliberately, not from devil-

30

ment or to provoke him, but because she wanted it. She put her arms, strong and smooth, fast around his neck, and her mouth settled upon his, and she hung there, letting her mind slip away from her into a haze of distant happiness, compounded of a cottage, and cooking, and chintz curtains in a shining parlour, and walks on Sunday evening after chapel on her husband's arm; she in her green edge-to-edge coat and the hat with the veil, and Jim in his walking-out uniform, for all the world to see and say: "There goes a fine-looking young couple!" As they would, for who could resist remarking upon Jim's stature or her beauty? Yes, she would have him. He'd improved, or else she saw him larger than life-size for having missed him so much. He was more self-confident since he'd been away; he had even a little assured swagger, one that didn't disappear when seen among the hundreds like it at Ecclesham. Even there you would notice him. She liked to think that her husband would be noticed. She liked the breadth of his shoulders in battle-dress, and the narrow waist and long-flanked, easy walk of him, and the way he set his feet down lightly, without sound or effort, and the way his cap clung impossibly to the side of his head, riding his thick brown curls like a small ship breasting a rough sea. And most of all, she liked him because he wanted her more intensely than she wanted him. That made him, with all his strength and size and energy, dependent on her. That was power, and Delia liked the taste of it.

It wasn't that one wanted so very much from life; but a man had his ideas of happiness and surely, thought Jim, feeling her heart surge against his heart, he might be forgiven for letting his mind dwell on the things of the future, the home she would make for him, the life they would share. Now, now above all, when he had France so closely before him, and the reality of the war drawing near; for though he had not told her yet, he knew that this was the first and last leave both, the first of his career, the last before he went to France. And after that who knew when he would see her again?

He remembered her vividly in that moment, every facet of her, from the first time they had met. He saw her striding through the modest chapters of his life, letting in the wind and the sun. Ecclesham had admired her slavishly, and envied him beyond reason. It had been rather like squiring a queen around the camp. When he danced with her in the Parish Hall he had been conscious of many eyes upon their progress. When she sat beside him at the Ensa concert in the camp common-room, and sang chorus songs at the full fearless stretch of her lungs, he had known that because of her they, whose render-ings of "Run, Rabbit, Run", and "Goodbye, Sally", were wont to make the corrugated roof shake, were grown too shy to let themselves go. After that visit he had known better how to value her. Her magnificence, too long familiar, was renewed because it fell so newly upon his companions. It was then, he supposed, that he'd made up his mind he must have her.

All this went over his mind again in Delia's kiss, before she put her hands up to his chest and held him away from her, and said: "Amen!" in the voice of a replete and self-willed child, and laughed upon the word. "No, Jim—really! I've got to go now. There'll be time—we've got all the week. No, truly, I *must* go in. You don't think it's because I *want* to, do you?"

"All right," he said, relenting, "I won't be awkward. I'll see you in the snug. And, Delia——" She had whipped away from him, but she halted in mid-flight, looking back at him over her shoulder. "—not a word to anybody—about us. Not yet——"

Delia uttered a small, complacent laugh. She was quite sure of him. "You're not ashamed of it, are you?" And without waiting for a reply, she turned and ran away from him into the house, leaving him holding in his arm the greatcoat still warm from her body. By the time he reached the front door of the house she was in the bar, drawing beer nineteen to the dozen, and exchanging Christmas greetings with her customers, her most bewildering smile thrown in with the pint for season-able measure. He could scarcely believe that this was the same Delia. One moment he had her to himself, the next moment she shone upon the world, and with equal beneficence for all who came; though perhaps the extra glow she had to-night was one man's gift to her and them.

Fred Blossom was in the snug, and Clye, and Robbie Wayne the warden, and Sam Reddin, and half a dozen boon compan-ions, Clye had his concertina going—the genuine old English kind it was, with a good mellow tone—and they were singing carols. They were near enough to Wales to sing, on the whole, exceedingly well, and their harmony was good; but Jim's entry put an end to the concert for that night. They looked up and recognised him as he entered, and the local setting of "While Shepherds Watched" exploded in a shower of exclamation and welcome. "Well, look who's here!" "Well, hullo, Jim lad!"

"Here comes the British Army, chaps!" "Hey, Lydia, fill one for Jim."

"Great stuff, this Bass!" remarked Jim, emerging from his first depleted pint with a sigh of satisfaction. "I haven't run up against draught Bass in months. How's things around these parts?"

They told him, singly and collectively, all the latest items of Sheel Valley gossip, who was born, who was dead, who had joined up and who been called up, what the weather had been doing, how the last A.R.P. practice went, what happened when the A.F.S. fired Monkman's derelict farm buildings only too well, failed signally to put them out again, and found too late that they were still insured for three hundred pounds. They told him who was courting whom, and how long it was expected to last; and which local ladies were queening it over the various jobs no one else would take on, such as the reception of evacuees, and the collection of salvage, and what small jealousies and warfares had arisen therefrom; and what the little evacuee townies had done to local house property, and how their long-suffering hosts were standing it. The details changed, but the outline was the same, Morwen Hoe yesterday, to-day and for ever. They said it was good to see him back, and he said it was good to be back; and suddenly the words stabbed inward, because this return was so brief, and prelude to so much wider and more unpredictable a journeying.

"The next round's on me," he said, "if you fellows can stand the shock. Fill 'em up, Delia."

"They must be paying the army these days," commented Clye.

"It only comes once a year," said Jim, defensively.

"What, Christmas, or your treat? All right, don't shoot. Thanks, Delia, love! Well, here's to you, Jim—may you be home long before next Christmas comes around. But I wish I thought so." And that was Clye to the life, thought Jim; he meant well, but he wasn't cheering.

Delia moved benignly in the hazing background of his vision. Every time he caught her eye she gave him a quick, intimate smile, reminding him that she was only being civil and friendly to these others by way of business, that her lavish broadcast kindness, her roguish glances and quick repartees meant nothing. Under the spell of that secret joy he endured silently his small instinctive stabs of jealousy, though his impulse was to warn them off from touching her, even from looking at her too

33

closely. When she leaned over Sam Reddin's shoulder to set down his beer, and he put up his hand quickly to touch her breast and draw his fingers down the soft flesh of her arm—it was hardest of all to keep quiet then. It wasn't the first time he'd seen Sam Reddin do that, not by many a one. It wasn't the first time he'd wanted to flatten his face for it, either. But he controlled himself by reflecting that a hog can hardly help his nature. And Reddin was just a hog, after all, especially with a few drinks inside him. He'd had more than a few to-night, they all had; what else could you expect on Christmas Eve?

No one remembered to turn on the news in the bar. No one would have heard it if they had. The piano was going madly, and at least two rival parties of songsters were in full voice, the "Washing on the Siegfried Line" cancelling out "Good King Wenceslas". Funny to think that probably not one of the carol-party know who Good King Wenceslas was, or that his country had been the first sacrificial victim, the first forgotten casualty of this war. That was something Jim had learned since leaving home, thanks to a Czech Pioneer named Jacek who frequented the same canteen; not the only thing, either, not by a mile. He'd known Jacek for a fortnight, just casually, before he'd found out he was a Czech; and the discovery had come as a shock, for he'd somehow taken it for granted that people of other nationalities should not, as Jacek did, look and talk and think exactly like English people. That made you think. Jim was not, perhaps, a thinking man, but at least it reduced the barriers which, in his mind, segregated the English from the Others. And it made him feel a sort of twinge of shame when he heard "Good King Wenceslas"; as if he could have helped, had he tried, to stop the things which Jacek said had happened to Prague. Which was unreasonable, because he was doing the only thing he could; that was what he'd joined up for.

The snug was blue and quivering with smoke, and more than comfortably warm. Everybody had paid his round, everybody except Sam Reddin, and he was singing very dark, keeping a noisy conversation going at the other side of the room, so that he could pretend not to notice when his turn came round. As it was Christmas Eve no one was saying anything. Goodwill to men, even if there's no peace on earth. But if they got much higher, or if someone came to the conclusion that there might be amusement in it, something would be said. He wasn't what you'd call a popular chap, and there could be fun in baiting him. No wonder Sam was getting the name for being wealthy,

34

said Morwen Hoe, with all the money he saved on drinks.

Look at him now, creating a diversion while Robbie paid for the round. He had a small spray of mistletoe in his hand, and was stalking Mrs. Goodwin round the corner table. Pretty far gone he must be to begin on old Lydia Goodwin, harmless old dragon though she was. Not even Joe could ever have got much fun out of kissing Lydia, even if she had changed a lot since he courted her. Now a girl like Delia. . . .

It was then that Delia came in, shutting the door behind her with a twitch of her elbow. Her face was at once bright and pale, and she walked with more than her usual magnificence, so that no man in his senses could fail to notice her that night; and Sam had always admired her, having good sharp eyes where women were concerned. She saw him come casually round the end of the big table towards her, keeping one hand out of sight behind his back; and as she set down the tray she asked disdainfully: "Well, Sam Reddin, what's the matter with you?" But she was not sufficiently concerned to look for an answer, and turned her shoulder on him without a qualm. His arm took her round the waist, so hard that she gasped, and his kiss fell short of her mouth and landed in the soft smoothness of her cheek. And the odd part of it was that it could have happened just so any other night, and she would only have pretended to resent it, laughing even as she scolded; but to-night she plucked herself away from his touch like a bent tree recoiling, her breast surging and her eyes wild, and sprang to put the table between them.

"You *dare!*" she said, panting. "You beast, Sam Reddin! Just you *dare* do that again!"

It was her voice that got into them both, like a very potent spirit, making the one come after her joyously with his sprig of mistletoe, and the other one heave himself from his chair and stride round the gaping group to stand in front of her. If she had not suddenly conceived that this small simple thing mattered so much, neither would they have been goaded; but it was suddenly more enormous than the war, and their senses were lost in it. Jim's hand took Sam in the chest, not a blow but with all the force of one, and they leaned there looking at each other; and Delia put her hand on Jim's arm, and said his name pleadingly, but no one paid any attention to her. Everyone else in the snug was interestedly watching Sam Reddin and Jim Benison, and settling back to enjoy a scrap which had been due for a long time. Delia scrubbed at her cheek where the kiss had landed, and tugged at Jim's arm, and entreated: "Look, Jim, it don't matter. It was only tomfoolery. We don't want no trouble—not on Christmas Eve." But even she could scarcely keep the exultation out of her voice; it wasn't in nature she should fail to enjoy being the cause of a promising fight.

"Well, well!" said Sam. "What's your hurry, Jim Benison?"

"You ain't looking for trouble, are you?" said Jim gently. "You tell Delia you're sorry, now, nicely, and maybe I won't push your face in. Or maybe I will, at that; I don't like it— I never have."

"That's pretty big talk," said Sam, grinning. "Let's see you make it good. Anyhow, what business is it of yours? How long have you been Delia's keeper?" He closed a large fist about Jim's braced forearm, and tried to jerk the spread hand from his chest, but it wasn't so easy as he imagined it would be. A few months of army life had hardened what was already a formidable body. "You get from out of my way, Jim Benison, while you're still safe," he advised, failing to remove the obstacle by sheer weight.

"Will I hell! You're going to keep your hands off my girl from now on—or I'll knock your block off right now. You can take your pick."

"Oh yes? Since when has Delia Hall been *your* girl? Seems to me the door's open to pretty well anybody with an hour or two to spare——"

Then Jim hit him, a short-arm jab that took him in the side of the jaw and lifted him clean back into the table. Delia shrieked: "No! *Jim*—don't!" There was a crash of glass, and every soul in the "snug" rose to salvage the remaining beer-mugs, not without impatience for the necessary interruption. Clye put himself between the combatants, in time to fend off Sam's wild rush, and Robbie and Fred caught Jim by the arms and held him from following up that happy beginning.

"Sorry, chaps!" said Clye reasonably. "No use in breaking up the happy home. Besides, Joe wouldn't like it. Outside, or pipe down!"

"Good!" said Jim. "Outside it is. More elbow room in the lane, anyhow."

Sam said only: "Let me get at him. I'll murder him!" Which was exactly the sort of thing you might expect from him in the circumstances. He was always going to do wonders, no matter what he put his hand to.

Forthwith everyone drank up, and out they poured through

the bar, gathering numbers on the way, to see the fun in the lane, under the snapping, impartial stars. With luck there would be time to finish the fight and cram in a last round before the pubs closed. They were willing to risk it; anything for a bit of excitement, anyhow, there hadn't been much since the war started.

Jim was plunging out with the rest when Delia threw herself upon him and clung to his right arm with all her weight. "Jim, you don't want to take it so serious. It was only a bit of softness—if he hadn't took me by surprise there wouldn't have been no fuss. You don't want to go fighting over nothing, like a couple of silly kids."

"You call that nothing? I don't. I saw him fingering you before, and I never said anything—but it's the last time he's going to put his dirty hands on my girl."

Following him out into the night, clinging to him, she persisted through tears: "Oh, Jim, don't hurt him! He didn't mean no harm—he's drunk."

"He's no more drunk than I am," said Jim, with more truth than he realised. "Drunk or sober, he can't maul you about and get away with it. If you don't like it, kid, you'd better go in."

It was a command; but Delia did not go in. She followed them round into the lane, under the quiet stars, the remains of the snow crackling under their feet; and there she stood, forgetting to be cold, while they stamped up and down between the interested spectators, encouraged impartially, for the habituees of the "Clay Pigeon" saw no reason to take sides in a fight which had obviously been brewing for months, long before Jim Benison went away and acquired his new assurance. No one was really sorry to see Sam Reddin get his nose punched, but young Jim wasn't needing any help to do it. Delia, being a woman, was partisan all through, but she was too excited to utter a word, except that now and then, when Jim took Reddin's heavy swings to his face, she gave a small, smothered shriek through her fingers, feeling herself bruised with him. No one noticed her, except Jerry Clye, and he, having advised her kindly to go in and not worry her head, saw that she had not even heard him, and, further, in some odd way of her own was enjoying herself immensely. So he left her alone; you could never tell with a woman.

It was a good fight while it lasted, the best since Coronation Night; but it didn't last long. They were much of a height, both big and both young, and both long in the reach, though the weight was mostly on Sam's side. But for the past few months they'd been living very different lives; Jim was in first-class condition, besides being in deadly, if slightly drunk, earnest about his cause; Sam was determined, and quite sufficiently angry to be dangerous, but he soon began to blow in an ominous manner, and after ten minutes of roundless combat, he was as good as done. Still, it was a good fight; it drew two gangs of small boys from their carol-singing, and an excited red setter next door to the end of his chain, where he barked and danced until the din subsided and the fun was over; and even one or two peaceful customers from the jug-and-bottle came round from the front door to see what all the pandemonium was about, and stayed to wait for a decision. They saw Delia Hall standing back against the gate-post, hatless, watching wide-eyed, and crushing back with both hands the tendency to scream. There was matter for scandal in plenty, and they did not fail to note the details of the picture for future reference; but as far as Delia was concerned, they did not exist. She saw only Jim. When his foot slipped in the powdery snow-ruts of the lane and he took Sam's swinging left full in the face and went down, she uttered a small bubbling shriek, thin between her rigid fingers; when he loosened two of Sam's front teeth with a lovely straight right, the impact jarred her to the heels with vicious joy, and she made an odd little sound, half laugh, half cheer. She was not aware of the girl who came leisurely round from the front door of the "Clay Pigeon" to lean upon the open gate and contemplate with a slightly jeering smile this manifestation of the adult civilised male. This one, too, though she did not look at Delia, saw how the wind set.

"I wouldn't worry, if I were you," she said, not without patronage. "Jim could break him apart."

Delia's head jerked round at that, and she saw Imogen Threlfall's child's profile clear in the soft starlight, the corners of her mouth twisted in that insufferably wise and experienced smile of the very young, her eyebrows raised and her slight shoulders hunched, the picture of blasé amusement at the follies of humanity. At any other time Delia would have smiled, and thought her a funny, old-fashioned little thing; but to-night she did not smile, she bristled. Everyone knew this chit had been Jim's protegée years ago, in school; but did she think that qualified her to tell Delia anything about him now, damn her cool cheek?

"I'm surprised you let 'em *fight*," said Imogen exasperatingly. "They might both get spoiled. Looks almost as if Jim might have a black eye to-morrow. I wouldn't be seen with a man with a black eye, myself. But the other one's lost a tooth, and that looks even worse." Her shoulders and eyebrows rose higher. "But you don't have to worry about who'll *win*," she added generously.

"Very nice of you to say so," said Delia, with an ominous sweetness.

"No, it's pretty obvious, really. If you knew him, of course. How did it all start?"

Delia could have boxed her ears. Instead she said softly: "Suppose you mind your own business!"

The dark-blue eyes, disconcerting as a sudden light in a dark room, met hers for a moment and were veiled again. "Oh, I'm not doubting it was over *you*, of course. I just wondered how you came to let it happen. But never mind, it isn't my business; you're quite right there." She went on helpfully: "I hope you know how to sober him up. Water and fresh air don't work, you know."

"I have some experience, thanks," said Delia in a thin voice. But it was too late to try and think of things to say in return, things which would crush and confuse this impudent child; for quite suddenly the fight was over, and the end of it remained for ever a lost triumph for Delia. If she had been watching Jim's left, instead of Imogen Threlfall's saturnine eyebrows, she would have seen it take Sam Reddin clean under the point, lift him off the ground, and lay him back in the crisp snow under the hedge; where he lay stunned for a moment, and even thereafter made no attempt to rise. And that, somewhat surprisingly, was that. It was all over; and thanks to the little cat Imogen she had missed the climax; for which she would never, never forgive her as long as she lived.

Jim, twisting a handkerchief round his skinned knuckles, turned somewhat unsteadily and pushed his way through the circle of spectators towards where Delia stood. The collar of his battle-dress blouse was wrenched open, his hair stood on end, and his face was undoubtedly marked; but perhaps not too badly, with a little care and some discreet and timely doctoring. His lip was cut, and his left eye——

"He's in a bit of a mess, isn't he?" said Imogen conversationally. "You'll need a little piece of beeksteak for that left eye, but I expect it's going to colour pretty badly whatever you do."

39

"You don't see me looking worried about his appearance, do you?" said Delia. "It's not a studio photograph I'm engaged to." She hadn't meant to say it, she was almost sorry she had said it now, but she had to score off this assured brat somehow, and that was a certain way. And Jim wouldn't know, because Imogen would never tell, never to a living soul. Delia was well aware of that.

Imogen laughed, it was true, but Delia was not deceived. "No, I wouldn't exactly call Jim that—not even when he hasn't a black eye. Look, you'd better go and be nice to him, hadn't you? He's still in a temper; he's always like that when he's worked himself up to a fight; you can't get him down again in a hurry." And she smiled, and nodded, and walked on abruptly down the lane, her walk unhurried as ever, her square shoulders swinging as if she hadn't a care in the world; and suddenly Delia thought wildly: "What's the matter with me, getting het up over a baby like her? I ought not to get nasty just because she's jealous. I ought to understand the way she feels. Poor kid, she isn't fooling anybody, not even herself. She thinks she's in love with him—she thinks it's the first and the last—— And me doing my best to break her heart—Me!"

Jim took her by the shoulders then, and pulled her round to him roughly, and kissed her with force and deliberation. The blood of his cut lip dewed her mouth; she forgot that abrupt sisterly tenderness for Imogen in this so much bigger and more exciting emotion; she forgot the interested eyes of the clientéle of the "Clay Pigeon", fixed upon her brightly and without pretence of discretion. When he released her for a moment she did say, teasingly: "I thought this was supposed to be a secret, Jim?" But she didn't care what he answered, or whether he answered at all.

"Secret be damned!" said Jim in a loud voice. "I don't care who knows it. Let 'em all come and watch, if they like." And he kissed her again, and she returned the kiss heartily.

The habituees of the snug reflected that it was time for them to go. They hoisted Sam Reddin, dazed but not greatly damaged, to his reluctant feet, and bore him away into the bar for that last round before the house closed; and over it they dissected the fight, happily, pleased with an eventful evening, pleased with young Jim and with poor old Sam and with the charming Delia; pleased, in a vague way, with the convoys of camouflaged lorries sailing by daily on the Caldington road, and the khaki-clad local boys on leave, and the pleasant club-nights at First Aid Post and A.F.S. Station, and the whole ever-present, ever-distant war. And young Jim and the charming Delia were left alone in the lane.

"Who was that you were talking to?" asked Jim, the immediate urgency of his need to touch and hold her satisfied at length.

"Oh, just a girl I know. Never mind her, Jim. Are you all right? Oh, look at your poor eye! Doesn't it hurt an awful lot?"

He let himself be petted; he didn't want or need it, but it pleased her, and it was rather nice to have her soft fingers smoothing the tender skin round his eye, and dabbing gently at his broken lip.

"I won't be pretty for a few days," he said, "but I never am, so you're used to that. And anyhow *he* won't worry you again."

Never, until that night, had the attentions of Sam Reddin worried her in the least; but she didn't say so. She said in a long, contented sigh: "No, he won't get up to his tricks in a hurry, after to-night." Poor Sam, it was a pity in a way that he had to be sacrificed to bolster up Jim's idea of his own self-respect; but there you are, somebody has to suffer when a man starts to build himself up big for a woman to look up to; and you can hardly expect the woman to have much time to pity the victim.

Jim said, sudden and low: "You're quite sure, aren't you, kid?"

"Sure? About this? Yes, I'm dead sure."

"Because, you see, I've got to know where I stand, before I go."

"Before you go?" She looked up sharply. "Jim, are your lot going overseas?"

He nodded. "Pretty soon. After this leave I shan't see you again until the balloon's gone up. I'm not supposed to tell, but I can't tell much, because I don't know, and anyhow *you* wouldn't talk. So you see, I've got to know."

"You *do* know," she said with a shiver of excitement and foreboding: "Jim, is it France?"

"Don't seem anywhere else it can be, does there? Yes, it's France." He saw her face pucker and cloud with fear, and caught her to him again tightly. "It can't be for long, old girl. You'll see. It won't last, once we get our plans moving. I'll be back before you know I'm gone."

She looked at him wordlessly for a long time, and then plunged her cheek into his shoulder and wound her long, fair arms about him. "Oh, Jim, Jim!" she said, and clung to him, and wept. From excitement, perhaps; she wasn't normally the weeping kind.

8

When his leave was over, she saw him off at the station at Sheel Magna. His ring was on her finger by then for all to see, not the ring he would have liked to give her, but the best he could afford, a modest diamond twist. She kept taking off her glove as she walked, and turning and flashing her hand in the winter sun, fascinated by the little explosions of coloured light which sprang from that hard whiteness; and as often as she looked upon it with love, he watched the pleasure of her face with equal ardour, so that they presented a picture as attractive as ridiculous, and indulgent smiles followed them all the way.

They timed it so that the waiting should be short. Scenes on departure platforms should be brief, and so in their hearts they felt, though nothing had been said. Just a few minutes of sitting by the waiting-room fire, and then the fussy muttering of the train coming down the incline and round the bend, and: "Well, here she comes!" and a matter-of-fact kiss, as if they'd been married for years. Delia wanted to talk, quickly, wildly, as if you could hold on to the moment that way; but she knew better than that. Everything sayable and worth saying has already been said before this extreme minute; better silence than that rush of small-talk which washes away the big, clear outline of good-bye. And they were silent as he climbed into a smoking compartment and let down the window, and put out his hands to her again.

Something had happened to her face, he didn't know what. She had always been lovely, but now as she looked at him, her beauty hurt like a steel constriction upon his chest, *"peine forte et dure"*. He had never seen her utterly still before, never seen her eyes widen and dwell upon him with so clear and constant a regard, nor her mouth soften and grow mild with such a burden of gravity and wonder. He wanted her to stay like that in his mind, to stand there behind his eyes and look at him so, wherever he went, with the faint, sombre smile and the awe-struck eyes, and the wind unnoticed in her red-gold hair. Nothing must be changed, nothing defaced, until he came to see her again.

He leaned down and kissed her, keeping his hands from her, as one kisses a child; and as a child she accepted the kiss quietly, tilting up her face. She had never been like this before; she would never be like this again; he felt something of the uniqueness of the moment, but she knew the full of it, and it frightened her. "Good-bye kid!" he said, through the steam of the train. "Take care of yourself, and be good till I come back."

"Good-bye, Jim!" she said, and lifted her hand, as he was drawn away from her, in a strange, solemn gesture until he was lost to sight. When he was gone, she came back with difficulty to the world about her. There were no tears; something too distant and dream-like about the whole thing for that. "I didn't know it could get *me* this way," she thought as she walked home. "I thought I'd missed this stage. I thought I was safe." And she trembled because she knew now that she was not safe; but already something of the rare quality of her emotion was gone, as if she had come down from the peak on which his eyes had set her into the softer air of the valleys, where by rights she belonged. "I suppose it's bound to wear off a bit," she thought philosophically. "It wouldn't do if we all walked round in a dream like that all the time. Nothing would get done. Besides, it isn't comfortable." She liked her comfort. "Ah, well, I suppose it's all for the best. What use should we be to ourselves or anyone else, for ever mooning around cow-eyed with love?" But she knew she was losing something, she knew something was going away from her; something she only realised she had had by the chill of disappointment which told her that it was over.

Jim tucked his kit onto the rack, and sat down in the corner seat, and looked without interest at the girl at the opposite window; and looked again, with a surprised grin, because the girl was Imogen.

"Well, hello, goblin!"

"Hello, ghost!" she said, unsmiling.

"I never expected to see you. I thought you were in Caldington."

"Mrs. Ridley asked me up for Christmas," said Imogen. "I'm going back now. Did you have a good leave?"

"Yes, fine, thanks." He caught her eye then, full and solemn and amazingly blue, and wondered what was going on in the unpredictable young mind behind that apparently crystal glance; for there was something different about her, something adult and demure which put him at a distance in spite of the easy old greeting. He didn't like it. Enough bits of his life were shifting around already, without Imogen growing up and pushing him back into line with the ordinary young men of the village.

"So you made it!" said Imogen casually.

"Eh? Made what?"

"Delia. I couldn't help seeing just now."

"Oh!" said Jim. "I see! Yes, I made it." But he really saw very little, she thought crossly, he was as dumb as they made them; and just as she was thinking so he said, surprisingly: "You don't like her, do you?"

"Oh, she's all right. Why not? What am I supposed to do, fall on your neck and weep for joy?" Her eyebrows, always agile, slid up into her hair.

"You could wish me all the best, I suppose—or couldn't you? A chap doesn't get engaged every day. Besides, I shan't be seeing her again for a good bit."

She sat up sharply at that. "Oh! Why? What do you mean?"

"Because my lot are hopping it across the Channel pretty soon, that's why."

Imogen said, punctuating with quick indrawn breaths: "Oh! —Oh, good for you!" and again: "Of course I do wish you all the best." And abruptly and with passion, leaning forward and pushing *Men Only* from her so that it skidded on to the floor: "I wish I could go with you. I wish I were a man!"

Well, that was more like her, anyhow; he could understand that. He was even looking forward to it himself. It was colour, it was adventure, something different to look at, something new to do. War was automatically pretty grim, of course, but there might perhaps be something to be said on the other side. Why not? With a cause so utterly right as this cause and a quiet conscience because you are doing what you know you must do —yes, that was it, the excitement in him which made Delia seem already rather far away, the eager feeling of action ahead, which made danger shrink to a small insignificant thing—yes, why shouldn't a man, in those conditions, settle in to *enjoy* his war? And why shouldn't a woman envy him?

44

PART TWO

FRANCE: ADVANCING

"Aux armes, citoyens!
Formez vos bataillons."
ROUGET DE L'ISLE: *Marseillaise.*

I

THE lorry ahead slowed, the ruby glow of its tail-light expanding and brightening as the drift of snow thinned between. Jim leaned out from the cab and peered forward. In the light of their subdued headlamps the night was a snowing-globe, faintly golden, perfectly spherical, suspended in an opaque blackness; very small and strange, very lonely. In this surprisingly shrunken world there were no people except himself and Tommy, and half a dozen disconsolate fellows leaning on the tail-board of the lorry ahead; and no soil, except a disc of frozen and rutted Artois road fringed with thin low hedges which made the edge of the light jagged; and the silence swallowed up the noise of voices and the roar of the convoy's engines as a sponge swallows water, and made it futile to talk and ineffectual to sing, though they had sung their way across the Channel, and from Cherbourg half across France. From this de-peopled world, swung like a lantern in the hand of the night, it was a long, long, impossible journey home.

"Where the hell are we?" asked Tommy, leaning forward over the wheel and narrowing his eyes against the dazzle of the snow.

"Lord knows! What you'd call somewhere in France. According to Scotty, we ought to have been in half an hour ago."

Tommy grunted. "Another draughty old market-hall, I suppose—or somebody's ex-stables." They crept forward over the frozen snow quietly; the soft, furred noise of it crushing under their wheels made the surface of the silence quiver from within. "Not that I wouldn't welcome a nice stable and a layer or so of straw right now," admitted Tommy thoughtfully, "bugs or no bugs."

"He's moving on," said Jim. The ruby speck around which the visible world revolved withdrew itself, diminishing into the dark. "Hello, he's turning in! I believe we're here."

"About time, too!" said Tommy, and shot the big lorry forward in pursuit. The low black fringes of hedge ran into ribbons, the lane unrolled in a striped cloth of grey ruts and creamy-white ridges. Another star, dulled gold for red, showed in the dark. A man's voice chattered in French, and the new star became suddenly the pivot of the world as the rear-light of Scotty Walsh's lorry thinned sidewise and slid from view. Jim interpreted the speech of his allies by inflections and signs; the words meant nothing to him, but he had a quick ear for the mood behind them, and had already, though not with Tommy's finesse, begun to blarney his way round people without much need of words. He knew friendliness when he met it, he knew when folks were going to be difficult, he knew when he was being overcharged, and how to knock down the overcharge without offending. This voice was brusque, voluble, and well-disposed; it was also rather pleasurably excited, rather important. It took charge of them with unnecessary firmness, and steered them to the right through a broad open gate, with all the persuasion and authority a mother might use upon an unreliable child.

"Somebody's having a good time, anyhow," remarked Jim, as they drew nearer to the waving lantern and the beaming voice. "Watch out he don't hop up and start driving her in."

"Not him, he'd miss the rest of the fun if he did. It's a bit like being in a circus, isn't it?"

Behind the canvas cover of the lorry someone chuckled, and the red head and freckled face of Bill Gittens was thrust out. "You thinking of that nice little piece on the quay at Cherbourg, Tommy?"

"Shut your head!" said Tommy, but he smiled at the memory. "Anyway she was a good picker. You're jealous, that's your trouble. I haven't noticed any nice little pieces wasting lipstick on your ugly mug."

A hand like a ham reached out and half-lifted him painfully by the hair to dump him back again in the driving seat. "Lay off, you fool, I'm supposed to be driving this grid. D'you want me to put the little fellow's light out?"

The waving lantern showed, in erratic glimpses, a small man in a beret and a blue coat belted tightly about his round waist. He stood against the gate-post, in the frozen muck of the yard, waving them in. His face, seen and lost and seen again by flashes, was weatherbeaten and hard, deeply-lined with outdoor living, and far older than his voice had led them to think, but mobile as a child's, and voluble as his tongue. As they drew level with him and turned slowly in through the gate, he looked up at them with excited black eyes and shouted something welcoming and shrill, and half a dozen lusty voices shouted back untranslatable English greetings. He looked very happy, receiving the salutes of so many young men.

"I suppose," thought Jim, "this is by way of being a bit of excitement for them. If those French johnnies with the giddy blue uniforms came driving into our village, I dare say we'd be out opening gates for 'em—yes, and shouting, too." But for some reason it seemed more logical that way round. He could never quite get used to being fêted, even though the eighteen days of leisurely procession from Cherbourg to Artois had been gay with gifts, and girls, and flowers, and music. "As if we'd already won," he thought, and his mind skirted the thought cautiously, and looked the other way.

"I can't see where the heck I'm driving," complained Tommy, and raised his headlights full. "What is this place, anyway?"

"Farm. Can't you smell it? Sizable, too, by the look of it."

"Sizable by the smell alone, for that matter."

"I like the smell of a farm," said Jim.

"You would, you've never worked on one."

"No, but whiles I've thought I'd like to. Watch out, there's not much clearance this side, they've left a cart lying on its shafts." He leaned out through the half-open door to watch Tommy's progress, and the snow drove in over them, hard and fine. Vague outlines of buildings showed through the fall of it, drew nearer and became solid; barns, and stables, and the house standing apart; a broad farm-yard, rutted with frozen mud and ringed with byres, opened ahead of them, and the first lorry was just drawing up beside the long wall of the barn which closed the circle. "It's a prosperous-looking outfit, this," said Tommy approvingly. "We might do all right for butter and eggs if they're well-disposed."

They were becoming accomplished scroungers, the 4th Midshires. They knew how to get the best out of their entertainment, in France as in England. If there were eggs and butter to be got out of this well-to-do Artois farm, eggs and butter they would have.

A dog barked within the shadowy house, in a deep bell-voice that drew at Jim's heart unexpectedly. He was glad there were dogs; that was one grand thing about farms, there were always dogs, even if in some of these foreign villages they were not the companionable creatures he knew at home, but mere beasts of burden with no claim to life but their usefulness to their owners. He had tried talking to them as he talked to Sue, handling them as he handled her; and they had shied away suspiciously from his advances; but some of them he had wooed to rest between his hands at the end, and some of them would have trotted after him gladly when he left their villages, so that he was in constant danger of acquiring a comet's-tail of four-legged camp-followers. But this was an imperious voice, the voice of a lordling of a dog sensing a strange foot upon his territory. Jim wanted a look at him; he sounded a big fellow. A sheep-dog of sorts, probably.

The lorry drew closely in behind its fellow, and the noise of the engine purred away into silence.

"We're here," said Tommy, sitting back from the wheel.

"All right, now let's have a look at the set-up. Come on, I want to stretch my legs after that little session."

A bustle of men already filled the yard which had received them so quietly, so emptily. Bill Gittens and the rest of the load were clambering out over the tail-board and tumbling kit down to one another with a speed and efficiency which said plainly that they were sick of the road and anxious to settle in. Jim climbed out and joined the rest. It looked a pretty good billet to him; the barn was new and solid, and the farm buildings, though seen dimly in the dark, were extensive enough to impress him. There was something about the place—he found it in most farms—which took the knife-edge from the cold; a presence of living things, a sense of company. Even the smells were warm and alive.

"I'm going to like this," he said, and from pure curiosity walked up towards the house to take a closer look at the place. Two people were talking in oddly contrasted French a few steps from the closed door; even to Jim, who knew nothing of what either of them was saying, the difference was very clearly marked; the one spoke French French, and the other English French, high-school French, used diffidently for the first time upon the natives who were born to it. This was Second-Lieutenant Ridley, lately Brian Ridley, the vicar's eldest, and an imp if ever there was one. He'd had to grow up in a hurry, like a lot of other kids who should by rights have still been at school; he was nineteen and a few months, but he took life and his job very seriously these days, and it was no light ordeal to have to expose his copybook French to the critical ears of farmers' wives who spoke it at incredible speed and not uncommonly finished his lame sentences for him. This one, however, was strangely easy. For one thing they were in the dark, where effort and embarrassment were less apparent; and for another, the woman herself was unexcited and kind, and seemed content to let him do his own talking in his own way. So Second-Lieutenant Ridley was rather enjoying himself.

Jim, hearing these two voices in the dark, did not at first realise that one of them belonged to a woman. Even when the figures took shape, both silhouettes seemed to be those of men, the one slight and unmistakably military, the other somewhat below medium height, but upright and sturdy, in a shapeless woollen sweater like a fisherman's and trousers tucked into the tops of heavy boots. But when the dog whined at the door, and the second speaker turned to call backward over one shoulder to him, the voice was suddenly full of character, at once a reproof and a caress, betraying much, so that the darkness seemed less complete about the speaker. It said clearly that here was a woman, that she was young though not very young, that she was with authority in this place, that if she said "Be silent!" one should be silent. But the voice had not even raised its pitch, nor quickened upon the words.

"Tais-toi, grand babillard! Ne connais-tu pas tes amis?"

The headlights of the last lorries, as they eased their slow way into the yard, caught and shone upon her so, her chin upon her shoulder; and Jim saw her face full. A broad face it was, strongly featured and of a severe stillness, coldly gentle like the early winter evenings before the frosts begin; the eyes of some indefinable dark colour, deep-set and heavily-lidded, the mouth both long and full, and denying the generosity of its shape by the rigid set of the lips when she ceased speaking. He had seen a woman's mouth drawn tight like that when she was angry, but never when she could bear to speak in a voice so level and calm; and he saw that this was not a matter of mood, but of something which had happened to this woman, something from beforetime, which could not now be undone. She was bareheaded, and he could not tell where the black of her coiled hair ended and the black of the night began.

Brian Ridley, in his shy, half-audible French, asked something about the dog. She turned and looked at him without a smile, but after her composed fashion kindly, for he looked a mere child to her, and his dignity touched her. *"Les soldats Anglais aiment les chiens, n'est-ce-pas? C'est bien connu."* And she raised her voice suddenly, and called towards the house: *"Simone, ouvrez la porte!"*

The dog came like a flash of tawny light when the door was opened, and having thrust its head under her hands, began to circle them in wide, easy leaps, no longer belling nor whining, but uttering in its throat that torrent of dark sound which dogs use when they come nearest speech. The Ridleys loved dogs, but this one would not let Brian touch him; he talked, but he kept his distance. Jim thought: "I'll have him within a couple of days. I'll get him before to-morrow's out." And it was suddenly important, more important than almost anything in the world, though he could not tell why; so that he could hardly bear to go back to the barn without trying his wiles then and there. That was a silly thing to want so much; but what he really wanted was to see the woman's face when he whistled her dog from her side; and that was worse than silly, it was damned mean.

He shook himself. and turned back to rejoin his fellows. They were already making themselves comfortable inside the barn, which was weatherproof and comparatively warm, and smelled heavily sweet and musty with straw. The company's cooks had been there several hours, and there was tea on the go, and bread and bully-beef; and the air was beginning to haze with cigarette smoke, as always where they were. There was a small portable oil-stove raised upon a low platform of glazed bricks for safety. It gave a respectable light and at least a suggestion of warmth. Altogether it was not bad; they had been in very much worse places.

"Quick work!" said Jim. "Where did you pinch the stove?"

"You think again, my lad," advised Tommy. "This was all done before we came. When we walked in here that stove was lit ready for us; *and* there's a little dump of paraffin-drums in a shed outside. There's somebody round here doing some very sound thinking on our account."

"Home from home," said Scotty Walsh, rolling over on his belly to reach out a long arm and turn the flame higher. "Proper motherly touch about it, ain't there?"

Jim took his mug of tea, and sat down in the straw and stretched his legs out before him. "There *is* a woman. She seems to be boss around here, too. Think she did have all this done for us?"

"Could be. You never can tell with a woman; they take us in some rum ways. Remember that old girl in Vitry-le-vieux who used to stand in the garden in a howling east wind to keep an eye on her washing? And the grocer's wife who sent her daughter out of the shop every time she saw us coming? Never knew we looked such hell-bats." These were the extremes upon one side, but Tommy's memory found more to ponder upon the other, without going back to the nice little piece on the quay at Cherbourg. He settled back in the straw with a reminiscent smile. "We ain't done so bad, all things considered. What's this one like?"

It wasn't easy to answer that, remembering the quiet, hard face in the gleam of the headlights. You could say she was youngish, and dark, and strongly built, and dressed like a man; you could say she was good-looking if you liked, because, by God, she was now you came to think of it; but nothing you could say would give them any idea of what she really looked like. Let them weigh that up for themselves, when they had seen her.

"Oh, I don't know. Not bad. She's outside talking to little Ridley. They're getting on like a house afire, too." He added with enthusiasm: "She's got a nice bull-mastiff. Right good-looking beast, he is. You wait till you see him."

There was some laughter over this, for it was exactly what they would have expected him to note and report. Bill, now, would never have seen the dog; Jim didn't seem to have seen the woman. He let it go at that; it was simpler. He didn't like explaining things at the best of times, and the woman outside was not the best possible subject on which to begin. But before he settled down for the night, he went out into the yard again to smoke a last cigarette. She was gone, and the bull-mastiff with her. The yard was empty but for the sentries at the gates, and the house was dark and quiet, wooden shutters closed tight upon the ground-floor windows, and the door fast shut. He stood bareheaded in the night for a while, looking up at the stars. It was a long way back to Morwen Hoe from there, and a long way forward to victory, but sometimes the way ahead seemed only a day's journey by comparison with the way back. For days and days at a stretch he never thought of home; it was queer that a man could travel so far in only twenty days. At the end of December he had said good-bye to Delia; and it was not yet the end of January. Yet she was so far from him that he might have known her in another life, in another world;

51

while the one in which he lived now was peopled rather with trim little sloe-eyed Parisiennes, and the volatile mixed company of French trains, and weather-beaten old peasants nursing the fields of their absent sons, and the sons themselves, gay and voluble and eager in uniform, and the occasional white-coifed old Norman woman, and the skirted curés, and the dark, quiet mistress of this Artois farm.

He supposed he ought to write to Delia. There was plenty to tell her, these days. He would go in and do it now, before he slept. Or better still, perhaps, wait until to-morrow, after he'd had a look at the village. It was not such a bad night, after all; the snow had stopped, and the sky was clearing fast. He believed it was going to be a fine day to-morrow.

He dropped the butt of his cigarette into the snow, and ground it out. He was quite content. There hadn't been much action yet, true; but on the whole he was enjoying his war.

2

They were the third company to make use of the farm at Boissy-en-Fougères, and the village had become accustomed to being over-run by English soldiers, and already had a smattering of the language. It was a small community until the English came, and had welcomed the first visitors with hysterical excitement but some distrust. For the 4th Midshires the ground had been well prepared, and from the first day they settled down to strike roots.

It was a pity that they saw it first in winter, when even the chilly sunlight could do no justice to the village; but there was promise of pleasure enough should they still be there when Spring came, for half the garden hedges were lilac, and behind Georges Lozelle's farm three acres of orchard climbed a gradual slope towards a beech-wood. Beyond the beech-wood again there was a folded valley with a stream, too small to be called a river, threading its heart. It was strange that the war should bring them to a spot so peaceful. As for the village itself, it was a single long, meandering street, joined here and there by narrow by-lanes, with a mill at one end beside the stream, and a fringe of small out-lying farm-steads. There was a little white-washed church with a single bell, and a curtained café in the front room of one of the houses, a café which in summer expanded into the garden, but just now stayed snug about the fire. There was a *bistro*, the nearest approach to a village pub they had found or were likely to find in France, though it served them with vin rouge or pernod or crême-de-menthe instead of beer; but the company was there, and the talk, and the atmosphere of a local club which can nowhere be found in a town, even in England. The proprietor was a middle-aged man, short and monstrously fat, who padded about all day in his shirt-sleeves, with a white apron tied around his enormous waist; and sometimes he was joined behind the bar, on brisk evenings, by his daughter Eliane, who was nineteen, blonde as a lily and almost as lovely; so that very soon the susceptible young men of the 4th Midshires began to drop in regularly at the hour of the apèritif.

There was a Post Office, and a grocer's shop, and a green-grocer's, with a modest nursery-garden attached, and a queer little family business something between chemist and herbalist, kept by an old man who had three sons in the French navy. There was Mêre Jeantot's cake-shop, where every day fresh home-made pâtisseries and sweets made the morning fragrant with delectable smells, and the warm air blew through from the bakeries behind the house. There was everything the free heart could desire, including a dearth of young men which gave the invaders a flying start at dances in the little schoolroom. But Madame Lozelle did not come to these dances. Sometimes she came into the café, sometimes they saw her in the farm-yard, but she remained the most elusive person in Boissy-en-Fougères, and this without in any way shunning the company of her fellows. She worked from dawn to dark, said the village, and had no time nor energy left for anything but work; the farm had lost so many men, her husband among them; she ran it now with the old man Jean and a couple of boys too young to serve in the army. Yes, she was well-liked, never think otherwise; a good mistress, a wonderful neighbour; but they did not expect her to have time to be gay.

In the *bistro*, with Papa Brègis for instructor, the visitors learned a certain amount of clipped colloquial French, and taught him in return a good deal of unapproved but useful English. If the language difficulty ever cropped up, there was usually someone to interpret. Several of the Midshires had school French to fall back upon; and Monsieur Peyron the schoolmaster, who dropped in every evening, had once been French master in an English preparatory school, and retained a brand of pedantic English which amply filled the remaining gap. He was still of military age, poor Monsieur Peyron, but

53

alas, his lungs—you understand. He was a thin, worn young man, with a neatly trimmed chestnut beard against which the pallor of his face was truly startling, and his emaciated hands were hysterical with gestures at once eager and deprecating. He had the spirit of an ardent boy, burning with enthusiasm to perform feats of heroism for France, which he loved as extravagantly and shamelessly as the bull-mastiff Chicot loved Miriam Lozelle; but he was physically and mentally quite incapable of bringing to birth even the least of his dreams. They liked him; they would willingly have been sorry for him, but he did not seem to realise that he was in a fit position for pity, so they contented themselves with liking him. His delight in their company was alone sufficient to assure him of that.

"The last time the Germans came," said Monsieur Peyron, waving his glass of crême-de-menthe in a trembling hand, "the last time, *vous voyez*, they took us by surprise, a people unprepared, unequipped, complacent. This time it will not be so, *je vous assure*. This time we have *la ligne Maginot*, we have guns, and tanks, and aeroplanes, and men—and most of all, messieurs, we have the mind to fight. It is they who will be taken on the hip. *On les aura!*" He clenched the thin fingers which could not even have held a rifle steady, and his hazel eyes grew golden with fever. *"On les aura!"*

"On les aura!" echoed the 4th Midshires, and Papa Brègis, and Eliane in her clear high voice.

"Let us drink to it," said Monsieur Peyron. "To the day of the meeting! To the day of their disillusionment!"

They drank it with roars of approval. Yes, there was something in pickle for the Germans, something they wouldn't like. To over-run Poland, a half-armed plain without planned defences, was one thing; to tackle France and Britain together would prove quite another. The man was mad to attempt it, but as sure as night followed day, his madness would recoil on his own head. When the slow dispositions were complete, the Allied armies would move, and then the clash would come, the day of meeting, the day of disillusionment.

"And the sooner the better," said Jim, setting down his empty glass with a clatter upon the green-tiled table. "All we want is a crack at 'em. What are we waiting for?"

"Monsieur, in France we do these things with method, with deliberation. We dispose ourselves to hoard men's lives, not to spend them. It must be done with economy; but never fear, it will be done. General Gamelin, he is a great man, he knows his business very well."

"So they say. Old Gort, he ain't so dusty, either. Well, all I hope is they'll get down to it soon."

"Rest assured. *Ça marche,* monsieur."

"*Ca marche!*"

Papa Brègis waddled and wheezed across to his spindle-legged cabinet gramophone, and sorted out a record from the many.

"A little music, *hein?* You like well the patriotic song, *n'est-ce-pas?*. This is one of the pillars of France."

They half-expected the "Marseillaise", which had played and sung itself into their consciousness very thoroughly. It was everywhere, ready to spring to the lips of ordinary men and women in the streets. Funny if little bowler-hatted businessmen in Caldington suddenly started rendering "God Save the King" on their way to the office; but nobody thought anything of it here. However, this was not the "Marseillaise", but another tune, almost as inflammatory but less familiar.

"What is it?" asked Tommy, beating time to it thoughtfully with his empty pernod glass. "It's a bit like the 'Death of Nelson'. Listen! ' 'Twas in Trafalgar Bay——' "

"*C'est le 'Chant du Départ'!*" said Eliane, and she sang it through, not shyly, as sometimes she sang for them, but full-voiced, with surging breast and brilliant eyes. That was the effect of French patriotic song upon the natives, Jim had found; they threw away all their reserve and went at it madly, with a fervour the English reserved for "The Washing on the Siegfried Line" and "Run, Rabbit, Run". Well, if it sat a trifle oddly on solid middle-aged men like Papa, it was a crown, a cap of liberty, upon the ash-blonde head of Eliane. It turned her into one of those posters of La France, one of those frail tigresses of the barricades. Her slim straight body arched itself like a rapier flexed in the hand, and her dark eyes, at all times arresting against the pallor of her person, flared into a red like that of gillyflowers in the sun. When she ended her song, they applauded her, though not for her voice; and she flushed, and hurried to refill Tommy's glass, to cover in some measure the triumph and joy she felt in stirring them so.

"That was really something," said Tommy. "What's it all about?"

Monsieur Peyron turned the flaming French into pedestrian English for them. "It is the song of troops setting out to a great

55

battle for right, monsieur. It is the song of leave-taking, perhaps not to return, perhaps to be brought back captive, perhaps to come home victorious; but whatever comes, to fight to the end for a great cause, messieurs. They will play it, I think, in your own Canada, as the French troops embark for England. As it might be we would play it for you here, when you go forward towards the enemy."

It brought a moment of solemnity in at the green-glass doors, to stand chillingly among them, and be as quickly dissolved in the next burst of speech and gaiety; but while is lasted, Tommy Goolden's eyes were fixed upon Eliane Brègis, and hers upon him, wonderingly, as if they saw each other for the first time, and were in some way disquieted by the encounter.

"But it won't be for long," said Tommy, as if he were answering a question no one had asked. "This time we're ready for 'em. It'll be a matter of months this time, not years, before we all come home."

"*C'est certain, monsieur,*" she said in a low voice.

"It is the comfort of many to believe that," said Monsieur Peyron. "Your hostess of all people will be glad when the men return. Consider what it means to handle so extensive a farm, when one has not been born to it. She has barely six months of experience on which to draw, *cette pauvre* Madame Lozelle, yet she does not hesitate. And a success, *vous voyez*—she has the place in most excellent order."

"It's pretty trim," agreed Jim. "She's not a native, then? She looked to me as if she belonged to Boissy, all right."

Monsieur Peyron smiled his deprecating, well-informed smile. It might have been hard to forgive him for knowing so much about everyone's business if he had not been so ardent a champion of the whole village. His gossip was all sympathy and praise. "You mistake. Monsieur Georges, her husband—Monsieur le Sergent—but yes, Boissy to the backbone. But Madame —oh, no. Madame is not of Boissy, nor of France itself except by her marriage."

"Not French?" said Jim. "Go on, you're kidding! She speaks the lingo all right, nineteen to the dozen."

"Nevertheless, monsieur, *c'est vrai*. I swear to you I do not kid. Madame Lozelle is Czech by birth. She met Monsieur Georges just over six months ago in Paris, and married him there. She is a woman of learning, a graduate of Prague University, with more languages than French only to her tongue. But unfortunately she is of Jewish blood—you understand.

When the Germans entered Bohemia, it was best for her to go. There was nothing there for her. She escaped to France, by what means I do not know, and settled down happily here in Boissy-en-Fougères. *Hélas*, the war has followed her even here; her husband is with his regiment near Sedan, and she farms his land, as you have seen.''

"I knew a Czech once," said Jim, thinking of Jacek the Pioneer, who also had once lived happily in the city of St. Wenceslas. "He was a good chap, too. It's a damned shame they should have to run from their own homes, like that."

"It is damn' shame for very many people, monsieur, but those days are over. Ah, we were too patient, too ready to believe that others were as well-intentioned as we. But now all that is changed. There is no more going back. We have drawn the line at last, your country and mine, and sworn that further than this they shall not go. It is the end of tyranny when France and England take their stand together. Soon she shall go back to visit her Prague, *n'est-ce-pas?* Cleared of its usurping Prussian pigs—yes. You will see. It will not be long."

"That's it," said Jim. "Here's to it! We take a lot of starting, but when we get going we go all the way."

"*C'est entendu!* Certainly it is good to be *en route*, is it not? We shall squeeze them as they have squeezed their neighbours. It will be the hour of the exile, *non?*"

"Sure enough! The hour of the exile. By gum, yes, that'll be something to look forward to."

He thought, suddenly, of how her face would look when she walked again in the streets of a free Prague; her quiet eyes everywhere soothed and comforted by the remembered buildings, the late-lost trees of home, her feet ringing upon the familiar pavements, the kind air in her nostrils. And he wondered if she would be changed then, if the set of her lips would soften and return, if she would be eased of the thing which never left her by night or day, healed of the thing which had been done to her and never could be undone. Because if so, he thought it would be worth a great deal to see Miriam's face that day.

3

They were firing in the deserted quarries outside the village, one day at the beginning of February, and a small dark speck began to run along the grass in front of the bobbing targets. Tommy, behind the sights of a machine-gun, was the first to notice it, and straightened himself to discover what it could be. It was one of the dogs from the farm, a little cross-bred spaniel bitch, heading confidently for her usual hunting-ground across the full line of fire. Tommy yelled his discovery and held his fire. So did Alec Ross on Number Two, in response to the Sergeant's agitated bellow. But above the noise of the guns a shout could carry no further, and no one beyond seemed to have noticed the intruder, for the grass was growing lush and coarse, and she was very small. Alec yelled through his hands, and was either not heard or not understood. He picked himself up from the ground in a hurry, and began to run towards the next gun-team.

"He won't make it," said Tommy. "He can't. My God, what do we do now? They haven't seen her."

Jim looked at the grass and soil spurting where the shots fell short, looked at the racing man, looked at the spaniel. She had almost reached the fourth target, and suddenly she was frightened and confused, she ran a little way back, a little way forward. She lost her head and cowered, the black line of her back all but buried in the grass.

"Oh, to hell with this!" he shouted, and began to run at full speed towards her, diagonally into the field of fire. He did not see Madame Lozelle as she came racing madly up the slope of the quarry, nor hear Sergeant Blackie's furious curses which followed him in his flight. He had never been capable of thinking of or doing more than one thing at a time, and just then he was bent on reaching the dog in the shortest possible time. He shouted himself, unprintable imprecations upon her, wasting precious breath in telling her to "Get the hell out of here! Blast you, get under the target, it's the safest place with these bum shots around". But she was incapable of making a sensible move, bewildered out of her wits by the noise, terrified by his mad rush at her; she lay down in the grass and whined. Even when he had her in his arms, and was loping aside with her from the danger zone, he called her a blasted little black bitch with far more than literal meaning, at the same time smoothing her quivering head with one hand, and holding her against him very gently, for she was just beginning to feel the weight of her next litter. She flattened her head against his chest, and lay trembling spasmodically; and the two of them together ran full tilt into the arms of Miriam Lozelle.

She had run so fast that she could not speak for a moment, and it was obvious that if he had not made that rush for the dog she would have done it herself without an instant's hesitation. Her hands took Jim by the shoulders, and held him tightly while she struggled to articulate, her breath singing through her teeth, her hair fallen from its neat coil in an ebony flood about her shoulders.

"It's all right," he said, "it's all right. I've got her. She isn't hurt." And he shifted the spaniel's weight and put one arm about Miriam, for he was half-afraid she would collapse. He had never seen her shaken before, so that all his senses were concentrated upon her, and only gradually did the rest of the world come in. He did not realise for a full minute more how quiet it was, there in the uneven grass-and-gravel floor of the shallow quarries. Several people were tearing towards them from the range, young Ridley, and Sergeant Blackie, and Captain Halliday; and all the guns had ceased firing. He wondered how long it had been like that; probably they had fallen silent well before he completed his grand and rather silly gesture. "In which case," he thought, "I've made an even bloodier fool of myself than I realised." But it didn't seem to matter very much; anyhow there was no one hurt. If he hadn't moved perhaps they would have been running towards what was left of Miriam, a tumble of black hair and white flesh in the grass.

"Don't! Please don't! You see she's all right—only scared, and she'll get over that fast enough; she's got cheek enough for two."

"It was my fault," said Miriam, hoarse and quiet upon her first controlled breath. "They told me, but I forgot. I opened the door, and she——" She touched the apologetic head, smoothing her fingers along the woebegone cheeks with a soft, cajoling motion. She looked up at Jim suddenly, and said, as if it explained something, as perhaps it did: "She is with young."

"Yes," said Jim, "I know. Should be some nice pups."

"I am not fluent," she said, "but I think you know what I would say." Her eyes held him, wide and dark. "You might have been killed; you know that, too."

"So might you."

She looked at him in surprise then, as if the comparison had never occurred to her, and even now she could not seriously entertain it. The shadow of a smile fluttered her lips, and the indifferent ghost of a shrug lifted her shoulders. The significance of it might at any other time have passed him by, but just then he was so intently aware of her that every gesture she made assumed importance in his eyes; and this deliberate refusal to be at all concerned about her own life, while she agonised over his, took root in his mind, and grew, and troubled him from that moment. It wasn't natural, in anyone, much less in anyone still young and handsome and happily married, as she was. What was it that set her so far apart? So far that even when she came towards you, even when she ran headlong into your arms, she was still a whole world away.

The pursuit closed in. Brian Ridley was ahead, being so young and fleet of foot; but he did not particularly want to be first on the spot, for he was not at all sure what one ought to say in such circumstances. There was nothing in the drill-book about it, and besides, he was unfairly handicapped by a sneaking admiration for the aplomb with which the thing had been done. Of course Benison ought not to have taken the situation into his own hands, and very certainly ought never to have exposed himself to such a crazy risk, dog or no dog. But Brian had almost hopped out from behind Number Five and gone tearing down the quarry himself, which would have been infinitely worse; so the less he said in the affair the better. He checked discreetly in the last hundred yards, and let Sergeant Blackie pass him. It was very much easier to leave it all to him.

"They will be angry with you," said Miriam.

"I'm not worried," said Jim, smiling at her. "I think you were a bit angry yourself."

She shook her head. "It was just that you should not have done it. I could not have forgiven myself if you had been hurt. But angry—Do I have to say how grateful I am to you —how deeply I am in your debt——?"

"Please, don't talk like that. You don't have to say a thing —not a thing. I just—well, there wasn't much time, you see. But anyhow, there's no need to think any more about it. It's all over and no harm done. Don't worry about me."

Sergeant Blackie came up in good order, his face purple with inexpressible curses. Jim supposed he had better get rid of Madame Lozelle, and let the old boy get it off his chest. He could hardly be expected to do his best swearing with a woman in the audience.

"You'd better go along home, Madame. Will you be all right alone?" And he held out the dog to her, and she took it in her arms gently, and stood away from him; but she did not go home. She was completely herself again, now that there were other people there; only he had seen her calm broken; only he

knew how lightly she regarded her own life, to shrug it aside
with a faintly amused smile that anyone should expect her to
put any value upon it. She shook back the torrent of black hair
from her face, and took a step towards the angry Sergeant.

"*Monsieur le Sergent*, I am to blame. It is all my fault. I
had forgotten there was to be firing to-day, or I would not have
let Sarka out of the stables. I am very sorry."

Sergeant Blackie, gruff and breathless as he was, could hardly
choose but be gallant to a handsome woman with her hair
down.

"Your fault nonsense, ma'am. The sort of unlucky thing that
might happen at any moment. Have to be prepared for these
things. But they must be handled in a responsible manner, not
by the first suicidal halfwit who thinks fit to step into the lime-
light. Are you quite all right, ma'am? It must have shaken
you up."

Captain Halliday, ending his run at an easy lope, came up
with Brian Ridley at his elbow, and took charge of matters in
his normal decisive way. He never seemed greatly disturbed by
anything.

"Everything all right here? Nobody hurt? All right, Sergeant.
I'll see to this." He turned to Miriam, and went into fluent
French, a flood of easy words which made Jim's heart tighten
with envy. She answered quietly, her voice now level and
strong, reassuring him, deprecating his concern for her, blaming
herself all over again because she had opened a door and let
out with Sarka the whole storm of feeling. They became ani-
mated with each other; it was plain that Halliday thought her
pretty marvellous, as they all did; but even as she talked away
in French she turned and cast one quick glance full at Jim, and
he remembered with pleasure, almost with triumph, that she
had talked to him in his own tongue, not with this voluble
circumstance of words, but as her mind moved, without concealment or elaboration. He knew her better than any of them;
the merest chance, the stress of a bad moment, had opened her
mind to him, but she would not close it again now. He felt
that about her; everything she did she did once for all.

"Perhaps," said Captain Halliday, with meaning, "Ridley
here will be so kind——"

"Delighted," said Brian, with obvious truthfulness, and made
his mission of seeing her home an excuse for taking Miriam's
arm. "Let me carry the dog—she's much too heavy for you."
Sarka, half-resigned and half-complacent, went to him without

protest, satisfied to be nursed and petted by whoever cared to do it. Miriam made then her most deliberate, her most betraying gesture; she stood there for a moment with her face turned to Jim, and then she crossed the few yards of broken ground which separated them, and with the fingers of one hand touched his arm, a touch so light that he scarcely felt it, but prolonged for a few seconds that there might be no ignoring it, no forgetting it. Young Ridley would have taken a bigger and colder blast than was coming to Jim, just to have had that accolade. Captain Halliday himself must have felt that after that he would be talking to no purpose; but after she was gone, he did his best to reduce the halo Jim Benison was wearing to the dingy fool's cap it really was and he could be effectively cutting when he chose.

Jim learned what sort of a soldier he was, in clipped phrases which might have had the intended bite but for the memory of Miriam's hand on his arm. In any case he had had from the beginning no illusions about his action. He had simply thought: "To hell with it!" and said it, and done exactly what he had wanted to do. But it didn't make a good defence, and since he was expected to say something, he took the opposite line from the truth.

"I'm sorry, sir. There was no time to reach you or Second-Lieutenant Ridley. Somebody had to do something quickly."

"And you considered yourself to be that somebody?" The thin eyebrows rose. "Sergeant Blackie, I believe, was close beside you at Number One?" He knew damn well he was, the pedantic little devil.

"Yes, sir."

"He had, I presume, taken some steps in the matter?"

"He stopped Number Two, sir, and sent Ross ahead towards the others. But it would have taken too long, sir. The men on the far guns couldn't see her."

"So you felt called upon to throw away your life in a grand gesture on behalf of Madame Lozelle's dog. Apart from any other considerations, your life is considered, for some incalculable reason, to be of value to the war effort. In the circumstances, I can't concur very warmly, but it's not for me to decide. Nor for you! Do you understand? You'll risk it where those in command over you decide that the risk is justifiable, not when you see fit. Sergeant Blackie ordered you back to your gun. Why didn't you obey the order?"

"I didn't hear it, sir."

"I find that hard to believe," said Captain Halliday drily.

"I heard him shouting all right, sir," Jim explained cheerfully, "but I didn't get the words."

"You took damned good care not to, I expect."

"Well, sir, quite frankly, I didn't just set out to get killed. I figured the chaps on the guns would have the gumption to cease fire when I started running. They couldn't see her, but they could see me. And it worked out that way." There was nothing in the least frank about this statement, but it offered to the casual listener some hope for his sanity, and it spiked at least one of Captain Halliday's guns. He dismissed him unblessed to the receptive arms of the Sergeant, who dealt faithfully with him. Towards the end of this second resumé Jim stopped listening, so that it was difficult to make the correct replies in the right places. Apart from certain aspects of it, he was rather bored with the affair by then. He went back thoughtfully to his gun-team, and grinned at Tommy, and turned his thumbs down.

"Dead and damned!"

"You asked for it," said Tommy. "What did he say?"

"Oh, the usual. I could have said it for him. Who's worried?"

It was talked about, diminuendo, for the rest of the day, but by night it was all over. Every occasion of excitement and discussion went the same way in the end; that was one comforting thing about making a fool of yourself, it was all forgotten long before you really began regretting it. Jim, on sentry-go at the gate of the farm-yard that night, no longer felt any desire either to congratulate or kick himself.

It was a cold, drizzly night, thick with mist out of which the grudging rain dripped as if wrung from a sponge. Not a night for contemplation, but he was quite content to stand there in the miserable darkness and let his thoughts wander. A rum sort of day it had been, and he didn't want to remember all the details of it; but there were things—the feel of Sarka alive and agonised with self-pity in his arms, and the sudden apparition of Miriam Lozelle as a woman after so long of thinking of her as a farmer. She had been admired from the beginning as the equal of a man, but not as was her due; and that abrupt vision of her in a dark-red frock, with disarranged hair and distressed eyes, had shaken them all. But they had not seen the truth of it. He remembered most clearly of all how there had sprung from behind that composed and indifferent front of hers the momentary revelation of

an ultimate agony of pity, how her voice had sounded some
sort of an answer in his mind as she said: "She is with young."

4

He saw her again the next day, drawing water at the pump
in the yard; and though he would not, until then, have ventured to speak to her at all, this time he picked up her heavy
wooden buckets quite simply, and asked her where she wanted
them. She had looked up at him as he approached, and given
him the matter-of-fact smile she would have bestowed upon
Jean, or one of the boys who worked about the place; and now
she turned and led the way across the yard and through a
corner of the newly-turned kitchen garden to the rear of the
house.
"In here. It is my washing-day, you see. Pour them into the
copper, if you please. They are too heavy for me to lift alone,
and Simone is busy baking, and does not like to be disturbed."
It was a pleasant place, the scullery of Boissy farm, with a
red-tiled floor and scrubbed white tables, and all along one wall
windows which looked out upon the neatly-ruled rows of
cabbages in the garden. All these windows were standing open,
although it was February, for the heat from the brick copper at
one end of the room made the air more than comfortably warm.
A round wooden lid, blanched white with much washing,
covered the boiler. Jim lifted it, and was blinded by a gush of
steam which shot upward like a giant geni escaping from its
bottle. He hadn't been so warm since he left England.
"Both buckets in?"
"*S'il vous plaît*, monsieur."
The steam subsided with a hiss of satiety, and the lid was
replaced. She had one batch of whites already blowing merrily
in the garden, and some more in her tub. "It seems wrong to
see you indoors," he said, thinking aloud.
"*Comment?* Wrong?" She smiled. "I am a farmer's wife,
and one must wash."
"I saw you ploughing the other day," he said; but he did
not say how grand it had been, the assurance of her, the ease
and rhythm of her walk along the furrow, the poise of her head
against the skyline.
"Yes. It is very late, it should have been done long ago.
You look at me as if you think there is nothing I cannot do.
That is foolish. I will tell you a secret—I cannot cook. If

64

Simone left me, I should starve, or eat roots and salads like a vegetarian." She smiled. "I think you do not altogether believe me. Some day I shall make you eat a meal of my cooking, and you will be cured of thinking me so competent. At my age it is not good for a woman to be flattered so."

He wondered then for the first time what her age was. Thirty, surely, at the very highest; and yet she spoke as if she had lived a whole lifetime out. He'd heard women use that phrase "at my age" often enough when they wanted to be laughed at and reassured that they were as young as the dawn; but that was not how she said it.

"I'll fetch you some more water in, shall I?" he said, reaching for the buckets. "You'll be needing some later on."

"Thank you. That is kind."

He refilled the buckets, and brought them back and stood them in a corner until they should be wanted. "You know," he said, wiping his hands, "you ought to sing out for one of us chaps when you want any fetching and carrying done. We'd be glad, and there must be a lot of odd jobs we could take off your hands around the place. You've done a lot for us, and you never ask for anything."

"*Et vous n'avez rien fait?*" she said gently.

"Please, don't laugh, but I want to ask a favour. Will you always talk English to me?"

"It would be good for your French to talk with me in that language, would it not?"

"I can do that with Papa Brègis, or Jean, or Michel Peyron. But not with you. It's different."

She plunged her arms to the elbow in the whispering suds, and considered for a moment before she answered. Her voice was very low and quiet as she said: "Very well, I do not think so fast in English as in French, but I will do as you ask. You say I never ask for anything. I said, have you then done nothing for me? Yesterday, was that nothing?"

The shock of that memory came in upon them again with a curious intimacy. Yesterday it had all happened so simply; to-day he flushed at the thought of it, for it was too revealing.

"I know," she said, as if she could read his mind. "We shall not speak of it again. You do not like putting me in your debt. It makes you uncomfortable to be thanked. But I warn you I shall not forget that it happened because I do not talk of it." Her tone changed: she said briskly: "If you wish to be useful, bring me that wicker basket; and in a moment you

65

shall turn the wringer for me until you are tired, no? I will make you sorry you ever offered to help me."

He sprang to do her bidding, in high feather with himself and all the world. This was more like it; this was like home; when he was a little boy he had taken great delight in making himself useful in unexpected ways about the house; afterwards, of course, it had worn off, as this queer zeal always does. Now it came back as a kind of novel game, a change from the usual fatigue and guard duties. He set to work merrily to help her rinse and wring the sheets. It was a two-person job, in any case, and he took considerable pleasure in showing her how handy he could be.

"You have done this many times before," she said, smiling at him as he folded a sheet lengthwise to feed it into the wringer. When she smiled, all the rigidity of her mouth was broken and softened; and now that he had found his way into her confidence, she smiled often. "It is the hand of an expert."

"You're making fun of me now; but mind you, I know I'm good. I used to do this for my mother, sometimes when she had a big wash. She used to say I was a great help to her." He looked sideways at Miriam, and gave her an impish grin.

"You fish," she said severely. "You are shameless. But I shall not encourage you. Later on I will tell you if you have been a great help to me; and I am not easily pleased, let me assure you."

"You can't scare me, I know my worth. Look at that—neat as ninepence." He folded the sheet away into the white wicker basket, and reached for the next. "I suppose the little dog's all right now, is she? Not feeling mopish any longer? I haven't seen her to-day."

"A little subdued, perhaps, but it wears off very quickly. I was afraid the shock might affect her litter."

"I wouldn't worry, the pups are too far ahead for that. There'll be no harm done, you'll see. That's a funny name she's got—Sarka. Does it mean anything special?"

"I brought her from Prague with me. My poor little Sarka!" Her face was turned away from him, but not because it had anything to hide, for her voice was gentle and pensive upon the remembered name of her city. "Sarka was a Czech Amazon," she said, "who hated men and made war upon them by strange ways. There is a ravine in Bohemia where they will tell you she had her camp, she and her company of fighting women. But this will be strange to you. I am forgetting how

66

little we know of each other. Or have you heard, perhaps, in the village, that I am only a foreigner?'' She turned, and looked at him plaintively from under a fallen curl of hair, showing her hands and wrists covered with suds. ''Please! The pin has fallen out, and my hands are wet.''

She stood there like a child having its face sponged, while he tucked the moist black curl back into position and replaced the pin, slowly and carefully, for this was one task at which he was not adept, having had no practice. Delia would never have let him touch her beautiful hair, nor would one of those gleaming ringlets ever have been allowed to fall from its place in the presence of a man. Miriam did not even peep in the mirror afterwards to see what sort of a mess he had made of it.

''Keep still, or you'll make me stick it in you. Yes, Michel Peyron did mention that you came from Prague. What are you laughing at?''

It was the first time he had ever heard her laugh aloud, and it was a pleasant sound, clear and gay. That was some good he'd done in the second great war, anyhow, even if it didn't last; he'd made Miriam Lozelle laugh, tilting her head on one side so as to train one dark eye at least upon him round the obstruction of his engrossed hands.

''At you. If you knew how funny you look. You have the tip of your tongue out at the corner of your mouth. I thought it was only in fiction and films they did that.''

''Then you've never seen a lot of small boys doing fretwork. Watch Louis' youngest carrying the can home, next time he fetches the milk, for that matter. There you are, that's fixed.''

She shook her head, hard, but it stayed fixed. ''Thank you. That's much better. So you know I am a Czech? That makes it much clearer, and we have somewhere to start from. After all, we should know each other. I was Miriam Lisek, and I am Miriam Lozelle. It seems very strange and wrong to me that I do not know your name.''

''My name's Jim Benison.''

She said it after him, her hands and arms again plunged into the tub. ''Jim Benison. Tell me about yourself. Where are you from? Have you a wife? Children, perhaps? Tell me about England. I was there once, a whole university term, but I saw only London.''

''Is that where you learned to speak English so well?'' asked Jim.

''It helped me very much, but I learned the language much

earlier, I was studying languages, you see, and I wanted to teach in England, later on. But let us not talk of me. I want to hear of you."

"Oh, I'm not much. Never been anywhere, never seen anything, never done anything. I don't suppose I should ever have thought of leaving England if it hadn't been for the war. That's rum, isn't it? But for Hitler I should have gone on working with Collinson's road-gang, doing patent surfacing, until I retired on the old age pension—or got kicked out. And I'm not the only one by many a thousand. It seems as if this war might have its uses. We shall see a lot we shouldn't have seen, and learn a lot we shouldn't have learned."

"Yes," she said, after a strange little pause. "You think that must be good?"

"Don't you?"

"Tell me about your home," she said. "Is it in the country? But yes, I know it is."

"Oh, yes, it's only a tiny place, no bigger than Boissy. It's in the Midlands, on the river Sheel. It's not much of a river really, nice for boating but not big enough to make much of an impression, you know! but there's a sizable valley, with wooded hills both sides. At least, we call them hills, but I don't know how you think of hills. These are gentle, rolling hills, with meadows up the lower slopes, and trees on the summits. There are plenty of farms among them, and two or three villages down in the valley. It's not bad; I like it."

"But you did not farm? What was it you said—a road-gang?"

"Yes, my firm made concrete, and did special road-surfaces—lovely non-skid stuff that bedded down into position in a few days—hardly made a sound to walk on, and driving over it was a dream, but it wasn't as lasting as they'd have liked. That was the only snag. I expect they're still working on it." He looked out from the open window into the pearl-grey sky, and was silent for a moment before he resumed thoughtfully: "I was doing all right with them. Pretty soon I'd have been a foreman. That's good money at twenty-four. I could have have married on it easy, and stayed reserved, too. Even if they ever get to tightening up the reserved list, Collinson's would have hung on to me. It's funny, isn't it, to think I'm here, on army pay, instead of sitting pretty at home?"

"Is it?" said Miriam, squeezing the suds out of a pillow case "Do you regret it?"

"No. There was nothing else to do about it."

"That can make all things simple. But there are some who find other courses open to them—are there not?"

"Oh, well, we don't all look at things the same way."

"No," she agreed drily. "It is perhaps a happy thing for the world. But you spoke of marrying. Is there, then, someone who waits for you?"

It was odd that she should be able to ask all this, and never step out of character; no one else could have done it without freezing him into inarticulate embarrassment or setting him smouldering with sulky anger. If they were unconscious of trespassing it was bad, and if they were conscious of it, it was worse. Even his mother could never have extracted from him more than a few stiff monosyllables on the subject of Delia, had she been so unwise as to make the attempt. Yet Miriam Lozelle walked in boldly, and expected and obtained an answer without reserve. It was not even the intimacy of brief acquaintance, which impels people to tell their life stories to fellow-travellers in trains. There was something about her that put her out of that category. Presently the 4th Midshires would move on from the Boissy district, and she would be left behind; but it was impossible to believe that he would ever forget her. It would be like forgetting mother, and sister, and wife.

"There's a girl——" he said. "I'll show you her photograph some time. She has hair the colour of red wheat, and she's big—you could never pass her in the street without looking round to watch her out of sight. You know how big women move, when they've been raised out of doors; even when they get interested in clothes, and make-up their faces like mad, there's still the way they move—free and grand. The way the wind blows over open fields. We're going to be married, after the war. Her name's Delia—Delia Hall—Delia Benison." He said it thoughtfully, dwelling upon the sound of it. "I've got it all planned. I shall go back to my old job; they're keeping it open for me. We'll get a house with a big garden, out of Caldington, where the soil's right for roses; and in my own time I'm going to grow flowers for the market. I had some good roses at home, but it's too sandy there to do the job properly, and there isn't the space. I want to show my own roses at the county show, and for Delia to wear the prize ribbons in her coat."

He fell silent, having talked himself into a dream which sprang up magically about him, putting on colour and form.

It was so vivid that for a moment he did not see the red tiles and white woodwork of the scullery all moist with steam, and the quiet listener in her green overall standing there looking at him with fixed contemplative eyes; but a chintz-bright cottage living-room in Midshire, and Delia in a frilly apron, and summer and roses outside the window.

"It will happen so," said Miriam abruptly. "It must happen so."

"Maybe, but there's a little matter of a war in between, so the less I think about it, the better." He shook the vision away from him, and picked up the wicker basket of sheets. "I'm going to hang these out for you. I won't be long."

"I will come and help you."

"No, it's all right, I can manage. I told you I was good. If you'll just pop that box of pegs out on the window-sill for me to collect——"

"But this is wonderful," she said, looking round the room and wiping her bleached hands upon her apron. "I have only my few coloured things to do—blouses and overalls—small fry, and then we have finished. Your mother was right, you are a great help. Tell me, how often have you done this for her since you were twelve years old?"

"Hush!" said Jim. "You know too much." And he disappeared before she could ask any more awkward questions.

When he came in again with the empty basket, she had a tray upon the table with coffee, and was just coming in from the kitchen with a plate of steaming scones. "You see? If one is a good boy one has cake, no? These are straight from the oven —very bad for us, but very good. Simone has a touch with scones. Come and try!"

It was true enough. They were feather-light, crisp at the edges and molten with butter inside. He ate three, and drank two cups of coffee, sitting at the table with her. "This is a bit of all right. Did I fish for it, or did it just materialise?"

"Be easy, you did not fish. I cannot ever let Simone bake without robbing her ovens, and to-day we are two instead of one." She pushed her cup aside, and sat with her chin in her hands, looking at him with a faint, reflective smile. "Your Delia will have a useful husband, I think. One day perhaps I will show you my Georges for your Delia. He is a good husband, too, the best in France. More coffee? Or perhaps you have room for another scone? We are expected to eat them all, but it may be you are afraid of spoiling your dinner?"

70

"Not much! Might spoil it by comparison, but that's the only danger. Stuffy's cooking is on what you might call utility lines. But I really ought to go, I'm afraid. There's a few odd jobs I ought to do before dinner, and after that I'm on fatigues. I'd rather stay and help you finish, but there it is."

"But you have already done wonders. Will you come and talk to me again sometimes? If there is mending you have to be done, or washing, bring them to me."

"Oh, wait a minute, now. I didn't fish as deep as all that," he said hurriedly.

"No matter, you shall do as I say, or no more scones."

"I'll get round Simone, and be independent of you."

"She speaks no English, and will treat you like a troublesome little boy. You will get nowhere without me." She laughed at him over her shoulder as she led the way to the door, and halting there, let him pass her. "Remember, you and your friends will be welcome always. It is good for us to know one another; we are allies."

"That's how the washing gets done so quickly," said Jim, and waved back to her from under the rattling lilac-trees, and went his way to the yard and the barn, whistling.

5

All that day she was busy about the house and the garden, and had no leisure to remember him; but at night, with the shutters closed and the curtains drawn against the world, he came back into her mind. He was so like Walther, Walther as she remembered him, before the Nazis came, before it was a crime to sing scurrilous student songs in the streets at night, or wear more than one kind of favour; before the Sokols were broken up, and the university cloisters became execution-grounds. She put her hands over her eyes to hide the unbearable quietness and peace of her ornate sitting-room, which hurt her always with a redoubled hurt when the past came back upon her; and the darkness flooded in, chaotic, thundering, disordered with wreckage. Walther's face against the wall, pallid, streaked with sweat, rigid with the proud labour to hold himself erect while he died, though three of his ribs were broken and his spine so bruised that he could scarcely stand. Walther slipping down the wall, so slowly—the blood coming out of his mouth. And other faces—the face of Jan, who was seventeen and had to go on living—the face of the Ober-Leutnant from

Bavaria who, even with her eyes inflamed and her hair dragged unbecomingly back, had liked her far too well. The grinding of wheels upon the stones, as carts came and carried the bodies away—the blood where Walther had fallen, when he struck the Ober-Leutnant and was himself dragged down by three of the guards, and trampled, and knelt upon—the dull, dreadful sound of the rifle-butt thudding into his back—all these blew shrieking through her mind as if carried by a great wind, and something loosened and separated from the inner part of her and was swept along with them, like a broken shutter carried away in the gale; so that suddenly she began to weep, she who had not wept since the goose-stepping armies came marching through the streets of Prague for the first time, and had not expected ever to weep again; without reserve, brokenly, in quiet floods of tears that ran between her fingers warmly and washed away once for all the hardness of her lips and the ice about her heart. To remember was to endure again; to remember with more of grief than hate was to endure without alleviation, to be hurt again as vilely as before, and without the old cauterising fire of vengeful dedication. Oh, God, deliver us from remembrance!

Not that she hated the less, but that she had found in herself the capacity for affection still as deep and vulnerable as ever, after six months of believing it sealed. And all because there were still young men who smiled with Walther's smile, and whose hair grew straight up in a curling bush like Walther's hair; young men who sprinted across the muzzles of machine-guns to save foolish dogs from being blown to pieces, and carried water for Jewish women instead of kicking them into the gutter out of their way. Young men with eyes confident and shy, instead of bold and uneasy, for there was to her a great difference, she who had seen the swaggering Storm Troopers flinch away before the fixed glances of the conquered. Young men who took it for granted that decency and kindness should be the common coin of their exchanges with their fellow-men, instead of arrogance and cruelty.

There had been, perhaps, many such in France before he came; but they had not looked like Walther.

It did not matter that she wept, for there was no one to see; and it was good to weep, it exhausted her body and her mind, and a clean, quiet weariness came in and took her, as peace takes the new-washed meadows after a storm. She was eased of the débris of a year of keeping her own counsel, all the stagnant silence washed clean away out of her in that breaking

72

flood; and when it passed she lay back in her chair with a long sigh. This also, this most strangely and surely of all, he had done for her. He had made her laugh, and he had made her cry, and therefore she knew that she had still a living heart in her. Sometimes she had doubted it. There comes a time when in self-defence one must cease to feel.

She lay there in the long chair, and felt the worst and the best of it flooding her being again, the horror and the pain of seeing death in such hideous shapes, the unutterable dreadfulness of having to go on living, continually visited by unrelenting visions of the ruin of her dead. Not Walther only, but others, not of her blood, only of her heart; students, men and women, her friends, outraged and murdered as a warning to patriots that even wit must be used only in favour of the conquerors. Siebel, publicly raped by three German soldiers and then shot in the back of the head for having made and sung a new version of one of the students' songs, unflattering to the Fuehrer. Eugen, who staged the first great, ribald procession through the streets, and was machine-gunned at the head of his bitter-tongued legion, still shouting scurrilous taunts through the blood that bubbled in his mouth. Martin, who out of that massacre was taken alive, to a longer torment and as inevitable an end. Rachel, who was too pretty to die, Rachel who was taken away, and did not come back. Things for which there could be no words, things which could not be spoken or written, because there was a limit to the elasticity of language; things which, if reduced to the written word, would read like obscene burlesques of themselves. No, one does not speak of all one has seen—but one does not, on that account, cease to see or to experience it over and over in memory, without alleviation and without end.

That was the worst of it. There was also the best, the dark fire of courage, and endurance, and hope which outlived even the most lunatic and lasting despairs; the great splendour, in-articulate and defiled but splendour still, which had come to birth only in the abyss of adversity, and which made her, in the perception of it, equal to whatever man could do against her. To be equal to circumstances does not limit the agony one suffers from them, but that is a small thing by comparison with the great good of being unconquerable.

"We are a people who cannot be subdued," she had said to the German soldier who threatened her once because she would not dance with him. It was something even to remember that she had said that, though that was before the darkest time began, or she might have died for it. And she had not meant the Jews.

To the Ober-Leutnant she had said nothing at all, never one word in the hideous acquaintance, but only looked at him with coldly disquieting eyes, and deliberately drawn in the skirt of her dress whenever he came near to her, and withdrawn even her sleeve from the arm of the chair so that he might not brush it as he passed; and when she could not withdraw herself so, she had shut up her mind from him and endured with loathing; and her integrity had not been broken nor despoiled, though she was in hell. Even from hell, she had found, you can see heaven.

But Walther had come nearest to breaking her, and in the remembrance of him she died continually. Seven years younger than herself, he would have been just Jim's age if he had lived, and just Jim's build. She had been prouder of her brother's degree and promise than of all her own laurels; and he had come to such brilliant flower only to be clubbed and trampled into feebleness, and murdered against a wall of his own college, scarcely able to die upright. For that no one should ever be forgiven, in this world or the next. From that abyss she had not looked for heaven, not one star of it, until Sarka provoked Jim Benison, and the beginning of the thaw set in which had left her now so strangely comforted.

Marrying Georges had not given her so much ease. Itself a deep and narrow thing, her love for him had done nothing to betray her mind, nothing to unseal the fiery silences which lay walled within the ice of her heart. Yet she had loved him, and not lightly; their passion had been from the beginning direct, intense, almost wordless, an incentive to live, but not to release the pent storm which had raged in her from the time before she knew him. He had never heard of Walther; he did not even know that his wife had had a brother. Together, they had no past. She lived with him in the present hour, looking even to the future only for the fruit of their soil and the fruit of their bodies; the other part of her was a closed tomb, and he had never tried to enter it. But the English private soldier in his innocence had walked unaware into that desolation, and let out at the opened door all the past; and by the same door the future had followed him in. For suddenly there was a future; there was a world after the war, a world in which martyrs and their wrong would be remembered, but without bitterness, being avenged and their indignant ghosts laid long ago. And then

Walther would be quiet; and even her own soul within her, the ghost of the living, would make an end of its savage, insatiable crying, and lie down, and rest.

Sarka whined at the door, and scrubbed with an impatient paw along the panelling. Miriam rose, and let her in. The night was dark, and there were no stars, and a small cold wind blew through the garden.

"That is a very fine young man, Sarka," said Miriam, "your friend Jim. My sons will be like that." He had done that for her, too; he had made her believe in and look forward to her sons. There was still virtue in man; there was still hope for the young.

6

The 4th Midshires did not expect to stay in Boissy-en-Fougères for more than a month; they had never stayed anywhere very long; but either the powers that be had forgotten them or there was nowhere ahead to move them to, for February budded into March, and March into April, and they were still there. The curious cosmic pause, the hush before action, lengthened out over the world, embracing them unaware. Nothing had happened. In spite of the rumours of patrol activity and desultory artillery action which came back distantly from the Maginot Line, it was quite clear that nothing had happened. These were only a pretence, a gesture to break the tension, failing utterly even to shake its taut surface with a single ripple. And the impulse to long for the end of this apprenticeship became less marked, the end of battle less sharply defined. Boissy-en-Fougères began to digest its alien meal. By the time the apple blossom was out in Georges Lozelle's orchard, the 4th Midshires had sunk into the scene and were a part of the village.

The company at the farm were by then putting in a good part of their time in helping Miriam and Jean about the fields and byres. It was second nature to a man like Alec Ross, who knew all about horses, to turn to and make himself useful when one of the team sickened; and Jim, who had mated Sue more than once, took complete charge of Sarka when she had difficulty in delivering her litter. There were men in the company who had lived most of their lives by the soil, on small-holdings and market-gardens and little farms. They could not see a field needing the harrow, or fruit-trees wanting pruning, without putting their hands to it. The company at the mill had cleaned out the

75

race and mended the rotting sluices, and in their off-duty time went about happily with flour in their hair and their clothing, from hoisting sacks and supervising the grinding; budding millers every one, for even the laziest had energy to work off somehow, and the best means was the one which came first to hand. The company abandoned three miles away, at the factory, could not keep their hands from the lathes. It was the same everywhere. They put forth roots and took hold of the soil of France.

In a way they were home-sick; letters from England brought the atmosphere of the old life in with them, and there was restlessness, and longing to see wives and sweethearts and parents again. But that was almost a part of the routine, and did not persist when the letters were put away. It was as if they had been in Boissy-en-Fougères for years, instead of months, and to villagers a village, wherever located, is familiar ground from the beginning. They were comfortable, made welcome, even made much of; the men, those who remained at home, met them with exuberant friendliness; the women were lively, attractive and excitable. The 4th Midshires took life as it came, and were content with it; only now and again did they remember that there was a war on.

It was strange to feel that clutch at the heart again, that constriction of awareness that there had been bloodshed, that men and women had died, that men and women would surely die again before the end. The most unexpected things brought it in, leaping from the limbo at the back of the mind; a letter from home, a snatch of the Polish national anthem whistled in the café, a spurt of gravel cast up by machine-gun fire in the range, the distant report of a grenade at practice, the sight of a tank rumbling along the main road past the mill. Once Jim went into the little white-washed church, and sat down for a few moments before a gaudy figure of St. Michael with five candles burning at its feet, and watched a shabby old lady in new black come in and prostrate herself and make long, voluble prayers to it; and though this was nothing like the sort of religion he was used to, and though the old woman's mourning might well have been for a husband dead of mere age, yet suddenly the war came in, the war which was and was not, the war which had never begun; and he felt that she was confiding a soldier son to the soldier saint, and that she was one of very many who were on their knees that day. And on another night in April, when he came up the village from the mill arm-in-arm with Monsieur

76

Peyron in the dusk, he saw under the lilac hedge of Miriam's garden a man and a woman twined together, motionless, mouth to mouth; and again the unexpected stab made him wince and turn his eyes hurriedly away. They had come to France to fight, not to make love, even among the showering lilacs, even to Eliane Brègis.

Afterwards, when they had finished chopping wood for Simone, Jim sat down upon the frayed old tree-stump which served as a wood-block, and leaned the axe between his knees, and looked up at Tommy. "You want to keep away from young Eliane," he said bluntly. "She's a nice kid; you don't want her to go getting ideas." He didn't care much how he said it, or whether Tommy liked it. They'd known each other all their lives, and blacked each other's eyes more times than he could remember, and there was no need to go picking and choosing words.

"Oh, it was you, was it!" said Tommy in a dry voice; and he took the half of a cigarette from behind his ear, and lit it deliberately before he spoke again. "I'll do what I damn well please," he said. "You look after your own affairs, young Jim, and keep out of mine. I don't need no help, see?"

"That's what you think," said Jim.

"That's what I know, and you'd better get it in your head, and quick. You're no keeper of mine."

"O.K., O.K.! Watch your step, that's all. You've already got one wife who's a sight too good for you, and you can't have it both ways."

"You leave Nance out of it," said Tommy, with the same ominous quietness.

"All right, go to hell your own way."

Tommy finished the cigarette in silence, and stepped off his dignity abruptly as he trod it out among the wood-chips underfoot. "Matter of fact, it shook me, too. I never meant it to happen." He turned suddenly, and walked away into the twilight at a rapid pace, and vanished among the orchard trees bowed with blossom. Jim sat still on the wood-block and watched him go, and a surging restlessness troubled his mind. It had gone further than safety if Tommy could be tripped into kissing her without his will; and the memory of their stillness came back to him disquietingly, every line of her slender body and fierce young arms pointing the significance of the moment. There wasn't a scrap of harm in either of them, and they could have kissed a dozen times under the lilacs without doing Nancy any wrong, if only they hadn't fallen into the desperate mistake of growing fond of each other.

"We've been here too long," said Jim aloud to the gathering night. "That's the top and bottom of it; we've been here too long."

He was the more sure of it next day. A dispatch-rider passing through the village north-eastward dropped out to have his dinner with them, and brought the news that the Germans were in Denmark and Norway. It came like the crack of a whip. They felt themselves start, and instinctively lean back into disbelief. But the impossible thing had happened; there was detail and circumstance to back it, to give the picture depth and perspective. They had crossed the Danish frontiers two days previously, on April 9th, at Tondern and Flensburg. They had put troops ashore by sea at Middlefast, Korsör and Nyborg, and landed others from transports at the quays of Copenhagen to take possession of the fort and the radio station. The Danes had not fought. The Norwegians had, and were fighting still, though Oslo had fallen in the first attack. Bits of the British Navy were hotly in action, while the British Army sat back among the apple-orchards of Boissy-en-Fougères, and fretted at the quietness of their life.

They talked of nothing else that day; and at night, to have the latest and most authoritative report on the situation, they deputed Jim to borrow Simone's portable radio from the kitchen. They sat in a silent crowd around it while the full story of the first battle of Narvik was told, from the entry of the Second Destroyer Flotilla into Ofot Fjord to the withdrawal of the survivors. They heard it out, and then suddenly Scotty Walsh got up with a volley of curses and switched off the set.

"And we sit here!" he said. "My God, chaps, we joined the wrong service."

So they were all thinking, and so, in varied words, they all agreed. They had thought when they came to France that they were to be the spear-heads of the attack, yet here they were living like farmers and peasants, in the most dream-like peace, while the *Hardy* fought her way three times into Narvik harbour under fire from shore batteries and enemy warships, and unable to keep steerage way any longer, was beached at last in a glorious death and put the remnants of her crew ashore to continue the fight, like true English amphibians. That was the sort of thing they had joined up to do; to hear it recounted of others took all the bloom from their contentment. It had been

78

pleasant enough in the Artois Spring, among the fields and woods; but suddenly all the attractions of Boissy paled, and the old urge to be moving ahead took hold of them all. They had been there too long.

"I thought we came here to fight," said Tommy violently. "Instead, here we sit like a lot of old women in a workhouse, letting the blasted Germans hit us whenever they like. Maginot Line be damned! I don't fancy sitting the war out in a row of nice safe little blockhouses, while they take over the rest of Europe. What are we waiting for? Why don't we move?"

"Better write and ask Lord Gort," suggested Alec. "We wouldn't know, any more than you. Anyhow, what's the good? I suppose they know what they're about—they're the blokes who're in a position to know."

"So you'd think. But what if they're standing still because they don't know what to do next? What if we're lying low here believing in 'em, while they muck everything up? Every minute we delay moving is another minute for the Boches to get ready for us, seems to me."

"It's another minute for us to get ready for the Boches, too, don't forget," said Jim.

"Yes, if we used it. What have we done the last month or more towards getting ready for the Boches, tell me that. You can't tell me the Jerries over there have been planting potatoes and digging marrow-beds all this time. Trouble is they're taking it seriously, and we're not. What good are we doing, any of us? Dropping damned silly leaflets on Germany and sitting down here to wait for them to repent. It wasn't leaflets they dropped on Warsaw."

"Warsaw! There you go again! Why bring up Warsaw? What could we have done to help 'em, anyhow? And what good's it going to do Warsaw now even if we bomb Berlin flat? That's over and finished."

"Is it?" said Tommy, and the sudden quiet of his voice after his former violence said clearly that to him it was far from finished.

Jim didn't want to listen any longer. He didn't altogether believe in Tommy's judgment; that was the old, wild Tommy talking, impatient always when there was action toward and he was not in it, intolerant always of any policy which involved waiting or keeping still. Jim had no doubt at all that he was under the best possible leadership in the circumstances. He wouldn't have wished to criticise in any case, being reasonably aware that he was not well qualified for the job; and besides, life was going to be an uncomfortable business if a man began thinking as Tommy talked. No security that way, nothing to trust to, nothing to steer by. Tommy himself didn't mean it very seriously, or he couldn't have been so complacent about it. You couldn't argue happily like that about a thing that logically cut the ground from under your feet and ripped away the background of your life. No, Tommy was just letting off steam, talking for the sense of talking. And yet, having convinced himself so far, Jim didn't want to listen any longer. If it didn't cut the ground from under his feet it made it tremble a little, and he didn't like it. He picked up Simone's wireless and carried it back to the house.

Madame Lozelle was in the kitchen, sitting in Simone's huge rocking-chair, with her toes upon the brass fender and a sewing-basket beside her. She was making filet lace, leaning over one arm of her chair to get the best light upon her work. She had on a black dress, and more lace of her own making was at her neck and wrists. In the broad, heavy-beamed kitchen with its big presses and glowing china bright in the firelight, she looked so perfectly a wife and housekeeper that nostalgia for Delia and home went over him like a wave. The cottage kitchen wouldn't be as big as this, or the china as good, of course, but that was how Delia would look, sitting by the fire at night, sitting opposite him at their own fireside in the world after the war.

"It is you, Jim?" said Miriam, smiling at him across the twilit room. "Light the lamp, please. It is getting dark, and this work tries my eyes. I will get you some coffee, no?" And she pushed aside the lace, and made to rise, but he said quickly:

"No, don't move. Just stay there, the way you are. Please!"

She slid back obediently into the great chair, looking up at him with a smile half-puzzled, half-indulgent. "What is it? Is there then something strange about me to-night?" There was, but he did not say so. Something strange and lovely in the dusk, the softening of all that was bitter in her, the veiling of all that was marred. In full light her face had deep lines, her hands, which lay so gently along the arms of the chair, were seamed and scarred with work; but in this limpid half-light she was young, smooth, untouched by the world.

"It's just the picture you make," he said. "It's pretty good. It makes a chap think about getting home. Not that thinking will bring us any nearer."

She watched him for a moment in silence, her dark eyes shining in the shadow of her hair like limpid water, very steady and clear. Then she said gravely: "You want it—very much, do you not? I feel it in you always."

"Yes," he said, "I suppose so. It doesn't bother me so much between whiles; but to-night—I don't know—seems it's a long way off, longer than ever. Sometimes a chap's inclined to forget that, and then when something happens to remind him—well, it's a bit of a shock, that's all. You always want a thing worse the farther out of reach it is."

"I understand," she said, in the same quiet voice. "It is bad news, yes. There may be a long way to go before you get home." And though he knew her too well to think she had meant it so, there was something in her tone which made him remember in what circumstances she had been driven into exile, and how infinite a journey lay before her if she would return. "Listen to me talk!" he said hotly. "It's worse for you, and I never hear you complain."

She smiled. The significance of it eluded him. He had never reached the outer darkness where complaint is no longer possible, because the mere acknowledgment of your sorrows is a luxury you cannot buy for a lower price than utter, broken despair. That was far outside his knowledge.

"But if we were even moving," he went on vehemently, "it wouldn't be so bad. We know we've got to fight for our homes —that's why we joined up. But we're *not* fighting. What we want to know is, when are we going to begin?"

"Soon enough," said Miriam. "Too soon." And she said it as if to herself, in an undertone, with certainty and sadness.

"It can't be too soon for me. How can we ever come out the other side of it, if we never go in this side? A war's a thing you can't by-pass. I wish we could get started—then there might be some hope of getting finished."

"Don't wish for it!" she said sharply, her fingers suddenly rigid with command upon the arms of the chair, her voice thin as a knife.

Jim was amazed and at a loss. She was a realist, brave as the bravest, patient as a tree, uncomplaining at all times; and yet she baulked like any ordinary woman at the thought of making short, practical, economical work of this necessary if unpleasant war. Naturally, one knew it must be a beastly business, but why not face it from the beginning? Did she think he was a child, going lightly into something he hadn't even considered? He had thought about it long and deeply. He was as fond of living, as much in love with his own vigorous body as the next man; but if he died he died, and if he was maimed he was maimed. The thing had to be tackled full, and he was ready

He had never wanted anyone's approval quite as he wanted hers. He had to make her understand how he felt, and at least respect his attitude if she could not share it. He went forward quickly, and sat down on the rug at her feet, looking up into her face with the fading light full upon his own.

"Look!" he said, in a voice desperately quiet. "I'm not treating it lightly. Don't think me such a fool as that. I know it must be horrible—plain hell, no less. I know I shall be frightened, and wish myself well out of it, every minute of the time. I *have* thought of all that. But there's no other way; so if I've got to do it, I'd rather do it, and get it done. It's like any other nasty job, only a thousand times nastier. I don't want you to think I'm going into it with my eyes shut. I know what I'm doing, and I still want to get on with it *now*." All this he said slowly, with painful emphasis, talking of the hellishness of war, telling her he knew the stature of the thing he was tackling, while he looked at her with his earnest, candid, worried eyes; steadily and solemnly as a child assuring his mother he can do an errand alone.

Suddenly her stillness broke. She put up a hand to hide her face, and: *"Ah, que tu es jeune!"* she said upon a gasping breath between laughter and pain.

He flushed, saying quickly: "That's not fair. You promised always to talk English to me."

"N'importe! It was nothing. I cannot exclaim in English. I am sorry, Jim. It will not happen again. It was only as if I said, yes, you have indeed thought it all out."

"I'm not sure you aren't making fun of me," he said doubtfully.

"You cannot think that of me," she said. And he could not; it was not what he had felt, it was not what he had meant to say. She was too straight and kind ever to use his bursts of confidence so ungently.

"Of course not. Only when I let myself go like that I always have a sneaking feeling I'm making a fool of myself. That's why I don't do it very often. Anyhow," he said firmly, "you see what I mean, don't you?"

"Yes. I see what you mean."

"I should hate you to think I was just going into it blind—treating it as a joke."

"I know that is not so," she said softly.

He got up from the rug, satisfied. After all, he didn't want her to pat him on the back and say Amen to everything he said; all he asked was to be treated as a responsible adult. "Anyhow," he said, almost thankfully, "the way I feel about it doesn't make any difference; I haven't any voice in it at all. I just do what I'm told. Look, I shall have to get back to the lads. Will you say thank you to Simone for me?"

"Yes, I will," she said, and watched him to the door with dark eyes curiously veiled and still, as if she had shut him deliberately out of a part of her mind. "Good night, Jim."

"Good-night!" he said, and let himself out quietly into the deepening evening.

7

The Curé of Boissy-en-Fougères, the Abbé Bonnard, was a little, good, womanish man with a small, swift step and gentle eyes. He ran about his curacy indefatigably for eighteen hours out of the twenty-four, and on his way home in the young darkness often called for a few minutes upon the mistress of Boissy farm. He felt it was his duty to act as a friend to Madame Lozelle, little though he knew of her, and imperfectly though he was equipped to understand her. And after their fashion they were friends. His welcome was now so assured that it need not be expressed at all; he walked in and out as he pleased; and walking into the farm-house that night, he found Miriam still sitting in the dark, so still and lost in the depths of the big chair that at first he did not notice her, until she said abruptly and without preliminary:

"*Mon père*, why are there wars?"

Startled, he looked at her with a troubled smile. "Madame, why do you sit in darkness? It is not cheerful. Let me put on the light."

"As you wish!" she said indifferently. And when he had switched on the lamp, he saw her face fixed and resentful and sad. In this mood he did not understand her, he could only labour along honestly at the edge of her thoughts and try to answer her as scrupulously as he could.

"I was not very clear. I should have said: Why do we permit wars? Why do we tolerate that our young men go out

83

unprepared in their innocence, to a thing they know nothing about, to have the confidence and the youth and the manhood bludgeoned out of them? Why do we stand by and let this be done to them?''

''We have no choice,'' said the Abbé Bonnard. ''Neither have they. The greed and ambition of man bring about wars of aggression; there is as yet no effective weapon against war but war. The young men go of their own will. Is it easier for us who cannot go?''

''Yes,'' she said vehemently, ''it is easier. Unless, like me, you have already been where they are going.'' She leaned forward, her hands gripping each other tightly in her lap. *''Mon père*, it is easy to keep one's ideals in sight through all manner of vicarious suffering; but it is not easy to see those things done in cold blood which have been done in my sight and will be done in theirs, to live through the obscene humiliations, the degrading horrors and pains that I have lived through and they will live through presently, and still to keep one's eyes fixed on an altar, or retain the belief that one is taking part in a crusade. Pain is only a little thing, death is not very much bigger; it is humiliation, hate, deliberate cruelty, leisurely, bestial cruelty that break the heart and dirty the soul. *Monsieur le Curé,* have we armed our young men against these when we give them rifles and tanks? Can you kill with a rifle the horror a clean boy feels at seeing his friends made to do the vilest menial things for their conquerors, with naked hands, and afterwards to eat with the same hands unwashed the fragments of food their masters rejected? Can you heal with a field-dressing the poisoned wound in his heart made by the remembrance of his friends lying in the tracks of the flame-throwing tanks, faceless and blind and blackened and still alive?'' She saw the horror and distress behind his mild eyes, and knew that he thought her hysterical, a little mad perhaps with too much remembrance of past suffering. She stopped. It was not good to hurt him with this involuntary weapon of pity. He was useful in his degree, but it was not in him to answer such angers and fears as she carried in her.

She said more gently: ''They believe they know the worst man can do to them, and are armed against it. They know nothing, nothing at all. And we let them go out to be dirtied, and broken, and stripped, and flayed. *Monsieur l'Abbé,* it is not good to think of that disillusionment.''

''It is not,'' he said. ''But the best of them will surmount

84

it, and overcome the worst it can do against them."

"At a very high price," said Miriam. "And even so they will hate us in their hearts, because we knew and did not tell them."

"Are you suggesting, then, that we should ourselves take away their illusions from them, and send them out disheartened, so that we may be spared the accusation of having betrayed them?"

She rose from her chair then, and crossed to the window, and stood there looking out across the yard, where the young men moved about darkly in the darkness, coming and going about the barns. She took the folds of the curtain in her hand, and with a quick gesture drew it across and shut them out.

"If it could be done," she said, "I would say yes. But they would not believe us if we tried to tell them the half; or if they believed, they would still be none the wiser. If we could speak of it at all, it would be diminished. It is a thing we cannot communicate. It can only be experienced. No, I have no suggestion to make, no suggestion at all." Her face was turned towards the drawn curtain; he saw it in profile, still as stone. "I only know, *Monsieur l'Abbé*, that it is hell to be young and to have seen nothing; and deeper hell to be old, and to have seen too much, and never to be able to cease from seeing, or to make others see." She turned, and looked at him, and meeting his clear, compassionate eyes, said no more. She was speaking to another blind man; he had never been initiated.

8

Throughout April the fighting in Norway went on, and the unrest and excitement of it came southward to France clearly, in a crescendo of tension and a flood-tide of rumour. They felt that the hour was drawing nearer, that the long apprenticeship of digging anti-tank ditches and raising concrete pillboxes, of firing over the quarry ranges and lobbing grenades into the sand-pits, was almost over. It was common knowledge that once already, three days after the attack on Denmark and Norway, they had been for a time under short notice to move ahead, and an imminent invasion of Holland and Belgium had been spoken of openly as a probability; but it had not happened yet. Nevertheless, the under-current of excitement had not subsided. It was in the swarming flight of reconnoitring planes which went to and fro overhead between rear aerodromes and the Belgian frontier. It was in the high, confident tone of the talk at Papa

Brègis', in the brilliance of Eliane's eyes, and the gaiety of Monsieur Peyron's hectic chatter; it was in the eager way the 4th Midshires went about their unexciting routine work, and the new zest with which they sang their ridiculous songs about being on their way to Berchtesgaden; and it was in the intense quietness of Miriam Lozelle.

In the small hours of the morning of May 10th, Jim awoke in the barn, and lay for a few minutes wondering what had broken his rest. It was dark and close in there, warmth of bodies and warmth of bedding making the air heavy, and there were all the usual queer noises of sleep, from Tommy's deep sighing breath to Alec's lusty snoring; but something from outside all this had penetrated his sleeping senses. He lay listening intently, and presently he knew what it was.

He had heard it last, that continuous throbbing hum, in the First Aid Post at Morwen Hoe; but on that occasion it had come, and lingered overhead, and finally departed, without sequel. This time there were other noises, dull and far and yet making the ground under him tremble ever so gently with sympathetic foreboding. The reverberation rather than the noise stole into the minds of other sleepers, and troubled their rest. Tommy rolled over impatiently in his blankets, and said: "What the hell!" in a loud, clear voice, and for a moment slept again. Then sharper, nearer, an ack-ack battery went into action, crashing upon the quiet with an irresistible shock. All over the barn men stirred and sat up, listening.

"What goes on?" said Tommy, fully awake now.

"Bombing. Started a little while ago. That's the battery the far side of the flying-field firing now. Wonder how near they are?"

"So it's started!" said Tommy, and was out of his blankets in a moment, and padding across to the door, stepping over bodies as he went. Jim followed him more carefully, and they stepped out through the narrow wicket door which had been made for men so much smaller than they, and stood under the clear, gleaming sky. Searchlights wavered upward from distant points, hesitant and pale in the glorious night which retained in itself, moonless and almost starless as it was, such a wealth of innate radiance. The thrum of the engines sounded clearer, but the bombers remained unseen, molten into that translucent zenith. Then, near and far, batteries slashed into the silence again, and the air was dazzled with tracer and star-shell and flare, like a grand firework display.

"They're over towards Arras," said Tommy. "They'll be after H.Q." And he leaned in the embrasure of the doorway with his face upturned gladly, greedily to this first onslaught, and said again: "So it's started!" as if he could not sufficiently convince himself that the lull was ended. It was the gratitude of the soil for rain, after the too-sultry tension of the thunder-calm of midsummer. "We'll be moving on now. It's come."

"It might be only a tip-and-run affair," said Jim cautiously. "They could have done it before if they'd wanted to; it may not mean much now."

"They wouldn't be doing it now if it wasn't time. Haven't you noticed? Everything they do is planned and works like clockwork. No, they've got to the bit where we figure. It's beginning. You wait a day or so, and see if we're still in Boissy."

Jim said nothing. In the face of this furious prophecy he felt no desire to look forward. Whatever was to follow would follow. He was content now to wait for it. He stood there for almost half an hour, watching the night blossom with curious flowers of fire, uncurl carnival streamers of tracer-shell, and quiver now and again to the impact of bombs. It was exciting, and bewildering, and quite unreal, more like a peace-time gala than a determined attack upon their usefulness through their G.H.Q. and aerodromes, which was what it proved to be. Only the recurring note of the bomber engines was sinister; it got into your head, if you listened to it, and went on and on round your senses like a tightening spring until something burst. Jim didn't like it. It brought the future darkness of the abyss into this jewelled, unreal, distant warfare, and suddenly he was afraid of the things that might follow. He thought then of Miriam saying: "Don't wish for it!" He thought of her covering her eyes as she cried out at him in French something she could not contain, something he was not meant to understand.

"So they're ready for us," said Tommy. "Now we shall see some fighting, anyhow, now it suits them. Why do we have to sit back and wait for *them* to make the moves, I wonder?"

"Because Belgium and Holland are still neutral, that's why. You can't just move your army across neutral soil when you feel it might be useful."

"Neutral!" said Tommy scornfully. "Much good it is trying to be neutral in a war like this! If they're not for us they're against us. I always said we were too damned law-abiding. We could do with a few realists in charge, if you ask me."

87

"Nobody did ask you, and nobody's likely to. Come on, let's go back to bed. It's chilly out here. Besides, if you re so sure the real thing's starting, who knows when we shall sleep again?"

The argument, though he did not believe in it, was not without weight, for Tommy went back to his blankets docilely, and fell asleep again with the aplomb of a small boy, which, according to Nancy, was all he was. Nevertheless, Tommy was right, as the morning proved.

The order to move came at eight in the morning, and zero hour was fixed for ten. Both the Dutch and the Belgian frontiers had been violated by German troops, and rumours flew through Boissy thick as flies, contradicting each other as fast as they came. The Dutch Queen was dead, prisoner, flown to England, or sitting tight in the Hague. Brussels and Rotterdam were bombed flat, or had brought down enormous numbers of Nazi raiders and were themselves intact. The invaders had advanced too rapidly to be held by the Dutch inundations one minute; and the next, men and guns were awash in the inroads of the Netherlandish sea. No one knew what was, and what was not. The one thing the 4th Midshires had clear and definite in their minds was that the Low Countries had been violated, and that they were to cross into Belgium to man the line appointed to them.

They knew this because Captain Halliday had told them, and he was a man of few and definite words. They didn't like him, exactly, or considered that they didn't; but they could depend on anything he said being the straight goods.

"It's begun," he had said, "and we are now going forward to finish it. You all know it will be no picnic, so no need for me to say anything about that. We are going into Belgium, to take over a forward sector in support of the Belgian Army. We move at ten."

So there was a frenzy of purposeful activity in the farm-yard at Boissy-en-Fougères, as all the evidences of occupation were packed away, all the transport lorries overhauled, all the kit loaded. It was the end of an era in the history of the village; without their particular *Anglais* there would be a great quietness in the *bistro*, an emptiness about the street in the evenings, a zest lacking in the schoolroom dances. The news of the departure travelled, and the villagers drifted to the farm gates to watch the preparations go forward. They knew, none better, what was toward; excitement was in the air, like vapour, like an infectious disease; it would not even let them regret the loss of their *Anglais* as at another time they might have done, because it filled their minds so full of action and glory and victory that there was no room for any other emotion. They cried: *"Vive l'Entente Cordiale! Vive l'Angleterre!"* over the hedges and the gate as they passed, and: *"Vive la France!"* shouted back the 4th Midshires, tossing kit-bags from hand to hand and tinkering with the innards of lorries in the yard. *"On les aura!"* they triumphed all together. But twice as they exulted the bombers passed overhead, and the rear batteries spat their alarm; and twice the slow-dissolving smoky dust of bomb explosions columned up into the sunny sky in the direction of Lille, and disintegrated with an undulating, leisurely flight into the dazzling day.

Brian Ridley was about among them like a desperately happy small boy who finds the weather unexpectedly fine on the morning of the big cricket fixture of the season. His face was taut and white with anticipation, his eyes brilliant to fever. He looked even younger than nineteen-and-a-half, and his French, as he talked for the last time to the wonderful Madame Lozelle, lapsed more and more into the stumbling, incoherent schoolboy tongue he had brought hopefully across the channel with him. She laughed at him, and lectured him in the voice of a mother, almost; for the Midshires had been there a long time.

"Lentement, lentement, mon brave! Est-ce que vous avez oublié? Je ne suis pas Française, moi. Parlez lentement, s'il vous plaît."

"Madame, vous êtes une citoyenne du monde," he said, gallantly.

"Vous avez raison," said Miriam, with a sombre smile. *"Je suis sans patrie."* But she did not linger upon so bitter a note, for it would have been against her nature to send him on his way discomforted, no matter what theories she held concerning the weapon of disillusionment. She was very kind to him; she said so little, and made it count for so much, that the white heat of him was at once stimulated and eased. He said shyly that he would have liked a photograph of her to send to his mother, who had admired her so much in his letters. She went instantly into the house and brought out a passport photograph, the best she had to give, disappointing but recognisable, and sent him back to his thousand and one last-minute jobs a happy man. He was of the right age to adore her without the least damage to himself or her. It had been a casual and comfort-

89

able contact; there were other, and deeper, ones to be broken in their turn.

Jim was in the back of a lorry when he saw her coming down the yard towards him, dressed for the fields in her blue overalls and boots and an open-necked shirt, her hair tied up unbecomingly in a gaily-coloured handkerchief. Even so she was a good-looking woman. He put out his cigarette and jumped down from the tail-board to meet her. They regarded each other for a moment without words, for it was important that the right things should be said now, and the worthy note sounded. After all, they would not see each other again.

"Well—this is it!" he said, and it was not what he had meant to say at all, so lame it sounded, and so naked; but she understood.

"It is what you wished for," she said gently. "My husband, Georges, he was like you in this; he also wished to come to grips. I shall think of you every day, and pray for your success always."

"I shall think of you, too," said Jim. "When all this is over maybe I'll see you again—we'll be able to talk it over, then, and see who was right and who was wrong." But he didn't believe it. One so seldom meets people again.

"Perhaps," she agreed with a sceptical smile. "At least we shall be marching together in thought, if we go by different ways. Your part is to fight Germans, and mine is to hoe potatoes, it seems. I shall be in the fields when you leave, but I did not want to let you go without saying good-bye." She held out her hand. "Good-bye, Jim, and good luck."

"Good-bye," he said, and took her hand, which was strong and hard, and neat, like a boy's. He said quite simply: "I shall never forget you, Miriam," and did not even notice that he had called her by her name.

"Do not say that. I know of nothing in me you should remember."

"I know nothing in you I want to forget. You've been grand to us all, and specially grand to me."

"I have been a shadow in your path," she said unguardedly, and instantly recovered herself. "There was Sarka. Have you forgotten?"

"You should have done," he said, flushing, "long ago. It only happened to be me, anyhow. If I hadn't gone crazy one of the others would. Look out, here comes my sergeant. I shall have to get back on the job, or he'll be after my blood." He gave her hand a quick, last pressure. "Good-bye, Madame."

"Good-bye, Jim." And she turned and walked briskly away towards the gate, only looking back at the last moment to wave her hand before she disappeared. And Jim went back to the heaving of kit-bags.

"Queer girl, that," said Tommy, looking over his shoulder reflectively.

"Who, Madame Lozelle? How d'you mean, queer? What's queer about her?" He was bristling at once. He had not a detached mind where his friends were concerned. Once he accepted people, everything they did, everything they were, everything they said was right and justifiable and not to be called in question by himself or anyone else.

"Oh, forget it!" said Tommy recognising the symptoms. "If she's in, she's in. Anyhow you're not the only one that thinks a lot of her. Come and give me a hand with this mortar." And after a few minutes of strenuous lifting, he said suddenly: "I wish we'd known last night. I'd have liked to go down to Papa's for a last drink. There'll be great excitement there to-day, I'll bet." But it wasn't of Papa he was thinking, or the *pernod* and *vin rouge* which he didn't really like, or Michel Peyron, self-appointed interpreter to the company; and Jim was glad there had been no warning. The briefer and more distant the farewells in that direction, the better for all concerned.

At ten, prompt to the minute, the first lorries moved off. The motor-cyclist runners had gone ahead by half an hour to take control of the cross-roads en route and keep the way clear. Jim was in one of the first transports, in the cab beside Tommy. By that time the entire remaining population of Boissy-en-Fougères was lining the lane, intent on giving the *Anglais* a memorable send-off. Sarka and her five puppies were playing in the gateway, but Simone came bustling out of the house like a hen calling her chicks, and gathered the entire litter into her capacious arms, and flurried away with the anxious mother at her heels. The lorries rolled steadily forward, out of the yard, advanced cautiously between the ranks of shrieking villagers; small boys ran alongside them for so long as they had breath to run, girls threw flowers, the sun beat down brilliantly, and a dozen songs at once fought for a hearing. It was a triumph; premature, unearned, but intoxicating. Jim's good sense turned from it, but his spirit was caught. He leaned out from his cab and returned the valedictory shouts of *"On les aura!"* and *"Vive la Victoire!"* and the frantic thumbs-up signs

91

made by panting little boys. The day rained sun and flowers upon them, bombarded them with song, tangled them in hysteria as in a gauze scarf. And so they left Boissy-en-Fougères for Belgium and the Dyle and the long-desired, suddenly-approaching, inescapable battle.

At the cross-roads well out of the village, when the greater part of the people were left behind and the convoy was gathering way, they saw Eliane. She was standing upon the hedgebank, embracing the signpost with one arm, and watching for them eagerly as the head of the column, heralded by motorcycling outriders, came into view. She was in a thin blue frock, and hatless, her pale golden hair lifting in the breeze like a halo worn awry, her face at once ardent and anxious, joyous and sad. She scanned and rejected the first three transports, and her eyes fell upon Tommy driving the fourth, and she flamed into such beauty and passion that it seemed she had suddenly been lit from within. In this last moment she had no interpreter, no leisure to remember her few phrases of English, no privacy to make her good-byes articulate by making them silent; she could only cry out to him, as he went by, in unintelligible French, satisfying herself if not him by the open expression of her feelings. In reply he could only lean across Jim and wave to her, and shout: "Good-bye, kid! Keep smiling!" before she was left utterly behind. Yet they were as deeply shaken, and Jim as disquieted in beholding them, as if momentous utterances had passed. Why did she have to be the last bit of Boissy they saw as they went away? Why did they have to carry with them, long after she was lost to sight, the echo of her voice, high and clear and gloriously unselfconscious, bursting suddenly into the "Chant du Départ"?

PART THREE

BELGIUM

"The so-called policy of independence which he announced . . . .
was inspired by the hope, which developed into an obsession,
that in this way alone would he be able to save Belgium from
the horrors of war. This obsession made him blind to other
considerations."

SIR ROBERT CLIVE, BRITISH AMBASSADOR TO BELGIUM, ON
KING LEOPOLD III.

" .... a darkling plain
Swept with confused alarms of struggle and flight,
Where ignorant armies clash by night."
MATTHEW ARNOLD: *Dover Beach*.

I

NEVER had there been such a welcome. From the frontier
to Tournai, and beyond, through the fringes of East
Flanders, along the hard, straight white causeways, it was lilac
and early roses and cheering and song all the way. For miles
and miles ahead, along those unwavering stretches of road, for
miles and miles behind, there was nothing in motion but lorries
and guns and transport wagons and more lorries, proceeding at
amazing speed, and keeping intervals of a hundred yards or so
between vehicles. As an advance it was exemplary; as a
pleasure-trip it was exhilarating. You felt irresistible, crashing
along in the radiant day, with your arms full of flowers, and
sprigs of lilac stuck in your button-holes, practising the Belgian
National Anthem and waving back to the girls who ran out from
orchards and farm-steads by the road, and the urchins who
popped up from canal barges as you passed to shriek greetings
in unintelligible Flemish and be answered in less intelligible
French. Before the greetings had passed, you were a hundred
yards away, and the next load of khaki-clad lads on limber or
lorry inherited the tail-end of the exuberant welcome you had
begun. "La Brabançonne" had a rousing tune, almost as good
as the Marseillaise, and the weather was set fair, and things were
the move. What more could you ask?
The speed they made during these first few hours surprised
them all. The traffic controllers had done their work well, and
the population appeared to be quite unalarmed, secure of the

93

outcome, and perfectly willing to give the newcomers a monopoly of the roads. Over the country stretches, between well-cultivated fields and by chateaux and gardens, they flew headlong; only as they passed through the little, compact, cobbled towns, with their step-gabled Hôtels de Ville and graceful slender belfries, did the pace slow to a steady, droning twenty, and occasionally halt altogether until some cross-road was cleared or some bridge opened to let them through. Then the eager Brabanters came running out of every house and shop and garden with their hands full of gifts, piled the limbers and cars with lilac and fruit, embraced every British soldier they could reach, brought them coffee and beer and cakes and anything eatable or drinkable on which they could lay their hands quickly enough, and chattered at them all the time in French and Flemish intermingled, so that they understood not a word, but only beamed back, and answered with a language of their own, and gave hearty kiss for kiss. At Tournai the girls came racing out of the carpet factories at the word that the English were passing through, and there was an orgy of rapid flirtation conducted without a coherent word. At country cross-roads children ran with dewy arm-loads of more and still more lilac. It was lilac all the way. They had never seen so much of it; they would never think of it again without remembering this day, the first day of Belgium.

But beyond Enghien, going down towards the Senne Valley in the last of the light, there was suddenly another side to the day's journey. They were driving along a narrow road between low hedges, with flat fields on either side, but ahead the undulations of small broken hills began, with scattered copses and fawn-coloured outcrops of sand. They were not far from Brussels, or the southern outskirts of Brussels, which they were intent on by-passing; and the quiet road had been earmarked for their use because so many columns were racing north-eastwards out of France that day, and it was expedient to disperse them as far as was possible over the whole field of approach. It was almost the end of their day's journey, for on the other side of the Senne, in the glades of Soignies, there was to be a halt for the night. They were already ahead of their time, and beyond Soignies they could not yet be dealt with. So there was food and rest to look forward to, and they were making a merry speed along the causeway when the lorries ahead slowed, and Tommy drew up in his turn.

"What's up? What's holding us?"

They were too far back to see, though there were voices in excitement at the head of the column, and the sound of engines running furiously.

"Get out and have a look what's doing, Jim," said Tommy. "Something's gone wrong up forward. I hope we're not here for long."

"O.K.," said Jim obediently. He opened the door and leaped down into the road. "No funny stuff, mind. If you start up without me, I'll skin you when I do catch up with you."

Tommy leaned from his cab, grinning. "You and what man's army? And what makes you think you'd ever catch up with me? When I drive, I drive." He had then been driving, with two short breaks, since ten in the morning, and was beginning to look grimy and tired, but he was quite happy.

"Some call it that," agreed Jim austerely, and went off at a casual lope along the grass at the edge of the road, towards the hold-up ahead.

Some few hundred yards from the foremost lorry of the column, a by-road from Brussels joined the causeway on which they were travelling, at a sharp angle, and partially blind by reason of a clump of trees. From the narrow way a stream of vehicles of all kinds projected itself out upon the main road and turned to meet the convoy. A thread of cyclists detached here and there from the mass and continued its way, but the main body was held as if by a dam. A powerful car had tried to overtake when barely out of the by-way, and fouled a heavily laden fruit and vegetable cart, smashing one wheel and ripping off its own door. Round the wreckage, among the fallen cabbages and potatoes, a noisy battle raged. The driver of the car, a middle-aged man in expensive town clothes, screamed at the driver of the cart, and was screamed at again with interest. The car's passenger, a fat, fair woman as overdressed as her husband, lamented volubly on the edge of the pandemonium, and though he understood not a word of what she said, Jim gathered that her only concern was for her suitcases, which had been broken and spilled into the dust in a cascade of georgette and lace. What was she doing, going south from Brussels with so much gear at a time like this? What were they all doing, all that accumulation of people in cars, on motorcycles, walking alongside pony-carts, all that procession, that river of humanity dammed into the side-road? They were in haste. They shouted and hooted and rang bells at the two who

95

were holding them up. Some of the men, all sorts and conditions of men from slick metropolitan Brabanters to farm-steading peasants, pushed their way furiously forward and joined in the screaming-match with all the breath they had left. No one attempted to get the wreckage off the road; no one did anything about the pony, standing trembling and uneasy in his sagging harness, which was dragging one shoulder raw, until Alec Ross skipped out of the back of one of the lorries and quite naturally appropriated the job to himself. The pony started under his hands, and felt the security with which it was handled, and was soothed. He got it from between the shafts, and led it quietly away off the road, and stood gentling it, having no further interest in the battle on which he had turned his back.

Sergeant Mace, who had little French and no Flemish, but an illimitable belief in his ability to make himself understood in any circumstances, was trying to get some sense out of the situation, shouting his loudest to make himself heard above the hub-bub, and holding firmly to the carter with one hand and the car-owner with the other. He was getting nowhere, for all his careful and vociferous French phrases, because no one was paying any attention to him; and it took him only a few seconds to realise it.

"Oh, to hell with this!" he said in very distinct English, and turned towards the head of the column, whence several of the first load were rapidly joining him. "Come on, lend a hand! Get this wreckage off the road; we'll do it quicker ourselves. And stand by the head of yon blasted holiday-excursion queue. I'm not losing the right of way along here if I have to fight for it."

They went in merrily, glad to have something positive to do. The obstruction could have been cleared long before they arrived upon the scene if anyone had made the attempt. The car's engine was undamaged; it steered awry but it was drivable. The cart, though heavy, had one good wheel and was not beyond the power of half a dozen or so determined men to move. The 4th Midshires made short work of both, backing the car away into the hedge and lifting the cart bodily aside after it. A litter of cases, silks, cabbages, wheel-spokes and onions lay derelict in the road. The fair woman looked at her draggled possessions as they were gathered up piecemeal and shoved into the back of the car, and said to her husband something which sounded vicious and tearful.

"What's she saying?" asked Jim, ducking back under the

shaft of the cart; for beside him stood Ben Rogers, who had, apparently, enough French at his beck and call to raise the shade of a smile at this. It was a sour smile; but then, Rogers was a sour companion, and liked his fun with a bite in it.

"She says they ought to have been in Enghien by now, and all her lingerie's ruined, and why did she marry him, anyhow, it's all his fault."

"And what's he say to that?"

"Says it was her idea to go to Paris, in the first place. He wanted to stay in Brussels. He thinks they should go back."

"So do I," said Jim. "My God, if this is the first day, what will it be like in a week or two? The roads'll be solid. You won't be able to move."

Half a dozen of the fellows were bullying the excited crowd back to the margin of the road, and holding them there by sheer force of personality and the fascination of speech in a tongue not understood. No one seemed to resent being handled by them; there were even smiles for them, and the tone of the voices was friendly. But there was fear loose among the hampered travellers, an impalpable, uneasy passenger in car and van and wagon, the quiet beginning of something incalculably damaging. It was in their eyes, and in their voices, and the way they leaned forward anxiously along the road south-westward, into Hainault and France. It worried Jim. It was like the first cloud on the horizon, which suddenly takes the sunlight from the day.

He went back to Alec, who had the pony's patient nose against his breast, and was massaging between its eyes with the fingers of one hand. It was a plain little brown cob, in good enough condition but hard-worked and not accustomed to being petted, and it didn't know what to make of Alec.

"Come on," said Jim. "We'll be moving off again any minute." For the road was all but clear, only one heavy van still faced out into the fairway, and even that was being manœuvred aside steadily with a Midshire lad on either running-board. It was almost over, this odd, disquieting incident. So he thought, and the drone of aircraft engines, startlingly crescendo, ran in his mind for a moment unrecognised, and at the end of the moment he knew, with a sickening shock, that the thing was only beginning.

It had come out of the north-east, that sound, that arrowhead of purposeful specks upon the lurid twilight, rushing in upon them with headlong speed, so that at one second it was not, and at the next nothing else existed. They were all, soldier and civilian, staring upward with taut faces and straining eyes, in a hush like nothing he had ever known, so that the sound took the sky over them with fear and power. This for a moment, and then the flanking aircraft on the nearer edge of the formation heeled over them with a screaming roar, and dropped head-on, like a hawk stooping. The blonde woman shrieked thinly. Sergeant Mace, leaping out of his startled immobility, bellowed: "Take cover! Jerries!" and charged upon the petrified tangle of civilians with wildly waving arms, as if he would sweep them bodily from the road. Before his ferocity they scattered, and ran, out into the level, coverless fields, and the scanty clumps of trees, and the banks of bramble and furze which offered some shelter. An uproar of screams and curses made the air mad. It was like a corner of Dante's Inferno. They were so many, and the time was so impossibly short.

The Midshires, those who were not already hanging avidly upon Bren guns and pumping away at the plunging Junkers, dropped over the sides of their transports and went to ground. Alec Ross looked up, saw no special advantage in running or turning the terrified pony loose into the fields, and coaxed him closer into the shadow of the nearest heavy lorry, and stood with an arm round his neck, talking away unheard under the uproar above. The second Junkers tilted and dived. The first was in the back of their necks by then, with Brens spitting at it madly.

Jim had gone to earth in the nearest furrows, but it was impossible to stay there while that tangle of people ahead struggled to disintegrate in time, and made so little headway. Sergeant Blackie had appeared from somewhere, and Brian Ridley, tearing madly up the grass verge and uttering the most appalling curses at the top of his voice. Half a dozen of those who were near enough picked themselves up and raced after them, full tilt into the hopeless, screaming, struggling mass, and began to pluck people out of it by hair, or arms, or clothing, or whatever came handiest, and push them down on to their faces in the furrows. Speech was in any case useless. There was no room in the air for any noise but the demoniac drumming roar of the diving bombers. The blonde woman stood among her trampled lingerie with her hat off and her hands at her face, and shrieked and shrieked and made no sound. She worried Jim. He had to get her out of sight, to shut her up somehow. He ran at her and took her in the hollow of his arm and dragged her off the road. They fell together, face down among the young barley, and he held her there, lying over her with all his weight, feeling her struggle to rise and brace her hands into the soil with desperate strength. She was mad, off her head with fear. This was why she had made her husband leave Brussels. He thought, with a strange lucidity: "These Junkers have been over Brussels. They can't have much left for us."

The first aircraft flattened and climbed again, so near that the wind of its passing tugged at them, and the noise of it was like a ton weight on their backs. The bomb fell forward of them, off the road, and a slow tower of soil and smoke and turf and stones went up, and hung, and expanded upon the darkening air, toppling apart in a rain of rubble. Stones and clods dropped heavily upon Jim's back, and he doubled the arm which was not preoccupied with the blonde woman over the back of his neck to ward off the blows. She had either fainted from sheer fright, or else she was just too scared even to struggle any more, for she had become very quiet, and lay still under his arm. It was a relief to be able to ease off the pressure with which he held her. He lifted his head in time to see the second bomber straighten out, and the second bomb fall, full upon the cause-way well ahead, among the cars and wagons, in an appalling explosion of fragments of wood and metal. Débris fell round him again as he dropped hurriedly into the loam. He was struck in the shoulder by a piece of a cart-shaft, and knocked silly for a moment with pain. But the noise was subsiding; it no longer deadened his other senses, though his ear-drums were still numbed with it. He was getting the thing in perspective.

He looked up again. Scotty Walsh in the nearest Bren-carrier was swinging his gun round upon the plummet flight of the third bomber. It looked hopeless, like trying to stop a charging elephant with a pea-shooter, but Scotty plugged away steadily. The other two planes were wheeling for a second sweep, and it seemed to Jim that their objective was the civilians rather than the convoy of Army transports. It was mad. There was no end to the damage they could have done had they wished upon that stretch of road, yet they detached only three of the formation, and apparently with orders to harry the inoffensive Flemings rather than the hated—and uniformed—British. Vaguely, be-hind the battering of the moment, he worried at this inexplicable circumstance. Then the howling plunge of the bomber brought his thoughts up standing, and lifted the short hairs along his neck. Something had happened to that confident roar. It was

99

interrupted by a strange, intermittent hiccough. The engine cut out, sputtered a time or two, and failed altogether. Scotty, open-mouthed behind the Bren gun, unbelieving, stood to see his victim fall. It had happened, the improbable thing. The Junkers sailed across the causeway, all but grazing the canvas of the transports, and sank itself two feet into the centre of the barley-field. Smoke gushed upward and hung dispersing upon the twilight, and in the heart of the smoke there licked outward sudden tongues of fire. No one came out of the wreckage.

They were so engrossed with their success that they emerged from cover to watch the death-agony, forgetting for the moment to keep track of the evolutions of the other two Junkers. It was so that the returning swoop of the first found them, and with a shattering outcry of machine-guns cut a swathe clear up the causeway. It was like the passage of a mower. Men folded at the belly and crumpled down to the hard white road, and were rolled along it like rags spun by a ground wind. Jim saw Brian Ridley, forward among the Belgians, take a screaming girl by the waist and throw her down into the ditch, and fall after her. Sergeant Mace toppled into the barley, too, but as it were in two sections, doubled over at the waist like roughly folded paper. Living and dead fell down together, and having learned wisdom, did not move again. The Bren guns went on chattering as the bombers passed and repassed, raising spurts of soil and stones. The smoke of the blazing wreckage blew across the road and made a thin screen against the attack. But no one made the mistake of lifting head or hand again until the recurring roar of the engines as the Junkers banked low grew more sluggish in returning, and at last failed to return. The diminishing note they made as they climbed, majestic and leisurely, receded into the distance. An immense quiet settled slowly upon the pitted fields. The smoke of the wreckage, no longer troubled by the passing of wings, gathered into a thin column and went up straightly into the sky.

Jim lay for a moment absorbing that grateful silence, relaxed and weary in the ghost of a grave his body had dug for itself among the barley. He felt himself trembling from head to foot, and waited until he had himself under control before he even took his face out of the loam. There had never been so complete a silence, never in his knowledge. They let their senses bathe in it; it was luxury unspeakable. The trouble was that they had to move, and break it. Time was precious; they had to get on.

He raised himself painfully, flinching as the bruised shoulder took his weight. It was all over, and a nice mess left to clear up. Along the straight road, pock-marked with craters and débris-holes, the living were stirring slowly and sorting themselves out from the dead. Here and there a transport sagged upon shattered axles, and trailed ribbons of drab-painted canvas in the dust. Forward, something which looked like the top-dressing of a refuse-dump, old clothes and cabbage leaves and splinters of timber and iron, marked the margin of that vociferous river of vehicles which had accumulated so short a time ago on the way out of Brussels. Brian Ridley was up, sweat-streaked and black as a nigger, holding up the girl he had thrust under him into the ditch. She went where he put her, like a docile child, and she was not screaming any more. As for him, he came up the road with a brisk step, and his voice as he shouted the first clipped, obvious demand for helpers was sharp and steady and practical, as if he was back on the Club ground at Morwen Hoe, placing his field. Nineteen and a few months! My God!

Jim touched the blonde woman's arm, and said, though obviously she would not understand the words: "It's all right now. It's all over. You can get up." Queer to hear yourself speak again; for nearly twenty minutes he hadn't been able to hear himself think. But the blonde woman didn't move. It took him a few minutes to see why, and he put his hand on her shoulder to shake her into sensibility before he realised that there was anything wrong with her. The back of her head was queer, a muddy red and the wrong shape, and a bunch of her fair hair fell aside as he shook her, and came away bodily over his hand, and the ends of it were red too, and sticky. A piece of metal, maybe a bit of her own car, had smashed her skull as she lay under him. She had gone quiet, all right, once for all.

2

Afterwards Second-Lieutenant Ridley, propping his grime-ringed eyes open with his fingers, reported to Captain Halliday that it might have been a lot worse. They had lost four lorries smashed beyond hope, and one Bren-carrier partially disabled, which might eventually be patched up sufficiently to overtake the main force; seventeen men killed, and eleven wounded more or less seriously, besides the walking and working cases. The badly wounded had been removed to Brussels, and the convoy had been delayed four hours in clearing the road and helping to give some sort of stop-gap assistance to the shattered civilians.

The advance across the Senne to Soignies had been made at last by night, and the halt could be of a few hours only. But it might have been a lot worse.

Jim, jolting down into the hollow glade where the convoy was drawn up for the remnant of the night in muster order, lay in the back of the last lorry, flattening his shoulders against the boards to ward off the agony of bumping his bruised flesh at every jolt, and staring at the sky. His mind was blank with weariness, though many a time at home he had come through a day physically twice as heavy without even noticing that his flesh was tiring. Winter-time in the woods of Sheel, when he had worked all day and poached all night and never been an atom the worse for it. But that was from love, when even the risk was a game and even the enemy a friend; there was no fear in it, nothing ugly or unpredictable, nothing to make your flesh string itself taut like a bow to keep the terror fast bound from the light, nothing to make your innards turn to water and the deadly sickness surge up and fill your throat. Maybe that was what bred this murdering lassitude now, after the strain was over. But he did not think about it; he did not think about anything; only in the back of his mind images flashed clear for a second like projections on a screen, and were lost again before they could mean anything. What were they seeing, those others who had declared themselves to be accomplished in First Aid as he had, and voluntarily stayed behind with him to salvage what could be salvaged from the mess of broken carts and cars in the lane? The old sweat with the grey moustache, sitting opposite with his tin-hat on the back of his head, and a cigarette drooping from his lip—what was he thinking about? And the serious young man with glasses, whose voice was so refined and whose manner so old-maidish—what was he seeing, after the first taste of being dive-bombed, and the more awful ordeal of trying his hand at putting bits of human wreckage together afterwards? There hadn't been time, thank God, in all that unutterably long two hours before the first doctor arrived, to feel the nausea to the full, or realise the hideous ugliness of the injuries you handled. No time to remember how inelastic, how book-learned and impractical was your knowledge of First Aid, Jim; or how long it was since you had used it, old sweat; or how intolerably ill the sight of blood made you feel, young man with glasses. There was the shattered line of vehicles, mere scrap metal and matchwood, still palpitating with threshing humanity, and some-one had to do something about it, and immediately. It was just:

"Any of you chaps know anything about treating injuries?" and "Yes, sir, I did First Aid before I joined up"; and there you were, tearing yourself on the jagged wreckage of cars like a man possessed, lifting out screaming women, and children petrified into silence, rigging slings under old men with broken thighs to lift them over to the grass, clamping your thumbs over severed arteries which pumped bright vermilion blood over your hands, purloining towels from the Captain's car to cover abdominal wounds for which you dared not do more, finishing off horribly hurt horses which kicked madly among the ruin of their harness, aghast at yourself and all your works, deathly sick, but too occupied to realise it.

No, it was only afterwards you began to see things, when it was all over, and ambulances were taking the worst of the civilian cases to Brussels; when you scrambled aboard the last lorry which had been left to pick you up, and suddenly there was time and place again, and it was night, and you were the wrong side of the Senne, and had a long way to go, and nothing to do by the way to keep you sane; when you sat against the side of the transport, watching the poplars along the straight, hedgeless road lean towards you and spring away from you in the darkness which yet was not dark, this luminous Flemish darkness. It was then that without thought you began to remember, and from memory passed to involuntary disconnected imagination, so that monstrous things began to flower in your mind. It was then that you had to take hold of yourself, and hang on to the stable things that used to be before the war began, and remind yourself that this wouldn't last for ever, that you were you, not the caricature of yourself, lost in a nightmare, that now you seemed.

Little things would keep bringing back the inevitable nastiness, of course. When the young man with glasses said abruptly, in that sharply-rising voice of danger: "I've *got* to get somewhere I can wash my hands!" and you looked at your own and found them fetid with blood and sweat and dirt like the worst conceivable kind of butcher, that liquefaction began all over again in your belly, and the sick feeling of falling apart was in your chest. Well, what about it? That's natural enough. What the hell did you expect? It isn't any soft job doing First Aid even in peace-time. There was a poor creature in Sheel once who went peculiar, and opened up her old operation scars with a knife. Disembowelled herself, so they say, or as near as makes no odds. Somebody had to find *her*. And that was before the war; he wouldn't be keyed up to withstand horrors, as we are now. Nobody expects a war to be all fun and games and pleasant sights. We've got the pull there. We're pretty well proof against anything. And this wasn't so much, really, only a curtain-raiser lasting twenty minutes or so, before the proper show starts. It might have been a whole lot worse. It needn't even have been as bad as it was if we hadn't been careless, and new to the game, and over-eager. Well, you don't make that mistake twice. And as for the civilians, they should never have been there in the first place, at a time like this. No, the incident at the cross-roads was only an incident, to be put by and forgotten.

If only he could stop seeing her yellow hair, though, her artificially-burnished, artificially-waved yellow hair that came away dewed with red, curling aimlessly in the wind, interlacing the stalks of barley, twining round his hand. If he could only get the feel of the warmth of her body out of the crook of his arm, the way she had plunged and struggled against his hold, and then relaxed into so strange a quietness. Admitted she was a fool of a woman, the sort Belgium or any other country could very well do without; but to die like that,.grovelling in the soil, scalped by a piece of flying metal while he covered her soft body with his and believed he was protecting her, while he survived without a scratch to discover his uselessness—that was worse than she deserved, whatever he had laid himself open to. Besides, she had never had a chance to think better of things, to get acclimatised to these new circumstances and stop making a nuisance of herself. Just because she lost her head under pressure the first time, and ran before she was threatened, and screamed before she was hurt, didn't prove there was anything really wrong with her. She might have settled down to the idea and been a tower of strength. But now there was nothing she could do to justify herself. She was dead. All in a minute, like smashing a fly. Just wiped out. He saw it as desperately unfair. But most of the time he saw nothing but her hair, swimming between him and the dusk, blown in dewy, bloody strands across his eyes, veiling the stumpy forms of the pollards by the canal as they passed, and dimming the sheen of the water. He lay on his back and stared at the sky through the shivering leaves of the forest, out of the inner opaque darkness into the inexpressibly deep and lustrous light, and still the pale perceptible curtain stirred between, superimposing its colour and texture upon all things seen. He couldn't get it out of his eyes.

He was in a half-sleep, half-daze when they came into the silent camp, and the hoarse exchanges with the sentries did not penetrate his seclusion. The private with the grey moustache leaned over and shook him by the shoulder.

"Come on, chum. This is it."

Jim dragged himself up obediently, and climbed over the tail-board, and jumped down into the grass. Not that it mattered much where he went or what he did for the few hours before they moved on again, but he supposed he ought to find his own lot. He liked things done orderly.

"You all right, kid?" asked the old sweat, seeing him steady himself by the back of the transport before he moved away.

"Sure I'm all right. Why shouldn't I be?"

"Oh, nothing. I thought you came down a bit gingerly, that's all."

"I ricked a shoulder heaving at that blasted cart that started the trouble. It's nothing much—just stiff." He drew himself together and went forward along the massed lines of transports drawn up under the trees. Men, known and unknown, passed indistinctly in the darkness, and spoke to him, and were answered. He got a cigarette from one of them, and stopped to light it, and the two faces flamed out of the shadow suddenly over the match, strained and grimy and grey. Like coming too suddenly upon your image in a mirror.

"Seen anything of A Company?" he asked, as the match went out.

"They're up forward. Bear right as you go, and there's a clearing. How'd you get separated from 'em?"

"I was with the gang that stayed behind to do First Aid until the ambulances came. A dozen or so of us volunteered. We only just got in."

"My God!" said the half-seen private, "I'd rather do the busting than the patching-up, myself. What was it like?"

"Oh, a bit mucky, but not so bad, considering."

"Sooner you than me," said the stranger cheerfully.

"Oh, I don't mind. Somebody has to do it, and I might as well keep my hand in. Thanks for the smoke, chum. So long!"

"So long. See you in Berlin."

Jim went on between the trees, along the ranks of transports standing silent and shadowy, with tired men sleeping within and around them. He stumbled among the tree-roots as he walked, and here and there misjudged distances in the dark, and blundered into the knotty trunks, wrenching his shoulder again and again. The deadly nausea came back upon him suddenly, and he turned aside into the underbrush, well off the road, and was direly sick. After that he felt better, but light-headed and unsteady on his feet. Anything to sleep now, and get the drifting blonde curtain from before his eyes; anything to forget it all, if only for an hour or two; and to-morrow, when the sun rose upon their continued advance, the incident would already have receded, and there would be new distractions, thank God. You can't go on indefinitely breaking yourself apart over other people's deaths when your own is hanging round inconveniently handy, or remembering other people's pain when your own body hurts like hell.

He found his company in the clearing off the road, dead asleep round their lorries. It was lighter there, because of the open sky above, and a gentle wind stirred the leaves with a constant furtive sound. Jim came down the slope quietly, but two or three who were sleeping uneasily stirred and looked up sharply as he passed, and Tommy, starting out of a doze, called out: "Who's that?" and stared for a moment before he knew him and sank back into the grass.

"Oh, it's you!" Jim unslung his rifle and let it drop beside the running-board, saying nothing. "How'd you make out? You've been a hell of a time." Jim shook his head, but made no other answer. He didn't want to talk; he was too tired, and, anyhow, there was nothing to say. "What in the world did you volunteer for, anyhow? You've done a precious lot of First Aid before to-night, haven't you? One night a week practising on a casualty that keeps still while you operate—I bet that lot didn't. You ought to have kept your mouth shut, my lad."

"Oh, shut up about it!" said Jim sharply.

There was a surprised silence, though the surprise did not go very deep. They knew each other too well for that, too well to be disturbed by unexpected moods, too well to expect consideration or resent the lack of it. Jim lay down beside Tommy, stretching himself along the ground with a heavy sigh, and turned his face away into his outspread arm. The grass felt warm to his hands, and the smell of the soil came into his nostrils with a loamy, lush sweetness, like the fields at home after rain. He was not aware of any nostalgia for England, or any unsatisfied desires in himself; just to be there still, with his mouth against the quiet, stable earth, was all he wanted in the world. All the perplexity and weariness and shock flowed out of him and was received into that tranquillity and there lost for ever.

"O.K.!" said Tommy briefly. "None of my business, I suppose. It's your funeral!" And he turned over and went to sleep again, lightly, as was his way.

Jim saw within his closed eyelids the last drifting flash of the dead woman's hair, like a pallid transparent curtain caught aside in a high wind. She was gone; the mist of weariness took her like a shroud, and the indifference of distance opened as a grave to receive her. It was her funeral, not his. He stretched himself along the ground. He embraced the earth, and slept with it in his arms.

3

Forward of their trenches the ground dropped, through the hazel-woods tangled with underbrush and spiked with the iron and concrete teeth of tank-traps, sheer to the canal with its broad towpath and fringe of poplar-trees, so tall and slim and motionless in the sultry air. Beyond the canal again the woods rose, but on that side very gently, laced with clearings and ending soon, with the red roofs of farm-steads in their neat orchards making points of broken colour here and there where the belt of woodland was thin. Beyond again, so they said, was a place called Wavre, but no one in the company knew more than the name of it. It might have been as big as Brussels or as small as the hamlet at "La Belle Alliance" for all they knew, but very certainly it was over there. Over there, too, were the enemy. Their artillery had been in action off and on for two days. The Midshires had watched the shell-bursts fretting the gentle landscape gradually, as a dog might worry at a child's picture-book, tearing out a clump of trees here, flattening a small-holding there, tattering the outline of the wood and pitting the meadows with smoking holes. From that ragged countryside had come back to them, during the past two days, all the desperate rumour of war, but never a sight of it, except when the distant batteries lengthened their range and smashed in a Belgian-built pill-box, or the daily methodical flights of the dive-bombers left mauled gaps in the trenches. There was fear of the Germans, but there were no Germans to fear.

Out of that ruin of Brabant there had flowed back and over them, like the wash of a wave, a foam of human ruin. The farm-steaders, their homes and fields smashed around them, had packed up all that was portable of their worldly goods and started on the hopeless trek through Belgian lines and British to the rearward areas which represented to them safety and rest. They had taken their cattle with them, and their dogs, besides every member of their families, even the decrepit and bed-ridden, pushing on top of laden hand-carts those who were in-capable of walking. On the first day, when Jim had looked down from the slope of the wood and seen the tow-path dark with people hurrying along hugging bundles of linen and food, and dragging tired children by the arms, it had seemed in-credible, almost comic. How could they fight a war with the civilian population strolling about between the two armies? Then there had drifted into that stream of people a salting of exhausted Belgian soldiers, sometimes travelling singly, some-times in twos and threes, broken men from lost units, drifting back to some sanctuary behind the lines where they could re-muster and find a place to stand and fight again. Many were wounded, some desperately. Most slept as they walked. All were red-eyed with loss of sleep, and limped upon blistered and bleeding feet. Questioned in signs, they only shook their heads and lowered their eyes and hurried on. They alone knew, but would not or could not tell, what was going on forward there, north and east of the Dyle. No one else knew anything. The inhabitants of the villages knew only that they were shelled and bombed, and that it seemed to them better to go away from the place where such things could be. No one tried to stop them. It seemed to be no one's business to try and stop them. So they went, slowly, painfully, tenacious in clinging to whatsoever they possessed of useful and movable, appallingly practical in abandoning everything else.

Jim was driving a small fast lorry northward towards Louvain one day to collect ammunition, and he heard as he drove through a tiny village something which made him pull up sharply. The place was completely abandoned, though apart from the loss of all its windows from bomb-blast, it was intact to the last tile; but somewhere there was a dog shut in, for he heard it scratching and whining. He found it in the third cottage he tried, the door unlocked, the living-room bare except for a few discarded pans and chipped dishes; he dared not think how long the dog had been there alone, without even water. It was a nondescript, chiefly collie, quite old and white-eyed with cataract, and smelled evil from age, dirt and confinement; but it wound itself around his legs in a trembling ecstasy of joy and gratitude, and it was a dog, and his heart was angry for it, all the more because he had sense enough to know that he had to do something with it, and that there was only one thing to do. Old and half blind, what sort of a chance would it have if he turned it loose and drove on? And it wasn't the sort of attractive beast a sentimental company adopts as a pet. He drew some water for it in a broken pottery dish, and fed it a bully-beef sandwich he had in a bit of newspaper in his pocket. He wished to God he had a revolver, but they don't issue revolvers to privates! While it was wolfing down the sandwich he did the cleanest job he could with his rifle. It wasn't pretty, but, anyhow, it was quick, and the poor old beast never knew what got him.

For an hour or so, almost until he had discharged his load and got back to his company, he hated the Belgians; but afterwards, while the procession along the tow-path continued under his very eyes, and probably many other cats and dogs were shut in to die of starvation and loneliness, he began to feel more gently towards them. They didn't feel the same way English people did about animals; and they were frightened for their own lives, which always makes people cruel; and nobody seemed to be giving them a decent lead, telling them what was expected of them, or how they could be most use. Nobody told them anything. Nobody put any restriction on civilian use of petrol, to judge by the number of cars on the roads. No wonder they panicked and ran. "The folks at home," he thought, with a shock of surprise, "might easily go this way if nobody got them together and told them what to do—or even if they weren't all doing jobs of their own. That's what it is—nobody's made these people feel it's their war. We jolly soon made it ours without being asked, but not everybody takes things that way. The bazaar has to be officially opened round these parts—and nobody's opened it."

It was a hot day, sultry towards thunder. As he tramped down into the traverse the heat seemed to close over his head, and he pushed back his cap and wiped away the triangle of sweat it left standing on his forehead. He wished the Germans would come, or better, that they could go forward to the Germans. It was overdue. He wanted action. Damn it, that was why they'd come into Belgium, wasn't it? They'd expected to sail into grips with the Jerries right away, and keep slogging until somebody gave in, and somebody meant the Jerries. But the enemy didn't seem to feel that way about it. Rumour said

the French 9th Army on the right had copped hell, and the retreating Belgians, afoot and awheel, spoke for themselves,
though silently, of the disintegration ahead; but along the
British sector there was little doing apart from scattered night
patrols, and bombing, and fairly heavy shelling at times. They
didn't seem to want to come to grips with the British. Three
days they'd been settled into their positions, and never a German
had he seen, except the one survivor they took from the bomber
that was shot down over their lines the second day. He wished
they'd get a move on; it might take his mind off the heat.

A despatch-rider was sitting in the traverse, hopefully tapping an unlighted cigarette and waiting for somebody to admit
to possessing a match. Jim gave him a light—the lighter he'd
bought at the little back-street kiosk in Paris still worked—and
sat down for a few minutes to swop a yarn with somebody from
outside the unit. It was getting downright parochial up in front.

"What's doing?" said Jim.

"Search me!" said the Don R. "I'd be surprised if God Himself knows. They're all chasing one another round and getting
no satisfaction, seems to me."

"I've just come from Louvain way," said Jim. "They were
saying up there that part of the French 7th is moving south-
east across the rear. I didn't see anything of 'em myself, but
there was a Staff car from H.Q. there, and the driver said he'd
had hell's own job getting there at all for these columns moving
over. Said the traffic chaps were doing a whale of a job, but the
roads were plain murder just the same."

"You're telling me!" said the Don R., with feeling. "I've
come up from G.H.Q., not a step over twenty miles, if that.
Took me two solid hours. So help me! The whole bloody
countryside's on the move."

"But why do they let 'em buy petrol? My God, they could
stop this run-out in no time if they wanted. Why the hell don't
they?"

"Don't ask me! I'm only the chap that ploughs his way
through it and hopes for the best. I've quit worrying about why
they do and don't do things. Let them worry about that. Thank
God it's not up to me."

"There's something in that," agreed Jim. "What d'you suppose these French units are moving south for? Is it true there's
a break-through down there in France? There's a rumour
around that they've had a bad time, but you don't know what
to believe in a muddled business like this."

"I never believe anything," said the Don R. "On principle."
He flipped the lengthening ash from his cigarette, and stared
moodily at the ground between his boot heels, where it fell.
"Talking of rumours—only this ain't no rumour—I suppose
you know Holland's stopped fighting?"

"Get off!" said Jim.

"Straight—no kidding! That's direct from Brussels. Laid
down their arms this very day, as ever was. Five bloody days!
Gorblimey, what a war."

"It don't seem possible!" said Jim, struggling to see it whole,
and failing, for it was too big.

"It ain't possible, but it's happened. Sure as death. It's all
over the place. If you'd had the forethought to fit a wireless
in your go-dammed limousine, you'd have heard it yourself."

"Strewth! It knocks you, don't it? Maybe there'll be more
doing round here, then—working on this here one-at-a-time-
please schedule they seem to fancy." The news which had
shaken the heart out of the Belgian people suddenly stirred a
current of excitement in him, apprehensive but stimulating. All
he wanted, all any of them wanted, was a go at the Germans.
They might get it now. He had to get back to A Company on
the canal, quickly, before the expected activities began. He
jumped up, slapping the dry loam from his seat. "I've got to
get on!"

"Me likewise!" said the Don R., grinding out the butt of his
cigarette with a large heel. "I'm late as it is, but who's
worried?" He got to his feet languidly. "Give my love to
Jerry. Tell him I'm hoping to see him some time, but not to-
day. It's too bloody hot."

"It is—stinking hot. Wish it would thunder, and get it over.
So long, chum!"

He went on down the trench, and by devious ways back to
his own people. It would come now, of course, just when the
clear mild May weather had congealed into this steadily clenching thunder heat which folded on them like a fist, sweating away
miserably all the energy from their bodies. But more than welcome, whenever it came, hot or cold, night or day. He wouldn't
be happy until he'd started in. It was like having a new and
intricate road-surfacing tractor to handle, and having the first
test constantly deferred until you grew nervous and jumpy about
it, and imagined yourself doing everything wrong and mucking
up the entire show. He found himself thinking: "Please, God,
let it start!" as he had prayed determinedly: "Please, God, let

it be fine!" when he was a kid of ten or eleven following the Morwen Hoe First XI from fixture to glorious fixture on summer Saturdays. But nothing seemed very much different. He went out across the canal that night, with four others, it was true; but he'd been out patrolling on the far bank more than once already, and nothing much had happened. Once they'd encountered an enemy patrol, darkly and distantly, but old Blackie, who hadn't the figure for these forays, had kept them back from attacking, and the Jerries had passed out of earshot unmolested. Clumsy woodsmen, too, that bunch had been. Jim could have picked off any one of 'em at almost any given moment, even in the moonless dark, by the noise they made. To Jim these night excursions were something in the nature of a game. He had amused himself in much the same way at home in Midshire, except that there the enemy had been only gamekeepers, and the danger more or less of a joke between the two of them; and it was difficult to realise now the magnitude of the difference that made. Because of his avowed experience in the difficult art of poaching he was a popular choice for night patrols; some day—who knew?—it might lead to something.

They were in the hazel woods, in the dark and the hot stillness, well away from the canal, just below the orchard of a ruined farm which sat in a hollow of the gradual slope. They were five in all, Corporal Williams, Brennan, Warrender, Bill Gittens and Jim, and they were looking for a machine-gun which had made itself very unpleasant all day long, having an efficient line upon the towpath. The corporal thought it was in the outbuildings of the farm; Bill held that it was more to the right, in the near edge of the thickest copse, where there was good cover. Jim offered to decoy it into firing, and was bidden to go ahead. They had grenades, and they badly wanted that gun out of the way.

He took his rifle and a coil of thin wire, and worked his way quietly round to a position where he was not likely to draw the machine-gunner's fire either upon his companions or the trenches across the canal. With a thrown pebble to rustle the undergrowth he had more than once drawn an unwary keeper in the wrong direction, and the old trick might well work again. He fixed the rifle in the crotch of a tree, taking his time, trying the feel of several before he found one which would hold it rigid, and made it fast there with the wire. Then he gave himself twenty yards or so of wire from the trigger, not daring to risk more for fear of dislodging the rifle and making the shot too wild to be convincing; and drawing to the end of this length of wire, by tentative pulls upon it decided how far to the left he could draw and still get an effective leverage on the trigger. Satisfied at last, he went back unconcernedly and pushed off the safety-catch, and settling himself carefully into the position he had chosen, fired the first shot.

He had set the decoy's aim perhaps a thought too near to the farm for his friends' comfort, for he heard the bullet whine off the white stone wall; but if they lay doggo as they should, they were safe enough. No rattle of machine-gun fire answered him, but he was not worried about that. The first shot was, so to speak, the preliminary tap of the conductor's baton, the second was the down-beat. He lifted himself out of his lush nest among the undergrowth, reloaded quickly, and dropped back again. This time they would be waiting for it; better get well down and be ready for anything. He wiped away on the back of his fingers the sweat that was trickling down his chin, and drawing the wire through his palm, rolled his weight back upon it a second time.

They were waiting for it, all right. Instant upon the spitting flash of the rifle a machine-gun gave tongue with a shattering crash, not from the farm-buildings, but from farther along the slope just beyond them, not a couple of hundred yards from where the rest of the patrol lay in wait. Jim did not locate it by that burst, however, if his friends did; he was fully occupied in flattening himself into the grass, holding his breath and wincing as he heard the scythe-swing of bullets cutting clean through twigs and small branches above him. A rain of leaves was shaken over him, slowly silting downward into the bushes. He thought: "I wonder if they got it? It was hellish near. Better give 'em ten minutes to work their way round, and then I'll create another little diversion." He felt with astonishment the thunderous beating of his heart. The burst of fire ceased, and there was a sudden enormous quietness. There was no wind, no sound, only the most profound and ominous silence, in which even the snapping of a twig might be the beginning of chaos. And Ginger could seldom move with any degree of finesse, being a townie born. Why did Corp. have to bring Ginger Brennan out on a show like this? Thunder rumbled suddenly in the distance. Or was it guns? There was seldom complete silence from guns, but this rolled in long, changing cadences and was almost certainly thunder. Praise God for it, anyway, and let it go on. Let it come nearer. No lesser sound would be noticed then.

Over Brussels, or what he calculated to be the direction of Brussels, the unresting planes began to circle, and the wavering rays of searchlights from far in the rear swept in wide arcs questing after them, and occasionally found for a moment only to lose again. It was over, that moment of terrifying silence, heaven-high and hell-deep. The world moved again, and the war went on.

He wondered if he dared reload yet. Had they chosen their position? Were they ready to play echo to the next echo? The thunder, bless it, was gathering steadily overhead, in long complaining groans. He lifted his head, and felt upon his face the first drops of rain, falling singly, heavily, bursting in explosions of smaller drops that dewed his eyelids with coolness. Yes, it was time. Do it now and the storm would cover the withdrawal.

The third shot seemed to touch off a whole train of violent and vicious sounds. Over the single staccato crack the machine-gun rattled wildly again, and this time they had shortened the range so that he heard the dull spattering impacts run along the ground behind him, and the short hairs at his neck erected themselves like a dog's hackles. He flattened his body along the ground, pressing his hot face into the soil, aching with tension, longing for the devilish moment to pass. Then the earth under him jumped and quivered to the explosion of a grenade, and he knew that the patrol were doing their part. None too soon; if the machine-gunner had shortened his range a shade more, the next swathe would have cut Jim Benison virtually in two. The grenade had got him, though, that far-too-accurate gunner; it was practically over, he thought, too hastily, and took his loamy, sweaty face out of the soil with a gasp of relief, and began to unfasten the wires which held his rifle to the tree. The rattle of the gun had snapped off with the grenade burst; but before the echoes had ceased their drum-roll it had clattered into action again, and Jim took his hands from the wire and dropped like a stone. It took him several seconds to realise that the field of fire had shifted, that the bullets this time were neither sowing the grass a yard from his feet nor ripping the leaves overhead. Someone had jumped for the gun and turned it on the attackers from the other quarter. A moment and the second grenade finished that.

This second interval lingered on and on. He got to his feet, quietly, holding to the tree, waiting for the next outbreak. Here and there rifle-fire broke out, more or less aimlessly, as the reverberations of the explosion diminished and were lost into the thunder above; but that characteristic stuttering roar did not begin again. That was the end of the machine-gun and the end of the job in hand. He wiped his face with his sleeve. More drops of rain fell with small, dull plops, bending the leaves, stinging his mouth. Lightning licked round the sky to westward and swallowed the searchlights. "That's that!" thought Jim. "Now let's get back to the rest."

There was something going on up there. The scattered rifle-fire, though blind, had an unpleasant thorny crackle about it. He pulled at the wire, tearing the tips of his fingers, but he'd done the job too well, and it took him a full two minutes to get it loose. All the time he was sweating and cursing silently because this was the first bit of real action they'd had, and he was missing all the fun. Starting it was all very well, but he'd meant to get off the mark quicker than this. He gave a venomous tug to the last turn of wire, leaving a strip of skin from his thumb adhering to it, and the rifle came away.

Stepping lightly between the trees, feeling as he went for the shorter grass which would receive his steps silently, he edged back towards his fellows. Now and again he halted, selecting the stoutest trees for cover, and took a careful shot at the most persistent of the enemy riflemen, slipping onward quickly between rounds to evade the answering fire. But they were quick to weigh up the workings of his mind. After the third shot, as he ran on stealthy feet for the next cover, mightily pleased with himself, a bullet cut through the leaves not a yard before his face, and pulled him up with a jerk. He crouched for a moment among the hazel-bushes and brambles, his heart pounding like a steam hammer, shaking his whole body with its blows. "Too damn' clever!" he thought. "That's my trouble!" But when he had steadied himself from the scare, he stood up and waited patiently for the next flash, and fired full into it; and this time the shot must have got home, for after that his opponent was silent. He tried the same tactics two or three times more, but without apparent success. One isolated rifleman didn't matter very much to them.

He had worked his way back, he found, at a slightly erratic angle, not along the slope, as he had intended, but climbing it, and he was now close beneath the roofless buildings of the farm. His eyes had become accustomed to the dark, and moving competently by night was one of his accomplishments at all times. He could see clearly the pointed outlines of the house gables against the sky, and the bulk of the barn, roofless both, and broken shapelessly downward here and there, good cover for guns. He crept through the torn orchard hedge, and went as near as he dared to the house walls. There were voices within. He heard brief sentences in a guttural mutter which must be German; many voices, so many that he began to wonder if he would not do well to get out of there quickly, while the going was good.

He lay still in the grass between the apple-trees, listening, and below the continuous complaint of the thunder, and the hum of distant aircraft retreating from the storm, he was aware of a multiplicity of small furtive sounds, the passing and repassing of muffled feet, exchange of orders and acknowledgments, voices near and far speaking in guarded undertones, and the constant unidentifiable suggestions of extreme activity. The place was alive with men. There was more going forward here than the mere establishment of a forward gun emplacement. There was preparation for battle, and imminent battle, too. There were lorries and gun-carriers, for he could hear the metallic familiar sounds of tools handled and laid down in the yard beside the barn, and presently a motor kicked into life and turned over for a few minutes with beautiful smoothness. They were getting ready to move, and so must he if he hoped to get out of there alive. He had seen nothing, but he had heard more than enough.

As he was worming his way back through the hedge on his belly, however, he heard something more, and stopped dead with shock and surprise. That was no lorry, and no modest Bren-carrier either, if he knew anything. They had armour there. He finished the passage of the hedge more recklessly under cover of the noise, and made the best speed he could towards the spot where he hoped to contact his friends. He guessed that they were retreating down the slope quietly in the hope of shaking off the following fire, which was converging in pursuit; therefore he set his own course down-hill, intending to join them unobtrusively in the thick hazel groves above the water. But either he had miscalculated their speed or they had been forced out of the direct course, for he was at the canal-side before them, and stood with one foot in the collapsible boat, holding it ready for their coming. As he waited, the lightning split the sky again, and the crash of thunder broke sheer over the passing of the light. It was coming at last.

Footsteps crashed stumbling through the hazels. "Ginger," thought Jim. But it wasn't Ginger. It was Corporal Williams with another man on his back, the head heavy on his shoulder, the right arm held across his chest by the wrist. He couldn't tell who it was, not until Ginger Brennan and young Warrender came out of the darkness behind, on their own good feet.

"Jim!" said Corporal Williams, low and urgently, and gave a long, soft whistle.

"Hsst! Here, in the boat!"

"Thank the Lord! Here, get a hold of him. Steady, he's dead out."

Between them they lowered Bill Gittens into the bottom of the boat and climbed down after him, and Jim pushed off from under the hollow bank. The water was miserably narrow, it wouldn't keep anyone on the far side for long; but if they thought they were going to bring their armour across the little bridge up the cut, they could think again, because it was very completely mined, had been for days, and an enthusiastic R.E. sergeant was sitting over it lovingly fingering the plunger.

"What happened your end?" asked Jim, dipping an oar silently, and watching the oily water shimmer under the lightning.

"Plenty. We got the gun all right, but that's not all—not by a mile. The place is alive. We had to beat it quicker than I'd meant, especially after Gittens got his."

"What was it?"

"Rifle bullet. They were thick as bees up there. Got him in the face. They were shooting stone blind, too."

"Bad?"

"I don't know. No time to find out. How did you make out?"

"Oh, not so dusty. Got 'em going easy enough, and then lit out. I ended up close by the farm. It's full of Jerries. They've got a lot of stuff there, ready to move—guns and tanks as well. They mean business."

"I know," said the Corporal simply. "I saw 'em. I should reckon around dawn we're due to get it."

Jim looked back across the narrow water. All aircraft had left the sky, and the searchlights had ceased from questing. The dark slope of hazels lifted gradually into the dark swirl of clouds, only a faint fringe of stormy dun-yellow cutting off earth from sky. The boat bumped gently against the bank, and he shipped his oars and bent to take a look at Bill Gittens, lifting him with an arm under his shoulders. The bullet had entered through his cheek at an oblique angle, smashing several teeth, making an ugly, painful but not dangerous mess, if only it had lodged there; but it hadn't, it had gone clean through and buried itself in the back of his throat. There was a lot of blood, because it had cut clean through the jugular vein. He was stone dead. He must have been dead before ever they got him back to the water.

The lightning seemed to dart upward out of the earth and clang like brass upon the zenith; and suddenly the rain came down, drowning earth and sky together, bringing a great cold wind in its teeth, making them gasp with joy to breathe freely again; the expected storm, the forerunner of the vaster storm to come. Jim stood up in the boat, raising Bill's body in his arms. The rain that gushed over them loosened the congealing blood from about his chin and throat, and flowed down into the hollows of Jim's chest and arms coldly, marking him with a mark no frenzy of waters would ever wash out.

"Come on!" said the Corporal, hauling the boat ashore after them. "We've got a hell of a lot to do before morning."

4

They couldn't believe it. It was crazy. Why should they move back? For just over twenty-six hours the Jerries had been trying to push them back, and hadn't managed it, not a yard; and now they were *ordered* to give ground, to move back within two hours to a rendezvous behind the lines, en route for the Senne canals as a first stage on the way to the Escaut. Sixty miles of good ground to be surrendered without a blow at last, when they had held it for so long against all the weight the enemy could bring to bear upon them. After all they had gone through, and all the men they had lost, were they to give up so tamely all that they had held with their bodies and knew they could hold still?

"Those are our orders," said Sergeant Blackie. "Don't ask me daft questions. I know no more than you. All I know is we've got to move, and move quick; and move quick we're going to, so come on, look alive."

They raged, but they obeyed; there had never been any doubt about that, of course. But the grievance was genuine and deep. They felt it a reflection upon themselves that they should be thus unceremoniously told to go, without explanation or excuse. They had stood their ground against armour, against air assault, against completely reckless expenditure of men and material, since five o'clock in the morning of the previous day, when the expected attack had been launched with a fury which bade fair to carry the enemy across the canal by sheer weight. Suddenly there were no more civilians. It was as if all civilians had been swept away out of the world, so that the war became universal, complete, all-absorbing. And all things in being fought in it on one side or the other. After that dawn they slept not at all, except perhaps for half an hour now and then in the lulls which heralded new and changed attacks; for there were no other lulls.

The shape of that battle, though crystal simple, was for ever obscure to them, who fought in it. It began with a wave of intense bombing, almost before the thunder of the storm had died. Up to then the Midshires had never seen or imagined what bombing could be like, but so far from subduing them it raised them to a pitch of blazing fury in which they were capable of anything. It was never safe to rile Midshire men. They were easy-going chaps in the ordinary sense, but apt to get uncompromisingly nasty when they were roused. They crouched under the rain and roar and mauling of bombs, hanging on grimly to their mounting grudge, nursing it, anchoring themselves in it, and biding their time, while the planes battered and gunned them into the mud. A good many of them died then, before ever the battle was joined; but the rest hung on sturdily, enduring stubbornly whatever came, and after a while so ingeniously obsessed with the meagre possibilities of present revenge that the natural human fear which is in most men's make-up was pushed away into the background of their minds, and it was as if they were working at their own proper trade. They discovered with satisfaction that it is possible to bring down a bomber with rifle-fire, if it flies low enough and you are persistent enough; just as, a little later, when urgency demanded it, they found that an army blanket in the caterpillars will stop a tank, and once stopped it can be dealt with. No one had told them how to do these things; as methods of warfare they would have been considered unprofessional and unreliable, even by those who used them; but they worked. They emerged naturally in the heat of the moment, out of the monumental, slow-roused, infinitely-slow-to-sleep indignation of the English when attacked; and they served their turn. Opposition, not precept, made soldiers of Midshire men, just as it made them, in peace, politicians and partisans. There was never anything like a persuasive push in one direction to make a Midlander go solid the other way.

119

All the same, they could have used a few more fighter planes that morning. It was too one-sided altogether, though what British pilots there were did very well, and broke up the worst of the attack time after time. But there were so many of the enemy that they had it more or less their own way, and all the defenders could do was dig in their feet and stick it out. And after the bombers the tanks came, suddenly crashing down out of the hazel coppices in half a dozen places, leaving torn streaks like the weals of whips down the soft flesh of Brabant. The bridge, the only remaining bridge for miles, had already gone up in a shower of dust and stone, and no one could quite see how the enemy hoped to bring his armour to bear on the opposite bank without a means of crossing; but the mere sight of those hurtling metal boulders raging down the hill with a tearing of branches and ruin of trees in their wake was enough to stop your heart for a minute. They were terrible in themselves, ugly, malevolent, nightmare creatures of unexplored possibilities. It was all very well to admire their speed and power on Salisbury Plain in peace-time; but meeting them in war was a very different thing, it made your hair stand on end. Nevertheless, they were land weapons, and however narrow the canal, they were on the far side of it; so the Midshires watched with deep interest to see what would happen, and the greater half of it had happened before they realised that there was to be no pause, no break at all in the rush of events. It was fantastic and appalling. The leaders of those steel columns roared full ahead, without so much as slackening speed, until the hollowed bank caved under their weight, and they plunged forward into the canal with rending splashes and were seen for a moment through colourless distorting curtains of water, erect and rigid as glass, before it slashed back over them in foam and washed outward angrily above their turrets. There was no hesitation; they followed one another at full speed. Two, three, even four in one place where they fell awry, immolated themselves to make a pathway for the others; and suddenly the Midshires realised that the enemy's armour was no longer on the opposite bank, but here among them, clambering ponderously out of the churned and swollen canal, nosing its way towards them up the steep incline, with devilish intentions and every possibility of carrying them out.

They had made the mistake of waiting, and every minute was time lost; but they moved fast then. There was no sense in waiting tamely for the impact. They climbed out of their trenches and went to meet them, with grenades, with Bren guns, with army blankets, with oil-drums, with their bare hands. Some of them went under the tracks, and some of them were dead before they reached them, and some leaped on to them and clung, and rode until they either fell off and died or found some way of smashing a grenade into one of the loopholes and blowing themselves and their victims into smoking ruin. If the Germans could turn suicide into a weapon of extraordinary ferocity, so could they. There was nothing the enemy could do in obedience to orders, that Midshire men couldn't do better of their own free will.

In that first hand to hand grapple fourteen enemy tanks got across the canal. Five of these fourteen were destroyed as they climbed the immediate slope, four more about the Midshires' disordered trenches, and the rest were pursued and stopped before they had penetrated more than a quarter of a mile through the lines. None survived, and no more crossed, then or at any later time, until the lines on the Dyle were abandoned. The corpses of these leviathans, burned out, black-hot, burst at the joints, littered the scorched grass, and the churned water and oily mud of the canal bubbled around their fellows. The bodies of over sixty Midshire men lay among the wreckage, smoking and broken past recognition; but there was no breakthrough. The infantry who had streamed across the water in assault boats after their armour never came to land, or never beyond the first step. They were mown with machine-guns and rifle-fire as a scythe mows grass, and lay rolled along the water and drifted thick along the hollow banks, dammed up into great swathes by their own wrecked tanks. Many of the defenders fell and were carried with them. Many more were blown to pieces by the unceasing rain of bombs; but they did not let go one foot of the ground they had been given to hold, nor suffer one German to set foot on it and live. There were few prisoners. Some who were disabled but still alive lay screaming for notice, but there was little time to give it. In the first lull, which came suddenly and from no apparent source, they snatched up their wounded and the few who survived of the attacking force, and whisked them back out of the desolation of the hazel-wood, with desperate haste lest the pause should end too soon.

They looked at one another, during that brief and incomplete breathing-space, as at strangers, people of another race, in curiosity and astonishment and respect. Jim, encountering Tommy in the bushes, not for the first time that day but for the first time recognisably, croaked at him: "Know something? *We're bloody good at this!*" and went back to his post grinning, as if he was enjoying himself to the full. In fact there was no time to feel any emotion at all. Every man was so fully occupied that although his senses recorded horror, his mind could not permit itself any reaction. They were transmuted into energetic forces compounded of an extreme stubbornness and a curious elated self-confidence. The real thing had begun, practice for all their theory. And it was all right—they were bloody good at it.

All day and all night and well into the next day they hung on tenaciously to that knowledge, while the bombers came over in waves, and the heavy guns across the valley blasted them where they chose, and periodically the questing tanks came down to the attack again, and the assault boats were launched by scores to overwhelm them. They had a good position, and the first shock had left them sure of themselves. What they had done once they could do again, and again, as often as it was required of them.

"They'll get tired of this before we shall," said Tommy grimly, lying along the flattened parapet over his rifle. "I'm just getting the knack."

"Ay, we're not doing so bad," agreed Jim. His hands were burned from a gun that had run red-hot and jammed on him, and he had lost a strip of skin from one cheek, but otherwise he was undamaged, and even at the twentieth hour of the battle, not particularly weary. "I could do with a pint, though," he said thoughtfully, easing his body into a better position.

"Who couldn't? Lucky to keep the throat to pour it down! They make good lager in Germany, so they tell me. How about you and me for the Army of Occupation?"

"Rot, that was in the last war. Hitler is a blinkin' teetotaller, they don't go in for beer no more. I say, though, Tommy——"

"Hullo?"

"You and Nance would do good business with a little pub. Ever thought about it? There's the 'Coach and Horses' could be worked up into a very pretty trade, with a bit of care."

"I don't know. There's the kid to think about. You don't feel like taking risks these days," said Tommy seriously.

"You'd be sure of one good customer, anyway." They dropped their heads then as the blast of a bomb from fifty yards forward dragged at the air over them; and emerging again cautiously as the rush of wind and flung débris subsided, Jim said: "I reckon they don't know what they're up against."

"They'll learn pretty quick," said Tommy. "We did."

Learn they did, and with complete and deadly patience went to work to use what they had learned. During the night they dropped parachutists behind the British lines, besides sending under cover of the darkness strong swimmers who succeeded in making landings here and there; and these also were all either prisoners or dead before morning. And constantly and unflaggingly they were bombed, until the very monotony of it grew maddening, and nothing was left of the Allied position but the bodies and spirits of the men who held it, and who knew now in some measure how great things it was in them to do. They died that night in great numbers; and having exhausted all their drinkable water without any hope of obtaining more, the living endured frenzies of thirst which almost tempted them, before morning, to envy the undemanding quietness of the dead. Such help as they could give to the wounded they gave, and were ingenious in improvising dressings and slings and splints when supplies ran low; and being for a while short of ammunition also, they fought off one landing with clubbed rifles which skinned their palms into blisters with the heat of the barrels. Most of them had wounds; all were in pain from smoke-scalded throats and flayed feet, walking with their boots sticky with blood. But they had not moved from their positions.

All this they had done and discovered and endured, and suddenly they were told to pack up and get out. They, who had settled down to things and made up their minds that the enemy should tire before they did! It was mad, and no one did anything to make them understand it better. Captain Halliday was not in the habit of explaining his orders or softening them in any way; and Brian Ridley, who heard the mutinous murmurs with which they made their preparations, lost his head and his temper and gave them hell for insubordinate battlefield lawyers, bolshies and mutineers, which even in their indulgent eyes lowered him to a schoolboyish status something below the level of being taken at all seriously. There was some excuse for him. He had been through the ordeal with them step by step, appalled and exultant both, and to him the order to retreat came more bitterly than to any of them, because he felt it for them all; moreover, he had never been encouraged to confide in his men. They were there to trust and obey. If he had followed his nature he would have told them all he knew—that down on their extreme right, in

France, there had been a break-through in strength, so that to hold their present position, however magnificently, was to be encircled and cut to pieces, a gesture suicidal towards themselves and benefiting nobody. To retreat was to fight again. All the truth he could not have told them, for in the maddening obscurity of the rush of events, too fast almost for the mind to follow, no one in the entire B.E.F. really knew all the truth. He could not tell them that the French 9th Army had been smashed to pieces south of the Forest of Mormal, or that five German armoured divisions followed by infantry were tearing through a twenty-mile gap due west for Amiens and Abbeville and the coast of France, across the British rear, across their lines of communication, making all their determination and accomplishment of no effect. The units of the 7th Army detached to reinforce the broken sector, had moved south-east too late to repair the damage. But this no one on the Dyle knew. They knew only that they had thrown away all the agony and horror and endurance of those twenty-six hours, all the lives of the dead, all the wounds of the living, because the positions they had retained by that bloody expenditure had now been wantonly taken from them.

It was in that mood that the Midshires began the retreat from the Dyle.

5

From the Dyle to the Senne it was a running fight, ferocious and exhausting, punctuated by shaken pauses of sleep as they relieved one another. And from the Senne to the Escaut, the poor shrivelled ghost of a river which they reached next day, the pressure eased only by infinitely slow degrees. Moreover, the nature of their warfare had changed. The first fine frenzy was over, the exhilaration and the shock together. They were fighting in retreat. It brought a cold anger into them, because they had not been defeated, but only ordered to go back; and this anger, like all the others they already carried in their ordinarily unretentive hearts, was turned against the enemy, so that they took their revenge wherever it offered, and in their depression and resentment were far more formidable than they had been in their hot blood.

"I'm bloody sick of this here defensive," said Tommy, as they jolted down what was left of a road between the tattered stumps of poplars, skirting bomb-craters and driving out into the margins of the fields streams of weary women and children who laboured along with bundles in their arms and cows lumbering before them. This was the commonplace of Flemish roads. It had reached the pitch where one hardly noticed them until the bombers came, as come they did unfailingly, sweeping at low level along those deathly straight roads, sometimes scarcely clear of the poplars, machine-gunning at leisure as long as their ammunition lasted or any demented child ran screaming to escape them. They were not so bold when British fighter planes were in the sky; but these were so scarce that no one looked for them any more, and their own Bren guns and rifles were the only defence they or the civilians had. The numbed, hopeless patience of the women's faces, the bewildered eyes which watched the retreat of the Allies who had seemed to them infallible, these were more wounding than the German fire. "I reckon we had too big a build-up," said Tommy bitterly. "It was asking for trouble."

"But we could have held on. We *did* hold on."

"Oh, don't start that again!"

They had had it all over and over, between heavy silences when no one could bear to speak of it.

"I will so start it again! What do they think we are? What did we come here for, anyhow? To run the first time we were hit, with our bloody tails between our legs? Did they think it was going to be all jam and fun? Or do they suppose we thought so?"

"We haven't got all the facts. They have. Can't you trust 'em to have *some* sane idea of what they're doing?"

"Can I hell! That's the trouble! Would they throw away sixty bloody miles of ground and a good solid position if they knew what they were doing? Does it make sense to you? I tell you, we could have held that sector for good and all." Scotty leaned forward and drummed upon Jim's knee.

"Tell me this, my lad. Could we, or could we not, have kept them b——s on the far side of that canal till doomsday?"

"It's my belief we could," said Jim honestly, "but——."

"But bloody nothing! Who said more than you when we were told to pack up and get out? You're trying to kid yourself everything's going to be fine and dandy, but you didn't think so then."

"I was browned off having to go. Anybody would be. I don't like being pushed around any more than you. But anyhow I don't kid myself I've got all the dope I need to prove

125

the General Staff are all bloody fools. I didn't expect to join as general adviser, like you."

"Maybe, but you're not so bloody happy about this as you make out. D'you know something? *We're retreating.* Think that out, and see how you like it. We're on the run. It doesn't taste so good, does it? Once it starts, you never know when it's going to stop. But whether you blasted well like it or not, we're on the run."

"Oh, shut your trap!" said Tommy. "The pair of you shut your damn' traps. We're sick to all hell of talking about the bloody business, anyway."

That was the only thing on which they were all agreed, however the words might burst out of them afresh when silence in its turn became unbearable. Therefore they took this violent request without resentment. They were sick of talking about the bloody business, and sicker of thinking about it; but with so much of fighting already before them, and behind, and around, there was no point in fighting among themselves. Jim with his anxiety to be reasonable, and Scotty with his bitter assurance, they were both in the same boat.

"It's just the thought of giving ground to the swine," said Alec Ross. "It makes you crawl. If someone was to order me to do something I could call 'attack' instead of 'defence' I believe I'd fall on his neck and kiss him."

No one quarrelled with that, it was so completely what they all felt. And on the fourth day after the beginning of the retreat someone actually did mention the word. By then the 4th Midshires had lost all sense of the country. They had been hurried along so fast and so far and through so many distractions that time and place meant little to them. They did not know where they were, nor what day of the week it was, nor where they were going. When they drew near to the frontiers of France again they did not know that, either. They were red-eyed from chronic lack of sleep, and all their muscles cried out for rest; they were dirty and lousy and unshaven because there was no time to bother with these little things; and they were inflamed with minor and neglected wounds, burns and blisters and festered splinter-punctures, discomforts which merged into the general discomfort and passed almost unnoticed. It did not strike them that they were being moved still farther south and west even than the new positions along which other British units were stolidly reforming their sector. All Brabant seemed to be afoot and awheel along those withered, chaotic roads, like a human tidal-wave washing south-westward; and with that distressful pilgrimage they moved, obeying orders, having no choice but to obey, but no longer attempting to understand. In this way they came back to the borders of France.

By that time, though the rankers were more completely lost than ever in their lives, and lived from hour to hour in readiness for anything, their officers at least had some sort of idea of what had befallen France. They knew that the flood of Nazi armour pouring through the Sedan gap had reached Amiens, and they knew also that since this news had had time to reach them, it was probably out of date. The next thing would be the fall of Abbeville, and they felt in their hearts that it would come soon, or that unknown to them it had already happened. On that very day, had they known it, fast armoured columns had by-passed the town and were thrusting for the coast at Boulogne, completely cutting off all communication across the Somme, and severing the B.E.F. from all their reserve stores and equipment. Even without these details it was patent that the situation was well out of hand, and that the only possible way of restoring it was by closing that southern gap. How wide it was by this time no one really knew, but there was nothing for it but to make the attempt. The dog-tired Midshires were not too tired to prick up their ears when the rumour of the counter-attack blew to them out of the smoky air, and they realised that they were cast for a part in it. It was like word of a victory, almost. They brightened, they were suddenly fully awake, voluble, eager. It wasn't only that this promised action and hope; it represented to them rehabilitation, a gesture not in compliance with the enemy's wishes. Besides, they had personal scores to settle, and personal scores still counted for something in 1940. A great many of their friends had died behind Wavre. Things had happened which were not good to remember, and would not be forgotten.

So they went south with a good heart on the 21st of May.

6

Jim sat under a tree in the yard of a little house in a village south-east of Arras, though he had no idea that he was south-east of any particular place; or even that he was in another country from the one in which the retreat had begun. It all looked much the same to him. The contours of the country were very similar, the villages, except in the degree of their desolation, changed not at all. He knew he had come a devil of a way, and was almighty tired. He knew he had swum a river under fire, and come ashore streaming water and blasphemy like a berserk Norseman, and that astonishingly the Germans on the bank had not liked the look of him and his fellows enough to stay and fight hand to hand with them. He knew, too, being surprisingly clear-headed just now, that they hadn't gone far, and wouldn't be gone long. He'd got past the stage of even pretending to believe in the "Run, Rabbit, Run"! line of psychology. He was beginning to know them; most of the time they were running they ran forward, not back.

There were six living men and one dead man in the yard. The dead man was a German, a very big, fair young man, not at all like the popular idea of a Nazi soldier, indeed he must have been good-looking when he was alive. The grenade that got them passage into the place had exploded right under the muzzle of his automatic gun, and blown him clean across the yard into the wall of the house, smashing the top of his head in flat. He reclined there against the wall in a curiously easy position, with his hands peacefully open, palms upward on the ground beside him. Blood had gushed out of his ears, and nostrils, and the corners of his mouth, and congealed in streaks down his chin, and the flies were settling on him. But for all the natural inclination to think: "Poor devil!" you found yourself stopping short of pity. Not simply because he was on the other side. It wasn't the ghosts of Bill Gittens, and Shorty, and Sergeant Mace, and all the rest of the Midshire lads, who grudged him a drop or two of sympathy: it was the blonde woman on the by-road south of Brussels, and the two little girls crushed in each others thin arms in the cellar of the house at Gembloux, and the draught-horses fallen kicking and screaming in their traces, and the woman who ran so heavily and clumsily along the causeway between the flat fields that one evening in Hainault, until the Luftwaffe machine-gunner got her, and she embraced her distended body, and wailed: *"Sainte Vierge, Mère de Dieu——"* and fell down and died before they could even reach her—Oh, my good God Almighty, to see that woman would cure even You of pitying Germans! Twice in a lifetime they've done this to the world, to the children, to the women with child. "She is with young!" The echo of a voice saying that came also, and strangely, between Jim and any relenting. Often, too often, he remembered the woman of Hainault, and always Miriam Lozelle was there with her in his mind. He had

128

no pity to spare. He looked at the dead body dispassionately, and considered whether the corner where it lay did not offer a better outlook across the fields to the ridge of trees where the enemy machine-gun was hidden. When he decided that it did he went and dragged it aside out of his way without a qualm, as if it had been a sack of potatoes. Compunction would in any case have been a bit of a farce, coming from him: it was he who had thrown the grenade.

The machine-gun duel had been going on for half an hour, and they were getting short of ammunition. From the low, broken wall, loop-holed and tottering, you could look out, if you were cautious, across a ditch grown with reeds and noisome with green scummy water, and a few scattered clumps of willow-shoots not yet grown even to shrub height, and a rose-red line of slender spears of willow-herb; beyond this thin but effective cover, a wide pasture opened, stretching away from them into marshy distances where there were growths of flowering rushes; and beyond again was the ridge, covered in what seemed to be thick groves of rose-briar and bramble, and dusted with trees. A natural barbed-wire entanglement. Plenty of men in it, too, to all appearances, but that wouldn't matter if they could only knock out the gun.

Jim settled himself more steadily into his new position, and nursed the stock of his rifle against his cheek lovingly, and waited on his sights for a movement among the distant bushes. One thing about being a hedge-side shot, you learn early to be frugal with your slugs, and wait patiently for a reasonable mark. No blazing away haphazard when you've been used to buying your own ammunition. The round of a steel helmet above the briars isn't enough to excite you, nor the flash of a bayonet turned in the sun. But let something provably human stick itself incautiously out of cover, and you're on it. Jim thought he had the machine-gun located; it was well hidden, but the centre of movement was there, and once after a burst of firing an eager gunner had raised his head to watch results, and Jim had got him, clean in the face he thought, for he had risen to his full height out of the brambles in a great leap, and crashed over backwards like a felled tree. Sooner or later he would get more of them the same way. It's only a matter of patience. "You can't go on for ever without showing yourselves, you bastards!" he said aloud. "I can wait." And he wondered how much more of the fabulous gap there was, once you were the other side of the ridge. They'd already come a hell of a way; there surely couldn't be much farther to go.

They wanted to get on. This half-hour hold-up was a nuisance. It gave them time to get their second wind, true, but it also gave them leisure to realise how tired they were, which up to then, in that wild dash across the Cojeul, they had not noticed. When they changed their positions, they found themselves stiff and sore, all their bones aching with the bruises and grazes of a fortnight's unresting movement.

"I'm sick of this," said Scotty Walsh suddenly. "I'm getting set. How about taking a running jump? It's not so desperate far across that field. Some of us might make it, anyhow."

"With that gun still in action, and over this open ground? Talk sense, for God's sake," said Sergeant Blackie. "If one of us could get near enough to lob a grenade in among 'em we might get somewhere, but those chaps up left are in a better position. They've more cover, and less distance to go."

"Ay, but they're not suffering—not from that particular b——. They've got their own problems and this is ours. How if I was to drop back and work round by the end of the ridge?"

"No need," said Second-Lieutenant Ridley from behind them. "Two of Williams' men are half-way there already. Sit tight for the bust-up, and then you can go in as fast as you like."

He came wriggling in through the shattered corner of the house, having worked his way along the hollow more or less in shelter. He had lost his steel helmet, and a stray rifle bullet had as near as nothing put paid to him, leaving a red groove clean along one side of his head above the ear, ploughed deep through hair and skin. It had bled profusely, making a devil of a mess, of the kid's face and neck on that side, but it was drying now. Abominably painful, but at any rate he was still alive. He wouldn't be able to sleep on that side in comfort for a bit, by the look of it; but then, sleep seemed a pretty distant prospect at the moment, in any shape.

Weariness and excitement between them had made him incautious, and another bullet whistled past his head pretty close as he came in, and whined off the wall behind. Jim took him by the arm and pulled him down out of sight. "Better keep your head low, sir. It's pretty hot around here."

"So I see." He had forgotten to keep himself aloof from his men. He was too tired, and, anyhow, they were all in this mess together, for it was a mess, no end of one if they only knew. There were supposed to be French in it with them, but they'd seen none. And the tanks—oh, lord, let's forget the tanks! It wasn't their fault they couldn't do better for us, the wonder is they did so well. They'd been on the road too long, the railway transport having failed them at Brussels on the retreat south. A machine isn't like a man; it can't go on for ever taking punishment and still hang on like death when by all the rules of logic it ought to be out for the count. Queer they used to think it was the other way round! "We're men, not machines!" they used to say, when they considered they were being hardly used. Well, these were men, and they went on when the machines had given up. To hell with keeping aloof from them!

"Any of you fellows got a cigarette?"

"Only these filthy French things. All the way from Boissy."

"Anything to keep me awake. Is that where you got the lighter, too?" The wheel flicked easily round, and the wick flared bravely. "My God!" he said blankly. "It works!"

"Never let me down yet, sir. No, that was from Paris, but I got the fags from Papa Brègis' place, the day before we moved." It seemed a lifetime ago rather than twelve days. You wouldn't think it possible for so much to happen in so short a time. "Takes you back a bit, doesn't it?"

Brian said, with his eyes on the distant hill: "We can't be very far from Boissy now. A few miles the other side of that ridge, I should say, and we'll hit the road we left it by."

Jim, who had been without a sense of direction or distance for three days, jerked away from his sights with a gasp. "What? Are you saying we're in *France?*"

"That's right. Didn't you know?"

"Know? I haven't known where I was for days. And Boissy-en-Fougères is down there ahead of us—over that ridge?"

"Yes, I'm certain of it."

"Then—you mean the Germans are in Boissy?"

"I'm afraid they've been there for days. I know—it got me that way, too. But they won't be there much longer, remember——"

"No," said Jim through his teeth, "so help me God, they won't!" But he did not say it aloud.

Suddenly he saw Miriam Lozelle, walking down a long straight road in his mind, with Sarka in her arms and Chicot at her heels, one of a nightmare procession of people, homeless and without hope; looking fixedly ahead of her with eyes which saw in all the world no resting-place, except perhaps a fold of the ditch by the roadside at the end of it, and no sleep but the last sleep, with the stooping bombers for a lullaby. He saw her very clearly, and her face was like a mask of marble, with bitter lips drawn rigid, and eyes withdrawn, recognising in all the world no friendship nor gentleness but bent rottenly under her hand. That was the worst moment he had had.

"We made an unholy mess of it," he said, "didn't we?"

"Somebody did."

"Everybody did, us with the rest."

Spurts of smoke began to jet out from among the brambles, and the intermittent bark of the enemy machine-gun broke off short and was silent for a longer while than usual. "That's them!" said Brian, and raised himself to look over the wall. Jim saw him take the bullet in his left shoulder, low, dangerously low, even before the exasperated Sergeant Blackie could shout to him to get down and stay down. The boy's knees gave, and down he came, clutching his wound tightly with the fingers of his right hand, and furrowing his brow in a surprised stare at the blood that oozed out and trickled over his hand. Jim's arm broke his fall and let him down gently on to the uneven quarries of the yard. "Sorry!" said Brian. "Bloody silly thing to do." And incontinently made to rise again, but found he could not.

"Hold still!" Jim began to unfasten his tunic and shirt. "Don't move that arm—you're speeding up the bleeding." The sound of an explosion from the direction of the hill brought Brian's head jerking round again. "All right, take it easy a minute. It's not so bad as I thought." He fumbled for a field dressing, and tore at the canvas casing with his teeth. The wound was clean, but the bullet had lodged somewhere in the shoulder, and there was a lot of blood, bright and bubbling. The dressing, bandaged tightly, might restrain the flow, or it might not. But there was no means of getting better attention for him here; as well take him ahead with them, if that were possible, as leave him here "How does it feel? Can you move that arm?"

"Yes." He did, and the blood sprang through the dressing instantly. "Sergeant, did they get the gun? I don't hear it now."

"They got it, I think, sir. There goes another grenade now. Shall we go ahead?"

"Yes, take them forward. I'm coming after, but I can't

make your speed." He shut his eyes upon a spasm of pain and nausea, and when he opened them again Blackie and Scotty and the others were gone, only Jim remained, holding him in one arm, steadying him against his knee. He said, staring down at his left arm, which was buttoned firmly across his chest inside the stretched tunic: "What the hell do you think you're doing to me? Making me into a bloody cripple? Here, undo the blasted thing, Jim, I'm no good like this."

"Don't be a fool! That's the only way you will be any good." The officer-ranker relationship had gone by the board without either of them noticing its passing. "How is it, kid? Does it stab when you breathe deep? Try it now."

Brian drew a long, slow breath, and perceptibly flinched. "A bit—nothing to speak of. I'm all right." But the flesh round his mouth had suddenly become blue-white, like veined marble. He put up his right hand, and began to unfasten his tunic again, but his fingers were curiously clumsy at it. Jim took him by the wrist and held his hand away.

"You pig-headed little devil! Let it alone, I tell you, unless you want to bleed to death. Do you think I fastened it up that way for fun?"

"Well, all right, but don't be so blasted managing. Here, give me a hand to get up. I think I can make it now."

Jim lifted him to his feet. The kid weighed next to nothing, and was thin as a lath, but these wiry youngsters had more stamina usually than their bodies looked big enough to hold. Brian stamped his feet experimentally against the quarries, and looked pleased and faintly surprised to find he had so firm a grip of the ground. "It's all right, I can stick up now. Come on, let's get on."

The ridge was a battlefield by now, the brambles threshing with men at grips; and if they were fired upon as they leaped the ditch and ran across the meadow it was only a desultory fire which escaped their notice. Brian was preoccupied with resisting the waves of faintness which attacked him, and Jim was watching him, one arm for ever extended to take him if he crumpled again. But he did not crumple. He raced across the marshy reaches of the field, water flashing from his heels, and dived into the briars; and Jim, following with a shout, heard his revolver giving tongue. The rest of the Midshires were halfway up the hill by then, leaving a litter of torn brambles and a maze of clawed pathways behind them. Other débris, also, as Jim found when his boot took a dead man in the chest and drove the breath from his lungs with a dreadful gasping sigh. The horrible protesting sound made him leap forward in plain panic, never looking to see what he had trampled. After that experience of the dead he fell upon the living enemy with joyful relief. The first he encountered had just plucked the pin from a grenade and had his arm drawn back for the throw when Jim sailed into him and dragged him down with an arm locked about his elbow. The grenade rolled out of his hand, and Jim whipped it up and threw it ahead. The explosion shook a shower of leaves down from the trees over them as they rolled among the briars, lacerated by thorns, their faces oozing blood from hundreds of scratches. They fought with fists, and knees, and heads, unable for a while to reach the rifle and bayonet which Jim had pushed from him when he made his lunge. Then Jim got his knees well under his opponent, and shot him off staggering but upright; and rolling violently into the bush where his rifle had fallen, had it propped before him, butt against the ground, when the German recovered his balance and literally fell upon him again. The weight of the massive impaled body knocked the breath out of him, and for a moment he lay with all his senses adrift in a sort of revolving opaque darkness; then the hot flow of blood soaking into his clothes revived him to a passion of nausea and disgust, and he struggled away, rolling the dead man aside. Dead or as good as dead; he twitched a little, but no more, and the mere relaxation of nerves after death can do so much. Jim reclaimed his bayonet, and drove it into the grass to clean it before he went on up the hill. He wondered where young Ridley had got to by now. He was a little anxious about him. After all, he was from Morwen Hoe, too. You're bound to feel an interest in a lad you've known all his life, and played cricket with, and taught to shoot, and clipped across the ears many a time for sauce before the army decided to make an officer of him.

He climbed hurriedly, and found the summit of the ridge re-peopled. The enemy had withdrawn, leaving the machine-gun to the attackers. It had jammed, but Scotty was working on it, with much blasphemous speech but with expertly gentle fingers. Brian Ridley was there all right, white and hollow-eyed but still on his feet. Blackie was there, and Corporal Williams and his men from the position nearer the end of the ridge, Tommy Goolden among them. He grinned at sight of Jim, and waved a derisive hand. "Late as usual, Private Benison! Arriving when all the work's done, I see." And then he did see; he saw

the blood with which Jim's waist and chest were soaked, and
his eyes and mouth dropped open together.

"Don't be daft!" said Jim, "it's not mine."

"Bloody good job for you—it looks like most of one man's
ration. Pretty tough from your approach, wasn't it? We saw
your first lot come in flying—never knew old Blackie could
move so fast. What happened to the kid?"

Jim told him. "Tell the truth, I thought he'd got it through
the lungs. Even now I'm not so sure; he's not as good as he
makes out, not by a long way."

"I don't know. He seems to be standing up to it all right.
Look at him!"

Brian was the only British officer in this forward position,
and knew it, and was trying to do his best with it; but waves
of dizziness kept spinning across his eyes and drawing him away
into cool distances of indifference in which the fate of this hog-
back of brambles and the decorous spaced beechwoods beyond
mattered not at all. Between these spasms he disposed his
meagre forces to the best advantage, and decided to go forward
himself along the crest of the ridge to take a look at the ground
ahead. They had now the German machine-gun as well as their
own automatic, but no great supply of ammunition for either.
He thought they would do well if they could hold this position
until supports came up from beyond the village; to go ahead
unsupported was to throw away not only their lives but their
gains as well. So he left them well established, Scotty purring
over the restored gun, and took Jim forward along the hog-
back with him. Jim knew why. When they were out of earshot he took Brian by his one good arm, and said plainly:

"You know damn' well you're not fit to be on your feet.
Come on back and let's see what we can do for you."

"No—I'm all right." A fleck of blood gathered at the corner
of his mouth and ran down his chin. He wiped it away and
repeated feverishly: "I'm all right."

"Like hell you are!"

"Do you damn well know who you're talking to?" flashed
the boy, still scrubbing at his mouth with a shaking hand.

"Yes—*sir!*" The emphasis raised a faint, worried flush, and
the ghost of a grin hard upon its heels.

"Sorry, Jim, I didn't mean that. But I'm not going to lie
down till I fall down; I don't want them to know there's much
wrong with me. We've come through well so far, and they've
got plenty to think about, without casualties hanging around."

"You—it's true, then? It's really bad? It scared me at first, but when you held up so well I thought——"

"I don't know. I feel like hell, but maybe I'm making a fuss about nothing. Come on, let's get the lie of the land first, and see what's hanging over us. Then maybe I will sit down for a bit." He laughed shakily as he started forward again. "Tell you the truth, Jim, I can't trust myself to keep still when it nags at me this way. I'd hate to give the show away."

There was nothing you could do with a brat like that, except go with him and stand ready to pick up the pieces; and Jim stuck close to his elbow as they walked softly between the trees on the crest of the hill, above the cleared track which coasted onward into the beeches beyond. They kept to the edge of the track, alert for the first hint of trouble ahead, but there was no near sound, only the unceasing rumble of gunfire, which had become the background of their lives. Their vigilance slackened gradually, not because they felt the danger to be any less, but because Brian's blind spells were perceptibly increasing. The weight of the revolver seemed to drag at his wrist, and from time to time he stopped to steady himself against a tree. Jim, for the intensity with which he watched him, had no eyes to spare for the way ahead. He knew it was madness to go on, but you cannot lay forcible hands on your platoon-commander and compel him to behave like a sensible casualty, even if he seems bent on committing ceremonial suicide.

At the distant edge of the hog-back the ground dropped into a gully, the path following; and across the gully the woods rose and rolled away again out of sight. There was not an enemy to be seen, but for obvious reasons those beechwoods must be full of them. There were felled logs, peeled and white, on the last plateau of the ridge.

"You could do plenty with the automatic-gun from here," said Brian, in an interval of complete lucidity. "We'll move it up, and make use of those logs to cover it, and bob's your uncle. All right, I'm satisfied now, we'll get back." In the act of turning, he stopped, staring down the gully. The gradient was not very great ,and before the shade of the beeches took complete possession of the ground there was a good deal of ground-ivy and underbrush crowding upon the path. "I'm seeing things," he said. "I saw the woods move. Birnam's coming to Dunsinane, I expect." He laughed, and bright bubbles of blood broke on his lips again. "Oh, hell! It's starting again!"

The woods moved; very certainly they moved, with a whining roar of engines and a crunching of caterpillar-treads biting into the beechmast. Before their eyes the bushes sprang apart and exploded like dehiscent plants hurling out their seed, monstrous seed that rushed towards them up the gully, slung low upon flat tractors, with jutting guns slewed from their squat turrets, and black and white German crosses marked upon their sides. A rain of snapping twigs and a ruin of branches surrounded them. They came soaring into a wild speed, medium-light Nazi tanks moving upon the captured village by the least expected and best concealed way, the woodland track along the rear of the ridge, just below the summit. On that road they would sweep up casually, as a dog licks up cake-crumbs in passing, the handful of Midshires and their two inadequate guns. If they fought they were dead men; if they escaped notice by hiding, they were fugitives until they died more slowly or became prisoners. No, it was almost too late even for that. They would have no warning. The treacherous fold of the ground which had cut off the noise of the tanks' approach until now would cut it off still from Blackie and his fellows. It would break on them at the last moment as the enemy topped the rise, and crashed past their position; and it was a thousand to one against escape.

Brian gave a short cry in his throat, meant for no one, uttered in the last extremity of rage and despair, but Jim heard it and his own nerves erected themselves. "You've got a grenade left?" panted Brian, springing back into the shadow of the trees, and wheeling on him as if he were the enemy. "Give it to me!" And as Jim stared for the fraction of a second before obeying: "Quick, give it to me!" he repeated furiously, and wrenched his injured arm out of his tunic to receive it. Sweat broke on his forehead and stood in beads, and all in a moment the small red patch in the chest of his shirt expanded like the opening of a scarlet flower. "Now run like hell! Tell 'em to scatter and lie low, and get out as best they can."

"You're crazy! There's no time to reach them."

"There's going to be time."

"What are you going to do? My God, man, you can hardly stand. If there's anything to be done, let me——"

"Don't be a bloody fool! Why you? I'm as good as dead now." And suddenly he screamed at him wildly: "Do as I tell you—get to hell out of here!"

Jim turned on his heel and ran, with that raging voice in

his ears dulling the advancing roar of the tanks. He kept within the shelter of the trees, and once, checking in his stride on the edge of the slope, for a broken second he looked back. So he saw, and all that day while he had sight continued to see, young Ridley leap over the barrier of logs and go bounding down the rough escarpment, fending himself off from trees with one arm, falling and rising again, like a madman, like a demigod, right for the narrowest point in the path where the tanks must come, the one point where the trees drew close about the rutted track, leaning to each other. He saw Brian and the leading tank converge, saw the boy hurl himself at the machine, and cling to it, spread over the flat grey side like a cross, hiding the other cross, as it swept into the darkness of the trees. So much he saw, and turned and ran again, madly, the memory pursuing him; but he could not outrun the dull exploding roar that followed, the bursting of his own grenade. As he ran he found himself sobbing and cursing, in horrible words he did not recognise as possible from his own lips, words he had not realised he knew. Get to hell out of here! Warn the others! That was all he was good for, while little Ridley went down like a comet, with destruction in his hands, to meet and embrace the enemy. The bloody little fool—the bloody little hero!

It was a madman or a ghost who ran back into the little group above the path, or so it might have been by their faces. They came to their feet everyone, eyes flaring, aware of disaster before he spoke, keyed for battle or whatever their part might be. Sergeant Blackie took him by the arm, and demanded urgently: "Where's Ridley? What's afoot?"

"He sent me back—Nazi tanks, medium light devils, coming this way up the cart track towards the village. A lot of 'em—don't know how many—coming fast. Any moment now! He says get under cover quick and stay away from them, and fight your way back if you can."

"Stay away?" growled Scotty, stroking the newly-acquired gun. "What's the matter with fighting?" He spoke for them all.

"Plenty. There are over a dozen of 'em, maybe more. And you've got next to no ammunition. Anyhow, fight or run, but for God's sake get out of sight before they drive over you."

Sergeant Blackie took the words from his mouth then, and the burden from his mind, and with brief and scalding sentences drove Scotty into the high bushes with the machine-gun, and Corporal Williams and Tommy haring across the track into the brambles with the automatic, while the rest dropped to earth singly in the best cover they could find, and the woods took them as a fish takes mayflies, and they were no more seen. Jim was left standing, emptied of all sense of responsibility to them, adrift from them, now that the message was delivered. He knew they meant to fight. That was not as Ridley had meant it to be. But for all that they might, with what ammunition they had, so delay and damage the convoy of tanks that its effect upon the issue might be destroyed, and the village held; so the end might be served better by the means young Brian had not intended. At least they were warned. He could go back now, and look for what was left of the boy, there in the arching of the trees where he had dammed up the steel river with his slight body and very great heart. Jim wanted to go back. No one needed him; one man more or less here would make no difference. He turned and dived into the bushes, and began to work his way back, with no great care in his choice of cover. His defection was unnoticed; they were all intent upon the track by which the attack would come, and had no eyes for anything else. So he departed unchallenged, and dropping down the slope, skirted the cart-track closely.

The head of the column, breaking back to the track from a difficult detour through the trees, was on him before he was aware, with a sudden gust of noise and gush of wind. He had to leap back abruptly to give them passage, and he knew that he was seen. Bullets spattered through the leaves and buried themselves dully in the trees behind him. He knew then he was done for. He knew he wouldn't reach Brian. The last thing he saw was the forward gun of the leading tank slewing, the sunlight sliding along its barrel. The last thing he felt was the pains of hell seizing him by the left side and the scalp, before a veil of blood' flowed down before his eyes, and the darkness took him.

7

When he opened his eyes the moon was up, shining through the splintered branches and raising into exaggerated relief the pits and ridges into which the soil was churned. He saw the clean white silence of the sky through his blood-matted eyelashes as if through bars, and wondered at it for a long while before he knew what it was, its serenity seemed so far from anything he had ever known. He was not conscious of pain; it was the cold that brought him to, the cold and the stillness together penetrating his stupor. He wished to move, but found his arms unwieldy, and his body heavy and sluggish. He could turn his head, though he felt the crust of blood which covered one cheek cracking painfully, and the sting as it tugged out hairs from over his cheek-bones gave him a strange, stimulating pleasure, because he knew then that he was still alive. When he looked along the floor of the forest he saw as it were mountains and gulfs close to him, but when his stiff eyelids yielded and opened wider the mountains receded into erections of soil, gouged out by the passage of the tanks and overhanging the gulfs which were stamped out by their tractors. He remembered then what had happened, and his senses came to life with a perceptible leap, and the night assumed shape and colour and sound and time around him. He braced his hands into the beechmast under him, and dragged himself up into a sitting position, and looked round. Loneliness rushed in on him; from every aisle of bone-white moonlight and the shadow of every tree the night looked upon him with cool, disquieting eyes, and he was afraid. Like a child left alone in the dark; like an animal tormented by the memory of things past in the sort of house men call haunted. Shivering he got to his feet. His body obeyed him reluctantly; it wanted to lie down and sleep, and he was dimly aware that if it lay down now it would sleep for ever. It repaid him with pain, but he was glad of pain, because it reassured him at every shuddering movement that he was alive; you cannot be hurt when you are dead.

His head was the worst. If he could only get things clear in his mind he would know what to do; but whenever he tried to arrange the disordered pattern of his memory, the roof of his brain began violently to open and shut, like a fist clenching and unclenching. He put up a hand to hold it together, and the raw, scaring pain that savaged him darkened the world again and brought him to his knees. Out of that whirling darkness the blanched trees advanced again silently, and stood in a circle about him, impassive, incurious, waiting for him to die.

He was determined not to die. This was bad enough, but living was worth a lot; and the zealous First Aider in him was beginning to wake up and record impressions. His skull wasn't broken; he was only partially scalped by glancing hits. His ploughed head hurt him damnably, but it was intact, and so, he thought, were his ribs, though the soft flesh of his left side was a bloody pulp, and his clothes were shot away there into stiff maroon ribbons. What had happened to the rest? The very thought of his own people seemed to take the steel edge from the silence and the sharp white coldness from the moon; and yet he knew in his heart that there was nothing living in that desolation except himself. Even the birds had been frightened away from their woods by the gunfire and smoke and noise of the battle; in a day, perhaps, they would come back, for birds are not easily driven away for long, but no wing stirred in the branches now, and no foot in the beechmast. He was the only one; in the wood or in the world.

He wandered back towards the place where the Midshires had made their stand, not because he wished to go, but because he had to go. There was a bit of history there waiting to be picked up, and somebody had to look for it, and he was the only one left. It had been a battle. For fifty yards or more the brambles were ploughed into the soil, and raw dark patches of loam lay bare where the deep turf had been. He found Sergeant Blackie's body, face-down in the briars, with half the clothes blown off him; and all that was left of Scotty Walsh lying bowed forward over his beloved captured gun, now a bit of twisted wreckage. There was a tank lying collapsed in the centre of the trampled arena where they had fought, burst asunder like an over-ripe orange, and spilling the remains of men from its seams. There were two more a little farther along among the trees, one still quietly glowing with the heat of its burnt-out fire. The rest had passed, but three at least would never reach the village; three might make the difference between holding it and losing it. But either way, the dead men on the ridge would never know.

He walked about helplessly from bush to bush across the silent battlefield, turning the bodies over and looking at their battered and blackened faces, but he couldn't find the one he was looking for. He found Corporal Williams, lying quietly along the grass under the bushes as if he were asleep, and thought it like him to die with such decorum. He found Alec Ross, and Steve Brookes, and George Hayling, and many more whom he knew; but he couldn't find hide or hair of Tommy Goolden. There wasn't even a body among the worst mauled which could conceivably be his. He might be a prisoner, but somehow it didn't look as if any prisoners had been taken. Or he might be alive and free, wandering somewhere through the eerie stillness of the wood, looking for the mortal remains of Jim Benison.

At the thought a sudden warmth sprang to life in Jim's stunned mind, and he came back out of his trance of pain and self-pity, and began to walk purposefully back down the hill-side, straining his senses for sight or sound of another forlorn wanderer in the woods. The deadly cold receded from his body; the pain quickened, but he closed his heart against it, and went on. If Tommy had looked for him on the ridge, and failed to find him, he would look for him next where Brian Ridley was, guessing that he had gone back to help him. So he went in a top-heavy fashion down the cart-track, pushing himself doggedly along from tree to tree, and came to the narrow place where the trees crowded in. Give the kid his due, he'd done a damned good job. The leading tank of the column had broad-sided and burst in the very doorway of the gap, forcing the others to make a hard detour, and so giving Jim time to reach Blackie with his warning. You could see the great weals in the ground where they had turned off the track, gouts ripped out of the bordering grass, and a massacre of bushes. Yes, he'd done a beautiful job. Four enemy tanks that one gesture had wiped out, if you looked at it the right way. The sort of job fellows gets V.Cs. for; only fellows like young Ridley don't—they get an obscure death and a place in the casualty lists, generally, and all the glory they enjoy is the unrecorded glory they wear to be buried in. Maybe after that any other would be a bit stale and tawdry, anyhow.

Brian was lying where the shattered tank had thrown him, just clear of the track. From the hips upward he was still whole, but for the wounds he'd had before, which did not greatly mar him; but from the hips down he was a bloody pulp, flattened into the grass, with white slivers of bone protruding. The second tank, turning in haste, had driven over him. It had been done wantonly, for there was room and to spare; the track it had left swerved from the straight to reach him, and having encompassed his murder, turned back again. Jim stood over the body, and his bowels contracted and knotted themselves with hate, and grief, and rage. Sudden great racking shudders began to sweep through his flesh, making his teeth chatter and his wounds break again in a dew of clotting blood. He knelt down, and lifted the boy's head upon his hand, and as his fingers touched the cheek, he knew that Brian was still alive. His flesh was cold, but not with the piercing coldness of death. All those hours of lying here, deserted, broken in pieces, with time interminable and pain limitless, and still God couldn't let him die! What have men done, anyway, that they should be treated worse than domestic animals? You'd be run in for keeping a dog damaged like that in peace-time. Even in war they go on caring for the four-legged soldiers, don't they? They shoot horses. "Well," he said to himself viciously, "what's to stop you? There's no one here to split on you. What are you waiting for? If you had the guts of a louse you'd put a bullet through the poor kid's head and finish him." But although Brian's revolver, fallen clear of the dark furrow, lay invitingly near his hand, he could only kneel there trembling and retching, his body crawling with cold sweat, without the courage to take hold of it. It was no good. He couldn't bring himself to do it. He knew it was the only service he could do the boy now, but still he shrank from it. It was murder. What the driver of the tank had done was only war, of course! And yet, for the love of God, what was he to do if he couldn't raise the pluck to shoot him? He couldn't go away and leave him alone. He might not die for hours. He might linger for days, even. Such things had been known. Suppose he regained consciousness, and couldn't reach the revolver? Put it in his hand, then. Suppose he couldn't lift it? What's the matter with you, anyhow, you snivelling humbug, putting the job on him? Do you have to shift the responsibility? *You shot the dog, didn't you?*

He reached out a shaking hand and took hold of the revolver. The heavy head that rested upon his knee was disturbed by the movement, and suddenly the stained eyelids lifted, and Brian's eyes, faintly distressed and almost visionless, looked up directly into his. He saw only the flooding pallor of the moonlight, and its emptiness troubled him, lighting as it did the inmost corners of his desolation, so that the composure of his face, from which all feeling had at last been smoothed away, was broken again by fear and loneliness rather than pain. He lay still, being incapable of movement, and stared up at the light, and presently the recognisable shape of Jim grew out of his blindness. A wonderful wave of ease and gratitude and weariness went over the young, bruised face. He relinquished his hold of time, which was so cruelly lame, and let the world slip out of his heart. It was all right. His own people were here. The soiled eyelids closed again. He said: "Jim!" faintly but quite clearly, in a child's sigh, and turned his face into Jim's sleeve, and very quietly died.

It wasn't like any of the others. The first one, the Belgian woman, hadn't even been an acquaintance, but just someone who brushed by him in dying, and meant nothing to him living and nothing dead; and yet she had haunted him unabashed until the others came to dispossess her. Even they, even Bill Gittens and the rest of them, with whom he had lived in such close companionship, even they had left him as they came, without undue stress, because they were the kind of deaths he knew to be inevitable in war, and against them he could arm himself with the indifference of reason. But this . . .

He couldn't grasp it; he didn't realise at first that it had happened. He knelt there for a long time holding Brian; and then suddenly, without feeling for heart or pulse or breath, he knew that he was dead. He knew it because some hitherto inviolate part of himself seemed to break and bleed. He laid the boy gently down, and took his quiet hands, grubby, immature, adolescent hands, and crossed them on his breast, like the recumbent Crusader monuments in Morwen Hoe church. He looked about sixteen, all the sharp and painful lines of his face relaxed in that last deep sigh of relief and ease as he embraced his rest. And yet it was impossible to look at him, however fastidiously, without being aware through every sense and nerve of his dreadfulness; of how his mangled flesh cried out, not only for vengeance, against the enemy, but for understanding, against his friends. "This is the real thing," it said. "You thought you knew! And this is only a very little bit of it."

That was it. You thought you knew! War is beastly, brutal, and bloody, you said to yourself, facing facts squarely. You thought of it in the right terms, but you didn't know how much they could mean; you pictured it as brutal and bloody along reasonable, conventional lines, and within human limits, when it was the smashing of all conventions and the bursting of all limits. You felt that it would at least adhere to some sort of cruel laws; and the more fool you, for it was the negation of law.

And biggest fool of all if you tried to arm yourself against it by teaching yourself to be ready and willing to die. Death was a holiday you couldn't be sure about, a leave that might continually be stopped at the last moment. To know the worst you had to quit thinking you could count on dying. This was more like hell, you had to learn to live with it.

Jim stood there and looked at Brian's body, and the desire to avoid looking below the waist went out of him, and he stepped back a little to see it whole, the corpse and the catafalque and the pall of moonlight. A thing he wouldn't forget. The summing-up of all he'd seen and learned, of the strangely glorious, unbelievably bestial potentialities of man. If you turned your head away from one, you turned it away from both. But oh! my Christ, how much of this can you bear?

He looked for a long time, and then, because he could do no more there, and the sinking moon reminded him of time, he took the revolver and set off through the woods. He had no idea what time it was, but he judged that the night must be half over, and to him, cut off as he was in lost territory, the day was of no value. He had to get back to his unit, or to such part of it as still existed. The German attack had washed them back towards Lille, and in the same direction he must go if he wished to overtake them. His mind was clear enough; crystal clear, but his senses were dulled with wounds and weariness, and he was incapable of fulfilling the designs of his brain. He made the mistake early of leaving the path, hating the nakedness of it now that his only hope was to hide himself; and when the moon sank out of sight he lost his sense of direction, and went on and on blindly, bearing right as strongly right-handed people do, working round in a wide and wasteful arc to the eastern edge of the beechwoods, and there losing himself.

The trouble was that the inward vision, incredibly vivacious and insistent, would not be dulled with the outward one. He began to see bodies, crushed and angry and piteous, where none were; even on the straight, steel-grey road, when he came to the limits of the wood, he saw corpses of men and women and children lying, gunned and bombed and ridden down, soldiers and civilians alike. He was glad that the moon was gone. Even without it he could see too much, things nobody should see and live, sights that should have destroyed the seer where he stood. That was the hell of it, that it did not strike you blind or dead, but was continuous and inescapable, something you had to accept and live with. Because these were not the reflections of Brian Ridley lying crushed and dead within his memory, as at first he had thought. They were the victims of the same crime, multiplied to infinity along that dreadful road, the débris of another of those processions of the homeless which had made Flanders a place of horror. But these had made the fatal mistake of choosing one of the main roads by which the enemy's armour was advancing. Jim had seen the way the pilgrims moved, so confusedly, so laboriously, dragging their few possessions with them in handcarts, and perambulators, at their swiftest no better than tediously slow. The German tanks, overhauling them at speed, could not wait. Many a time had the Midshires waited and cursed, but waited. But the invaders could not wait. The marks of their tracks were stamped along the highway in a dark, encrusted mud between the ruin of the dead and their possessions. That was how the New Order had come into France.

He left the shadow of the last trees, and slithered down into the ditch. He wasn't sure which way he should go, and since waiting would not tell him, he turned right, and went stumbling along the edge of the road as fast as he could, stepping clear of the dead. He saw babies among them, fallen with their mothers, and young children, stone-dead, still clutching at the skirts of older girls. He saw *poilus* of the French 7th and 9th Armies, who had been caught in that human stream on their retreat, and been scythed down with the rest. He saw an occasional Belgian soldier with them, though how they had wandered to that Artois road he could not guess. All these lay down together in a dreadful death, draggled and uncomely, robbed even of repose, along the road which was to have been to them the last way of escape. He stepped carefully among the bodies, and the deepening darkness hid much, but there was much it could not hide.

A small garden bordered the road where the woods ended. It had a high dark hedge, and there was the glimpse of a roof over it. He hesitated for a moment whether to go in and ask for help; surely any of the people here would hide him and put him on his way; and he was beginning to have light-headed spells which frightened him. But an hour's rest and a meal was not worth the risk. He took his hand from the gate and went on. A moment later a voice cried from within the garden, a sharp exclamation of challenge that froze him in his tracks. He had come very near to giving himself up; there were Germans in the cottage. The shock drove it deep into his consciousness that he was in lost territory, surrounded by enemies; that they were on the roads, in the fields, in the villages, under the stones for all he knew. He heard the sound of boots upon the road ahead, more than one man coming briskly. In all that wide wound which scored the face of France that night only members of one race walked thus boldly.

Jim dropped quickly into the ditch, and lay down among the dead. A crushed *képi*, fallen from a lolling hard head, lay against his face. He edged close against the broad shoulders of a French sergeant, and lay over his rifle for fear it should be seen and considered worth acquiring. Even in flight he knew it was the first rule, the only rule, almost, that he should stick to his rifle closer than a brother. If they started raking among the corpses he was done; but why should they, unless he betrayed himself by a movement? They came ahead steadily, the sharp staccato of their tread monstrously swollen in the silence, broken only by the dulled intervals when they trampled clothing or flesh or both. As they drew near he felt the skin drawing tight along the back of his neck, and the beat of his heart was thunderous in his throat. He believed that they must hear it as he heard their footsteps, as a great, nerve-shaking noise filling the night. A red mist flowed over his eyes. He didn't know what it was that ailed him. He wasn't used to hate, and he didn't recognise it when it took him by the throat, and filled him with the desire to leap from cover and kill and kill until he was himself killed. He didn't do it. There was enough sense left in him for that. He didn't want to die, or to be captured, and if he revealed himself one or the other would most surely happen. He lay in cold sweat, grinding his face into the dead sergeant's dusty coat, and trying to suppress the storm of his breath as the hard, indifferent steps went by.

They were close above him now. He heard the exchange of clipped remarks, and laughter, quiet but careless, as if the night belonged to them and they could not be awed by it. Once there was a stumble and what Jim took to be an oath, and the dull soft sound of a boot driving into flesh. A body rolled over the edge of the road and slid down upon Jim's legs, by the pitifully slight weight of it, a child's body. Then they had passed, and their steps were receding into the silence, and their voices. The beauty and horror of the night came down again unmarred, unmitigated.

For a long time he was afraid to move. He lay there relaxed into his great weariness, sobbing into the blood and dirt of the sergeant's coat; and then suddenly he felt time skidding through his fingers, and was more afraid to stay than he was to go. He raised himself very cautiously, straining eyes and ears along the road, but once again it was unpopulated but for the dead. He patted the sergeant's solid shoulder, and said insanely: "Thanks, chum!" and was taken with a weak desire to laugh when the body rolled over stiffly at his touch and lay upon its back, staring up at him with wide-open, outraged eyes. He tried to close them, a service he had never yet done for anyone; but the lids were stiff and would not stay shut. Jim was childishly sorry. The sergeant had stood by him nobly, helping him to remain alive and at large; and there was precious little he could do in return.

He leaned close above the dead man, and threaded a shaking hand into his breast. He'd been young, this thick-set Frenchman, not above thirty-five, at any rate, and decent-looking, what you could see of his face under its mask of dirt and growth of beard. Somebody somewhere would be glad to have word of him; even this word rather than none. There was a bundle of papers in his breast pocket, matted together with dried blood at one corner, and a piece of stiff card which Jim took to be a photograph. He transferred the lot to his own pocket, and went on along the ditch, not venturing on to the road again.

He walked until the darkness began to dissolve eastward in a dewy greyness. He made what speed he could, keeping close to the road, but circling into fields and coppices whenever houses or humans loomed through the fading night. He did not know how long he had laboured along nor how far he had come, but his strength was giving out, and the treacherous day would betray him soon. He turned aside into the fields, and crept into the deepest thicket of the first belt of woodland he found, and lay down there to wait for another night. Hunger and the cold of exhaustion lay down in the leaf-mould with him, and a loneliness like the end of the world. The loneliness was the worst of all. Because the only island in it was the bundle of letters in his pocket, evidence at least of human intercourse and surely of human affection, he took them out and began to run them through his fingers, separating the blotched pages carefully; and in a moment he came face to face with the photograph.

It was of a woman, a head and shoulder study no bigger than a postcard, but quite clear except for the lower left corner where the sergeant's blood stained it. The dawn-light showed a broad face, dark-eyed, clear-featured, with strong straight brows and a mouth sternly set. She had heavy coiled braids of hair wound round her head. She looked out squarely at him, and he knew her. He knew, too, against whose shoulders he had taken shelter in the darkness when the enemy passed by. The farm at Boissy-en-Fougères was masterless. Monsieur Georges— *Monsieur le Sergent*—would never come home from Sedan.

PART FOUR

FRANCE: RETREATING

What is freedom? Ye can tell
That which slavery is too well,
For its very name is grown
To an echo of your own.
          SHELLEY: *The Masque of Anarchy*.

I

THAT day Jim neither ate nor drank anything more than
the drop of stale water he still had in his water-bottle; but
at night the pain within him got the better of his pains without,
and he was driven to hunt for food. Again moonlight as white
as day made advance perilous, but he could not wait for moon-
set. He found a small cottage, deserted by its owners and
stripped bare by the invaders except for the heel of a mouldy
loaf and the bottom of a sack of potatoes. But at least there
was water to help down the sour dry bread; and he not only
refilled his canteen, but took away a small covered milk-can
as well, for thirst had already impressed itself upon him, in
that very short acquaintance, as the most to be dreaded of all
evils. He might have done better still if he had not been interrupted, but the Germans came, as they always did now wherever
he turned, wherever he set his foot; and he went to earth in the
ruined garden until they had passed and he could make good his
retreat. In one way they did him a service, for a clucking hen
took flight from the bushes close beside him, and he found
where she had laid astray. The egg was still warm as he sucked
it. That helped considerably. He was still hungry, but he
began to feel better, more in control of his faculties, more capable of planning his journey in pursuit of his friends.

Lying there in the coarse grass under the hedge, he tried to
think it out. It was very clear that there were neither British
nor French troops left in this part of the country, for he saw
no fighting and comparatively few planes; whereas the Germans
were everywhere. Small orderly streams of them had detached
themselves from the steel river flowing westward across France,
and penetrated southward into villages and towns, feeling at
the French defences and finding them none too secure. Jim was
sure by now that he had lost his sense of direction and gone

149

astray on the previous night. A good head for country he might have, but it had not been in very good shape, and had done him on this occasion no credit. He could take a directional bearing by the rising and setting of the moon, if need be; but he wanted more than that. He wanted to know something of the lie of the land, of the roads, and in particular of where the Germans were thickest. That was a lot to ask, but not too much, given one promising contact with a friendly Frenchman.

So all that night he wandered, hiding and running and hiding again, looking for an inhabited place where the Germans were not; but there was no such place. They were everywhere. Towards morning, hurrying for the only cover he could find, a hillock of furze bushes across a brook, he even stumbled upon one soldier lolling upon the grass with his bare feet in the water. They looked at each other for a second in ludicrous astonishment, and then the German turned and reached for his rifle, which lay behind him upon the bank. He was quick, but from sheer desperation Jim was quicker. He plunged forward through the water, which was little more than knee-deep and very clear, and throwing himself upon the other man in a low tackle, pulled him down into the brook with him. For a minute it was touch and go who drowned, and then Jim, feeling down through the water, clawed up a jagged stone and smashed in his opponent's temple with it. The German slid down into the bed of the brook, and did not get up again; only a few bubbles came in a sultry fashion to the surface of the soiled water and broke there. Jim, on hands and knees from the drag of the other man's weight as he fell, watched them burst and disappear. Threads of blood crept out from his left side, where the deepest furrow had re-opened at the first strain, and ran through the water, widening as they went. He wondered why the fool hadn't shouted for help. He might have been alive still if he had; nobody wanted to kill him, and if he'd given the alarm to a dozen or so more, there'd have been no point in silencing him. There'd have been nothing to do then but run like hell as long as there was any hope of out-distancing pursuit, and stop and shoot it out when there was none. But he'd kept his mouth shut, and he was dead, and in as good a place as any; for who would think of looking for him in the brook?

Jim took the dead man's boots and rifle, and threw them into the thickest of the furze-bushes on the stretch of waste ground beyond. Then he went on to the far side of the hillock, and found a high growth of flowering broom, with paths run amongst its stems by marauding animals, compact tunnels in the green. Along one of these tunnels he crawled, and lay for a moment with his head down in his arms, suddenly deadly sick. It was the drain of blood from his side again. Unless he could somehow get it bandaged properly, the wound was going to burst open like this every time he exerted himself, and bleed him to death in the long run. "To-night," he thought, while the morning was still only a glimmer in the greyness, "I've got to get hold of somebody who can start me off on the right road. If I go on like this, I'm sunk, I'll finish by getting captured." And that was the last terror, hand in hand and equal with the terror of death.

He lay still until the sickness subsided, and drank a little of his precious stock of water, and longed for the night again. He knew now how the hunted animals feel when they run from the daylight to lie quaking in cover until the darkness delivers them for a while from fear. And he wondered if there were not, perhaps, others running wild in the dark like himself, struggling to remain uncaptured and get back to their friends. It was strangely clear now that their friends would not, for all that impetuous rush across the Cojeul, be able to come back to them. Northern France was a lost land, and they, the stragglers, the survivors from many such clashes as that on the ridge among the beechwoods, were lost with it.

The wave of weakness passed. He began to edge himself deeper into the fortress of broom, drawing himself forward carefully upon his right arm, and holding his left hand tightly over the hot stickiness of his side. Then he stopped, with a sharply indrawn breath, as his fingers, groping ahead, touched cloth, and warm flesh under it that started at the touch.

Under the arching bushes it was still dark, though here and there the dawn filtered through. He could see nothing more than a movement in the darkness as the unknown man started away from him; but clearly he heard the snap of a rifle-bolt going home, and dropped flat into the broom-roots and lay motionless. He was afraid, but of one thing only, that the unseen man would fire first and ask questions afterwards; because there could in reason be nothing more to fear from him. No German would be hiding in the undergrowth; no Frenchman, either, unless he still carried arms and hoped to use them again for France.

"Hold your fire!" said Jim, rapidly. "I'm English!"

There was an instant of silence, and then a remembered voice, hoarse and tremulous but still recognisable, croaked: "Jim! Good Lord Almighty—Jim!" And laughter, breathless and painful, choked whatever else he would have said, for all Jim heard afterwards was a crackling like thorns burning, and short, gasping outbursts of coughing; but he knew already who his fellow-fugitive was. He crawled forward into a small circlet of thick grass, roofed with interlacing bushes, where the light came in more clearly; and he got his arms round the tattered, red-eyed, shrunken ghost who was Tommy Goolden, and patted him, and laughed with him, until he was exhausted with hysterical joy, and had neither breath nor strength to do more than lie in the grass flaccid and soothed and sleepy, like a dog worn-out with his own exuberance at a home-coming.

"Thank the Lord you didn't fire right off! Even you couldn't have missed at a couple of yards."

"Keep your voice down," said Tommy urgently. "Fire? I should have fired when you touched me if I'd had any cartridges left. I haven't got one slug to my name. I wanted to get out and try and get some last night, but it wasn't so good. I don't know—seemed I couldn't even walk far without breaking myself in two. I had to come back. Jim——!"

"Yes?"

"You wouldn't have any water, would you?"

Jim raised himself on one elbow, and unslung his water-bottle. Now that he had time to realise it, there were things about Tommy that worried him. In the unspeakable pleasure of seeing and touching a friend again, he had accepted without question the breathless voice, the short, hard cough, the hot hands and forehead, the sunken eyes like dark-red coals burning their way deep and deeper into his head; but now all these significant details seemed to spring to sight at once. While Tommy drank, Jim kept his hand upon the bottle, because it shook so violently that he was afraid it would be dropped altogether if he released it.

"Have you been without water since the night before last?" he asked, drawing the bottle gently away before Tommy would voluntarily have given it up.

"I had a drink at the brook just below here, but I couldn't get back to it again for Jerries. I lost my canteen somewhere in the fields back there. The webbing must have been nearly shot through, and I never noticed it. I went back looking for it, but it was dark, and I hadn't got time to do the job properly. Then I went in the pond to get out of the way of the Jerries, and lost my ammo., too. Fell down before I meant, and soaked the bloody lot. Hell of a night I had!" he said, querulously.

"Have you had any food since then?"

"I got some part-grown turnips out of a garden on my way here, but they weren't properly fit to eat. I hung about the village hoping to get into one of the shops, but there were Jerries everywhere. You daren't go near a house, or a road." He lay back in the grass with a sigh that rustled in his chest like dry leaves in a wind. "What happened to you, anyway? I looked everywhere for you."

"So did I for you. You must have been away ahead of me. I started back to where little Ridley was, but I got knocked out on the way. I was dead out for hours, and off the track. When I came round it was all over. I meant to strike back towards the village, and see if I could catch up with the rest of the company, but I went wrong somewhere."

"I thought it was you who had the head for country," said Tommy with a wry grin.

"Did you do any better?"

"I got where I aimed to get. It wouldn't have done you any good if you had found the village, there was nobody there but Jerries. It was hell trying to get through. I wasted hours and had to give up in the end. Then I came on here. But I don't know what went wrong—maybe it was that blasted pond— I don't seem to be a hell of a lot of good now I am here——"

"What in the world made you take cover in the pond, anyhow, of all the damn-fool places?"

"There was nowhere else. The place was as flat as the palm of your hand, and not a tree nor a house nor a hedge within reach. It was that or run slam-bang into 'em. I never meant to go right in. There was a good thick growth of reeds. I turned dizzy, and fell flat on my face in the water, and it's lucky for me I managed to drag myself in among the reeds without drowning. All that water, and nothing to drink. Hell, it stank!"

Jim felt his forehead, and it was hot and hard and dry to the touch. "Your clothes dried on you, I suppose."

"What about it? I've done as much many a time and got away with it." But he was shaken even as he spoke with a spasm of uncontrollable shivering, and his teeth chattered in his head. He knew very well what ailed him, however feverishly annoyed he became at the suggestion from someone else; and to judge by the expression of his eyes he was already somewhat

153

frightened by the state to which his normally adaptable body had been reduced. So was Jim, though it wouldn't do to show it. How was he to make his way back to the retreating British forces with a sick man on his hands? And obviously he could neither leave him behind, nor stay with him and let him die slowly of pneumonia here in the wilderness. An ally was more than ever necessary, an ally with a roof and a bed to offer. Afterwards it would be time to worry about getting away.

"And I don't even know where we are!" he said aloud.

"Didn't I tell you? We're just over the rise from Boissy-en-Fougères. I knew where I was going, if you didn't. I came to see if Eliane was all right—yes, and to get Papa to help me, too, if I could. But anyhow, if I had to go like that I wasn't going without seeing her again. But it's like everywhere else. They're going through on the main road all the time. They're in every house that isn't damaged too badly. There isn't a minute of the day or night when they aren't in the *bistro*. I hung around until it was nearly light, but I never got a chance to get in the place or to speak to a soul." He looked up into Jim's face with a bitter smile. "You think I'm wandering, don't you? Go and look for yourself to-night, if you don't believe me. If you go across the fields from here and through the wood, you'll come to the orchards of Madame Lozelle's farm. Go and see!"

"I will," said Jim. For even if his heart contracted at the thought of it, he had business at the farm of Madame Lozelle.

Tommy turned his hot face into the cool of the grass. "They dropped bombs at this end of the village. One in the farm-yard. Most of the house is gone—there's just one end standing, and the stables and lofts built on to it——"

Jim thought: "How if she was killed when that happened?" and didn't know whether to hope for it or dread it. Remembering the body of Georges Lozelle lying in the ditch beside that northern road, he thought it might be easier on her if she had died, too; but he needed her, he needed her just now most desperately, for Tommy's sake as well as his own. Who could take her place if she was gone?

"They didn't all walk out of Boissy, then?" he said.

"All those who had carts did—or bicycles, or cars, or ponies, or anything that would go. You see a few of the local people about, but mostly it's nothing but Boches—everywhere you look, Boches."

"And Madame Lozelle? Did she run, too?"

"I don't know. I saw Simone in the street, going up towards the farm. I don't know about Madame Lozelle." He said, suddenly, shuddering: "I'm hellish cold, Jim."

But what was there to be done about it? They could not possibly move out of cover now until the dusk came again, and Tommy would have none of Jim's battle-dress blouse, though he died for want of it, while he had consciousness to resist the offer. Only when he fell into an uneasy doze did Jim manage to get it over him without having it indignantly thrust away again. Well for them if they could both sleep, and so wear out a little of the endless time between them and the friendly night. Jim lay down close to Tommy, flank to flank with him, to give him warmth, though it was like lying down before a fire. He did not sleep; he kept the revolver in his hand and his rifle close beside him, and lay watching the sun rise and climb the interminable whiteness of the sky, and listening to Tommy's shallow, dry breathing. He had stopped looking back at all, and he looked forward no farther than the first hour of darkness, when he would go down into the shadowy desolation of Boissy-en-Fougères. He had left it only fourteen days ago, but in the interval its gentleness had been violated and its ebullient heart broken. He had left it as a saviour; he came back to it as a fugitive. He was one of the men who had failed it; how if it failed him now?

2

In the orchard the young apples were forming, green and small and hard as walnuts. The grass under his feet was dappled with moonlight and tremulous with the shudderings of leaves. It was like an English garden in peace-time, but for the noise of the guns and of distant bombs, a music which never ceased now by day or night. Sometimes he could close his ears to it altogether, and let it slip away into the background of his mind; but to-night it was in his consciousness, fixed fast, refusing to be ignored or forgotten.

He had walked into the orchard through the gap where the hedge had been blown out of the ground. He didn't know what he was going to do. If she was gone, he might at least find Simone still at the farm; or failing that, he knew where Jean's cottage was. Tommy had wished to make contact with Papa

Brégis, but that was the last refuge Jim would consider. In the first place, it was too dangerous; there would be too many German soldiers in and out of the *bistro;* and in the second place, it was no part of his plans that Tommy should, even to save his life, lose it ever more deeply in the profound beauty of Eliane Brégis' dark, responsive eyes and moon-pale hair. It wouldn't be fair on Eliane herself, to look no farther afield. She was a nice kid. She could get hurt badly, for no better reason than that Tommy was good-looking, and impressionable, and helpless. Women went for that. Sick he would be twice as attractive to her as he had been in health. Likely she'd forgotten him by now; and heaven knew every man, woman and child in Boissy had enough of pain and chagrin and despair to bear just now, without adding to the burden. It was only because Tommy's mind was fevered with wounds and sickness that he had ever considered appealing to her. And Jim did not consider it.

Softly, stepping from shadow to shadow down the harlequin slope, he went through the orchard, and came to where the bulk of the farm-house shone clear in the moon. It had been a gracious four-square house, not beautiful, except with the beauty of undecorated honesty; but now all the nearer part of it was a heap of rubble, and the kitchen end, which alone remained erect, soared jaggedly against the sky, tall and slender and strangely graceful, blanched white as snow in the full rays of the moon. The torn face which looked upon the ruins projected into the ice-cold light a first-floor fireplace of marble, with rounded Grecian pillars on either side; and in between them the shadows were ebony-black. It was like the façade of a temple opening upon air.

Then he saw Miriam. She was walking round the rim of the bomb-crater, down there in the farm-yard, and looking up at the white jade spirit of her house, where that appalling beauty clung and clothed it from head to foot like a wedding veil or a shroud. She walked slowly, which was not her habit, but there was no mistaking the short, upright figure or the carriage of the dark head. She was in black, with a scarf over her hair; and when she left the yard and came wearily between the trees, he saw her face clearly in the moonlight, motionless, white as bleached bone, the dark eyes cavernous in it, the mouth frozen and austere. He knew then that he had been mad to think for a moment that she would go with the refugees. She could be deprived of one world, perhaps, under pressure, but never of a second. She might, in the first shock of the realisation of evil, consent to run from fate once, but if hell itself fronted her, she would not run a second time.

She had not changed, though her life had fallen to pieces around her. She had only withdrawn into herself, and drawn the curtains, and barred the doors. He supposed the first German motor-cyclists, sweeping through the town on their way westward, had found her picking her way thus deliberately through the ruins of her home, with this same icy composure, as if she scarcely noticed the onslaughts of fate; only her eyes betraying what was within the drawn curtains and closed doors, and that only to those who knew already something of her mind. As he did, too well for his own peace.

He watched her, and his heart failed in him. If it hadn't been for Tommy he didn't believe he could have faced her at all. If it had been for himself only he was seeking shelter, he would have dropped back into the shadows and let her go by him without a word, rather than go through the ordeal of breaking the last, worst news to her. But she ought to know, and no one else could tell her; and only with her help could he get himself or Tommy Goolden safely away to fight again. He waited until she drew level with his hiding-place, and then he said her name, in a queer, brittle voice he scarcely recognised as his own:

"Miriam!"

It startled even himself, it rang so clear in the silence. As for her, she stopped upon the instant, and her hand went up to her heart as if the sharp intake of her breath had stabbed deep. She did not turn her head; he thought she was afraid to. He struggled to speak again, to say that he was only Jim Benison; but his throat contracted upon the utterance, and he could not get out a word. Her profile was towards him. He saw clearly how the cold Spartan lines quivered and broke before the uprush of piercing joy, so that light seemed to stream from her and irradiate the aisles of the orchard and soften the whiteness of the moon. A thing you could never forget—a thing you could never be satisfied until you'd seen again, in another face—— To be loved like that! What else was there worth looking forward to? To have a woman look like that for you, when you came home! But Georges Lozelle hadn't come home; he would never come home.

She put out her hand a little from her side, as if she felt for him. *"Est ce-toi, mon âme?"* she said in a whisper. Her eyes were closed, and along the lashes there were tears. *"Bon Jésu, je vous remercie!"*

Then she turned, and looked at him full, and the light of her face went out like a snuffed candle.

He turned his face away; he couldn't bear to look at her. Even the small, famished, frustrated moan she uttered as hope went out of her was like a knife turned in his flesh. He said in a very low voice: "Yes, it's only me!" with desperate humility, as if he was to blame for not being the man she had thought to see. "I'm sorry!" he said.

Then with a sharp sigh and a rush of cool air she was breast to breast with him, her hands under his arms, holding him, feeling at the ploughed and crusted flesh of his side where the blackened rags of his shirt hung stiffly, touching with great gentleness the raked, raw wounds in his hair. "Jim! *Vous êtes blessé!* You are hurt badly. Tell me, they are following you, no? You cannot go on like this, *mon pauvre*, even if they are on your heels. The body can go uncared for a certain time, but you must not drive it too far. Have we time? Are they close?"

He stammered: "No, there's no one after me—no one knows I'm here."

"*Tant mieux!*" she said with a grateful sigh. "There is not such urgency, then; we can afford to be less hasty and more careful." And by the touch of her hands and the contact of her body, he felt the tension go out of her. "I have thought of you much," she said. "Now I see you again, and you will not look at me."

Wondering, suddenly adrift in warm seas of comfort and compassion and hope, he did look at her then. She was smiling very faintly, and her face was alive again in fullest measure, the deep eyes heavy with concern, the strong mouth moving upon whispered phrases of reassurance. "There are no Germans in my house. It suffered too badly for that, they do not like to live with their crimes, those. But there are still dry rooms there, and there is a bed for you, and food. Only we must keep out of sight of the road. Always they pass there, and the light is strong."

"You don't know what you're doing!" he said.

"I know what I do very well. I offer hospitality to my friend. Why should I not?"

"That isn't what they'd call it." What was he saying? He'd come there to ask her for shelter, hadn't he? And yet now that she offered it with both hands before he could so much as ask, he was warning her off, trying to persuade her to think of her own safety, and be wise in time. Miriam, who knew more about the enemy than he would ever know!

"I know what you would say," she said, with a sombre smile. "Believe me, I am not a fool."

"But if they ever find out——"

"I know. Do not bother to speak of it. It is my life, that is all. You have not been very careful with yours, I think." And when in despair he made to argue further, she put her hand over his lips. "Hush, it is waste of breath and time. Are you to teach me how to hoard my safety now, when there is so little left? Let us go in, quickly, before the moonlight reaches the garden. I am not easy until I have you safely within and the shutters closed."

"Wait a bit! It isn't even just me. There's another man—Tommy Goolden—he's ill. I left him among the broom-bushes back there."

"He cannot walk?" she asked, accepting two as readily as she had accepted one.

"He might manage. It isn't far. If not, I can carry him."

"There is no other way. You cannot go near the roads. What is wrong with him? Is he worse hurt than you?"

"It isn't wounds. I think he's in for pneumonia. He hid among the reeds in a pond when a convoy of Boches went by. He has a bad temperature. I was frightened to leave him, but what else was there to do? At least he's well hidden there. I couldn't risk bringing him away until I knew if you——"

"If I would take him in?" she said quickly.

"If you were still here. There was never any other question."

"But yes—forgive me. One is no longer sure that the earth remaineth and seed-time and harvest and friends will not fail." She put a hand upon his arm. "Wait here! I shall come with you. A moment only! I must warn Simone. Do not turn back without me."

She ran from him, her feet swift and quiet in the grass, the rays of the moon touching her briefly as she passed, until the black shadow of the house took her and she was lost to sight. While he waited for her, obediently still upon the spot where she had left him, he wondered how in the name of pity he was going to tell her about her husband. It had been bad enough before, but it was a thousand times worse now. At the thought of that wonderful and dreadful moment when she had believed that Georges himself called to her, Jim's heart turned over in him. Bad enough to have seen that joy snatched away from her, without holding out to her in its place this unspeakable sorrow. It should have been done at once; that was the only fair way, if only that instant of piteous joy had not stopped his mouth. But surely there would be an opportunity once they were within doors, some mention of the tragedy of Sedan to give him an opening, anything to get it out. He was no good at this sort of thing. He wanted it over. It wasn't that she could be less than magnificent, whatever was done to her; but it would be easier on her if somebody more adroit broke the news. No hope of that now. It was his responsibility; he would have to go through with it. He sat down wretchedly in the grass, and dropped for a few minutes into a tormented sleep, from which he was roused at length by her hand upon his shoulder.

"*Pauvre garçon!* It is a shame to wake you. An hour more, and you shall sleep as long as you can, and no one shall wake you. It is a promise. But now I shall need you. There is no man here, you see."

"I'm ready," he said, getting stiffly to his feet.

"I have brought you a coat of my husband's. It will not fit you well, but at least the silhouette will be of a farmer, not of an English soldier. I have also one for your friend. And you have rifles? They are with him, perhaps?"

"Yes, but I doubt if we'll ever manage to get away with them. Men with rifles are too conspicuous to get far—especially British Army rifles."

"That is in the future," she said practically. "We shall not neglect the little things. Two British Army rifles in a French thicket might start a house-to-house search. Whether they go with you in the end or no, very certainly they come with us now. I shall carry them." She stood back a pace to look at him, in her husband's coat, the buttons strained across his chest, his wrists protruding five or six inches from the sleeves. "But it is a youngest son in outgrown clothes which cannot any longer be handed down! No matter, we shall do better when the time comes. *Marchons!*"

Across the fields, once they left the shelter of the orchard and the beeches, the moonlight was naked and flat, throwing long black shadows even from the mole-hills. There were no hedges high enough to cover them, but for much of the way there was the dry ditch of which Jim had made full use earlier in the night.

Into this Miriam dropped without waiting to be instructed, and set a pace he could keep only with difficulty. On this second journey of the night the way did not seem so long; that was because she was with him. A flight of planes went over them, flying westward very fast, like hard white birds stretching out towards a summer feeding-ground. She said through her teeth: "Boches!" and watched them until they were out of sight, lost in the radiance of the moon; but she did not speak again, either to complain or condemn. When she was gravely moved, she did not speak often or at length; as he knew her, that was her nature.

They reached the hillock of broom and furze without incident. Miriam crept through the tunnel into their fortress, and bent over Tommy, who lay staring at them wide-eyed and made no sign. He was shaken from head to foot by long, spasmodic tremors, and his teeth were chattering, and yet a heavy dew of sweat stood in beads and runnels on his forehead and upper lip.

"He's worse," said Jim in a whisper. "He doesn't know us. When I left him he was muttering to himself. I was scared he might get noisy, and someone might find him while I was gone."

"Few people come near here, except the women and boys who drive cattle out to pasture in these fields. But it is going to be difficult, this. So little cover, and so long to wait for the moon to set." She sat back on her heels and looked at Jim. "What do you say? I think we should not wait. An hour might mean life or death to him."

"I can get him along the ditch," said Jim, "if you can carry the rifles."

"*Bien*, we shall do that. Let us get him into this coat, quickly. If we hurry, the end of the garden and the door into the kitchen may still be in shadow when we get back."

That was no easy journey. Tommy was not heavy in the normal way but now he was dead weight, and Jim was in no case to carry him even upright, much less upon his back and shoulder as he crawled on all fours along the ditch. Nevertheless, because it had to be done it was done. Towards the end of the ordeal, just before they reached the beechwood, the wound in Jim's left side burst again, with a sickening onset of pain, and blood ran down his hip in hot, sluggish threads. Miriam was ahead, and she looked back and found him lying flat on his face under his burden, with his hands clenched into the grass. She ran back and crouched beside him, and half-rolled, half-lifted Tommy's burning body aside, so that for a few moments he breathed in a wonderful ease, and almost fell asleep again under her hands.

"Only a little farther," she said, "and then you shall rest—but really rest. But not now. We must get on. I beg you, Jim, help me."

Happily her husband's coat hid the momentary copious flow of blood. She knew he was desperately, inhumanly tired, and feverish with untended wounds, but she did not know that blood was trickling down into his boots as he raised himself from the grass again and drew Tommy's arm across his shoulder.

"*Mon pauvre*, it is too much for you so. We will take him between us, upright, like this. It is only a little way now."

"Go on ahead," said Jim. "I can finish what I've started."

Finish it he did, though he all but finished himself in the process. In the orchard, where he could at least get the inert body of his friend well over his shoulder, it was somewhat easier; and as Miriam had foretold, there was still a narrow strip of kitchen garden in shadow under the wall of the house. He came to the same door by which he had once carried out a basket of linen to dry, and once again it stood wide to receive him. Simone, silent and impassive, held it open for them, and closed it quietly behind them, and shot the bolts. Jim heard the heavy chain flung across and snapped into place, and a wonderful sense of security came upon him, and a desperate weariness.

"A moment!" said Miriam. "We are well sealed in now. I will put on the lights."

At her direction he carried Tommy up the stairs, and into a cool, cream-coloured bedroom where an old mackintosh was spread upon the bed and hot water steamed in a copper jug. Miriam's arm steadied Tommy's head down upon the pillow, where he lay between stupor and sleep, his eyes closed.

"That is enough. Now forget your friend for a while. You can—Simone has four sons, and is an accomplished nurse. There is a bath drawn for you, and you will wish to shave——"

It sounded like heaven; but there was still something worrying him. He looked back at the white bed and the creamy hangings, seen now through a blinding mist. "Wait a minute! How much of the house is left? A bed in the loft would have done for us. This is your room, isn't it?"

"Does it matter? I shall go in with Simone. It is much better that I do. He must have the best of care, your friend. To-morrow, if I can, I shall get hold of a doctor for him. I know we must let in as few people as possible, but you will trust me? Doctor Vauban is an old soldier himself, he will do anything. but *anything*, to keep you safe and free. And your Tommy is very ill—I think you know that."

"I do trust you," he said fervently. "You know I do. Anything you say is O.K. with me."

"Then I say, leave everything to us until you have slept. It is for you I am concerned now. Bathe, and shave if you like, and then there will be food waiting for you. And you must let me look at your wounds." She had her arm about him as she led him from the room, for now that the immediate stress was over, he was swaying on his feet, and she was a little afraid of a complete collapse. She drew him to the door of the bare little box-room where Simone had filled a zinc bath from the copper, carrying bucket after bucket of steaming water up the stairs, for the bathroom was gone with the bulk of the house. There were towels laid out for him, and pyjamas which had belonged to Georges Lozelle, shaving tackle from the same source, and an ancient dressing-gown. "You will still be the youngest son in outgrown clothes," she said, with a wry smile, "but when the time comes we shall find some to fit you better. If there is anything you want now, if we have forgotten anything, you need only call. I shall be helping Simone, just across the landing; and I will leave the door open. You are all right? You can manage alone?"

"Yes—thank you, I can manage."

"Call us when you are ready," she said, and went back to the other room, where Simone, with an arm under Tommy's shoulders, was just turning back the coverlet of the bed. Washed and cooled and eased, he had fallen into a strangely calm sleep, and looked, for all his sunken eyes and flushed face, very young. Between them they got him safely between the sheets. Miriam, on her knees, was still for a moment, looking down at him with a faint smile.

"It is like having sons, no? Suddenly one has two boys to look after, and almost one forgets that outside the house there is only ruin and death and a world of enemies. Simone, he has eaten nothing."

"He needs sleep more."

"Yes, you are right, Simone—it is bad, is it not?"

"I think so. It will be well to have the doctor, Madame, if you can trust even the doctor now."

"I trust no one," said Miriam bitterly, "no one but you and

Jean. But one must take a risk, that is all. I cannot let these two die in my house because I am afraid to confide in a doctor. Even if he betrays us, they are prisoners of war, and will at least be allowed to live. They are young. There will be a world worth living in again some day."

"And you?" said Simone, very deliberately.

Miriam dropped her head into her arms upon the bed, and lay there silent for a moment. At thirty-one, and with so much of darkness behind and around, one has not relinquished the bitter desire of life; for every wasted spring, for every year of frustrated youth, the passion to possess and enjoy happiness, freedom, and peace becomes more intense. Nevertheless, other things move resolutely in the mind after so long of suffering. She was not a woman fighting for her own security; she was a partisan in a world at war. The longing remained, but her reason turned from it·in indifference. She looked with a distant sadness upon the future she had planned to encompass, and knew that for herself she had never believed in it. After the agony and conflict of Prague, where she had left her youth, she had tried to wall herself into a narrow world bounded by her husband's fields and her husband's love, where the wrongs of the living and the dead could not torment her. You cannot escape your nature so. Her warfare had followed her into France. What use to run from it again? She turned and took it in her arms.

"Simone—I wish that you shall go away from me. No, do not be in haste to refuse. I mean what I say. It is not economical that two should involve themselves in such a risk where one would do. I know you are not afraid, I know you would conduct this thing better than I, but it is my responsibility, and I can very well carry it alone. Who knows when your own family may not need you? Or even some other such fugitives as these? No, it is wasteful that both of us should be spent upon the one adventure. It is my wish that you shall leave me."

Simone gave a short, sharp snort of laughter, and her broad brown face settled again into its lines of competent and tolerant age. "And who would feed you all if I went and left you, tell me that?"

Miriam smiled. "I should. Not so expertly, I grant you, but still I think we should contrive to live." She reached out a hand, and with her handkerchief wiped away the beads of sweat which were gathering again upon Tommy's forehead. *"Pauvre petit!* It is a mere child. I look at him and feel old, Simone.

Do you hear anything of the other one? It may be he will fall asleep in the bath. Simone, you have not answered me."

The old woman said: "I will not leave you. Not to-morrow nor at any other time. If you order me to go I shall not go. You will need me, and I think you will not grudge me a share in this thing. We shall give two soldiers back to the cause of freedom; that is something at least for an old woman who can do very little now for France."

"You understand it is a capital crime we are committing?"

"I understand it is very good to have the opportunity of committing a capital crime against the Boches."

"You are a stubborn old woman," said Miriam, and laid her cheek for a moment against the wrinkled old hand. *"Bien,* you will have your way. This one cannot do better than go on sleeping for the moment. Let us go and see what we can do for the other."

There was no more mention of sending Simone away. In her heart she had never believed it could be done. To Georges' nurse all of Georges' possessions were her own particular charges in his absence, and none so jealously guarded as his wife. Since all her own sons had married and scattered, she had known no home but Boissy farm, and no interests outside it. Better, perhaps, to risk even one's life than to uproot oneself after so long, and in such hopeless circumstances, and attempt to conserve what had no longer any savour.

Miriam went out to the landing and listened at the door of the makeshift bathroom. There was no sound at all from within. She tapped softly, and called: "Jim, are you all right?" but he did not answer, and remembering how weak he was from loss of blood and lack of sleep, she pushed open the door in quick alarm, and looked in.

He was lying on his face, close beside the steaming bath, with the towel crumpled under him. She marvelled that she had not heard him fall. He had just pulled on the pyjama trousers, but had not tied the girdle, and the wet red swamp of his left side was exposed, three irregular furrows like the marks of a harrow, two of them healing inward from both ends, but the deepest still wide and gaping-lipped, the lush, brilliant red of the petals of a poppy. Blood dripped from it slowly and spread in a pink stain across the wet towel.

Miriam called: "Simone—quickly!" backward over her shoulder, and ran to ease him on to his side and lift his head into her lap. When the old woman entered, she was pressing together with her fingers the lips of the wound.

"You see? I did not know—I did not know he was like this. He did not tell me. There will need five—maybe six—stitches before this will ever heal. Quickly, the lint and bandages."

"It is a doctor's business," said Simone, watching the quick hands work upon him.

"Yes. To-morrow, whatever happens, I must get help for them both. But for to-night we can only make him comfortable and let him sleep." She made the first turn of the bandage around his body, folding in the padding of cotton-wool. "Finish it, please, Simone, while I hold him. I cannot reach, he is so big."

He did not move while they swathed and dressed him, and bandaged the scalp wounds which were drying in his hair. They did not know when unconsciousness lapsed into natural sleep, but certainly when they carried him between them into the other room and settled him carefully upon his right side in the camp-bed placed for him, he was in a deep sleep, breathing long and luxuriously. Miriam drew the sheets over him and left him so, relaxed like a child, sunk very far into his insatiable weariness. She thought he would not move again for a long time.

She put out the light, and went back to where Simone was stolidly emptying the bath. Jim's discarded khaki lay in a heap on the floor, where he had let it fall. Miriam picked up shirt and trousers, and looked with a shudder at the fresh blood which had soaked them both on the last stage of that moonlit journey. No wonder he had collapsed in the end; the wonder was he had held up so long.

"When one must," she said aloud, "there is nothing one cannot do."

Simone straightened her back. "What was it you were saying, Madame?"

"Nothing. We must get these clothes out of sight. There is no privacy now. Who knows when we may not be visited?"

"But how can we hide the young men—if they come? That is not so easy."

"I don't know. It depends on circumstances. There is the door straight through into the loft from that room. You remember Georges used to store apples there? They would not find that too easily; it fits well, and it was papered over neatly in order not to spoil the room. I think one could go back and forth there without being detected. But it is all in the future. Whatever plans we make will be made to no purpose, so why should we plan? When the time comes, we shall know what to do."

She took Jim's battle-dress over her arm, and carried it away with her into the room where the two men lay sleeping. Simone had left the clothes she had stripped from Tommy draped upon the foot of the bed, and as Miriam gathered these too upon her arm, something fell from the breast pocket of the torn blouse which lay uppermost. In the darkness she could not see what it was, but she groped along the quilt for it, and found a small packet of papers, held together by an elastic band. Letters, perhaps, from the girl of whom Jim had told her, the girl Delia at home in England; who thought of him now, very probably, as missing, believed killed. Well, if all went right, Delia should not lack her Jim in the end.

The clothes she shut into the wardrobe in Simone's room, and the letters she carried downstairs to put them for safe keeping in the cabinet where her own small valuables lay. But as she entered the kitchen the light fell full upon the packet in her hand, and her own face looked back at her. She saw blood upon the lower corner of it, and thought at first that this was Jim's mark; then she remembered that in the breast of the blouse from which this packet had come there had been no stain.

Very slowly she walked to the table, and drew the letters from the elastic band, and sifted them through her fingers; her own letters to her husband, every one she had written to him since he had left her, and all with that crude black encrusted seal in the corner. He had kept them very carefully; she had not believed that he was a man who would carry old letters against his heart. Very strangely they came back to her now by another man's hand, but the message from her husband was implicit and complete. She would not see him again. The Germans might swarm through Boissy-en-Fougères in their millions, and the heart of France be broken, but Georges Lozelle would not know. He had finished with fighting; his war was over.

3

Miriam went out into the darkness where the moonlight had been, and walked about the pitted yard. She heard the stirring of her diminished stock, uneasy in the byres, and the continuous

167

rattling hum of traffic along the high-road, and the mourning of Sarka in the scullery after her lost litter. These sounds touched her as if from afar off. All her senses had become remote. She stood in the midst of a turmoil silent and intense, sustained upright by the whips of circumstance like a top in motion, complete, sufficient and alone.

She had done, in the past week, things she had not believed it was in her to do. When the byres were damaged she had helped Jean to extricate and kill the maimed cattle and the better of the two draught-horses. She had seen the first of the puppies go from her, unnecessarily, wantonly, under the wheels of a German lorry, and the second kicked aside in her own garden when the fatigue-party came and stripped her of every cabbage she had, and everything else worth the taking. After that she had drowned the injured one and all the rest, with her own hands. The flow of Nazi columns would go on for a long time. No little living thing was safe; nor, while they survived, would there be food for them, for Boissy was already so destitute as to be scarcely able to feed its human inhabitants. She had it in her mind that even Sarka would be better dead, if there could be some way sufficiently gentle and swift. Jim had a revolver, true, but the shot must not be heard by alien ears. If in the issue it could and must be done, she felt no desire to have any hands but her own perform the last service; but with Jim in the house, Jim who had once amazingly risked his own life for Sarka's, it seemed worth while to prolong the struggle a little longer. She would, after all, stay close enough to her home to avoid contact with the beast unless it followed her in; and though she grieved now for her young, she would not always be inconsolable. "At the worst," thought Miriam, within herself, "I will not let her live after me."

As for Chicot, a German bullet had put an end to him at her very side as she walked along the main street of Boissy on the first day of the occupation, her eyes fixed ahead, her neck stiff as Lucifer's. Not even a piece of deliberate brutality, that, merely a drunken boy-beast awash from Papa Brégis' bar staggering out to prove his vaunted deadliness with the revolver. And that honey-coloured, svelte, loving magnificence had fallen together and moaned at her feet, and she, distracted, had put her hands over his bleeding nostrils to help him to go, and had rocked him in her arms until he died, while he looked at her with surprised, reproachful, forgiving eyes because she was his heaven and his god and yet she could not or would not help

168

him. All this they had done to her, and still she had held on tooth and claw to the illusion of human happiness; because with Chicot lost, and the puppies, and her home, and the livestock, and freedom, and France, and the ordinary dignity and decency of human intercourse, she still had one thing left to lose, and out of that one thing alone she could make another world.

But it was different now. He was gone with the rest. Georges was dead. Her last stake was lost. What could be done to her now? Lightened of hope, she knew for herself the ending of fear. Of grief there was no ending; it must continue while she continued; it was a part of her, and she believed it was the greater part. But now, stripped of all possessions, she felt in herself power to do whatever she set herself to do. What happened to her now could cause him no further pain; she need have no care of herself, she could venture arrest and humiliation and death with an unmoved heart. She stood by the gate with her head upon her hands, and said to the darkening night: "It is timely!" And when a passing German under-officer stopped to warn her to go in, and asked her the significance of the remark she had made, she repeated it for him pleasantly, and let him take it to the credit of his own people with a surprised smile of gratification and wonder. He said good-night to her when he moved away, convinced of a sympathiser. She could afford to let him believe that of her now. The hate which had been hot in her was colder than the Pole Star. She could wait to bring her forces into the battle; she could be cool, and deliberate and subtle in deceit. There was only one thing she could not do, and that was to forgive.

She went away from the gate after the under-officer had passed, because it was her part to be pliant and accommodating, and he might look back to see if she had obeyed. She walked about the garden until she grew tired, and time came back to her; and then it became clear to her that it was late, and she had need of rest that her wits might be sharp, for she had no other weapon. When she turned back to the house, Simone was waiting for her in the kitchen, and the silent anxiety of her face made it clear that she had seen and understood the letters and the photograph spread fanwise upon the table. She saw how impenetrable a calm had settled upon Miriam's spirit, and her eyes wondered at it. This was not the frozen mask she had worn over the boiling spring of her anger and pain when the fall came. She moved with a steadfast gentleness, confident, considerate, assured. The bereaved are like that sometimes, when they have loved the dead very greatly.

"It is all right," she said softly, seeing Simone's concern. "I know. I understand. It is what one foresees, and I am one of very many. Do not speak of it, and do not be at all anxious for me, I beg you."

"Madame, there is someone else who agitates himself to see you. The big one, he is awake and asking for you."

"I will go to him. Is the milk for the coffee still hot?"

"Yes, Madame."

"*Bien!* Go to bed, Simone, and do not worry any more. I shall come presently."

"Very well. Good-night, Madame!"

Miriam went up the stairs with a candle in one hand and a cup of very weak coffee in the other. In the room over the garden Jim was lying wide-eyed, waiting for her step, and when it came he raised himself on one elbow in a fever of eagerness and apprehension. She came to him quickly, with a small, soundless exclamation of reproach. He was hot from too deep sleep after extreme weariness, and his heart was racing so that it shook him from head to foot.

"*Mauvais enfant!*" she said in a soft whisper. "You excite yourself. That is not good. Why are you not asleep?"

Lost and confused as he was, he would have smiled and been soothed by her deliberate maternal cajolery but for the guilty memory of the thing he had left undone.

"I couldn't sleep until I'd seen you. Sorry I passed out on you—damn' silly trick! I meant to tell you before, but I'm no good at—at—and I thought there might be a chance if I waited. I was just too—too gutless to come at it straight——"

She slid a cool hand under his shoulders, and presented the cup to his lips. "Drink it, and do not talk. It is coffee, but it will not make you wakeful, I promise it."

"No, but there's something I've got to tell you first. Please, I've got to get it off my mind. It—it's about Monsieur Lozelle——"

She caught the terror and distress of his eyes in the candle-light, and was unspeakably touched. "*Mon pauvre,* do not up-set yourself so. There is nothing you have to tell me, nothing in the world. I know what it is you would say. I have the letters he carried on him. We shall speak of it to-morrow, but not a word more will I hear from you now. It is my wish that you shall sleep. Come, drink your coffee."

He drank it. He would have drunk hemlock for her without a question. His eyes closing again, he said in a deprecating murmur: "I ought to have had the pluck to tell you—I'm awfully sorry."

"You have done your part. There, go to sleep, and do not distress yourself for me." And seeing his haunted face relax: "*Bon garçon!*" she said gently.

The kindness of her voice, the kindness of her hands, soothed him away from the world. She stayed beside him until his breathing grew long and quiet and deep, and then she rose and went slowly from the room. Slowly because, although she still carried the candle, she moved like a blind woman, groping her way with foot and hand. To her the small flame was a yellow flower shining dimly in a great darkness; she saw it through an infinite weight of unshed tears.

4

Miriam went down into the village at mid-morning, decorously, grasping her shopping-basket, almost as if she expected to find all things running normally, and plenty of food displayed for sale. She avoided the main road for the greater part of the way, choosing instead a bridle-path which brought her into the village close beside the church. It seemed to her, as she stood at the corner of the narrow pavement and looked up and down the winding street, that the nature of the occupation had changed. All morning the sound of convoys rushing westward had halted from time to time in its rhythm, and marched now to a less hurried beat. She saw one long column pass, heavily laden lorries full of infantry, all uniformly young, all with faces blankly similar. They did not even look exultant in success; they stared at the few silent Frenchwomen and the subdued groups of children, as if they did not exist. It was like being over-run by a race of machines gifted with malevolence but having no other attributes of humanity. But now, apart from this uninterrupted flood rushing across France for the Channel, there were more stable signs of occupation. There were German soldiers bivouacked at the school; she saw them as she passed. That was new. And at the door of the Mairie stood a short man with a duel-scarred face, his well-cut uniform very carefully brushed and his boots glossy as satin. His was a face so marred by the sword-slashes down one cheek that it was impossible to decide whether he had any readable expression, or how it could be interpreted if he had. He wore a revolver in a beautifully-kept leather holster, and an armlet blazoned with a swastika.

"So you also are here," she thought, for she knew his significance only too well. "Our status becomes established, it seems." And she looked at him carefully, while she seemed to ponder the meagre goods in the grocer's window; for on him much might depend. His eyes, which were like opaque brown pebbles, seemed to pass indifferently over the whole length and breadth of Boissy, and see nothing worth noting; but she was not deceived, however dull those onyx eyes remained, however motionless that face in which only the thin mouth retained any coherent form. She had seen Gestapo men who looked just so as they sat watching the advanced examination of recalcitrant graduates and professors after that impasse in Prague, waiting for them to let fall one word of self-betrayal, or, better, betrayal of others. She knew they were all dangerous; the only question was as to the degree in which this one was likely to be dangerous to her. She was almost surprised that they had thought it worth while to place so elaborate an establishment in a place so small as Boissy-en-Fougères. Perhaps, after all, he was only a very little desperado, or he would not have been there.

Others, besides herself, were studying him furtively from behind drawn curtains. The local population, apart from the shopping women, had disappeared from the streets, but from the windows of their homes they looked out with stunned, incredulous faces, and called in their subdued children within closed doors. Boissy was dead. Its heart was broken.

Miriam bought what food she could get. The shutters were still closed at the butcher's shop, because the convoys had taken away all his stock. Mère Jeantot had only a meagre showing, for much of her allowance of flour had also been appropriated. Grocer and greengrocer had suffered the same depredations. Wherever she made her inadequate purchases service was given in haste and silence, with averted eyes and trembling hands. No one spoke of the darkness which had fallen upon Boissy; no one could bear to speak of it. The time would come when their tongues would be loosened, but it was not yet. The German soldiers, too, appeared and disappeared with sinister suddenness. They loomed at her shoulder as she bought bread from Mère Jeantot, and looked her over disconcertingly. She raised her eyes, heavy from loss of sleep, and gave them only the sullen, fearful glance they met with everywhere in this town of ghosts; and they saw in her nothing out of the ordinary, and did not follow her further.

There were more of them sitting in front of the café, off duty and very much at their ease around the little green tables; and still more, and a great noise of their singing, in the *bistro*. The place had changed completely since the days of the 4th Midshires, when the raucous noise they made at their leisure had been at least a cheerful noise, preoccupied with a ribald aspect of war and peopled with figures of fun. This song was arrogant as a goose-step, and shouted like a threat, and the young men who sang were deathly serious about it. Even the blue-checked curtains hung awry now; there was something distraught and hysterical about the whole place. When Miriam passed the door was open, and she caught a glimpse of Papa Brégis behind his bar. He looked an old man, all his fat hanging in unhealthy grey folds, his cheeks and chin unshaven, his hands unsteady upon bottles and glasses, where once they had been so nimble and light. Eliane she did not see, and she hoped within her heart that he had hidden her away in some secure place; but it is not easy to hide a creature so full of beauty and youth. At least he had kept her away from the bar, and by the face of him would go on keeping her away while he had breath.

Miriam had considered whether it would not be better to approach Doctor Vauban's house, which was her real objective, by a roundabout way, but on reflection had rejected the idea as a dangerously premature subtlety. She walked up directly to the front door and rang the bell as anyone else would do when calling out of surgery hours, and he opened the door to her himself. He was in no hurry about it, and his broad face was by no means friendly, even when he recognised her. She was not French; a Czech woman with a French husband might be accepted while all went well with France, but when the night of disillusionment fell, her alien origin was remembered. She had been fully prepared for that, but perhaps not for so early a manifestation. However, he stood back and let her in, closing and bolting the door after her; and in his surgery he set a chair for her, but she crossed first to the window and looked out. The room overlooked only a sunny garden, neglected, high-walled. She turned back to where the doctor stood watching her.

"Doctor Vauban, you have yourself fought against the Boches. I am putting my life and some others, I think, in your hands. There are two British soldiers in my house. It is my responsibility that they shall stay at liberty and get back to their own people in safety when they are fit to make the attempt. But for the moment they need you more. Will you come?"

Whatever he had expected, it was not this. He stared at her, and his heavy features warmed suddenly into interest. "Madame, you are undertaking a very dangerous business," he said; but she knew he was tempted.

"I know it. I have trusted no one but you. But they must have your help."

"But of course! Why else am I a doctor? You wish that I shall come with you now?"

"No, there are too many German soldiers in the streets. It is best that we go singly. I wish to keep your visits as inconspicuous as possible, and to attempt to be too stealthy would be to invite notice; therefore come quite openly to the house. You have attended Simone Lacasse more than once for rheumatism; that is cover enough, do you not agree?"

"Certainly it is best not to complicate one's plans without need. If any questions should be asked—who knows when it may not happen?—I am visiting Madame Lacasse. These young men—what is wrong there?"

"The one has pneumonia from shock and exposure. He is the one for whom I am most afraid. But you will also need sutures and dressings; the other has at least one wound that will need stitching."

He nodded. At the prospect of having something positive to do in Germany's despite, his normal brisk alertness had come back, and he looked almost happy. "I will leave the house about half an hour after you. Presently, Madame, you will want also clothes for your protégés, a little less conspicuous than their uniforms. I can help you there, perhaps."

"I shall not fail to call upon you. These details can and shall be arranged; but now I am anxious only that they shall not die on my hands."

"Very well! First things first. I shall follow you home as I have said." He ushered her out, and at the door, for the benefit of the scarred Gestapo man, who was strolling past at an easy pace, he was heard reassuring her grumpily that he would come when he had had his coffee. She went away well pleased with her accomplice; conspiracy was in his nature, and he might yet be useful in many ways, for his wits as well as his professional skill.

She had intended to go straight home, but as she passed the church, a little girl ran across the pavement in front of her and into the whitewashed porch, holding a bunch of white half-opened roses in her hand. Miriam sensed something strange in the manner of her running, furtive and frightened, as if some-one had prompted her from behind: "Now! Run quickly, while no one is looking!" Children are not afraid of un-accustomed people and things unless adults whom they trust and believe implicitly create an artificial fear in them. She wondered why a mother whose first instinct would be to call her child in behind locked doors should, instead, send her scurrying to the church with roses; and because it was expedient that she should know everything invaders and natives did, and said, and thought, she turned in after the child. She had now the instinct to close all doors carefully and quietly behind her; and so she did with this one, before she looked down the narrow aisle.

It was cool, there within the church, and the light was brightly blue as it fell through the tinted irregular panes of the windows and touched the vivid tinsel jewellery of the saints. In the dim open space where the light did not reach, a trestle table had been set up, and upon it lay a long, narrow shape swathed in black, with a white cloth draped over the face. The child had laid her roses on the black shroud above the dead breast, and was slipping back between the pews, sidelong, as if she struggled to make herself invisible. They met within the doorway, as the little girl stretched out her thin fingers to the holy water.

"Jeanne!" said Miriam softly.

"Madame?" she said in a whisper.

"Who is it?"

"It is Monsieur Peyron," she said, her voice scarcely audible.

"Monsieur Peyron? Dead? I did not know."

"It was yesterday, Madame. We are forbidden to speak of it, or to come to his funeral, because they don't want people to know how they killed him; but my mother gave me the roses to bring for him, and that is why I had to hurry." She drew nearer, aching to tell what she knew. "It was when they took over the school yesterday afternoon. Monsieur Peyron was giving a singing lesson when they came in and said that we had to go, because they wanted the building for their soldiers. The officer made a speech, but his French was very queer, and we could not all understand him, so he made Monsieur Peyron tell us. But Monsieur Peyron didn't tell us the way he wanted him to, he just said that we had to go home quietly because 'les sales Boches' were now in command in Boissy for a short time, and until we could eject them we must behave with the dignity and composure France demanded of us before an ignorant and barbaric race who could only learn by example, having no civilised tradition of their own to give them poise." All this she had by heart, and it came with something of its original fire, though she dared not raise her voice above a whisper. "He said it all very quickly, Madame, and they could not tell what it all meant, but they knew he was making a mock of them because we laughed; and they were angry, and struck him, and we were frightened, but he smiled at us and told us to sit down quietly and remember who we were, and it would be all right. Then the officer shouted at him, and pulled out his revolver and pointed it at him, and told him to sit down and play 'Deutschland Uber Alles'. He sat down just quietly, and looked at us, and said would we all sing with him; and then he began to play 'La Marseillaise'."

"I see," said Miriam in a very low voice. "Poor Michel!" But she felt even then that pity was inappropriate; but for that grand gesture his would have been a long, slow, sickly death. It is not given to many people to live their dreams of glory, even at such a cost. "They took him away with them then?"

"Oh no, Madame. Before we had sung two lines of 'La Marseillaise' the officer fired, and Monsieur Peyron fell down, and then the officer was frightened, I think, and he fired at him again; and then they carried him away quickly, and brought Mademoiselle Meunier and made her tell us we were not to speak of it to anyone, or it would be the worse for us. They made her say that Monsieur Peyron was a degenerate and a traitor to the best interests of France; but after they had gone, she told us that he was really a hero, and that we should always remember him. I wanted to bring some flowers; my mother was frightened, but she said yes, go, and she gave me the roses. You will not let anyone know I told you?"

"I will not ever admit that I have seen you, Jeanne. Tell me, who brought him here?"

"They sent for Monsieur le Curé, and said that he must take away Monsieur Peyron and make arrangements for the funeral as early as possible, so that no one would know. But they do know, Madame; they all know."

"It is fitting that they should know," said Miriam.

"Yes, Madame. I must run home now, or my mother will be worried."

"Yes, indeed. Good-bye, Jeanne."

When the child had slipped away through the porch, Miriam went forward to the uncoffined body, so flimsily thin, and turned back the cloth from his face. He was unmarked, and looked curiously alive except for the more-than-living calm of his expression, in which something of the exaltation and surprise of his farewell to the world still lingered. His flesh was waxen white, and the fastidiously trimmed chestnut beard jutted from his chin like a dark flame. He looked confident, and pleased, and even a little complacent, like an ambitious young soldier unexpectedly presented with the Croix de Guerre. A life thrown away, if you looked at it from the strictly practical viewpoint. And yet was it? He had subjected those children to a horrible experience to satisfy his vanity—yes, but he had given them something to live up to, something to live for, while this darkness lasted and after it was ended. His memory might yet be worth a regiment to France.

She looked down at the clay-white face for a moment only, and then laid the cloth over it again. "There are some here who will not forget you," she said.

When she left the church, she all but cannoned into two young German soldiers who were strolling along the narrow pavement and left no room for her. The nearer one seemed inclined, for a moment, to fall behind his companion and leave her a clear passage on the inner side of the walk, but the other one kept fast hold of his arm, and forced her into the gutter. She stepped past them lightly, as if she did not even notice their existence; being fully aware that they preferred to be noticed at all costs, whether with cringing subservience or anger or open hate, rather than make no impression at all. Then she remembered that she had a part to play; it would not do to have even the meanest of them look twice at her because she acted like one accustomed to encountering and dealing with the gestures of the master race. That would encourage investigation of her identity and past; and if they ever discovered that she had escaped from Prague while under suspicion of assisting in anti-German agitations, she would be at best a marked woman and at worst a dead one, in either case of no use whatever to the two Englishmen in her house. One must be more nervous, more ingratiating; the accomplishment of seeming unmoved in such circumstances is not learned in a few days.

177

She had expended almost half of her half-hour's start, but she was home by her short cut to the orchard in ten minutes more. Simone was in the bedroom when she came in, and came hurrying down at her call.

"He is coming? But I see it in your face."

"Yes, very soon. I thought it best we should not come together. And Simone—you will have to keep close within, and be ready to act the invalid should it be needed. I made your rheumatism the excuse. Oh, not to Doctor Vauban. He knows why he is wanted. It is just that our stories may agree, if there should ever be any questioning."

"It will scarcely even be a lie," said Simone, "for it never leaves me."

"You should make me do the running up and down stairs on trivial errands. I can very well wait upon our guests in small ways, even if I am not so handy at nursing as you. Tell me, how is he now?"

Simone's broad shoulders lifted helplessly. "Madame, I dare not try to guess. He has spells of calm when the fever seems to leave him, and he sleeps quite easily, yet at other times he raves. He has taken milk and beaten eggs, but nothing more. I think it is the one lung only. With the doctor's help surely we shall save him. As for the other one, he is awake and has eaten a good breakfast. He wishes to get up, I think, but I would not give him his clothes. In any case, he will not long remain awake; he has still nights of sleep to make up, that one, I see it by his eyes."

Miriam smiled. "He has also things to say that will not let him sleep. Let us by all means keep him awake until the doctor has sewn up his side, and after that he will need to rest. Will you send Doctor Vauban up to us when he comes?"

She went up the stairs. Tommy was lying in an uneasy sleep, a steaming handkerchief soaked with eau-de-Cologne spread over his forehead. Jim was awake and watching the door, for he had heard her step upon the stairs, and he was agog for news. Almost before she was in the room he asked in a quick undertone:

"You've been into the village?"

"Hush!" she warned, looking over her shoulder at the tormented sleeper in the double bed. "Yes, I've been. The doctor is coming to see you both very soon."

"Oh, I'm all right!" said Jim. "It's him I'm worried about. I don't need a doctor."

Since he was apparently determined to talk, she went close, and sat down upon the edge of his bed, so that they might hear the merest breaths of whispers, each from the other. Strangely bereft now, it seemed to her that besides Simone she had no one in the world so near to her as this young Englishman she scarcely knew.

"He must see you, none the less," she said firmly. "If your wound is not stitched, it will be slow in healing, and leave you with an ugly scar. How do you feel, now that you have slept? Better?"

"Oh yes, thanks, I'm fine, really. Well—you know—not so bad, anyhow. Do you think he's any better? He's been pretty quiet most of the time, but a while ago, before Simone came up, he was talking to himself. Miriam—do you know whether Eliane Brégis is still in Boissy?"

"I don't know. Why do you ask?"

"He talks about her—calls for her now and then. It was while we were here before; they were very friendly—well, too friendly, if you know what I mean; but I wondered if it would do him any good to see her now. Ordinarily," he said frankly, "I'd rather steer him off her, because he's a married man, and Eliane's a proper nice kid, too, and you know how a chap could feel about her. But when he's like this——"

"Yes," said Miriam thoughtfully, "I know how a man could feel about her. But let us not talk of letting too many people into what is after all a dangerous business. It is enough to have brought Doctor Vauban in. The risk is greater to us and to them if more people learn that you are here."

"All right," said Jim readily, "you're the boss."

She was silent for a moment, frowning down into her linked hands. Then she said: "The Gestapo are in the village. That means that the occupation is becoming firmly established. They are a people who do not speculate; they must be very sure of themselves to be setting up already their little inquisitions. Soon, I think, they will have a dossier upon every person in Boissy, and a close watch on every house. They trust no one, those people; happily I have learned from association with them how to behave when I am suspect, and to trust no one in my turn. But I wish they were not here. It means that they are confident of holding this territory they have taken. There will be much travelling for you to do through enemy country."

"As soon as he's on his feet again," said Jim, nodding towards Tommy, "we'll get on. I don't like the thought of making trouble for you, and, anyhow, we want to get back to the boys." The words brought back to his mind how few of the boys remained alive. He supposed A Company was virtually wiped out in the repulsion of that one counter-attack. There was no one to get back to; some composite battalion, probably, re-formed behind the lines westward towards the Channel. "It's queer," he said. "When we left here I never thought we'd be coming back like this. You wouldn't believe so much could happen in so short a time—and all go wrong—would you?"

"You will be here a long time," said Miriam deliberately, ignoring the dangerous question which needed no answer. "Even for your own case I think a fortnight of rest at least would be needed; but with him as he is, I cannot even begin to guess. To take him away and drag him across France before he is fit would be murder. There is no help for it. I know you long to get back to your friends, but it must not be until the doctor gives the word. You understand?"

"I'm in your hands, and almighty lucky to be there. I'll do whatever you say. Miriam—did I ever get around to telling you, last night—about those letters, how I got them?" He had been trying to ask her that from the beginning, she knew.

She looked steadily away from him, to the opened window where the white curtains swayed in the wind, and the crests of the orchard trees foamed away from the house like dark green waves of a turbulent sea. "You tried to, but I did not let you. It is all right, I understood the only thing of any importance; but if it will satisfy you at all, tell me now."

He told her, and now that he had at last plunged back into that remembered sea, he told her more of it than he had meant to tell to anyone. She knew already so much, and she was so unmovingly quiet, sitting there upon the edge of his bed, receiving his staccato, muttered confidences without comment or exclamation, so that he was not constantly brought up against the mirror of his own horror. He had not, until then, ever had time to look back and examine again his impressions of that unbelievably brief and horrible campaign; now that he ventured it her calm maintained in him an answering calm. These things were. It was useless to try and cover them over with gentle phrases to keep yourself sane, and worse than useless to turn your head away. He told her about the position behind the incomplete Belgian tank-traps upon the canal, and the three-day battle, and the crazy retreat, and the massacre in the ridge among the beechwoods, and the finding of her husband's body.

About the woman on the Hainault causeway, and the mothers and children on the moonlit road where the tanks had passed, and the aged dog shut into the cottage to die, he did not tell her, but he felt that in her heart she knew. He told her that Second-Lieutenant Ridley was dead, but not in what manner he died; and then her fixed eyes widened but did not waver, and her linked hands closed but did not tighten, as if all the fierce tensions in her had been somehow severed. Yet even in that great tranquillity of hers he was aware of warmth and resolution and pain at least equal to his own. Nothing had died; only something had come to birth, like the cone of stillness in the heart of the whirlwind.

When he was silent at last, himself shocked into silence, she put out a hand and gently touched his shoulder. "You have been through very much," she said. "You have changed." Her voice regretted what she had known to be inevitable.

"Yes," he said. "I didn't know it could be like that. I didn't know anything could be like that."

"It was so with me. But we were not even at war. What was done to us was done in cold blood and at leisure." She got up abruptly, and went and leaned upon the window-frame for a moment, with her face raised to the breeze; a moment only, and then she turned and looked at him across the room. "What am I to say to you?" she said; and she said it as if he had accused her.

"You've been through more than your share," he said, more pre-occupied with her wrongs now than his own; which was Miriam's peculiar gift to him, the more strange because never until now had he heard her utter anything which could be called a complaint.

Speaking to each other thus, over the width of the room, they had insensibly raised their voices; but now she broke off with warning finger lifted as Tommy stirred and turned with a restless moan upon his pillow. He did not fully awake, nor feel her touch as she took away the handkerchief, and having dipped it again in the saucer of eau-de-Cologne, smoothed it carefully back across his forehead. He subsided again into his uneasy sleep with a long sigh. Miriam came back to Jim's bed.

"If only we had ice," she said, in a whisper.

"Yes. No one in the village would have any?"

"No one in the village has anything any more. Remember the locusts are here."

"Oh, God, yes! I *can't* realise it. It doesn't seem possible.

Boissy, of all places—— You can believe in it when it's miles and miles away, but when it happens to a town where you've lived, where your friends are—— What's it like down there? Is it—very bad?"

She only shook her head, but her face answered him. He said: "When I remember how sure we all were—how we sat in Papa's and drank to the day of disillusionment! My lord, that's rich, isn't it? The day of disillusionment! I wonder what Michel feels like now? It was his phrase, that. He used to race along in the most dazzling English, with bits of French thrown in wherever he was sure we'd understand them, wobbling his glass around all the time, the way it's a wonder he ever got a drink at all. Poor old Michel! I can't imagine him without that grand bombast of his."

"No need," said Miriam; "he has it still."

Jim looked at her narrowly. "There was something in the way you said that—— What's happened to him?"

And she told him; in the softest of undertones, as it had been told to her, and almost in the same words. At the end of the story he lay quiet for a long time, staring wide-eyed upward at the ceiling on which the reflections of sunlight among the orchard leaves danced with a ceaseless motion. She thought that he did not wish to speak of it, that with this last hurt she had driven him back into the prison of his own overburdened mind. It was a pity, but to try and follow him would do no good. She made to get up quietly and go away from him until he should want her again, but instantly he put his hand over hers on the edge of the bed and held her so, and his eyes, still sunken and tired and bewildered, came urgently back to her face.

"It seems a queer sort of thing to feel about it, but gosh! what a way for him to go. It was the sort of thing he dreamed about."

"So I have told myself," she answered softly.

"You know, when some of 'em waved banners and shouted about 'La Belle France' it just made me get pink round the ears. But somehow with him it was different, even when he waved harder and shouted louder than all the rest. It was like a kid playing King Arthur and the Round Table. He used to make up big scenes in his mind, so real he almost believed in them. And then all at once one of 'em comes to life, and he really does it—and nothing lets him down."

"He is dead," said Miriam, but there was no rebuke in her tone, if the words implied one.

"I know, and people here will miss him. But he did it."

"Yes," she agreed, "he did it very well."

In her mind, as in his, the scene took form, the little school-room, and the audience of children, and the amazed, amazing, grandiloquent exit of Monsieur Peyron, with "La Marseillaise" on his lips.

> *"Allons, enfants de la patrie,*
> *Le jour de gloire est arrivé——"*

And there his voice had snapped off upon the sharp cry of the revolver. Yes, certainly the day of glory had arrived for him.

"My God, yes. They'll talk of him behind their closed doors, all right, even if they keep quiet in the streets. But can you conceive of anybody doing that to him? The most harmless creature that ever walked, and they—they have to—— With the kids looking on!"

"He was not harmless to them," said Miriam. "One such unbalanced enthusiast as Michel can do them incalculable harm. Perhaps he has. They are adroit enough to realise the danger, but not profound enough to know how to deal with it. They should have disarmed him by making him a figure of fun. Instead, they have made him a martyr. It is not altogether their fault they are such bad psychologists. They have been taught to make sure, not to experiment. Where the règime is resisted, kill. They have killed. They will be seriously surprised when the story of Michel Peyron rises against them in the day of reckoning; they do not expect their dead to rise."

"The day of reckoning!" he repeated, in a low and bitter voice. It sounded too like Monsieur Peyron's "day of dis-illusionment", two-edged and delicately-balanced, liable to fall the wrong way.

She looked at him with unsmiling gentleness. "You do not believe in it," she said.

"I don't know what I believe in. I don't know what's happened, nor what's happening now, nor what's going to happen. I don't even know where I've been. All I do know is that you can't be sure of anything. Look at us! We couldn't wait for it to begin, we were so damned sure of ourselves. We wanted it. Action, we said. Well, we got it." He turned his head away, but still he felt her eyes upon him. "Our chaps are on the run—those who're still alive—and the Jerries are in Boissy, I'm doing no more betting."

"I also," said Miriam slowly, "have been through this phase. Do not persuade yourself that it will last for ever, nor that it is the ultimate discovery you have made. *Mon cher*, it is not so. You have not learned the half. I also, when the night fell upon my country, wished to join battle. Listen, I tell you what I have never told to anyone, living or dead. I also rushed into my warfare gladly and blindly. It was only a very little combat, ours, but it was a great and terrible defeat, and after it things which for long I have not dared to remember, nor been able to forget. I also conceived that neither flesh or spirit could bear more, that good was wiped out from the earth as incompetent and unintelligent and weak. All of which things, I think, the good of this generation has been, but it is not wiped out, believe me. I also wished to get the evil out of my eyes and the bitterness out of my heart, and to turn my back upon this doomed world and fill my hands with what consolation I could find. Jim, I tell you, this also passes as the blind confidence passed. I have lived through them both, and I know. There is no despair that lasts for ever, there is nothing that cannot be borne. I say it from my heart. There is nowhere you or I can hide from the nature that is in us. I am not an optimist. I see all manner of follies and crimes and spites and rotteness weakening our cause even now, making the scales heavy against us; I see years, perhaps a whole generation, of struggle and slavery; but I know that the fire of freedom and progress and devotion to right cannot be stamped out of the world. It may burn low for centuries, but it cannot go out. I feel its continuity in me, and therefore in others. Do not believe, however it uses you, however many times it abandons you to the pains of hell, however it cheats you, and plays you false, and lies to you—do not ever believe that you can abandon it, Jim, your cause. It has only hurt you yet; that is the beginning, it can do far worse things than that, it can turn in your hands, it can wrap itself in a darkness of words and cause you to strike at your friends, it can open the earth under you and let you fall, it can promise you rewards and progress and turn its back on you and give you nothing, it can dirty your hands, it can make itself cheap and hideous where you believed it so clean and comely. But it cannot drive you from it. You will still go on hoping against hope that a spark of the truth survives in it, and for that spark you will fight against all the devils in hell. And it does survive," she said, "it does survive."

She stopped. She was exhausted, as if she had run a long

way; she wanted to rise and dared not trust her knees to bear her. It was very quiet in the room, unnaturally quiet. What had she said? She, who had cried out once to the Abbé Bonnard that this armour of experience could not be handed on, was trying now to buckle hers upon this English boy, whether he would or no. It was folly for him, and strange pain for her. She leaned over him. His face was still turned away, or she could not have spoken so; he had said no word, or she could not have gone on speaking.

"Jim!" she said softly.

He made no answer. She looked more closely, and saw that his eyes were closed. Scarcely asleep, he was certainly not awake; he could not have heard more than the beginning of that slow and quiet statement of faith which had so wrung her. A great spring of relief seemed to break out within her, cool and sweet and full of comfort.

"I give you the heart out of my body," she said, silently moving her lips upon the words, "and you fall asleep!"

Then she heard from below her the kitchen door opened and closed, and the doctor's step upon the stairs.

5

On May 28th, the King of the Belgians surrendered to German pressure and issued orders to his armies to cease fighting, thus leaving the left flank of the B.E.F. uncovered, and making the retreat upon Dunkirk even more hazardous than it already was. The Allied perimeter had by that time contracted so drastically that to dream of pursuing it was madness. Three days later the embarkation at Dunkirk began, that miracle of improvisation.

It was on that last day of May, too, that the Gestapo came to Boissy farm.

Jim was out of bed when they came, and padding about the room in his inadequate pyjamas and dressing-gown, fetching and carrying for Tommy. It was about noon, and Miriam was out somewhere about the farm, and Simone busy in the kitchen. It was not a time when anyone was expected to come to the door; yet someone was rapping there, for he heard the light wooden noise repeated imperiously three or four times before Simone could grumble her way to the door. A queer knocking it was, like the butt of a revolver beaten upon the panels; and impatient, not accustomed to being kept waiting. Uneasiness awoke in Jim's mind. He crossed barefooted to the bedroom door and softly set it ajar.

In the shell of the old house sounds carried with dazzling clearness. The conversation below was a quiet one, yet he heard every inflection of the voices; Simone's grudging and unfriendly, but not unduly frightened; and two strange voices, one high-pitched, speaking metallic, carefully-articulated French, the other a strangely pleasant baritone, speaking French also, and fluently, but with no pretence at correct pronunciation, and robbing the language of much of its nasal quality. He did not know what any of them said, but he did know that neither of the two visitors was French, and there was, after all, only one other thing they could be. He was seriously alarmed. What if they wanted to go through the house? Not in a conscious search for two English stragglers, for they would not have entered thus peaceably if they had come looking for prisoners, but upon some other pretext which would reveal their presence just as surely; for how can you remove undetected, from a room which has only one entrance, a sick man and all the evidences of his occupation, with the enemy standing in the kitchen immediately below you?

A slight sound behind him made him turn with a bounding heart. The flush door in the wall behind the bed, papered over and then carefully slit round with a sharp knife, had caught his eye before, but he had never seen it open, nor thought to see it so. It swung now, and was pushed wide, and Miriam came in from the musty darkness beyond, in an open-necked shirt and breeches, as she had raced in from the yard. She had left her boots in the stable, and trod silently as a cat along the floor-boards. He turned upon her with a breath of relief, but before he could utter a sound, she put her hand sharply upon his arm, and her face silenced him.

"I know. I saw them come. Quick, help me to lift him into your bed. The blankets, too, or they will strip us. It's bedding they want."

She was like a small, sudden wind blowing through the room, carrying him with her. Between them they swept up Tommy and his sheets and blankets, and lifted him into the camp bed. The door into the loft—by the smell of dusty hay, sweet and heavy, it was a loft—was wide enough to admit of the bed passing through it, though there was an awkward ten-inch step down on the other side. Miriam backed through it cautiously, and by following her movements Jim also made the passage successfully. It was very dark in the loft, but she drew him after her adroitly, and the white of her shirt gave him a beacon to steer by. As they set down the bed, he felt straw under his bare feet, and the dust of it came into his nostrils dry and aromatic and faintly acrid.

"Stay here!" said Miriam, and slid past him and back into the bedroom. She put her hand upon the exposed mattress of the double bed, and finding it warm, set her knee upon the edge of the bedstead to prevent the castors from moving and making a noise, and hauled the entire mattress over in her arms before he could raise a hand to help her. He took the two pillows, however, and swept up the tray of glasses, bottles and instruments from the table, and carried these also away into the loft. She gave him a quick glance of approval, and stopped on the threshold for a last look round the room, but it looked bare and untenanted. Their boots and khaki she had long since hidden in the stone roof of the covered well in the garden; their rifles were wrapped in oiled rags and a tarpaulin sheet and buried under the flagstones in the kitchen. She saw nothing that could betray them, and there was no time to linger for double certainty. She drew the door to after her, and locked it. The key she put into Jim's hand, drawing him to her in the darkness which was now beginning to lift from his eyes.

"Listen! Stay here and keep him quiet. If they come into that room you will hear what passes. If it seems necessary, after they are gone, get him back into there. I will try and keep them out of here, but if they insist, I shall bring them through the stables, so that you can have a few minutes at least. If need be, take Tommy away and pile straw over the bed and the other things. You understand?"

"Yes. I'll manage all right." She had taken something else from her breeches' pocket, and was pressing it into his hand. "What's this?"

It was Brian Ridley's revolver. "If need be," she said, "they are only two, but they are both armed, remember. You will see better than they; I shall not bring a torch." She took him suddenly by the arms for a moment, and pressed her body close to him, and he felt the tumult of her heart. Then she turned her back, and stooped to wrench up the small trap by which she had entered from the stables.

He whispered after her, in an agony: "Take care of yourself, never mind us." Which was folly, for they were inextricably bound together; but she turned up her face to him for a moment as she slid through the trap, and gave him a smile which glowed even in the dimness. Then she lowered herself from view, and let the trap slip into place between them.

Before she walked out of the stable she stooped to beat the dust from her elbows and knees, and the cobwebs from her hair, and to put on her boots. She could be as dirty as she liked, but cobwebs in the hair are not acquired in the open air, as a rule, and she had, as far as the visitors were concerned, come in honestly from the fields. She was careful to tramp the length of the yard, and clatter into the scullery loudly, but she hoped not too loudly, briskly but without haste. There was no sound from the kitchen. She washed her hands under the tap, and walked into the kitchen, calling out: "Simone, is lunch ready?" And there upon the threshold she stopped, visibly drawing back into herself, her wet hands stilled in the folds of the towel, her eyes dilating. For a second she stared inimically, and then inclined her head in a stiff bow, and in a very small, wary voice: *"Messieurs!"* she said.

The man with the scarred face was sitting easily in a chair beside the window, his opaque eyes looking through her, his thin, shapely mouth smiling vaguely. Six inches below the rug on which his glossy boots rested were the two British rifles; she thought of them, and prayed that she had painted over the new mortar carefully enough to satisfy him should he kick the rug aside. No prodigy of suspicion or clairvoyance on his part would have surprised her; and it was of him she was afraid, not of the young army officer who stood poised in the middle of the floor with his hand on the butt of his revolver in its holster. A big, blonde arrogant creature, with hectoring eyes and, she thought, a dangerously touchy temper. Perhaps the same who had taken fire in the schoolroom, and shot down Michel Peyron.

As soon as she halted in the doorway, he straightened up and shot out his arm in the conventional gesture, but with more than conventional fervour. "Heil Hitler! You are Madame Lozelle?"

The Gestapo man neither moved nor spoke. Simone, in the shadow of the great china-press, stared and trembled, and was glad she had no more to do.

"Yes," said Miriam, "I am Madame Lozelle."

"You appear alarmed at seeing us here, madame. There is no need, provided you co-operate with us sensibly."

"I have no choice," she said woodenly, and came forward into the room and let him look at her. She was deeply sunburned, and in the creamy golden-brown of her face her eyes were ebony, polished and hard. "Neither by French nor Germans have I ever been consulted. They took my husband, and it is not to be expected that I should conserve from you anything of what is left."

"Madame, we shall not be hard to satisfy; if you are reasonable, we also can be reasonable. Your husband, then, is a soldier in arms?"

"He had no more choice than I," she said bitterly.

"Where is he now?"

She lifted her shoulders. "I do not know. For sixteen days I have had no word of him."

The man by the window said abruptly, in German: "Sergeant Georges Lozelle was with the 9th Army at Sedan. You know he is dead?"

She thought: "They know who I am. They know everything." Despair came into her for a moment, until she remembered the body upon the moonlit road, not so very far away. Jim had removed part of the evidence, but from what was left they would find it easy to identify him. Yes, that was it. They knew what Georges' papers would tell them; of his past, and hers, they had nothing at all, nothing but the suspicion which came to them so readily. At least behave in accordance with that belief, and if they have more they may even come to doubt its authenticity. She stared back into the onyx eyes, and shook her head patiently, and said: "Speak French, if you please. I do not understand that language." And when he looked back at her in silence, she appealed fearfully to the officer: "What did monsieur say? I did not understand."

"It does not matter," said the Gestapo man, in his fluent but ill-pronounced French; and with a gesture of his hand seemed to withdraw himself again from the scene. But she was conscious of him at every second. Plainly he suspected her of knowing German; that casual remark had been designed to make her betray herself. "You know he is dead?" Happily she was proof against any shocks upon that score; but how if she had *not* already known? How if the news had come to her for the first time in that baited trap? She believed she would have cried out, or grown pale, or in some way given him satisfaction.

"All goes well," she thought grimly, catching a glimpse of

her own sullen, subdued face in the mirror. "That is not how one looks who hears of her husband's death suddenly."

"We have need of food and bedding," said the young officer. "You will give us whatever blankets, mattresses, sheets you may have in the house, apart from those for your own use. Also if you have stores of flour or sugar or preserves you will make these also available to us. Two of my own men will come in an hour after I leave, and collect what you can provide. You are a solder's wife, Madame Lozelle; you know that a protective force such as ours must be sustained by the territory it occupies. It will be well for you to recognise at once where your best interests lie."

"I understand my position," she said dully.

"Also, there is for the moment a failure in our supplies of fresh meat. It will be necessary that we ask you to supply a beast for slaughter. The disorganisation is temporary only; there will, I trust, be no second demand."

"I shall have a bullock ready for you," said Miriam in the same flat voice.

"My men have orders to view all your stock, and make their own selection. I am more satisfied of their single-mindedness— forgive me—than of yours." He smiled at her, the kind of smile she had believed herself too old to incur. It was, perhaps, the high colour in her brown cheeks, and the curling disarray of her hair, that drew that hateful, insolent light to his eyes.

She shrugged again. "You shall do as you please. But you see we have very little left—except our lives, and that by mere chance. What we had is gone with the house."

"I regret it should ever have been necessary to bomb. But France made an unhappy mésalliance, Madame, and has reaped only the harvest of her own short-sightedness. They were unprofitable allies, were they not, the English?"

She said nothing. The scarred man, still lounging at his ease beside the window, said softly in German: "It would be well if we saw the house for ourselves." He added in the same tongue, and still more quietly: "You will show us, Madame?"

She made no move, but only drew her brows together in a hopeless frown, and protested indifferently: "I do not understand you. Please say it in French."

"You understand me very well," said the low-pitched, musical voice. "Why pretend otherwise? Is it then a crime to speak German?"

She shook her head with a sigh. *"Monsieur le Capitaine*, your friend perhaps has little French? I am sorry, I know no other tongue. What is it he wishes to say to me? I am only anxious to do as you tell me; I want only to live in quietness with you." She spread her hands. "If you will interpret, I shall answer truthfully."

"He wishes to see the house," said the officer deliberately. "You will show us, please, what you have of bed-linen and of food stores as we go."

"Very well. It will not take long. There is but the shell to see. There is, it may be, something you wish opened in this room before we go further? None of these presses or cupboards is locked, except the cabinet of Sèvres yonder, and Simone has the key to that. Simone, if you please!" She was brisk with relief, now that she had something definite to do; and determined, besides, to set a pace they might be induced to keep through the rest of the house. But it was, as she found, impossible to hurry or delay them. They did not seem to be looking for deliberate concealment on her part, they were simply very thorough in examining all that did present itself to their eyes; and for this she was ready, having removed adequate stores of all that was preservable to a cache among the ruins. She was therefore acquiescent in their search, but not too complacent, for fear they should suspect that she was coming better out of this stripping than she wished them to know. Dissimulation was, after all, no more new to them than it was to her.

She showed them the larder, and the scullery, and what had been the stillroom once; and was fully aware that the officer noted down as he went whatever seemed to him worth looting. She would have led them away from the cellar door, but shrugged and showed them a light upon the broken stairs when they refused to be decoyed away. She supplied what information she had concerning the age and quality of the wine, and being pressed, went resentfully but docilely to fetch glasses and draw off samples for them. Wine went down upon the list of booty to be collected.

Miriam's linen chests, cedar-lined, aromatic, proved disappointing. They stood in the hall of the house, with one damp-marked inner wall between them and the open air; she opened the heavy lids, and scent of cedar and lavender gushed out.

"That is all," she said, "except for what is upon the bed we sleep in. Nothing else was salvable."

"There is one bed only in use in the house?" asked the officer.

"Yes, monsieur, one only. There are only three rooms still safe upstairs, and only one at all comfortable for sleeping in. One is not weather-proof when it rains, and one is dry but too near the stables. There are rats. I have tried it, but they run, and cry, and I cannot sleep because of them."

She had hoped that they would take her word for it, and possibly the officer would have done so. She was not as handsome nor as spirited as he had at first thought her, and he was becoming increasingly bored with the fragment of an incident. But the scarred man began to climb the stairs.

They followed him, as he looked into the three rooms one after the other, coming last to the room next to the loft. To all appearance what she had said of it was true. No one inhabited it, and it had the derelict look of a place seldom lived in even when the house was whole. The Gestapo man, who had done no more than pause upon the threshold of Simone's room, here walked into the centre of the floor and stood looking round him at leisure. Miriam came and stood just within the doorway, her hands folded sullenly before her, waiting with fixed, resentful eyes until they should have done with her. Her face did not change from its impassive enmity as she watched the scarred man drop a casual hand upon the mattress. Cold from the iron of the bedstead, that would tell him nothing, and she doubted if, short of concrete material for suspicion, he was sufficiently in earnest to go further.

He turned away, and he saw the thin line where the wall-paper joined at the edge of the door into the loft. She watched him run his slender finger-tips round it, and find the best purchase, and lift at it strongly; nor, when it failed to open, did he try a second time

"This door is locked," he said. "The key, if you please, Madame!"

"There is no key, monsieur. The door has not been opened for years. I do not know what happened to the key."

"For—years? How many years?"

"I cannot tell you. Before I came here. I have never seen it open."

He turned his opaque eyes on her, and for the first time she saw a gleam of light in them. "It is unfortunate," he said, in that deep, sweet voice which came so strangely from his thin mouth. "I have a fancy to see what is on the other side of this wall."

"A loft, monsieur, over the stables. There is nothing there

but straw. At one time apples were kept in store here, but the attics are—were—better, and this room was abandoned."

"Until it became a bedroom?"

She gave him a thin smile. "I slept here for two nights. Even during the day one hears them, but at night the noise is inconceivable. There! Do you not hear them now?"

What she had heard, and she believed he had, too, was a sudden rustling mutter, infinitely brief and soft, but to her recognisable enough, for she had heard it often from her bed at night, and Jim scuttling across the room to answer it, like an anxious mother with an ailing child. It was Tommy, fretful in delirium, talking to himself. Only the first protesting utterance, and then silence. She prayed for the quiet to continue, and in her mind she saw, as clearly as if there had been no wall between, Jim on his knees in the straw, holding Tommy in his arms and tightening a terrified hand over his mouth. Flesh could not stand very much of that. She dug her finger-tips into her palms to hold her hands steady, and said:

"I can show you, if you wish, but there is nothing there."

"I wish to see everything."

"Very well!" she said clearly. "We will go through the stables." And she turned to lead the way.

An awful fear was in her that he would order the young officer to remain in the bedroom while he himself went through the stables; but apparently she had been sufficiently unconcerned throughout to discourage any inordinate interest he might have felt in a locked door, for he followed her in silence. They went down the stairs in single file, and in the kitchen Miriam caught Simone's eye, and gave her a look which sent her scurrying up the stairs as soon as they were out of the house.

When she ran headlong into the deserted room the papered door stood wide, and Jim was just stepping through into the light, struggling to lift Tommy bodily in his arms, and making heavy weather of it. Simone took the better half of the weight from him, moving with the agility of a cat for all her bulk. They laid him in his blankets upon the mattress, and sprang back to carry in the camp-bed after him, and the tray. The door closed again, softly, and the key turned, a clear two or three minutes before Miriam brought her shoulder against the trap into the loft and lifted it. Pressed against the door, out of range of the tiny key-hole, Jim heard her let it fall heavily aside, and next minute the straw rustled under her feet. He looked at Tommy, moving uneasily among his rumpled sheets upon

193

the bed. The draped head-board would prevent anyone from seeing him from within the loft; but if he should cry out now, or even moan, they were finished. Jim turned the revolver in his hand, and braced his weight lightly upon spread feet, ready to move first and fastest if the need should arise. They were only two—two of very many, but just now two alone. Unless they had notified others of their movements, they could very well disappear, those two, and no one need ever know. Then he thought of Miriam, and it seemed to him in his extremity that whatever he did she would get smeared with crime and suffering more indelibly than before. In that moment he wished that he had never come there for shelter; even for Tommy's sake it seemed to him unjustified.

But Tommy did not cry out again. That bad minute crouched in the hay, threshing and panting for breath under Jim's agonised palm, had been the end of Tommy's strength. He lay silent while Miriam talked desultorily to her enemies, and waited for them to tire of the exactness of their own investigations. She was wearily obliging; she showed them the byres as they crossed the yard, and stood ready to make patient answer to whatever else the scarred man should ask her, so that for the moment it was obviously pointless to ask her anything. They finished their list of booty, a formidable list enough, and went away from her without another glance; but more than ever, as she walked back into the house and up the stairs, she was afraid of the stony onyx eyes of the scarred man.

Jim had lifted Tommy into the camp-bed when she came into the room, and was re-making the big one, but with hands that shook so violently that he was not doing it well. When she entered he turned and looked at her, and for a moment could not speak. What was there you could say to a woman like Miriam? Simone was busy with the sick man, sponging his face with cold water, and lifting him into an easier position upon the pillows. Miriam went without a word to the other side of the double bed, and helped Jim to finish it. Not until they had Tommy safely relaxed into an easy sleep again did Jim manage to ask:

"Was it all right?"

She smiled, perhaps through a deadening weight of preoccupation with graver matters than the sheltering of his self-esteem, but still she smiled "Yes, it was all right. You did very well."

"If it hadn't been for you——" he began, and let the sentence trail away into a sigh. "What were they after? They didn't suspect there was anybody here that shouldn't be?"

"No. They were after food, and bedding, and anything we might have that would be worth their while to carry away, that is all. In a little while men will be here to fetch away the booty." She saw the question tumbling from his lips, and was quick to reassure him. "No, they will not wish to see the house. They will come armed with a list of those things their officers found desirable. See, I have a copy of it here—he gave it to me when he went away. They will take only what they are authorised to take, and it will be ready and waiting for them. No, that pinch is past. For this time all is well."

"For this time? Do you think they'll come again?"

"Do you think we shall ever be rid of them?" she said abruptly. "No, it is a warning to hasten our plans. You will never be safe here from one minute to another. We must have all things ready to move as soon as he is fit, perhaps even to move him before he is fit, if need be, rather than see him taken prisoner."

"It's for you I'm worried," said Jim. It was the uppermost truth in his mind, but he was quick to disclaim the heroic self-forgetfulness it implied: "At least, I'm pretty concerned about myself, too, but I mean—well, it would be worse for you if they got us. We're still carrying army pay-books and wearing identity-discs that mark us as soldiers, but you——"

She smoothed the corner of Tommy's pillow, and went practically back to the immediate task in hand, attacking the rumpled ruin of the camp-bed with an energy which restored it to order in a few minutes. "There, please get into bed again, Jim, I am a little uneasy about your side as yet, and you have been lifting heavy weights, which you should not do. It was my thought that the doctor took out the stitches too soon."

"I'm all right," he said, but to please her he did as she wished. She made no reply to the fears he had expressed for her; she had not realised that he had thought deeply of what her fate would be should he be taken, and was unwilling to encourage him in this line of thought, even by admitting its existence. As for her own reactions, she had none. She was not indifferent, but she was incapable of being swayed.

She said to Simone, as they went down the stairs: "He will come back!" And she did not mean the looting officer; it was the other man who recurred to her mind as the point from which danger flowed, now as before.

"We shall be ready for them," said Simone.

"Perhaps. Let us at least be ready for them now." And she shook away from her the thought of the future, and began the systematic denuding of her house. Better to be fully occupied; she found her mind worked more clearly while her hands were busy.

6

He came back. Not suddenly, not accusingly, rather drifting in as if the house pleased him, or there were something about the woman he found congenial. He came in quietly, without knocking, and sat down in the chair by the window. She found him there when she came in from the garden, and although her exclamation at sight of him managed to be no more than conventionally surprised, she felt for a moment her world, her last remaining world, collapsing. How long had he been there? Had he climbed the stairs, or in any way made use of his time? There was no sound from above except Simone's thin old voice singing a French nursery rhyme. Perhaps she had heard the stranger come in, and had warned the two young men to keep silence and be ready to disappear into the loft. At least there was not a murmur of them, no feeling of their presence, in the whole house.

"*Bon jour*, Madame Lozelle!"

"*Bon jour, monsieur.*"

They looked at each other, and for some minutes neither of them spoke. Then Miriam said wearily: "What now? Is there *more* one can be asked to give?"

She had left the scullery door open and a warm soft wind blew through the house. Over their heads Simone sang to herself carefully with a note in her voice which made it clear, quite suddenly, that she knew the enemy was within the gates, and had made her dispositions accordingly.

> "*En revenant de Versailles,*
> *En passant devant St. Cloud,*
> *J'ai trouvé un petit bonhomme*
> *Pourtant sa femme à son cou.*
> '*J'ai assez de ma femme,*
> *L'Acheteriez vous?*' "

So sang Simone, polishing busily at the black panelling of the landing, and watching for the first sign of the Gestapo advancing up the stairs. In the bedroom Jim and Tommy sat on the edge of the bed together, straining their ears in vain to catch some echo of what went on below. Tommy had not so much as put his feet to the floor until the previous day, and should not have been allowed to do so even now, but he was so much restored already, in those seven days of early June, that he had more energy to insist than Jim had to deny him. He could at least walk into the loft this time, if there was need; and he was sane again, thank God; no more of that hellish business of throttling him to keep him quiet. Tommy, emerging from the dark, hot mist of delirium with characteristic suddenness, had no memory of that moment in the straw. So much the better for them both; there were a lot of other things he need never remember.

Miriam felt them at her back, their readiness and resolution solid with hers. There was none of the tension there had been the first time; they knew what to do, now, they and she, a free army fighting subtly with the means they had at hand, until the time should come for more open warfare. She looked at the scarred man without dislike, unless it be dislike that moves a soldier to train the sights of his rifle upon his opponent. He was completely untypical, older than the enthusiasts brought up in the Party, of a very different type from the born hooligans who had found an outlet for their own malignant natures in becoming the hired thugs of the Party. No, this man was of another class. The soft voice, the easy poise, the hideously-scarred face which put his student days back to the period prior to the last war, marked him clearly as belonging to an older régime, and put a cynical opportunist light upon his adherence to the new one. She could conceive of such a man riding in easily upon the crest of the next wave as he rode now upon this. He had not, perhaps, become as yet anything but a very minor light in the Nazi sky, but for him even that would not be easy; and if there was one thing certain about him it was that he would never be altogether out of power. She thought he would be an effective and intelligent servant, but not an honest one; corruptible, though not by money or by anything she possessed, but rather by his own cold, appraising nature; brave, but not loyal to any force outside himself; consistent, but not calculable. A tool with a mind is a dangerous tool always, it may well make use of the hand which conceives it drives. Miriam wondered if there were not some way of approach to be made to him, some method of establishing contact with the potential adherent in him. She believed he had vanity, and could find pleasure in playing two hands at once. There were more ways of bending a man than by bribing him, with money or any other commodity. This man, she felt, could enjoy balancing two or three schemes at the same time, trapping with one hand and releasing with the other and keeping both partners lulled and complacent; that was in his nature; it was how he had lived. For a moment she actively contemplated making the attempt to use him.

Once before she had felt that impulse in her extremity, and had obeyed it. That was how she had got out of Czechoslovakia, by trusting the instinct that told her certain men were malleable. The wretched, homesick boy who had seized on her deft approaches then, like a drowning man clutching at weed, did not haunt her now. She remembered him only with distaste and a faintly pitying contempt. What softness there must be behind the brazen front of the master-race, when its exiles of conquest poured out their confidences with so little reserve to the first woman who would speak to them; dangerous confidences, so easily extracted with a smile and a few words of kindness. She had let him talk spasmodically for a long time before she went further, and began frankly to admit her Jewish blood. A quotation from Heine began it, and in a little while she knew all about him, that his grandmother had been a practising Jewess, that he had books in his possession which were banned by the Party, that she could damn him when she liked. After that she made no more concessions, but held the knife at his back until he had got her safely across the border. One fights as one can, and there are more weapons than ever came out of the Skoda works.

This man, of course, could not be frightened; but he might be flattered. He was fully aware that she was playing some deep game of her own. How if she should suddenly lower the curtain she had held between them, the pretence of not understanding him, and look at him with unconcealing eyes which said clearly: "I am fighting against you. Why? You and I are both playing the same hand. Neither of us owes allegiance to the Nazi Party. Why pretend we do? We might be useful to each other in many ways." There are sudden straight looks, after long evasions, which can say all that and more, and still are not evidence.

"Be easy!" said the scarred man. "Nothing more is required of you, Madame Lozelle." And suddenly, and very smoothly, so that there was no shock of awareness to brace her for the answer, he asked: "What was your name before it became Lozelle?"

She had a moment of fear, but she dared not hesitate; there were too many other people in Boissy who could have answered that question already. "Lisek. Why?" Happily they could have told him, however threatened, nothing more of her; there was little more than her name they knew, and perhaps that she was from Paris. Moreover, no one would willingly admit to knowing even that, unless closely questioned, for she was no one's enemy, and Boissy, even in fear for its own life, was a village curiously united.

"That is not a French name?"

"I have never thought about it, monsieur. It was my name. It was my father's name."

"And he was French?"

"I have always been led to believe so."

"You were born in France, then?"

Placidly she lied: "Yes, monsieur. Why do you ask?"

Foolish, perhaps, to claim French birth for herself, since it could so lightly be disproved; but not yet, not until the German armies had taken more of France than she hoped they would ever see. Paris was a safe place to name as her own, a distant, proud, inviolate place. The Battle of France was then two days old, and the Weygand line held firm everywhere, so that it was quite impossible to believe that the grey wave would ever lip at the bastions of Paris. The possibility of treating with the enemy had already receded from her mind; it was not for herself she rejected it, but for the two young men, who seemed to her still untouched by the dirtier side of the modern tragedy. It was not for them to put themselves on a plane with this man's kind in order to escape from the dungeon this man's kind were making of Europe.

"How long have you been at Boissy farm?" asked the sweet voice idly, as if he were making conversation over a tea-table.

"Nearly a year."

"You were married here?"

"No, in Paris."

"From what part of France do you come?"

"From Epinal in the Vosges, monsieur, if one goes back to

first childhood. I was born there. But most of my life has been spent in Paris."

"You met your husband there?"

"Yes." So much at least was true, and would be confirmed wherever he might choose to query it.

"What was your profession at that time?"

She said with a thin smile: "I worked in a modiste's shop, monsieur, fitting gowns, though you would scarcely think it probable now. It was not, however, a very good shop, and I was not sorry to get out of it."

He leaned back in his chair and looked her over from head to foot in one calculating glance. "Interesting, Madame Lozelle, very interesting. So you are not, it seems, a countrywoman after all!"

She opened her eyes wide at him. "Monsieur is a man of perceptions. He did not for a moment suppose that I was." And suddenly she leaned forward, her hands braced upon the table, and looked at him urgently. "You did not come here to ask these little unimportant questions. What do you want of me? I have done nothing. I have not stood in your way. I want only to work my farm and make the best of this business I do not understand. Why do you come here to this wretched fragment I have left? There can be nothing here to interest you."

He smiled. She had a momentary impression that but for the ruin of his face, that bravado of ugliness, it could have been an attractive smile, though she did not suppose that it could ever have been a candid one. In his small way, and without passion, this one had been a ladies' man.

"Madame," he said, rising from the chair and turning his face to the light, "all human creatures interest me, and you more than most. Why, for instance, do you sustain the fiction that——" He checked there, when she would willingly have heard more. "No, I do not think I will put you in a stronger position by telling you yet what I find bogus in you and what genuine."

"You haven't yet decided yourself how much, or how openly, or even in what directions I am lying to you," she thought, and was glad, because to keep that problem unsolved in his mind was the best way of delaying whatever action he might choose to take.

"Another day, perhaps!" he said, and again the sweet and ominous smile made the laced scars of his cheek stand out like white cords. He gave her the ghost of a bow, and walked out a quiet, aimless, unmilitary pace, as if he had nothing in his mind against man or woman. She flew to the window, once he was well out of the room, to see that he did indeed leave the premises. Upstairs, Jim was peering through the edge of the curtains, intent upon the same reassurance. But the scarred man—they neither of them ever learned his name—was not obvious. They watched him walk leisurely away up the yard, without so much as turning his head, and through the gate, and so out of sight. It seemed to Miriam that one so untypical would certainly have enemies among those of his associates who lived more conventionally; and that part of her which had been twisted into the shape of intrigue by necessity, weighed for a moment the idea of hunting them out and making use of them against him if she could. But that instinct, too, she rejected; there could be no parley with the enemy.

At the gate of the farm-yard she saw him meet Doctor Vauban. That was a curious moment, too, almost comic, they met and passed so casually. The doctor had a brisk professional walk, and the pre-occupied manner of one intent upon an urgent task. He almost collided with the scarred man before the significance of the Gestapo uniform seemed to penetrate his mind, and he made the supreme concession of stepping aside and raising his hat, with an ironical politeness which was accepted as blandly as offered. They exchanged a neat bow, and went on about their business; nor did the German look back to see what the doctor's business there might be, perhaps because he had not really noticed him at all, or perhaps because this was not the time. He was a very patient man.

Jim came hurriedly down the stairs, and took her by the arms as she turned from the window with a sigh. "I heard you talking. What did he want? He was asking a lot of questions, wasn't he? I don't like him coming worrying you all the time. He doesn't think there's anything wrong? I mean, anything wrong about you?"

She waved his anxiety aside with some impatience. "He knows nothing. It is his business to suspect everyone, me with the rest; that is all."

"But it isn't all. If he should find out that you escaped from Prague——"

"He will not. No one here will tell him anything. I have said I am from Paris, and in Boissy you are a foreigner if you come from Paris, just as surely as if you come from Prague.

He will get nothing at all. Now do not make more difficulties than we have, I beg you. Here is the doctor. Go up to your bedroom and let him look at your side, and then I will come; we have plans to make."

She drove him back up the stairs, and went to the door to let in Doctor Vauban. The doctor's bland smile had vanished now that the immediate need for concealment was past; his heavy face was grave and alert, and he patted his bag as he set it down with the gesture of one congratulating an ally.

"So they have been here again, eh! They are curious, these people, too curious."

"As you see."

"He did not get anything for his pains?"

"Nothing that will benefit him. But he knows I have something in hand; I have seen it in his face."

The doctor's broad shoulders lifted. "Who has not something in hand, these days? Every soul in Boissy goes furtively now; he is used to that, he will not make much out of it. Nevertheless, it is for us to make all speed, before the fist that closes on us is tight shut."

"How soon?" she asked.

"A week at the very least; more, unless the danger here is extreme. Your Jim, he will stand a great deal of rough handling and be none the worse, but of the other I am not so sure. However, there can be no harm in having all things ready. See what he would have found, that clever one, if he had opened my bag." And he tipped out the contents pell-mell upon the kitchen table, and stood rubbing his hands over them in high delight. Certainly the scarred man would have been more than interested in the nondescript collection of clothes which came tumbling forth, the pipe-stem trousers, the soiled dungarees and cloth caps, the greasy old gaberdine raincoat; and above all in the folded map which fell out on top of the pile, opening its concertina folds slowly. "So! Who would believe one could get so much in the bag which should hold only decorous little instruments! And what would not our scarred friend have given to see this?" He groped in the side pocket of the bag, and triumphantly produced his own ancient revolver, spinning it in his hand as if he had laid it away only a week ago instead of four years. "Rifles are too conspicuous. You cannot hide them about your person. This is at least portable."

"It will be dangerous to be found carrying arms of any kind," said Miriam, doubtfully.

"It is dangerous to live at all, but what of that? Come, let us take a look at these young men of ours." And he swept up the clothes in his arm, and led the way up the stairs.

7

After that day the darkness closed in very quickly. The receding edge of freedom seemed to them, who were already enslaved, to be drawn relentlessly away out of the borders of their knowledge, even before the day of final disaster, June 14th, when Paris fell and the light went out over France. They had had energy to curse Italy for stabbing their country in the back, four days previously, but after Paris was fallen it was as if the heart that beat in them had died, and they had no longer the spirit to curse their enemies. Later the paralysis might pass, but for the moment they were numb. There was so short a time to become acquainted with grief.

In Boissy-en-Fougères time stopped dead. Certainly there was day and very certainly there was night, and cloud and sun and rain came and went; but the people of the village walked through twilight and knew no change in the weather. They passed one another in the street like sleep-walkers, without a word or a sign, averting their eyes from the abomination of the sight of the enemy; and the enemy clattered their heels upon the Boissy trottoirs, and made overbearing approaches to the Boissy girls, and were puzzled by the impassive numbness against which they broke their shafts.

More than one man disappeared from the village during those long, drab days while the Battle of France rolled southward. Some went away in the darkness, intent on escaping somehow out of the orbit of the conquerors; some came home by day, fished out of the millpond, or found laid out neatly upon their own doorsteps with bullets through their heads. But for these reminders it might have been almost possible to forget that the men in grey were members of a conquering, not a visiting, army; for they were circumspect after their fashion until the first of them were found dead in a ditch outside the village. After that they walked in twos, and their walk became a swagger, and they gave up trying to ingratiate themselves, and asserted themselves instead, having all the weapons on their side.

As for the woman Miriam Lozelle, she gave no trouble. She went about what was left of her business in an apathetic fashion, worked hard and worried no one. Even on June 17th, when the word went round that France had requested an armistice, when everyone went in and closed their doors, and the very silence was like a lament, Madame Lozelle was seen about her byres, moving at the same practical gait, and with the same darkly patient face. And all this time the young men fretted and raged in her shadow, and unquestioningly obeyed her. To them the news came like whips, though it came only through the filter of her calm. France was lost, and what was to happen to England now that she stood alone? They were no longer sure of her. They were no longer sure of anything. The pillars of the house were trembling, while they sat here in Miriam's bedroom, intolerably tormented by the thought of all the things they could have been doing in England, and waiting hourly in dread of the news of another surrender. The longing to go became an agony; but it was not until the last week of June that Doctor Vauban shrugged his shoulders and Miriam let them go.

It was a rainy evening, and a grey mist had settled early upon the village, when Tommy Goolden walked out of the gate of Boissy farm with old Jean trotting beside him, and turned westward away from the main road, heading for the wooded valley where the brook ran down to the mill. Jean's cottage was there, on the edge of the trees, and it was the hour when the old man usually walked home that way, so that even the German soldiers in the street did not so much as turn their heads to look a second time as they passed. The old man was known to be harmless, and his companion looked innocent enough, a thin young man in cheap, soiled country clothes and a soiled cloth cap, with a stained grey mackintosh belted tightly in to his middle by a leather belt. The cap was pulled well down over his face against the rain, so that he might have been any one of a dozen young labourers from the outlying farm-steads on his way home from the town. He seemed to be a silent soul, for he made only wordless, grunted replies to old Jean's streams of idiomatic French; but there was nothing about him to attract undue attention, and no one felt any desire to know more of him. So they came to the grey edge of the woods without incident.

Two people were just emerging from the shelter of the trees, and met them face to face at the corner of Jean's garden hedge. A man and a girl, coming back from a walk in the rain, she with his grey military greatcoat round her shoulders, and the man's arm about her waist. He was talking eagerly into her ear in stumbling, uncertain, ill-pronounced sentences, and lapsing now and again into German, so that she understood only the half of what he said; nor was it his blonde good looks which drew her with him, for she never turned her head to look at him, but walked with her large eyes fixed ahead, and only the practised outline of a smile rigid on her lips. Her face was pale as snow, but the blind darkness of her eyes was indifferent and resigned; and she walked as one who knows where she is going, and does not intend to turn aside.

She saw the two men, and her eyes swept over them and rested upon the younger one's face, and suddenly her white rigidity was shaken from within. Her ivory smile was broken, and her lips, though they uttered no sound, certainly framed what should have been a cry of protest and pain. The dark gilly-flower red came into her eyes; he remembered how it had blazed there once, under the budding lilacs of Miriam's hedge. It seemed a long time ago, but she had not forgotten. The labourer's clothes, the upturned coat collar and peaked cap pulled low over his eyes could not hide him from Eliane Brégis.

There was a moment while they looked at each other in passing, while he wondered why she did not turn to her companion and denounce him. It would have been only logical. She was wearing a German greatcoat and walking in the circle of a German arm, so why not make her position secure by turning over an English runaway for imprisonment? She was a realist, wasn't she? She wasn't walking with this tow-headed young German officer because she liked him or his kind; if that had been true, wouldn't she have looked at him now and again? He was pleasant enough to look at, more wholesome than most of his kin. Hadn't she picked him out as the least damage? And an officer, too, the better to ward off the rest of the world. In a land reduced to ruin and despair she picked her way bitterly, with cynical care, using this stepping-stone and that as they offered themselves, treading upon anything to keep herself out of the mud. She was ordinary enough, after all; it was only by chance that she looked like Jeanne d'Arc.

But she did not speak. The instant of recognition went from her, and the last glance he had of her eyes was cool and incurious as marble, as if she had never in her life seen him before. Also she turned her exquisite pale head and deliberately gave her companion the first unveiled look he had ever had from her, so that he was aware of no one else. The two Frenchmen passed by him unseen. He no longer felt the rain. He was an ardent young party man from Bavaria, a professional soldier, cleaner than most of his fellows, and innocent enough to be unaware that a girl could look at him with that look and hate him as she hated him. His arm tightened about her with pride. She thought: "What does he believe of me? What have I done?" But it was not of the German officer she was thinking. She would never know what Tommy was doing there, where he had come from, where he was going. It was like seeing him in a dream; nor would she ever see him again, dreaming or awake. The mist and the rain drove between them. She heard her escort asking earnestly:

"Are you cold, mademoiselle? You are shivering, I feel it."

"No, monsieur, it is nothing. I am a little tired, that is all. Will you take me home? It is foolish, but you see, we are not yet sure of your people—I am afraid to walk alone."

"You are not afraid with me, *hein?*" he asked it eagerly, happily, holding her with foolish gentleness, as if she had been the lily she seemed, and he went in terror of breaking her.

"No—I am not afraid with you."

She hated him all the more then because he was a silly ram and not a wolf, because he meant her nothing but good, no matter what harm might follow him into her life. She hated him because she could not even hate him properly, nor take a fitting joy in dealing treacherously with him. But in her heart she was glad that she could no longer hold on to the hope of any happiness from Tommy Goolden. What use to fix your eyes on so infinitely small and distant a spark of light among such a waste of darkness? Let it go, and the last torment of hope goes with it. Better to get what you can out of the wreckage, and let the impossible future rest; at least there's a certain peace about being without hope. Besides, he is then free, he can go away with a single mind, and be happy; that is always something. So she let her body relax into the German officer's arm, and her shoulder press warmly against his shoulder; and Tommy Goolden passed on into the shelter of Jean's cottage, and sat down on a rickety kitchen chair beside the empty grate, and raged in silence because he also had seen a light go out.

He was still sitting there when Miriam and Jim arrived, twenty minutes later. There was, in any case, nothing he could do now until they came. He could not even understand what Jean was trying to say to him. There was nothing to be done but sit and wait, and then it was impossible to keep Eliane out of his mind. What was it in her that had failed to sustain what other people were suffering without a murmur? She, who looked like the virginity of France in person, and yet turned in the hand like a faulty blade. You could never tell with a woman. The ones that were blessed with faces to make a man fight like a hero, they were the ones that slipped away like flowers bending when he wanted to lean on them and draw breath. Nancy, now, she hadn't that blanched beauty, or that way of looking at a man that made him feel taller and stronger; her fairness was faded and dingy by comparison, and she nagged a bit, and the kid had done things to her figure; but she would never have turned her coat for advantage as this cheap little blonde bitch had done. More likely to get herself into hot water by telling the conquerors in the street exactly what she thought of them. And yet the eyes of Eliane, copper-red and wild with joy and alarm, looked straightly at him through Nancy's eyes, and would not waver nor turn aside. He was glad when Miriam came, and he could hope for movement again, and danger, and rest from too much of thought.

The light was failing by then, and though the rain had ceased the mist was closing in. Miriam closed the door quietly, and looked out from the window upon the murky green light under the trees. She was not displeased; the weather at least had befriended them.

"So far, good! You had no trouble? You met no one?" She took off her dark raincoat, and shook the moisture from it in a flashing shower. Nothing else in the room was bright. They looked at each other with shadowy faces in which only the lines of the bones stood white.

"We met a German soldier," said Tommy, in a flat voice. "But it was all right; he wasn't interested in us—he had a girl with him."

Miriam's brows drew into a dark line. "You are sure he paid no attention to you? The girl—did she know you? Did she look closely at you?"

"No," he lied tranquilly. "She was just out with a man. We weren't smart enough for her, anyway." He wondered in his mind, even as he said it, whether there was not wit enough in Eliane to betray him, after all; the allaying look for decoy, and then the death-blow; but even in his rage against her he rejected the thought. She was not the kind of girl to hate what she had injured; even her treachery had a sort of tragic candour about it. "You made it in good time." he said.

"Yes, we were fortunate. There was no one in the lane. From the orchard here we did not meet a soul. It was well begun. Let us see it as well ended." She turned upon Jim; the suddenness of her movements was startling now, and her face in the twilight had flowered into beauty, wide-eyed and aware. "Listen, this is the last halt. When it is a little darker we go, and after this we do not speak again together, except it may be a few words, and in a whisper. You understand what you have to do? You have the maps? And the food? And the guns?" They had them all. She felt at the butt of Brian Ridley's revolver through Jim's pocket. "Do not forget, they are dangerous to you, these. Do not be taken with them still upon you. If the crash comes, either kill your enemies with them or throw them away. They will be made an excuse to kill you otherwise. Remember you are not wearing khaki, there is nothing to give you the rights of soldiers except your identity-discs and pay-books; and if you continue in arms I do not think these will protect you very far." She stopped, seeing how Jim looked at her; the grave, intent look he had was a thing she had cherished in him. "Is it then that I talk to no purpose?" she said, with a sigh. "You do not listen to me."

"Yes, I was listening. We know what we're up against, all right. I said that once before, didn't I? Well, it's nearer being true this time. We know where we're going, and what we have to do. We've been over the ground with you a dozen or more times, and we've got a good map, and enough food to keep us going until we hit the presbytery at Perné. I only wish we could skip the first day or two, but it'll soon pass. You'll be happier when we're gone."

"It does not sound tactful," she said, with a wry smile, "but it is true."

"You know what I mean. We've been an awful worry to you. Sometimes I was sorry we ever let you do it."

"You would not take away from me the only satisfaction I have," she said. "Let us not talk of it, now, it is too late. There remains so little time. Another half-hour, and we must go."

"I wish you'd go back," said Jim, more abruptly than he had meant to say it. "I mean, I don't like you being in it at this stage. There's no need for you to wait, and it's mad to walk into risks you don't have to take. I'd be a lot easier in my mind if you were sitting quietly at home. Haven't you done more than enough for us already?"

She looked back at him gravely, and pondered in her mind how strange it was that she should arouse in him this instinct for protection; she was thirty-one, and looked older, and had left her beauty and feminity somewhere behind her among the graves of the martyrs in Prague. Even Jim thought of her as something between a mother and a male friend; and yet he was more concerned for her than he was for himself, even to death. It was an unfailing joy and refreshment to her, however she put it aside, that he should be so filled with care on her account; for as often as she looked at him she was reminded that there still were many young men such as he, who had gratitude and friendship in their natures. She said, not troubling that he would hear and would not understand:

"Yes, I have done something for all the world. I am quite satisfied." It was not everyone, after all, who had the opportunity of putting back two soldiers into the battle. "I will come with you through the wood," she said. "There is the right place to cross the stream; it is deep in parts, and your friend must not get wet feet so soon, or you will have trouble with him again. And then you will have to cross the railway track, and there are guards along the cutting, so it will be well if I see you safely across; but after that I promise you I will turn back. From the railway I can give you no help. If we had had more time I know we could have made a contact somewhere between, but that cannot be helped now. After Perné, it will be different. Monsieur le Curé is more practised than I at this sort of thing. Doctor Vauban says he has already smuggled away more than one straggler. I wish you were already in his hands."

"We shall be all right. We shall do fine. Thanks to you!"

She wanted no thanks. It put the suggestion of a price upon what was priceless. To avert it she turned back to the window, where the moist green dusk clung to the glass like wet silk, and the last of the daylight swayed with the branches and dripped with the limpid water from the eaves. "We chose the day well," she said. "They will none of them trouble to question two chance-met peasants on a night like this, without a general alarm; and there has been no supicion of an alarm. Remember what I have told you about the roads. Do not attempt to use them. I know it would be quicker, I know there will still be French traffic upon them; but where the roads are, there the Germans will be also, and they will ask more questions of those who ride them than of those who walk. Stay in the open country, and keep away from the towns; and do not talk more than you can help even when you must talk at all. I would say travel only at night, but that way it would be too easy to lose your bearings. There must still be many wanderers in the lanes. Some of them are returning home, they say. Why should you be noticed more than others?''

Home was a strange word to use, she thought, for that captivity. Even where the walls and the roof remained the spirit had died.

"You said my French had improved a lot," said Jim, smiling. He had practised it steadily upon Simone and the doctor for the past three weeks, for there had been nothing else to do with his time, apart from helping to look after Tommy. Stock phrases, but he could be a laconic sort of Frenchman, couldn't he? There were some who talked remarkably little.

"It is good enough for Germans who know little French themselves, yes, but not for Frenchmen," she warned, buttoning her raincoat about her again. It was now so nearly dark that he could just see how she smiled.

"Frenchmen wouldn't give us away, anyhow."

"You are still very young." They knew each other so much better now that she could say it in English, and need not turn her face away. "Trust no one, I beg you. It is easy to take your stand on one side of a rigid line in theory; but in practice the line wavers, and you are puzzled to know where you belong. It is not wise nor kind to burden bewildered and desperate people with a confidence which can be sold."

Tommy said, like an impatient child hedged with grown-ups: "Can't we go? It's practically dark. We want to get well away to-night." But the truth was that he could no longer bear to sit inactive, watching Eliane recede from him and return to torment him again, constantly, without pause or alleviation. If he could get moving, perhaps she would leave him alone.

"Yes, it is time. Come, then! Jean, when we are gone, lock the door after us and go to bed. You have seen no one; you know nothing."

The old man opened the door a crack and looked out. There was no sound but the soft shuddering of the leaves under a weight of rain, and the rustle of the grass, rhythmic and monotonous, as heavy drops fell from the branches.

"There is not a soul out. There will be no questions. But I

have seen no one, and I know nothing. I am good at that. They will get nothing out of me."

"Good! Keep close to me—we have a strip of open ground to cross, and then the trees. A moment only—now!"

She moved with an extraordinary suddenness and silence, slipping through the scarcely opened door and across the narrow belt of grass like a shadow, and melting into the green darkness of the trees. They followed her as adroitly as they could, though the pace she set was never an easy one. From then until the moment before they parted, there was no word spoken. She did not let them lag too far behind, so that at any time, if she heard a movement or a sound, a backward touch of her hand would find Jim's arm and bring them up standing. Twice she halted them so in the green heart of the wood; on the first occasion a man went by on the path, perhaps ten yards from where they stood invisible. There was no secrecy in his going; he was drunk, though not very drunk; he clattered his feet upon the stones where the soil was thin, and when he was only a few yards past them, he sang. He sang: "La Marseillaise", but with new and unrepeatable words, and in the accents of Alsace. Miriam was glad her companions could not understand the words, though the manner of singing was revealing enough. She thought grimly: "My friend, you too will be found dead if you go through Boissy woods alone at night singing that song."

When he was gone, they pressed onward, crossing the path at an oblique angle; and above the slight drop to the bed of the stream she stopped them again. There was a faint sound ahead, a soft slithering run and a splash; another second, and Jim knew it, and felt by her relieved sigh that Miriam knew it too. The otters, at least, were still free to play under the banks of French streams, if the people were in chains. When they came down to the edge of the water, in a spot where the undergrowth was thick and heavy with rain, they could see the long polished clay slide tucked under the bushes, glistening pallidly with its own lambent light. The brook ran broad and steady here, and a fallen tree, ridged with moss, spanned it neatly; a tree lost in its youth by a cave-in of the overhanging bank. It was so slight that it swayed even under Miriam's weight as she walked across, and Jim, with doubts of whether it would bear him, measured the span of it and took it at a light-footed run. It was like running along a slack wire, but the distance was short, and his sense of balance had always been good, so that he dropped safely into the grass beside Miriam. Tommy followed more cautiously, but then Tommy's weight was less. At the last moment he missed his footing, and had to jump for the bank, and a stick cracked under his feet like a pistol-shot. Miriam's hand closed sharply upon his arm, and they all three stood for a moment with senses strained, listening for some answering sound of voice or movement; but the woods were still. The drunken soldier from Alsace was already out of earshot, and no other foot stirred in the grasses. They had the night to themselves.

The rest of the way through the wood was a long, irregular climb through spongy deeps of leaf-mould, with the trees gradually thinning ahead of them, so that the line of saffron light along the edge of the world shone upon them pallidly between the branches. They came out upon a glazed highway, and had to wait for a quarter of an hour or more before it was safe to cross it, for even in the dark the lorries were still thick on the road south-westward. During that pause, while they stood motionless among the bushes, the light perceptibly left the earth. The grey-green mist closed down fully from the sky, thinning the stormy yellow skyline until it was no greater than a golden hair, and finally quenching it altogether. Jim heard Miriam sigh, and knew how she welcomed the darkness. Until then he had felt no fear, only a sort of excitement that gripped him by the pit of the stomach when he tried to think ahead; but suddenly his mind made strange contact with Miriam's mind, and he was afraid. It was all the stranger because she was not afraid, unless perhaps for them; for herself she had finished with hoping and fearing. She lived as she must, acting according to her nature, with nothing to lose but a life, and nothing to gain but the satisfying of her heart. They had so much to cling to, family, home, love, youth and the future; they were hampered by their goods, and tied down to their ambitions. She was erect and complete; within herself she carried her world. Even so poor and even so full of possessions was the Christian church, perhaps, before it acquired power and imprisoned itself in property. For Miriam carried in herself not only this world, but also her religion, and the world to come. In the green and amorphous night, while her face was only a lighter shadow among shadows, and he followed her movements rather by sound than by sight, he saw this very clearly, and it was his first true glimpse of her. That was why he was afraid. Was there still so much more of human pain, and passion, and cruelty that he had not seen? She was still young, there were not so many years between them. Over what white-hot plough-shares do you walk into that perfection of integrity?

Her fingers, wet and cold, touched his wrist, and she slipped out of the shelter of the trees and across the road, drawing him after her. They were barely over and out into the wet field beyond, when another heavy lorry passed behind them. They went with less caution and more speed here, where it was more than improbable they would meet a soul, unless it were another human creature in flight or in hiding like themselves. The ground levelled, and they crossed wide fields of beet and turnips, running between the hoed rows through thin, slippery clay mud that splashed above their ankles. But for Miriam they could not have made nor kept such a speed; but she was upon ground she knew like the palm of her hand, and they trusted her utterly. When she ran, holding fast to the hand of the nearer man, they ran blindly after·her, following close in her steps; and when she checked, the tightening of her fingers was enough to stop them in an instant. If she had walked into hell with them they would have followed her, trusting her to know the way through and bring them out safely at the other side.

They travelled so for longer than they realised, and having emerged upon a narrow lane, scarcely wide enough for a cart to clear the hedges, they ventured to stay in the open road for a while, and so saved themselves a long detour. They walked this stretch demurely, as bona fide travellers should, but they met no one. Ahead of them a train passed, the muffled noise of it drawn across the darkness in a tenuous thread of sound; they were nearing the cutting.

The ground fell away suddenly before their feet, steeply through a heavy fringe of trees and over broken, tussocky grass and stretches of rosebay willowherb to the metals. They threaded the trees cautiously, slowed now to a stealthy walk; and not far from the gravel edge of the track she halted them, and waited. Their eyes were used to the murky darkness by now, and vague but significant outlines lifted out of the night, the silver, snaky double line of the nearer metals, the loom of the bank opposite, lumpy here and there with hushes and low trees. They stood close together, motionless, Miriam leaning forward a little, with a restraining hand spread backward against Jim's shoulder, listening to the advancing tread of heavy feet along the gravel at the side of the track. Presently they saw him through the shivering wet leaves, a mere shape of grey uniform, streaming oilskin and helmet, with a rifle slung upon his shoulder; a young man by his walk, big, with the hint of a swagger even here, alone in the night and the rain. He passed them close, and they heard him whistling cheerfully between his teeth, out of tune, out of any tune they could name, before he passed on steadily and was dissolved into the grey gossamer air.

Jim turned and looked at Miriam, closely, fixing all his senses upon her; and answering the question he had not asked, she shook her head. "Not yet!" she said, her lips framing the words soundlessly, and put out her wet hands and took him by the arms, drawing him breast to breast with her, as once she had done in the loft over the stables at Boissy. The pacing sentry was away in the deadening mist, lost to sight and sound up the line. She had perhaps a full minute, perhaps not so long, for her last passionate instructions and all her farewells; and suddenly it was as if she put her hands into the last living place in her heart, and deliberately tore it. When he was gone, there would be nothing, no one left to keep the woman Miriam in mind.

Her lips close to his ear, she said in that quick, almost soundless voice: "He will come back. After he passes again I shall leave you. Wait for five minutes after I go—fully five. You understand? Then run across the track into those bushes opposite, and climb the bank quickly. Down the fields from there is the canal, and there are trees lining it for a long way. Keep in that belt of trees and you cannot lose your way."

"I know," he said in a whisper. "I remember."

"But give me five minutes to get clear. He will not turn back, and unless you make very much noise, he will not hear you. Downhill the track winds; and sound will not carry to-night."

"We shall manage all right," he said.

She turned her head for a moment, and with a swift gesture caught at Tommy's hand, but holding fast all the time to Jim's arm, that at the end she might sustain herself with the touch of them both. "God bless you! You will come back to Boissy one day. We shall wait for you."

She clung to them both. Her eyes were wide and luminous, and her face was young, smooth as a girl's in the dimness under the trees. When they would have spoken to her there was nothing to say, no words of any meaning; and already the sentry's step was clear in the gravel, drawing nearer upon his return journey down the line, and she was motioning them to stillness and silence. Never with their lips did either of them say to her that he would never forget her, that to her he owed not only his life but the impetus that made him wish to continue living, the power that made it impossible he should cease from fighting. Only their eyes, fixed upon her with agonised intensity, spoke what was in their minds, and she heard it, and was at once humbled and soothed and elated, filled with astonished gratitude and the desire to serve them more recklessly; for such a look as that is not easily repaid. While the German sentry strolled past them and away again, she stood so in the glow of her ultimate happiness, the most unexpected, the most perfect she had ever known. And when he was gone, suddenly she flung an arm about Jim's neck, and drew his face down to hers, and held him so for a moment against her cheek, feeling his arms tighten round her and strain her body to his; as if the same wave had swept over them both and carried away all the barriers of reserve and usage and restraint from between them, and left them trembling together in the night, sustaining each other against a world of enmity and despair and danger and sorrow; they two, little and lonely and afraid, but erect, but unbroken. Afterwards he could never remember that moment without wonder, and the wonder grew with time. How much of his life flowed into it and was lost? How much of her spirit flowed out of the moment into him, and transmuted him? For he was never quite the same man again; never again so simple, and empty, and small, never again so young, never so easily cheered nor so lightly disheartened. Her heart beat against him for an instant only, and then she slipped out of his arms and was gone like a wraith between the trees; but there was something of her she did not take away.

When she was sure that she was out of sight and sound of them she climbed the bank of the cutting until she was clear of the bushes, and began to run, heading down the track. She was ahead of the sentry as he whistled and tramped his way round the curve of the line; and when he met his friend and halted gratefully for a word with him, Miriam was in the bushes high on the slope above them. By then the five minutes she had demanded was over, and she had made of the brief pause a very different use from the one in which she had led her friends to believe. The crest of the slope was behind her, a short and easy climb; she looked over her shoulder, and measured the distance she had to run, and the quality of the cover she could reach most speedily, and marvelled at her own coolness now that the pinch was come. She saw nothing ahead, nothing behind, only the two glistening grey men, foreshortened into steel helmets and boots and little besides, talking there on the edge of the track below her; and she did not take her eyes from them as she dropped to her knees and groped through the sparse, sodden grass for small stones, prising them out of the hard ground with her nails. The sentries would not linger very long; they were dutiful creatures after their fashion, these soldiers of the Reich, they would do the job they had been given to do, however dull, however discomforting, however bestial. Why not? They had not the fertility of mind to move the opposite way, and they could adjust themselves to enjoy what they knew they must perform. A curious gift, she had found it; it made them happy and it made them formidable, until they were brought up short against the flexibility and strength of free minds; and then they were at a loss, for that very quality in themselves turned against them and destroyed them.

She waited until they turned to resume their patrol up and down the line, and then she began to throw her stones, not full out into the track, but into the grass below her, level perhaps with their heads, for the bank was steep. The first fell short and softly and was not noticed, and she knew an instant of fear lest they should truly separate, and the one of them return to surprise Tommy and Jim as they raced up the opposite slope. She threw again, and this time the man who was marching up the line plainly heard the hiss of the disturbed grass, and stopped abruptly, jerking back his head and swinging his rifle forward with appalling dexterity. He called back to his companion, who returned at a run, and they stood close together staring up the bank.

Miriam heard herself breathing long and steadily, as a woman does who wishes to hold back laughter or tears. She stood suddenly upright, full in their sight, and the spring of her rising shook the bushes as if with a weeping shudder, and showers of heavy drops fell over the skirt of her raincoat and her pulped shoes. She heard the two men cry out, not loudly, two clipped exclamations lost in an instant, scarcely noticed at all for the beating of her heart. She saw the younger one throw up his rifle, and the crack of the shot followed her as she turned and ran headlong up the slope. She knew they would follow; she meant them to follow; there were a dozen places on the road home where she could lose them at will, even one or two where with luck she might drown them. She ran like a deer, in long, leaping steps, over the crest of the cutting, and across the field, and into the thin coppices along the heathy waste, where she was lost among the treee-trunks silvered with moisture, a creature swift and invisible. Once she paused for a moment, and heard the clatter of their boots as they crossed the lane in pursuit of her. Since she was well ahead, and had the friendly woods before her, she gave them another clue, snapping the dry dead branch of a tree in her hands before she ran on, for it was no part of her plan that the pursuit should grow discouraged and give up too soon. Another shot echoed the sharp snap of the wood. She felt a small, inconsiderable pain cross the soft flesh of her forearm, no sharper than the scratching of a bramble; and presently blood began to trickle into the palm of her hand and grow sticky and hot between her fingers. "This is too near," she thought. "I must lose them before they kill me."

In the wood, therefore, where every leaf and every fold of ground was on her side, she exerted herself to shake them off, and found it easy. The tree by which she crossed the stream was not known to them, and she was too far ahead of them for her crossing to be heard. By the time she emerged behind her own orchards, circling the nearer houses of the village, she knew that she had shaken off the enemy. As for the English fugitives, they were in God's hands; but at least they were safely across the railway line and well upon their way.

Miriam was now very tired, and down her left arm the blood was congealing in thin, stiff streams. She went through the wet green orchard and the looted garden like a sleep-walker, eased of the necessity for speed or thought or any subtlety. It was all over. They were gone. There was a deadness about it. What more could one do? There might be others; or failing friends to be helped, there were still enemies to be destroyed. It was not the end of living, this night; only reaction and weariness made her see it so.

She eased open the scullery door, and closed and fastened it behind her with deliberate care, and for a moment leaned against it with a sigh, grateful at least for her life, for after all it is not a desirable thing to die in the dark, and alone. Then she crossed to the kitchen door, and opened it, and halted upon the threshold.

The room was very bright and quiet and orderly, from the

glowing fire to the polished china in the Sèvres cabinet. It was too quiet; the hush was conscious and breathless, as if someone had died; and Simone's old face, staring at her across the scrubbed white table, was motionless and shocked as if she had watched the death. Spread out upon the table, on the tarpaulin in which they had recently been wrapped, were a pair of boots crusted with mud, and two neat piles of torn and blood-soiled khaki. In the arm-chair by the fire the scarred man sat peacefully smiling, with Sarka asleep at his feet.

8

"You are late, Madame Lozelle," said the scarred man. "I have been waiting a long time." And his voice was as soft as a sigh. He was happy now; he was satisfied; he knew what she had been doing. Possibly he even believed he could undo what she had done. Miriam smiled; it was not so simple as that, for him at least. For her there existed now no problem at all; it was only a question of endurance, and she was by nature a stubborn woman. Simone knew nothing and could tell nothing, except that two English soldiers had come and gone, which the enemy already knew very well. If he had been as wise as he was subtle he would have known that Sarka could be held over her as a threat of the greatest possible effectiveness; but he was not himself a man who would allow himself to be tortured through a dog, and he would not suspect the flaw in her unless she gave him some sign of it. She had no qualms on that score. She was quite sure of herself and her own deftness. It was too late to attempt to conceal the state of her shoes or her coat, or the wound in her arm. She stripped off the mackintosh and hung it up behind the door, and kicked off her shoes before she went forward to the hearth.

"You are hurt," he said, in that dulcet voice of his.

"Yes; but so far only slightly," she said. "I shall not die from this." She turned her arm to let him see the shallow furrow, fringed with fronds of blood. "It is nothing, but if you will let Simone dress it for me it will offend your eyes less. I suppose you are not afraid to let her out of your sight? You cannot be alone here."

"You are intelligent if not wise," said the scarred man gently. "No, I am not alone here. There are four of my men about the house." He turned his head, and looked at the old woman, who had not moved, and seemed not even to breathe; only her eyes, flickering from her mistress to the enemy and back again, were tormentedly alive. "Well, Madame Lacasse? What are you waiting for? Did you not hear what Madame said?"

Simone stood, though her legs would scarcely carry her, and took a few uncertain steps forward, and stood staring at Miriam's arm. Miriam sat down in the rocking-chair opposite to the Gestapo man. By chance her foot brushed Sarka's head, and the spaniel thumped the floor with a drowsy tail, and nuzzled her mistress's instep. Miriam, bereft now of all other loves, knew a moment of longing to have the warm and adoring body in her arms again, the pulsing throat hot upon her shoulder. She need only say her name, and the bitch would come climbing against her heart; an easy moment of comfort, almost of happiness. For what else are we born but to love and be loved? No, that was a fatal weakening, one she could not afford. She had already failed Sarka; there was no time for more than a partial amend. "Oh, Sarka!" she thought, with a last spasm of agony behind the indifference of her face, "my poor Sarka, who will have the courage to kill you now?"

She looked up at Simone, and her eyes were brilliantly hard. "Go! What are you waiting for? And take the dog away with you. How many times have I told you not to bring her into the kitchen?"

"I am sorry," said poor Simone, too confused to understand or protest, "I am sorry." She went forward and gathered the small black body into her arms. "She was company," she said sadly, "I was afraid by myself." And she carried Sarka away with her, out of the room, out of the tragedy; but Miriam would have preferred that she should have been carried thus gently out of the world. She was small, loving, vulnerable; it was no world for her.

"You see," said the scarred man, suddenly leaning forward in his chair, "you cannot work against us and escape hurt."

"I had not expected to," said Miriam.

"At this moment you are as good as under arrest. You understand that?"

"Yes, I understand it."

"Upon a capital charge."

"I understand that, too."

"You are being very foolish. You have intelligence, you have real abilities, and yet you choose to expend them upon a course which cannot obtain you anything and may certainly lose you all. From the first time that I saw you, Madame Lozelle, I recognised that you had something to hide. I knew you lied consistently, with your eyes wide open to danger. Until to-night I did not know what it was you hid, I did not know which of your lies were true, and which were lies. And all this was for two men who would have been safe and well-doctored as our prisoners! Your life against their imprisonment? Not even Frenchmen? I tell you frankly, I do not understand you."

"It is not necessary that you should," she said. "You are not concerned with the workings of my mind. You see I can bleed."

"I would have preferred that you should co-operate," he said equably. "You have much to gain and little to lose. Listen to me, Madame Lozelle. I ask you, and I shall not ask you in these terms again, to do for yourself the little thing which will keep you safe even after this night's work. Give me full details of the owners of those uniforms, their appearance, their route, their plans, the time at which they set out. Tell me all this, and I will forget that it was you who sheltered them. You shall go free. I swear it."

Miriam folded her hands in her lap, and looked back at him with her tired and tranquil eyes. It was all curiously easy and smooth, not at all like the beginning of martyrdom either sudden or slow; and yet no ghost of hope deceived her. She knew she was a dead woman. What of it? Was not Georges dead before her, and Chicot, and Michel Peyron? There was good company among the dead.

"You want to make use of me," she said slowly, and smiled. "No, monsieur, I have lived through too much to turn decoy for you now. If I gave you this first thing you demand of me, I should have to go on co-operating, should I not, under the threat of death? I should live and do infamous things only to die in the end as miserably as I can possibly die now. No, I will tell you nothing. I do not build with so much care in order to knock down again what I have built."

"You are a remarkable woman," said the scarred man reflectively. "I appreciate you. I do not blame you. But that will not keep me from destroying you if I find you obstructive."

"I know it."

"It will not even make me reluctant to destroy you. Do not promise yourself any relenting in me, Madame Lozelle."

"I am not so foolish. I expect nothing. But I advise you to expect as little from me."

"We have resources of which even you know nothing," he said, with the thin smile which made his scars stand out in high white lights against the weathered brown of his face.

"So have I," said Miriam.

He had told no more than the truth. He would use all the arts of Nazi persuasion on her without the slightest compunction, not because he cared a button for Party ideology or military prestige, not because he believed for a moment in the greater Reich or the New Order, not even because she had dared to withstand him. He would torture her to extract information, he would kill her for withholding it, because the tortuous course of his fortunes, opportunist and cynical in every step, marched for the moment with the march of Nazi Germany, and in advancing one he advanced the other. He had no strong feelings towards her; he did not hate nor admire her, and he was incapable of anger or pity towards her. That was his strength; hers was in the quietness she cradled now within her, a living thing that grew in her body even as she looked at him, a serenity that grew like a child, until every nerve and particle of her being was absorbed into this miraculous womb of peace. She felt nothing but exaltation; fear was a long way behind her. She knew she would suffer, but she knew it gently and patiently, as old men know they will die, and it did not trouble her at all. It was familiar; it was like looking back sanely upon something once mysterious and horrible, like adolescence seen from maturity. She had outgrown all that.

Simone came in with a bowl of water, and dressings, and knelt on the rug at Miriam's feet and began to bathe her arm. Looking on from what seemed an infinite distance, Miriam thought: "How foolish all this is. Why let her repair me, when I am so soon to be altogether broken?" Yet he rose quietly from his chair, and strolled about the room while the old woman worked, humming to himself, and lingering before the Sèvres cabinet to admire the shining china, as if he had unlimited time to spare. She supposed that already he had men out combing the countryside for the fugitives, and considered that their capture was only a matter of time. Or perhaps the apprehension of the traitress was to him of more strategic importance than the taking of two prisoners-of-war. He was capable of turning her into excellent personal capital, and who was she to blame him?

He turned his head and met her calm, incurious eyes fixed upon him over the old woman's head. It was still true that he did not understand her. If she had looked at him with any hate or defiance, it would have been easier, but the eyes were so far from either that she might have been looking on from another world, she who had lied to him with so guileful a face not ten days earlier. It was a transfiguration. All the urgency of deceit and subtlety was gone out of her; she had made use of these only because she must, and now they were happily laid aside, and her empty hands folded upon quietness. He thought as he looked at her: "We cannot let her die publicly. It would be to give them another martyr. *They must not see her!*" From the tranquillity of one such face, he knew, more fires are lit than from all the incandescent rage of a Passionaria. And yet perhaps she could be marred before they brought her into the public eye for execution. The symmetry of her face once broken, the clarity of her eyes smudged with blood, and she would at best rouse only pity and fear and disgust in the hearts of those who saw her die. So he thought, knowing that pity is at best only a secondary sort of inspiration, not given to breaking tyrannies; and the fate of Miriam Lozelle crystallised in his mind. There was much in the human spirit he did not yet know.

"Are you rested?" he asked.

"I am ready, if Simone will get me some dry shoes." She looked down into the old woman's face and smiled. "Don't look so stricken. It is all right. I have to go away with this officer for a little while, to answer some questions. There is no reason for you to worry about me." No one in the room even pretended to believe it, but to hear her say it, in that gentle, assured voice, was strange comfort.

Simone got to her feet slowly and clumsily, as if she could no longer see what she did, and went out of the room obediently, and brought the shoes and a dark woollen coat.

"Should I also take other things with me for my stay?" asked Miriam, putting on the coat.

"Madame Lacasse may pack them for you, and one of my men shall bring them after you to the Mairie. There is no need to wait."

"Then I am ready," she said, and turned to the door almost with eagerness, or so it seemed to him. She did not seem to see the breaking grief of Simone's face; she only took her by the shoulders and kissed her lightly, as if she were taking leave of her for no more than a few days. The old woman did not move nor speak as they went out from her into the night; it seemed as if the silence they left behind had closed for all time over the house and the farm. Miriam, as the door closed behind her, felt it too. She said, with a gesture towards the byres:

"There is still good stock here, monsieur. Am I permitted to dispose of what is left? Or is my gear automatically confiscated now I am under arrest?"

"What was yours belongs now to the Reich," he said, though he said it as if he cared less than nothing.

"I am sorry," she said, "I should have liked to give something to Simone and Jean. But it does not matter."

As they walked up the muddy yard, she lifted her head and looked up into the sky. A wind had arisen, and the mist was dispersing before it in torn grey drifts, and overhead the clouds swayed like swathes of hair parted and drawn aside from a fixed and starry face. The noises of battle had all receded from Artois. She heard only the moist stirring of trees, a living sound, and the rippling of the wind in the leaves, songs of perpetuity. Her dark hair blew against her cheeks in wet, sweet strands. She was happy. She had outdistanced all that was to come; only her flesh would be aware of pain and mutilation. Already she had Georges in her arms again, she was dead and risen with him, her mouth upon his mouth. Already the departed armies returned gloriously, like the returning Spring, tormented with life and joy; and freedom was renewed upon the world from within, like a passion of flowers breaking over the fields of France. She breathed in the cool, soft air, and it was as if she drew into her heart all the promise of the future of the world.

"You think they will get clean away?" asked the scarred man gently in her ear.

"Yes. I believe they will. I know they will."

"It is a pity," he said, "you should build too securely upon it. If they should come back——"

She looked towards the west, where they were gone, and she made her last prophecy.

"They will come back!" she said.

9

From Perné, south of Agincourt, so small that no one bothered to send a single Nazi soldier to keep it in subjection, a funeral cortège set out in the early morning of the 22nd of June, the day of France's capitulation. The old man in the coffin had been a fisherman for the greater part of his life, until at sixty he settled himself and his small savings with his married daughter in the market garden at Perné. He had wished to be buried with his fathers in the rocky cemetery of the coast village where he was born, and not even the New Order could think of a reason why he should not. The Abbé Tissot had himself trotted timidly along to the nearest German post to obtain a safe conduct for his whole party, all the children and grand-children and devout friends of the deceased; some indifferent protest had been raised about the great number of them, and the little man in the shabby soutane had insisted pathetically that the list of names could not be curtailed even by one; so that in the end, because his frightened but persistent arguments amused them, and he was patently harmless, he got his own way, and the safe conduct was signed and stamped and thrown to him as a crust is thrown to a dog.

The cavalcade that set out from Perné was a long one, for the family of Pierre-Martin Dupuis was large and well-respected. The two adopted relatives from nowhere who appeared mys-teriously among all the legitimate brothers and cousins and nephews just before the journey began were soon lost in the crowd. No one seemed to notice that they were strangers. They were talked across and round and to, caught up in the pro-cession of family piety, as if they had been Dupuis' all their lives. Their stiff black was exactly like the mourning of every other member of the party, and among so many different faces it was difficult to pick out two which were so unlike the rest as to be noticeably un-French. The unanimity with which they were accepted made it clear that their secret was an open one; but partly by the bland and adroit fellowship of the mourners, and partly by their lack of French, they were prevented from expressing either anxiety or thanks on that score. Everything was done for them, smoothly and ably, even to the making of their conversation, and no one would let them worry even about their own lives, much less about the danger they made for others.

They had been just over twenty-four hours at the presbytery of Perné, having arrived in the small hours of the previous morning. The Abbé Tissot spoke no English beyond a few words picked up from the troops passing through; but the details of the case had obviously been passed on to him already by Doctor Vauban, and he had his plans made accordingly. All the fugitives had to do was to go where they were pushed, and do what by ready signs they were instructed to do, and preserve the silence which was almost second nature to them after more than two days of avoiding human company and making no sound. Even when they were alone together in the attic of the presbytery, sharing a make-shift bed, they talked very little. There would be time and leisure to talk later, in England, when the incident was safely over; and then they would be able to speak openly, without this superstitious terror that a word too many exchanged might break their luck and bring the whole extravagant vision of escape falling about their ears. They dared not believe too firmly in it. They ceased from thought, looking neither ahead nor behind, taking each step as it became necessary, holding their breath that the illusion might not be shaken and tear like floating gossamer on an autumn morning. They questioned nothing. If Pierre-Martin's funeral had not provided a means of getting them to the coast, the Abbé would certainly have thought of some other way. He was that kind of man. Slender, shabby, short-sighted, of a more than innocent countenance, he yet seemed to quiver with intense energy in all that he did, like a single-minded child. For him difficulties existed to be, not surmounted, but circumvented. Dangers did not exist; or at least he was unaware of them.

The mourners travelled in old-fashioned open brakes drawn by horses, because apart from the fact that the village had not enough cars to take them all, they were not allowed to use any petrol. It was conveyed, indeed, that they travelled at all only at their own risk, and that no one could guarantee when, if ever, they would get home again. They had a journey of between forty and fifty kilometres before them, with the probability of long halts whenever they touched a main road, and more than a slight chance of still further delays from air-raids; so it was well to set off with the dawn. Even so, it was late in the evening before they came in sight and sound of the sea, and there were times during that infinitely long and wearisome day when it seemed to Jim that the Channel was no true salt water, but only a mirage, receding as they approached it. Several times they were stopped for long periods while German military traffic tore by at high speed, lorry after lorry, limber after limber, tank after tank. Once the sky overhead grew frantic with a tangled fighter combat, but they did not stop for this, nor did they see the end of it. Once, also, a German soldier held them up at a cross-road, and by signs indicated that he wanted to travel some way with them. It was an order, not a request. They took him aboard the very brake which held the two Englishmen, and he elbowed his bulk in between Jim and his neighbour, and settled down and slept, his cap pulled low over his eyes, his head rolling sideways on to Jim's shoulder. He was no trouble, awake or asleep, for he had no French; the only danger he brought in with him was danger to himself, for it would not have been difficult to kill him while he slept; but of this he appeared to be arrogantly unaware. No one had grasped where he wanted to go, so no one knew when to awaken him. He slept until early evening, when the jolting of the wheels over an incredibly rutted by-road shook him awake, and he looked round wildly, clutching at his rifle and stammering out a sudden flood of speech, not a word of which was understood. The mourners looked back at him with faces blank and wary, as if he belonged to a different species. He jumped up abruptly, and pulled at the arm of the man who was driving, making violent signs that he wished to get out. Which he did, and they were rid of him. There were no more such passengers.

After sunset they came to the sea. The road dropped gradually, and in the dusk they saw how the few sparse trees leaned inland among the sand-dunes; and then the smell of the Channel came up to them, and then they saw it for a few moments before they began the descent into the town. A long expanse of brightness in the afterglow, paved with an insubstantial deep golden light, the English sea, the way home. They leaned forward, the two of them, leaned upon the sudden sharp, nostalgic wind that blew upon them from the sea, and the longing for home, entertained for so long unaware, rose in their throats with a desperate intensity. From that moment every delay was like another death. They scarcely saw the small houses and cobbled streets of the village as they drove through, or the few subdued natives who came to greet the Dupuis family, or the haunted faces of the women who passed them hurrying home. They saw only the phosphorescent lipping of the water against the jetty, and the barriers, steel, concrete and human, that stood between them and it. So small a village, and so formidable an erection of barbed-wire and so many Nazi guards to hold its beaches from violation! They would have been happier if they had even known what the next move was to be; but in the business of their own escape they were the only people who went blindfold, so that every turn to left or right seemed to be leading them into a cul-de-sac. They had been urged to trust, and certainly this complete surrendering of their fate into the hands of Miriam and her fellow-patriots had so far brought them to nothing but good; but they were human, and they would have been easier in mind if they had felt less like puppets dangled from the accomplished fingers of Miriam Lozelle, of the Abbé Tissot, of the Dupuis mourners. How if even now the strings should break? Better not think of that possibility.

And the strings did not break. The Abbé reported his whole party at the Mairie of the little town, as he had been instructed to do, and they were checked off one by one against the list of names on the safe conduct, and found innocuous. Several members of the family had already arranged for their night's lodging; those who had not were received readily into the cottages of the town, so that the party dissolved like smoke from the cobbled square, before the very eyes of the German sentries. Jim and Tommy followed the Abbé and the Dupuis elder who was to lodge with him at the presbytery. Pierre-Martin lay in his coffin before the altar of his own old church, and he at least was content with his bed. As for them, they did not know where they were expected to go, nor what would next be done with them; and now that they were no longer two among many, but two of four, they felt too conspicuous and too un-French for comfort, even in the enshrouding night.

In a narrow street, where the overhanging houses seemed to lean inward from the strength of the sea-wind, the Abbé tapped at a door sunk deep into a stone wall, and a man came out and spoke to him, breezily, without any attempt at concealment, one more townsman throwing open his house to the family of Pierre-Martin. It was so dark in the embrasure of the doorway that they could see little of him but a tall, high-shouldered shape and a shock-head, but his voice was young and full and gusty, though not loud. It was as if he knew but could not feel what need there was for stealth, for circumspection, now that the enemy was in the very streets; as if the tide schooled itself to advance discreetly upon its own beaches. The Abbé spoke to him in turn, gently, with gestures towards the two strangers; and in a moment they were inside the threshold, and the door was closing behind them. They had a last glimpse of the little Abbé trotting away placidly, without a glance behind. There was no good-bye, and no thanks. It was done without haste or confusion, as smoothly as if they would indeed meet next day at the grave-side. One more link of the chain which drew them to safety had slipped away out of their hands, and one more link had taken its place. At Compiégne they believed the war was over; yet here, and surely not here alone, the battle passed from hand to hand, silently, unceasingly, and the echo of the name of liberty was prolonged to the edge of the sea, and beyond. Between the soldiers of that army no word of gratitude or leave-taking was needed; no distance divided them, and the things they did were done not for one another but for an idea they shared, an idea which contained them all, like the air they breathed, and the sky that covered them. To utter thanks was to appropriate to oneself services done to the world; but at the time they did not see it so, and the rustle of the Abbé's soutane as he departed unthanked was a reproach in their ears.

From the darkness of the porch they were drawn forward through a second door into a small living-room lit by a smelly oil-lamp; and by this inadequate light they saw the fisherman André Lenormand, who was to be their companion on the last stage of their journey. A young man of perhaps thirty, with a weathered mahogany face as deeply graven as the rocks along the shore, and bright blue eyes, their vivid colour startling under his dark brows. His face was set in wrinkles which were chiefly of laughter; even the lines of his bones laughed, but there was a high, intolerant temper in them, too. It was easy to see why such a man must go, at all costs, at any cost, rather than stay here in this ghost of a town and try to adjust himself to the new mode of life under the Germans. To stay was to die as surely as smoke rises. The first self-conscious Nazi adolescent who tried to elbow him off the pavement would himself be shouldered into the gutter; the second might not live to tell the tale. Nor would André live long. No, he knew himself, he knew he had to get out while there was still time. Already he had a small bundle of food and valuables rolled up ready for departure, roped tightly together in an old tarpaulin coat. He kicked it aside gently to let them come to the stove, for the dark little room was curiously cold.

"You sit," he said. "Hours yet. We go when the moon sets."

"It won't be safe till then?" asked Tommy, and his face sharpened with desire. Every moment that divided him from home was like another lifetime lost; all along, ever since the night they had left Boissy, that fire had burned in him, until now there seemed little of him it had not consumed.

"Safe?" André lifted his shoulders. "What is safe? But we give ourselves every chance." He sat down, and looked them over with frank curiosity. "You surprised I speak good English, eh?" He was obviously proud of it, and indeed it was quite unexpected; and yet why should it be found surprising? He was a deep-sea fisherman, and the Channel was narrow. No doubt there were English coastal waters he knew like his own. "Very useful I should know English," he said. "Pretty soon I need it. Look, I tell you—Ten days I take to provision my boat, and to-night I fix to go; but better if I have companions, no? Then *Monsieur l'Abbé*, he send me word that you come with me. That is well for us all. *C'est le bon Dieu qui nous garde.*"

"It's to-night, then?" said Tommy insistently. "We don't have to wait no longer?"

"At moon-set. It will be five, six hours. We dare not move until the dark comes; we have the dunes to cross."

"Where is this boat, then?" asked Jim.

"In a cave in a rock island, a little up the coast. I took it and hid it there when we heard *they* were nearing the town."

"And you've been there since?"

"Three—four times, yes. There are things you must have in a boat."

"What if you've been seen? Suppose they've found the boat? Suppose they know about the cave?"

"Why should they? Nothing has been touched. The island is not an island when the tide is low, it is a bare rock at the end of a sand-bar. Also that is the only time you can enter the cave without diving. There is nothing there, no one lives there, nothing grows. What do they want with it? No, they know nothing of it. No good for guns, no people, no minerals, no fish—they do not want it. Those people, they do not see what they do not want." There was something in that, Jim thought. They had a way of fixing their eyes upon the thing they did want, and fighting their way to it, tooth and claw; there should surely be some blind spots at the edges of that fanatic vision.

"You be easy," advised André calmly. "I get you home. I make coffee now. You like to eat, maybe. Maybe you sleep a few hours, eh? Next time we sleep in England."

He brought them what was left in the house; it was not much, crusty cottage-baked bread, and cheese, and heavily-sweetened coffee, but it was more than welcome, for they had eaten nothing since leaving Perné at dawn. André was handy and silent about his house, as most lonely men are. He gave them not only food, but clothes for the journey, too, old, darned jerseys as thick as frieze, and oilskins, and even sea-boots for Jim, who was much of his own size; and the feet of several pairs of old stockings to wear over their boots as a measure against noise.

"What will you do in England?" asked Jim, offering the last of his last packet of cigarettes. Miriam had given them to him the day they left Boissy.

"Make ready to come back to France," said André, and all the lines of his face flamed into grim laughter. "When they go away in boats from the Flanders coast, your people, many of *us* go with them. They say French ships also have sailed to ports in England. Is it that they go to settle there? I think not. They go that they may make ready to come again. There will be room for André Lenormand among the seamen of France. One day they will need men who know this coast as I know it."

It was a child's faith, perhaps, but it was faith, and it was heartening. It caught them in the old contagion, and they took into their minds hopes they had been afraid to entertain. The three of them sat down together and smoked, and talked as only strangers can talk, congenial strangers whose paths touch and part without deflecting each other. They talked of their homes, of their jobs, of what living had been to them before the Germans came, and what it would be again some day, when the Germans were gone. The sea was near to them, and the sea was almost England, so that hope did not seem so remote and fragile a thing as when they saw it from the inland desolation of Boissy-en-Fougères. When the time came for them to set out on the last stage of the adventure, they were in the right mood for it. It seemed that the dreamlike quality had come back into their affairs, that a charm was on them, and nothing could go wrong.

Nothing did go wrong. They left the house and threaded the most devious streets of the little town through a darkness that clung like velvet. They made no sound. It was like being disembodied. In the sand-dunes there were gun emplacements and sentries along the rims of the beaches, but André had their positions by heart, and knew how to find his way through them. The sighing sound of the receding tide was small, but great enough to break the tension of the night's stillness. The sandbar, narrow even at the tide's lowest ebb, and taken step by step in the dark, was a schoolboy's thrill. So was the four-foot mouth of the tiny cave, and the boat swinging and creaking in the ebb, and the cautious stealth of the oars dipping in the first strokes, feeling for silence through the water, shaking away the phosphorescent lips of the ripples that there might be no light from their progress as there was no sound. It was all unreal. It was the kind of thing you could yarn about over a pub fire afterwards, and not be believed, or at best not more than half-believed. It was the only thing, the only thing since the whirlwind began, that they could contemplate telling to anyone; because the rest was real, but this was out of a thriller, the conventional kind, where the hero is the hero, and nothing can go wrong for him.

"It isn't this easy," thought Jim, sliding his oars into the dark water. "It can't be this easy." And yet they had done it. They were there, going out with the ebbing tide, receding steadily and invisibly from the dangerous coast, waiting only for a safer distance before they ventured to use the motor and set off at speed for home. Even in this fate was on their side, for before they were more than half an hour out from shore, the gathering hum of aircraft approached them from over France, the familiar thrumming crescendo of massed bombers heading across the Channel. It made the two Englishmen raise their heads in a wild disquiet, searching the darkness for the invisible source of that sound, the flight of the enemy crossing the sky towards England. André did not even look up; the only impression the noise made upon him was a very practical one; as it grew in volume he shipped his oars, motioning Jim to do the same, and turned eagerly to the engine, which leaped to life under his hands after a momentary hesitation, and tore them away from the receding shore at a moderate speed. The noise of it was lost under the greater noise from overhead. André sat back and wiped his hands on a piece of oily cotton-waste, well content. The wake they left was bright and thin and curved, like an osprey feather; but it would never be seen from the beaches through such a darkness. In a while, too, the covering noise would out-distance them, and perhaps they would have to withdraw again into the slow silence of the oars; but every yard gained was an added defence. He felt the rigidity of his companions, though he could not see the expression of their faces.

"That?" he said simply. "That goes on all the time. In the town we always used to hear them pass over."

"What, by day as well?" asked Jim.

"Night and day."

"How long has it been like that?"

"Seven—ten days, maybe."

They looked at each other, appalled, straining after vision across the width of the boat.

"My God!" said Tommy blankly, "what can there be left?

It wasn't such a bloody big place to start with. It must be flat."

"I don't know," said Jim. "I don't know." It seemed to him that once the shock of finding themselves vulnerable was over, people and countries could survive almost anything. Besides, he had changed. He no longer believed in easy victory or easy defeat; the one was as improbable, as much of a chimera, as the other. Nor did it seem to him that the maximum of destruction was the maximum of disaster. At the thought of England being turned into another Belgium his innards contracted and froze; but that would not be the finish of England. There was more to it than that, by a long way. And for his comfort, no matter how great a mess the bombers could make of it, at least there was this blessed bit of a ditch to keep the tanks out. "Let's get back," he said, "let's see, before we start going into mourning. I don't believe anything till I see it. I don't believe they can do so much as they think."

Tommy, turning up the collar of his coat against the spray they were taking aboard, laughed; a queer sound, without merriment, famished and bitter. "And after all you've seen 'em do?"

"Yes, after all I've seen 'em do. I've seen what they can't do, too. Besides, we've got an air force, too, if it comes to that."

"Have we? I haven't seen enough of that to believe in it yet." He turned abruptly upon André. "How soon do you reckon we shall reach England? How long does it take, this trip?"

"We are a slow boat. But by daylight we should be nearing the coast. It may be I have not kept as true a course as I would wish, but we shall not be long delayed beyond daylight if all goes well."

"That's another thing I believe in when I see it," said Tommy, very quietly, "the English coast." But with this no one quarrelled, for no one heard it. It was lost in the continuous rhythmic hiss of the waves against their bows, and the long, bubbling caress along the length of the boat, for the shrouding noise of the bombers and their escort was already withdrawn north-westward, leaving only a faint shuddering vibration upon the air.

Home by morning? Perhaps. Nancy and the kid, home, the congenial people of Morwen Hoe, all these distant, desirable things waited at the end of a long, long corridor of thought; and though the scurrying boat bore him nearer and nearer to England, the distance separating him from them did not seem to diminish at all. Sometimes he thought that it lengthened, that Nancy's face grew more and more remote. Sometimes he could not see it at all; sometimes he could not even remember it. It was all so long ago, so far away; it had happened to another man. What was the use even of longing to get back to it? Supposing he couldn't get back to Nancy, any more than he could get away from Eliane? Because he couldn't. Running was no good. She didn't have to hurry to keep up with him, she was in him, all the time; hers was a face he couldn't forget, nor were the lines of it dimmed even by this starless darkness.

Home by morning! Perhaps they would have been, but for the hour they lost in mid-Channel when the rickety old motor cut out, and defied all their efforts to coax it into life again. Tommy worked on it hard enough then, frenziedly, in a desperate silence, the most insatiable of the three in his appetite for England. It was he who induced it to show signs of life at last. It was old, and had seen hard work, and the days when it should have been left to battle with even a phenomenally calm Channel were long past; but after they had rowed for the better part of an hour it yielded to treatment, and they began to leave a feathery wake once again across the surface of the sea. Unhappily it was by then a strange, flat, grey sea, like the void before creation, over whose mysterious waters the spirit moved without a resting-place. It was not yet dawn, nor any longer dark, but the half-light between, the coldest, the unkindest hour of the twenty-four. There were masses, but no shadows, outlines but no relief. World and sky and sea, faces and bodies of men, had between them only two dimensions. The darkness withdrew but there was as yet no light, only an absence of darkness.

It was by their wake, not by the shape of the boat itself, that the aircraft found them. That slim white arrow upon the slate-grey water, perpetually producing itself forward and melting into the waste of sea behind, was clearly visible, the only thing moving with a purpose in all that seething monotony. The bomber formation, returning raggedly, passed overhead and seemed to pay them no heed, though perhaps not because they were not seen. It remained for one escorting pilot, in sheer wantonness, to undo all they had done, Miriam's work and theirs, all that erection of labour and hope and longing.

They had heard the thrumming approach grow out of the vast quiet until it possessed the sky, and they themselves moved under it without sound. This time they had no cloak of invisibility to cover them, they were naked to the sky, and in a

233

superstitious manner afraid. They held their breath, looking upward all three. So it happened that they saw the solitary fighter plane detach itself, and heel, and plunge upon them. The too brief night had withdrawn its favour from them, and left them to the mercy of the indifferent dawn, which was without mercy.

Jim heard himself cry out in rage and reproach; but what was the good of that? While the hunter stooped over them, something seemed to happen to time and space. He knew he had thrown himself down into the bottom of the boat, and yet an age passed before sea and sky ceased to stare back at him with their dwarfing grey eyes. All the known world was drawn together into the tight pain in his chest. He wanted nothing but to survive, only to live through this moment, not to lose what was so near now, and had been paid for at such a cost. It couldn't happen. Not now, not after all they had been through. He had never felt like this, never in all those days in Flanders, fighting and retreating. There was more in it now than his life; there was all the anger and hope of the people who had brought him so near to England again, there was Michel Peyron, and Simone, and Miriam. Miriam above all! He had to live. He couldn't die now.

The boat shipped water, zigzagging madly under André's raging hands. The roar of the plane as it straightened out tore the hair erect on their heads, and the shattering outburst of the pilot's machine-gun smashed all other sounds. The engine coughed and died, and oil began to expand along the water in a glistening, iridescent fan. If only he would be content now, and go! But they heard him bank, and climb, and turn, and swoop over them again. The boat rocked softly in the oily swell. They crouched low against the boards, their faces pressed into the wash of sea-water which had come inboard with André's last attempt at escape. Jim wondered what it was that ran so warmly down his chin, and drew pale dissolving whorls of pink in the wash. He wondered, too, who it was who cursed, in that high, monotonous voice, somewhere forward from him. He tried to lift his head and see, but a great, warm, smothering weight pressed him down, and he could not move.

The plane was coming back for a third time. They made sure, these bastards, bloody sure. They had made sure of him. It was all for nothing, all that magnificence of effort, and courage, and calm, all for nothing. Miriam had torn herself in pieces, and God could only turn his back, as if she offered him something not worth accepting. This was how it had to end, in this blood-stained weariness, past consciousness of the last burst of gunfire, past feeling the last crashing pain through his loins. Only this releasing of life from slack fingers, and the end of anger, and the dark beginning of a long sleep.

10

He opened his eyes, and the sun shone into them and blinded him with gold, and a quick flame of pain went through his head and stabbed him into consciousness. He heard a voice, quite close to him, so close and strange that it might even have been his own. The voice was cursing, not loudly, not hurriedly, going on and on upon a monotone, like a cracked bell, cursing God, or Hitler, or somebody, for destroying the speaker. He lay and listened, and did not even wonder who it was who was alive enough to talk that way. All he knew was the heat of the sun, and the pain that swung through him in waves as the boat lifted and lurched and creaked languidly, rolled like dead drift in the troughs of the lazy seas. Only the very aimlessness of that slow roll and sluggish recovery, repeated over and over, seemed to distend the sea mile beyond mile in his mind until it was shoreless, limitless, endlessly calm in an interminable noonday; a sea in which a small boat could rock for ever and ever without sight of land, or life, or hope, or human company. As it could, as it would, for he remembered now with a bitter sickness that the motor had been half shot out of it in that first chatter of machine-gun fire, and the oil had come swirling down into the two inches or so of sea-water aboard, in little coloured arabesques, iridescent, like a dragon-fly's wings, gilding over the pink evanescent thread of blood. And as for the oars, they might as well have gone with the motor for all the good they were to him. He knew that even before he tried to lift himself out of the wash of water, and oil, and blood. He could not have held an oar, for his left arm was broken just above the elbow joint, and his right hand was too feeble to lift itself between his eyes and the sun. He felt light, incapable of controlling or directing his body. Nor was there any movement from the others, though one at least was alive, for the voice went steadily on with its quiet, methodical denunciation. It did not quicken nor grow angry; it was too late for anger, but there was all time to spare for cursing.

Jim got his hand over his face, and opened his eyes again;

and between his fingers he saw the sky, all the immensity of it, diamond-hard and diamond-bright, without a cloud to soften its nakedness. By the heat of the sun it was full noon. The oilskin coat he wore was torturing him. At the least laborious movement he felt the perspiration crawl over his body in streams. And yet somebody had to move. They had been drifting for many hours, and in this sick, small wooden basin of a world, with the sky for a lid, they could all three lie and die while the coast of England shone on them quietly from a few miles away.

Getting his arm, his one good arm, under him to lever his weight up from the boards, was one of the labours of Hercules, and cost him five minutes of pain and dizziness before he could go farther; but he got his shoulder securely against one of the benches, and when the first nausea had passed dragged himself up to his knees, and after another rest clawed himself upright against the side. The swaying of the water was a blinding agony, monotonous, unresting, stretching away on every hand to a barren cobalt horizon against the marbled blue-whiteness of the sky. He hooked his right arm over the side to hold him in position, and strained his eyes to find the hint of a point of coast or another boat in the glittering blueness, but there was nothing. Turning his head, he was seized about the throat by a fiery cord of pain, as the string on which his identity disc hung, and the waterproof bag in which he had sewn his pay-book and money and papers, was drawn into the bleeding score along the left side of his neck. The sea swirled before his eyes in whorls of purple and black. To keep himself conscious, he clamped his chest down hard upon the side of the boat, and lifting his hand, clawed and tugged at the string until it snapped, and the collar of fire leaped from about his throat, and he dropped his streaming, jerking face into his arm, retching his heart out into the oil-dimmed, sleepy-swinging water. He never saw nor cared what happened to the string and the bag. What did it matter if they went over the side? What did a man want with an identity if he wasn't going to live more than a day or so? Nobody wanted to call him anything. Nobody cared what his name was. The immediate hellish pain was over, that was all that mattered.

He heard the voice again. It had stopped cursing. "What's the use?" it said, with a soft, detached bitterness. "What are you grumbling about, anyhow? It wouldn't have done a damn bit of good even if you had got home. You wouldn't have been satisfied, so what's the bloody good of making out you would? You wanted *her*." And suddenly he was off again, raging and gasping: "Damn you, you bitch, why couldn't you have the guts to stick it out like the rest? Oh no, that was a hell of a lot to expect from you, wasn't it? Other people could starve, and hide, and walk in the gutter, but not you. You were too delicate and sensitive, weren't you? Plain women might get pushed around, and robbed, and bullied, but you couldn't stand it, could you? You and your 'Chant du Départ'!"

It was Tommy, then. Jim let himself down gingerly to his knees again, and began to drag himself clumsily forward in the swilling sea-water, over the splintered benches. The field of his senses seemed curiously curtailed, so that he could see only a foot or so ahead of his single struggling hand. But in a moment he found Tommy, lying on his back in the wash between the benches, his head thrown back, and his eyes, wide open, fixed upon the staring zenith. His coat was open, his hands clenched upon his stomach; and between the doubled fingers dark blood oozed in slow beads, and gathered, and ran. His face, on which the sweat stood in quivering globules, was the drained ivory colour of parchment, and the pool in which he lay was a dark, cloudy brown. Forward from him, the big form of André lay in a huddle of oilskins against the engine, his outspread hands stained with black gouts of oil, his right temple streaked with blood. He was dead; the first burst had smashed him and his motor together. When Jim touched him he fell over forward, stiffly, and rolled upon his side. He was already rigid; he must have died at once. All the better for him in the end. There was no food on board, and not even a drop of water, no means of moving, no sight of land. André at least had got it over; they still had it coming.

He sat down in the bloody pool beside Tommy, and touched his shoulders, which seemed at least a whole part of him. He was afraid to try and lift him, having only one arm with which to do it. And how if he should hurt him? He looked broken in two; the least movement might kill him. He dared only press his shoulder gently, and say hoarsely against his ear:

"Tommy—come on, snap out of it! It's me—Jim! Do you hear?"

"What's the good?" said Tommy, the fixed stare never wavering. "It was all very clever, and they went to a hell of a lot of trouble, and don't think I don't appreciate it—but what good was it to me? It wouldn't have done me any good in the end. You think I was mad to get home, don't you? Well, I can't blame you, I thought so myself. But it was all bloody silly. You don't really believe I could ever have settled down again the old way, do you? My God, could you? With that girl always in your mind? If she hadn't looked like she did—— Why did she look like that? It wasn't fair on me. Why couldn't she look the cheap little blonde harpy she was? Then at least it would have given a poor devil a chance to hate her properly. You knew she'd changed sides, didn't you?"

"You don't know what you're talking about," said Jim shrilly. "You shut up, will you! Give yourself a chance, and stop wasting breath. We're not dead yet."

The fixed eyes dragged themselves reluctantly from the pale zenith and fastened upon Jim's face. Tommy laughed; it was supposed to be a laugh, at least, though it was more like an animal moan, and it made bubbles of blood break between his fingers and spatter the backs of his hands. "Oh no? How far off, do you think? My God, look at me! Do I look as if I'd ever be any good to the army again? Not dead yet! We might as well be; it's only a matter of hours."

"I don't believe it," said Jim, lying wildly. "We can't be far from the English coast. We're sure to be spotted and picked up in time. And as for dying, *you're* no doctor, *you* don't know how bad you are. I tell you we're sure to get back all right in the end. Think of Nancy and the kid! You want to get home to them, don't you?"

"No," said Tommy in a famished whisper. "I want Eliane." And suddenly he snatched his smeared hands away from his middle, and seized Jim by the arm, and clung to him; from the corner of his mouth a thread of blood ran down slowly, sliding through the standing sweat. "Don't you tell Nance that! But you wouldn't tell her. You're not that sort. She'll be able to think it was all right between us, right to the finish. That won't hurt, anyhow. That won't do any harm, and it'll be some comfort to her. Tell her she was the one, never anyone but her. No, don't say that, it'll only make her think there was something funny going on. We never did say things like that, it wouldn't do to start now. Tell her I thought about her and the kid all the time. There's not so much you can say, but tell her that for me, and she'll think the rest out for herself. But it won't be the truth, Jim. It's no good making out things are the same as ever—even if it mattered a tinker's curse now—even if I wasn't smashed to pieces this way——"

238

The impulse to protest further went out of Jim. He sat watching the light upon Tommy's ashen face, and the flecks of blood that formed along his lips at every halt of the hard voice. He said nothing. What was the good? It wasn't worth even trying to keep Tommy quiet, for quiet or noisy he wouldn't last long. And anyhow he himself was scarcely alive. How could he do anything for Tommy when the very face of his friend kept reeling away from his eyes, and its features flowing together into a greyness? Even the heat of the sun, and its blazing brightness, sometimes receded from him and left him alone in a waste of darkness; and which was more terrifying of this grim day and appalling night he did not know. He only knew that he was filled with pain, and that time and space had withdrawn in anger from the world. That was why the boat rocked idly here among the little, sunny, indifferent seas. What was the use of going, when there was nowhere to go? The shore, the desired shore of England, was a dream. There was no coast to this sea.

"Nothing stays the same," said the voice more faintly, but very clearly. "I didn't; but then, neither did she. Did you know she'd changed sides? Oh no, she couldn't stay with the losers—not Eliane! With a face like that, why should she? She could draw them after her the way she drew me, and they'd come like bloody fools, the same as I did. They'd put their coats over her shoulders, and their arms round her waist, and get her past the little restrictions that everybody else had to put up with, the way she'd hardly know there'd been a war or a defeat. That was what she wanted, for all her talk of France. She looked good, but she had no guts. As long as she's comfortable she won't care whether it's France or a bit of the bloody Third Reich." His hands relaxed; he was weakening rapidly; only his eyes kept their tormented life, staring at what was left of Jim Benison and seeing only the pale, illusionless head of Eliane Brégis, and her coppery eyes regarding him steadily, that should have evaded his. Unashamed, unforgettable, unattainable, she had gone her way and put no obstacle in his; and however he miscalled her now, however he desired her, she would not know nor care. That was worst of all, that he could not in any way trouble her, even by dying. "What is there," asked the voice, small and remote even in its anger, "about a bitch like that? Why can't you just think 'To hell with her'! and get her out of your mind? You can't—I can't, anyhow. She wasn't worth a single bad night, and yet she's had me in hell,

239

ever since that night we got away from Boissy, when I saw her
walking with him, and knew what she was. It was worse when
I knew what she was. Anyhow, I could keep her to think about,
and look up to, if I hadn't found out; but once I knew, there
was no good in her at all unless I could have her—and I
couldn't—I couldn't—Jim—why the hell don't you say something?''

"What's the good?" said Jim.

"How do I know you're still there if you don't talk? I can't
see you. Oh, my good Lord Almighty, I can't see nothing but
her.''

"I'm still here," said Jim.

"You won't go away? But you won't—I don't believe you
would if you could. I wonder why? Much good I ever did
you! It was me that brought you here. If I hadn't talked like
I did about the war—about saving the world—I bet you'd still
have been with Collinsons, nice and safe in a reserved job.''

"I'd have been here, anyway," said Jim.

"My God, it's funny, isn't it? All we were going to do, and
this is the end of it all. What a mess we made of it, what a hell
of a mess! Saving the world! There's not much left of that, is
there? All our talk didn't amount to much. Even people like
Miriam couldn't make a job of it. Look where it all ends!''
There was no word of protest, no movement in the blazing,
indolent sea stillness; but he felt how the rush of his anger and
despair was broken suddenly against something stony and
immovable. "You don't believe that, do you? You don't
believe it's ended. More fool you! You're only letting yourself in for a lot worse than what you've had already. Me, I've
had enough. But then, you were always that sort of fool. Slow
starting, and never stopping. I get off the mark as hot as hell,
and in a mile or so it's all over. And you start cold and lazy,
and work up a slow heat that keeps on burning for ever.''
Sudden panic took him because of the quietness. He reached
out his hands and groped blindly for Jim, and shrieked: "Don't
leave me!''

Jim took the nearer of the clawing hands. "I ain't going to
leave you. It's all right, I'm still here.''

"Keep hold of me. I don't like it when I think you're gone.''

"All right, I'll keep hold of you.'' He set his shoulder more
strongly against the bench, and allowed his hand to be carried
into the wet dark ruin of Tommy's chest, and pressed there
between Tommy's stained hands to help to subdue the raging

pain which devoured his body moment by moment. Like a swinging curtain his own suffering closed and unclosed upon his senses, so that sometimes he was aware of himself only, and sometimes only of Tommy, and sometimes of them both as one person, or at least as one pain. The sun upon his head was an agony, but he could not cover it without dragging his hand away from Tommy's hold, which he did not contemplate doing. He put his face down upon his arm, and lay with his eyes closed, seeing curious muddled memories rush through his mind. Sometimes he heard Tommy speak again, but so faintly now that it was needless care and distress to attempt to distinguish words. There was no need for more than a murmur in reply, or a slight movement of the head to show he still lived. And in a little while even these mechanical tendernesses obtained no response, no sigh, no answering pressure. In the gathering darkness of Tommy's mind only one memory remained fixed, like a star, and that was the face of the lost Eliane, for once at least her name was clear on his lips, and indignant, as if he confronted her at last. But after that he was quiet, and in a little while his fingers relaxed and slid away from Jim's hand, and Jim, who had not deserted him, was himself deserted.

He was past realising his loneliness by then. It was only another aspect of pain. He thought of nothing, for with so much of feeling there was no room, no time for thought. Only sometimes it seemed to him that someone who had been with him step by step along that broken road to freedom was now snatched away from his side. It was not Tommy, though Tommy was dead; it was not André, though André was dead. He did not know who it was, but the shape of the emptiness left behind was like the shape of the strength of Miriam Lozelle, like the part of herself which she had left with him when she drew herself out of his arms and ran away up the bank of the cutting. Why should she take it back now, or why should he lose it, when he was so nearly dying? It was not like her to withdraw her arm from about him for death or any pain, and he felt his courage lost with her, and was desolate. Was that why he suddenly saw her so clearly, not as he had ever seen her in the flesh, but as he had once imagined her, as once she had so nearly lain, a huddle of black clothes and white flesh and cloudy dark hair, in the thin grass of a waste place, where the machine-guns had cut her down?

II

No one would admit to knowing anything about it. There were intensive questionings throughout Boissy, but they elicited no information of any kind. No one had touched the body. No one had carried the flowers. To pursue the matter further was to publicise still more widely what was already becoming a legend in the neighbourhood, and might yet raise against the Nazis in Artois an invisible army more perilous than any open enemy. So said the scarred Gestapo man, and others, themselves less subtle, trusted his wisdom more than their own anger, and let the enquiry die by default. Nevertheless, the legend remained.

It was on the 23rd of June, the day after the armistice was signed at Compiègne, that they shot her, at midday, in the quarry where once the British had had their rifle and machine-gun ranges. She was, so said a witness who had known her well, so marred and discoloured by bruises and several unhealed weals as to be at first unrecognisable, but her walk was still unmistakable, and she climbed the slope to the quarry with so much vigour that it was clear she was unbroken. She had on a thin black dress, and no coat or hat. Her arms were bare and badly marked, and her long black hair, which was tied up in a gypsy scarf, she suddenly unloosed about her shoulders in the moment before the order to fire was given, as if to clothe herself with her one remaining beauty. She looked at the sunlight, and seemed glad that the day of her death could be so bright; and when she saw faces she knew among the crowd that followed her she smiled, but briefly, as if her mind was preoccupied with other matters, but not as if she was afraid. She looked as if she had walked right through fear as through a dark room, and come out again unshaken on the other side. She stood where she was told to stand, and looked straight at her executioners and straight through them, and her bruised face and suffused eyes were softened by the shadows of her long hair lifted in the breeze. And when she fell, said this witness, the black cloud still covered her features, but she was grim enough to make even those who pitied her turn their eyes away, for where her dress was torn away from her side there were marks of day-old burns, unbandaged, all around the new, neat black wounds. So the Nazis left her lying in the sand and gravel and thin grass, forbidding anyone to remove or touch the body for twenty-four hours, so that everyone might steal up and see what was the end of a French traitress, and be warned. They left no guard; they supposed, contemptuously enough, that they would be obeyed.

The body was not removed. When the next morning came Miriam Lozelle still lay in the quarry, but not as she had been thrown down by the guns. The body had been laid out with care, all the stains of blood washed away, the torn dress straightened, the large eyes closed, the black hair brushed and smoothed back from her temples. A small tricolour, a child's flag torn from its standard, was spread under her head, and her arms were laid close to her sides. She had flowers in her hands, and flowers against her blanched cheeks, in the dark coils of her hair.

But no one knew anything about it, of course; no one would ever know, except the person or persons who had so honoured her to their own danger. Before the Nazi authorities discovered the outrage almost every soul in Boissy had already seen the transformed dead, and the story was far afield. There was nothing to be gained by spreading her fame still further abroad; the only thing to be done was to pretend indifference, and permit her small, misused body to be taken away, roses and all, by the Curé, and quietly and decently buried, for fear they should draw yet more eyes upon her by acts designed only to rob her of all notice. They therefore signified to an undeceived people that the corpse was nothing to them after the twenty-four hours had elapsed, and might be removed by her family or friends; and Simone and the Abbé Bonnard came and took her away.

But it was too late to bury Miriam Lozelle by then. Legends cannot be shut into graves. She was in the blood of the French people, she who had never been French except by adoption. She was in the imaginations of the young and the memories of the old. On the night after her funeral the bell of the Mairie was rung at midnight, and a startled German soldier, opening the door, found his Captain, the military head of the village, laid at the foot of the steps with a table-knife stuck through his throat. For that ten people only were shot, these being the early days of the occupation, when there was still hope of placating the French, and retaliation on the later scale was too terrifying a prospect. Nevertheless, the scarred man in his own mind recognised the end in the beginning of this multiplication of martyrs. Often he remembered Miriam Lozelle. He remembered her because she had died and succeeded, whereas from that day there was always a suspicion in his mind that he and his kind had triumphed and failed.

So Miriam died, and was buried, a long way from her own country; and to some, less intelligent than the scarred man, it seemed that she was a momentary danger only, satisfactorily obliterated. It was not their business to look into the minds and memories of the conquered and recognise her there. They perceived only that she was dead, her house a ruin, her live-stock driven off to feed the army of occupation, her garden trampled, her orchards running wild. The wine from her husband's cellars made the command drunk for several nights. The only thing her woman-servant was allowed to take away was her small black spaniel bitch, and that, so they said, soon pined. Also her furniture, what remained of it, was divided up to embellish the quarters of German officers and men; and the new Nazi Commander, so the ranks boasted, slept in her marriage bed.

They did not say if he slept well.

PART FIVE

ENGLAND, 1940

"This fortress built by Nature for herself
Against infection, and the hand of war."
SHAKESPEARE: *Richard the Second*.

I

THERE was a man in Ward B who had no identity. He had been picked up by a motor torpedo boat in the middle of the English Channel, after the disabled boat in which he lay had been sighted by a reconnaissance plane of Coastal Command; and since he carried on him no means of identification, and was too far gone to speak for himself, and since his dead companions in the boat were a French seaman and an English soldier, he had remained nameless and without nationality. In any case, it seemed for several days that he would certainly die, and all he would want with a name was in the inscription on his tombstone. How long he had been in the boat with the two dead men was a matter of guess-work, but the doctor who examined him when he was brought in put it at between two and three days. His tongue and mouth were swollen, cracked and purplish-black; he had an infected flesh wound in the neck, a broken left arm, and two bullet-holes through his left thigh, though the femur was untouched. He had lost a great deal of blood, and was in a coma which did not lift for three days, and then yielded only to a sort of listless stupor. But he did not die.

Of the other two, who had obviously been dead for at least two days, the one carried letters which identified him as a fisherman from a small town south of Boulogne, and gave his name as André Lenormand; the other still wore round his neck a British military disc on a tarnished silver chain, and was wearing his issue boots into the bargain, so that it was not difficult to establish his identity. His widow, Nancy Goolden, herself confirmed the evidence of the disc, and so did the only surviving officer of his company, who had been shipped back from Dunkirk among the last of the B.E.F. They were as gentle as they could well be with the calm but broken young woman, and took care that she should see only the face of her husband, and that only momentarily and in a shaded light, for the sun had been hot upon the boat. She did not collapse. She said yes, that was

Tom, all right. She said she would make arrangements to have his body taken home; and then, having received the few personal things he had carried on him, she went back to her cottage in Morwen Hoe, and made practical deals with the undertaker and the rector, and set to work to take the coloured lapels and pocket edgings from her best black frock. She did not parade nor hide her feelings. People who knew Nancy Johnson knew there would be no fuss. Only from that day she somehow ceased to be young.

Perhaps if they had not been so overworked with the débris of the evacuation it would have occurred to them to ask her if she knew the other man. But they were desperately crowded, and exhausted with a multiplicity of pitiful claims upon their time and energy and will; and the one living man had misled them by wearing sea-boots and an oilskin coat like the Frenchman, so that it was with the Boulogne coast they had him linked in their minds rather than with the country districts of Midshire; and they did not ask Nancy what she knew of him, nor take her to look at him in his gaunt, unresting sleep. He was, therefore, still nameless when he suddenly opened his eyes sanely upon the sixth day of his stay in that inland hospital, and looked at the nurse who came hurrying in surprise at seeing him stir, and said clearly that he was Private Benison, and was looking for A Company.

He went on looking for them for over a week, very anxiously and patiently and doggedly. Most of the time he was in a nightmare countryside, denuded of trees and birds and grass, looking for them along giant tank-tracks and in shell craters as sterile and cold as the pock-marks of the moon. The sky over him was alternately a furnace of sun and an oppression of frozen darkness, under which he groped sightless and alone, trying to find A Company. He went on and on, falling and rising and wandering blind, burned and chilled, feeble with weariness and stiff with wounds; but he never found them. Only at last, coming out of the darkness, he opened his eyes upon the white, narrow hospital bed, and the cool sheets, and the pure daylight of a July morning flooding in through an open window. The fever had left him weak but alive. He did not know where he was, but he knew it was heaven by comparison with the hells through which he had been on that interminable quest. Moreover, it did not fade. He moved his fingers shakily along the white neatness of the sheets, and they did not dissolve nor change; he was not used to clean, cool, tangible things which did not elude him, and at first he did not believe in them. But he watched, and all this quiet whiteness remained constant before his eyes. Then, as the desolation and distress receded like the wash of an outgoing tide from his mind, and the room put on proportion and form, he saw a face leaning over him. But before the moment when he knew the face he fell asleep.

That was the first true sleep he had had, after seven days of raving in a fluctuating fever. When he opened his eyes again the steadfast quality of the room had not changed, and his mother was still there, sitting by his bed and watching him with her anxious blue-grey eyes. He remembered the black straw hat with the red rose in it, and the way she wore it, un-compromisingly straight on her grey hair, and the knitted black silk gloves, and the narrow band of black velvet round her neck, with the tiny pearl brooch pinned into it in front. He remembered suddenly how things had flowed along softly at home, before all this horror began; and he remembered that the horror was only begun. No going back yet to that heaven of quietness, no going back from the dreadfulness of the war. Only the sudden unbearable memory of calm to redouble the violence of the storm, so that enfeebled flesh could not support the burden, nor exhausted mind sustain the integrity of its resolve. In a moment of darkness he yet saw again all the deaths his friends had died, from Bill Gittens to Brian Ridley, from Michel Peyron to Tommy Goolden, processions of the dead marching through his mind in hideous suffering and bitter resentment, marching from despair to despair. Walls of experience of horror and dis-illusion rose about him and shut his mother out. And yet there was comfort in being reminded; the remembered light made the night darker, but at least there had been light once.

"Jim?" she said hesitantly, seeing how his eyes agonised upon her, and half-afraid to speak until they were eased. "It's me, Jim. It's your mother."

The voice broke him. He turned his face into the pillow, and cried, with physical weakness and homesickness for peace, letting his manhood slip away from him.

"It's all right," she said, patting him as if he were a fretful baby, "it's all right, my lovey, I'm here. You're home again." And when he had sobbed himself silently into a shuddering exhaustion, and the tension of his emaciated body had relaxed, she picked up his unresisting hands and nursed them in hers, and: "I know . . . I know!" she soothed him. But she did not know. She did not know how he was changed, nor what fires had burned him. She did not know how far away from her he was even now, nor how much of his life he would have given to get back to her again, and to the homely things and quiet days of which she was the symbol. She did not know about the ridge among the beechwoods, and the reddened tank-tracks furrowing it, and the crushed boy who took so long to die. She did not know about Miriam kneeling on the pavement outside Papa Brégis' with the bleeding body of Chicot in her arms, or the steady, insatiable rain of bombs on the position above the canal, or the pregnant woman running heavily along the Hainault causeway, steadying her burden with her hands, and shrieking for help to the Mother of God. She did not know—oh, God, she did not know!—about the red mud crusted along the high road where the German armour had passed, and the pale, soiled, childish faces open-eyed to the bitter moon. No one who did not know these things had any communion now with him. He was a haunted creature. If he lay awake he saw them with his wakeful eyes, the murdered children, the maimed men, the women bereaved and despoiled and without hope; if he slept he dreamed about them, and awoke sweating and gasping for breath. Shock, they called it; but like her, they did not know the half.

"You've had a bad time," said she, in the soft monotone which came straight from his childhood, "an awful time, you've had. But it's all right now, it's all over; you're safe in England. Oh, Jimmy, my lad," she said, "your father and me was getting right worried about you."

"I'm all right," he said impatiently, as always when his well-being was called in question. As a mere toddler, picked up after a fall with skinned palms and knees, he had plucked himself peremptorily out of her hands and frowned her away with: "I'm all right!" Now the voice was a mere husky thread of sound, but the tone was the same.

"Is Dad here, too?" he asked.

"He was here yesterday, but he went back. He's doing overtime, you know, besides his Home Guard duties; and he knew I'd send for him if need be."

"Home Guard?" said Jim. "What's that?"

"It's what they've formed in case the Germans try to invade England. All the old soldiers are in it. Dad's a sergeant, bless him. But when you come home he'll tell you all about it, more than you bargained for. He talks about nothing else. What with his Sunday exercises, and traipsing all over the hills in the rain, stalking the lot from Sheel, like a twelve-year-old Boy Scout—well, it's took years off his age, years, it has. Eh, these old men!"

Dwelling upon the one phrase of all this which he had clearly understood, he said in a wondering whisper: "Yes, I shall come home, shan't I? I shall have sick leave. They'll surely give me sick leave."

"Of course they will. All you've got to do is just get well quick, and not worry about nothing, my sonny. Just forget about everything but getting better, and then you'll be home the sooner."

Forget! How do you set about forgetting things like Tommy Goolden's voice cursing Eliane? He at least had made up his mind what should be remembered and what forgotten. And that brought back into Jim's mind another dreadful responsibility.

"I've got to talk to Nancy," he said.

"Got to talk to Nancy?" she repeated indulgently.

"About Tommy. He died in the boat." A tremor shook his wasted body from head to foot. "It was bad in the boat," he said piteously.

"I know, I know, fine I know it was bad; but it's all by. There's no call for you to say a word to Nancy. She knows it all, more than you can tell her, and all the better if there's no more said. He's dead and buried, poor lad. She's past the worst of it. You let her be, Jim. Nancy's all right."

Long after a harassed nurse had driven his mother away, Jim lay thinking of what she had said, and for the first time his mind seemed to be working clearly. She was right about Nancy. Better not to hark back to a thing she had already accepted. If, when he saw her, she should ask him questions about her husband's death, well, he would lie to her, tell her Tommy had died with her name on his lips, and loving no one but her; but he felt that she would not ask. She would be sure of him in her heart, and who could say she was wrong? There was more to it than a few minutes of hankering after a pair of dark eyes and a milk-white face. Nancy had lived with him, and knew him through and through; and if she was sure of him the odds were that she was right. And anyhow he was gone, and none of them could call him back. No, the best thing to do, the only thing to do, was to turn his back on all that was past, at all costs to put away the thought of it, and if his will was strong enough the very memory, too. It was the only hope for him. Surely, if he dwelt with all his strength upon the sane, pleasant things which awaited him at home he would be able to get these horrors out of his senses.

And then he thought of Delia. Strange to have let her wander so far out of mind, and stay away so long, she who was surely for him a shield against all these terrors which had never touched her nature and could not live in her presence. While he lived with the powers of darkness he had lost sight of her, almost put her away from him, because it was beyond bearing that she should be in the same world with them. But now he was back in an air which she might breathe without dismay, and with all his ruined might he drew her back to him. By the deliberate evocation of her face he shut out the dead men who would not leave him alone, and by the virtue of her smile, he slept. What good does it do, after all, to break yourself in pieces over something you can't stop? He had done what he could, and when he was better than a demoralised piece of wreckage hung round England's neck he would do as much again; but the mountain was not to be moved like that. How would it help to agonise over a thing which was, and could not be denied? No, better to conserve what little usefulness there was in him, even by a wisdom of defeat, even by an admission of cowardice. Better to shut his eyes and stop his ears, and take what comfort there was for him near at hand. And there was comfort. There was leave, leave in the Sheel valley in summer, with his own people, in his own home. And there was Delia.

Maybe, if his leave was long enough, they could be married this time. Maybe there was a cottage somewhere in Sheel that would suit them. Suddenly, in his weakness he wanted her, desperately, he wanted her by him in the day to reassure him when the very quietness and kindness of living and being home seemed too good to be true, and more than all he wanted her in the night, so that even when he dreamed he would not be alone. It was when he was alone that the dead men came in, and the children after them, the children with the wan, soiled faces, who had got in the way of the invaders. She would never let them come troubling him. The very bravery of her commanding eyes and arrogantly joyous face would send them back from him into the darkness.

He lay there in his waking dream, and the desire of her took his flesh with a strange and drowsy delight, shutting out from him all the pains of the world. In anticipation he possessed her, his fever was assuaged in the coolness of her yellow hair, and his memory dimmed in the white, delectable calm of her body.

He hid himself in her ignorance and inexperience, from the terror of all he knew and all he had seen.

2

It was towards the end of July that he went home. Even that was not as he had expected it to be, not as he had planned it, though it kept the clear sweetness of a dream. At first his mother had been afraid to tell him that the home to which he would come was not the home he remembered. He was so weak and thin and so easily moved to fits of shuddering dread, that she wanted to keep from him even the last, least anxiety. But afterwards, when he was able to walk out into the hospital gardens with her on her visits, and she saw the sun of July warming him and the English winds bringing him back to life, she ventured to talk more freely of what had happened in England. It wasn't, after all, so much; just a stray bomb or two jettisoned over Morwen Hoe one night by a scared Jerry who had been turned back from his target. No one had been killed. The only injury had been the deep cut father got in his forearm when the window was blown in, and that had healed clean and was now only a puckered scar. They had even salvaged most of the furniture before the roof collapsed, though the grandfather clock had gained madly ever since, possibly from shock, or more likely because in the new little house in Caldington father had insisted on having it in one particular corner, where the floor was uneven, and it had never really settled down properly.

He accepted this reluctantly, but tranquilly. Caldington or Morwen Hoe, what difference did it really make? It was all England. It felt steady under his feet, and its familiar beauty, unchanged by such small wounds as a bomb or two could make, soothed him like sleep.

She talked to him about the things he had forgotten existed, the Women's Institute, the soft fruit harvest, how the gardens were doing, who had bought Fred Blossom's best colt, and whose cake won first prize at the parish show. It was like a slow charm working on him, folding him in from remembrance. Had he really been away from it all? Had it really ceased for him for all those months, this life which had never wavered nor turned aside from its course for wars and rumours of war? For he felt it firm about him now, and leaned upon it, and was unspeakably refreshed.

As for his side of the story—well, there was nothing to it, really, mother. I mean, it was all in the papers, I expect. We didn't see very much. We just moved up, and there were a few days when it was pretty warm up there, and then—well, then we had to come back. It was pretty muddled from where we were. No, we sort of got separated from the rest, our lot did, that's why we never got to Dunkirk. The French people helped us a lot, they were good to us. And we got to this fishing village, and this chap, André had a boat, and so we started off all right, but on the way this Jerry shot us up and—well, that's all there is about it.

The French people helped. Not a word of the Czech woman, though. He didn't know why. It was just that he couldn't talk about her, not even to his mother, not even in this easy, bald way. He would have liked his mother to know about Miriam; he wanted at least, and even at this distance, to repay her the gratitude and love and honour of his kin, which fell at its greatest so far short of her due. But he couldn't talk about her. When he came to the point his mouth grew dry, and his lips stiffened, and the muscles of his chest seemed to tighten hurtfully round his heart. She was too deep in him to rise into the surface of speech. She was one thing he would never forget. Her hands upon him, that night when he had tried to tell her about Georges, her so gentle and strong hands pressing him back into sleep, and her voice reproving him: *"Mauvais enfant!* You excite yourself. That is not good."* And again: *"Mon pauvre,* do not upset yourself so. There is nothing you have to tell me, nothing in the world."* He remembered every inflection of her voice as she had hushed him, calling him: *"Bon garçon!"* taking away every burden from him before he could so much as lift it; she, with her husband and two countries lost, and her life broken in pieces at her feet. No, he could never speak of Miriam, any more than he could talk about God in a saloon-bar.

His mother saw nothing lacking in the brief account he made of his six months away from her. He had never talked much about his own doings, and anything he really cared about you couldn't prise out of him with a crowbar. So she was content. Soon he would come home; to Caldington instead of Morwen Hoe, certainly, but nevertheless home. When he was ready he would talk, and until then she had no wish to trouble him. It was enough to have him back upon any terms.

And Jim went home. There was still something dream-like about it all, even as he sat beside his mother in the crowded third-class carriage, listening to the happily grumbling English voices around him, and watching the sunlit greens of English fields and woods flash by him and yet remain, at once evanescent and steadfast, which was their whole secret. Presently he would wake with the pain of the salt spray in the raw wound in his neck, and open his eyes, and see Tommy's relaxed hand washing back and forth in the oily water to the swing of the drifting boat, as so often already he had seen it. But the train went on, and the lanky seaman opposite gave him a cigarette, and he did not wake. It was real. He was back with his own kind. Soon he would see Delia in the flesh, and she would be the final and glorious reality. He could believe in it all then.

At Caldington station his father met them, still in his working overalls, and with a face smeared round the hairline with a tide mark of machine oil. It was the first time Jim had seen him for six months, for his one visit to the hospital had been made while Jim was incapable of recognising him or realising that he was there. The old man was changed. It was noticeable at once. He had shed years from his age; his eyes were bright and alert, and his walk was elastic as a boy's. With the old house bombed over his head, he at least was still enjoying himself; and why not? After several years of feeling that his usefulness was ending he found himself suddenly in demand again, his work esteemed, even his spare time claimed by a service of the greatest urgency. No wonder he looked at life with a new regard, and manhandled it with a new zest. It was Sergeant Benison now, in and out of uniform.

"Well, Jim, lad!" he said, beaming but strangely constrained, as Jim remembered him sometimes after a great anxiety. "How's it going?"

"Oh, not so dusty. A bit wobbly at the knees, y'know." He found himself constrained, too. He knew he looked to them like the ghost of their son, and it troubled him that they should be anxious about him. He couldn't bear being fussed. "You're a nice one!" he said, to fill in the first strange pause. "The minute I turn my back you go breaking up the happy home."

"Oh, our bomb? Oh, yes, you'll have to have a look at what's left of the old place. It's a miracle we ever got the furniture out before the roof came in. And the crater! Right under the back-kitchen window, and that far across if it's an inch!" He was mightily pleased with his bomb, a blind man could see that. "I suppose mother's told you all about it," he said, almost regretfully; though that would scarcely prevent him from telling it all over again.

"Well, not all the details. Just that it happened." He walked out into the neat market square of the little town between his parents, possessing himself of an arm of each. After all, he could afford to be a bit more demonstrative than usual, couldn't he? It wouldn't hurt him, and it would please them very much. "How far have we got to walk? Remember this is all new to me."

"Not far. It takes about ten minutes to walk it, but I thought we'd get on a bus, being as you——"

He said: "My lord, do I look that bad? I bet I can outwalk you any day." But that was just talk, and they knew it as well as he did. He could stay on his feet for more than ten minutes, certainly, but he was in no state to take on his father yet. "Come on!" he said. "I want to have a look at this place you've landed me in—see if it'll do." And he set such a pace that he himself would have liked to relax it before they had climbed the steep hill out of the square.

"It isn't just like the old place," said his father deprecatingly. "There's only a bit of front garden, and a little piece at the back."

"Good! Shan't have to dig it."

"It's a different sort of house, too, you mind, one of a row. The rooms are smaller than they were in the cottage and it's all pretty new."

"Maybe the doors will open and shut without sticking, then. Remember how the kitchen door used to drag along the quarries? Set your teeth on edge to hear it! What sort of lighting have we got? Electric? Hurray, then I can have that mains set put in at last! Hear that, Mum? No more carrying batteries up and down, burning holes in your gloves. You'll always be able to have the news on full strength, too." That would please her, he knew. He could see her sitting over the wireless taking in every detail, doggedly settling down to endure and win this war about which, even with the celebrated bomb-crater under her back-kitchen window, she knew nothing at all. And only twenty-one miles of water and a few leagues of land separated her from the rivers of German armour which had swept away the flower of France, and the steel-fingered hand which had methodically stripped Boissy-en-Fougères of every comfort and every grace. Only twenty-one miles of water and a thin rank of old men as gentle and brave and unprepared as herself.

"I hear you're a blooming non-com., Dad," said Jim, reminded of certain filial obligations. "Wish you'd tell us how it's done."

His father said: "Get off with your soft-soap!" But he was obviously tickled pink to be stroked the right way, like that. "You know dam' well I'm only a sergeant through my record in the Great War. Couldn't hardly help it, with all the raw kids we've got; some of the old hands had to get a few stripes so's to get the lads started. I tell you what, though, Jim, we've got some grand little shots here. That red-headed boy who used to deliver meat for Billy Beckett—he's working at your old shop now—he's got the straightest, quickest eye I ever met with in a youngster. Never touched a gun in his life until he joined us a month ago, and we're putting him up for the county shoot in August. You ought to come up to the range with us some time, while you're here, and see the platoon do its stuff."

"He's on leave, you remember," pointed out his mother briskly. "Rest and good food and plenty of sleep is what he wants, no gallivanting around the countryside with your platoon, getting his feet wet and going down sick again, as like as not. He's done enough of that for a bit, I should think, and in dead earnest, too, not for fun, like you overgrown lads."

"For fun? Well, if that ain't just like a woman! Do you think I enjoy manœuvring all over the country in the pouring rain? At my age?"

"Sure you do!" she said, unshaken. "Don't you suppose I know when you're having a good time, after all the experience I've had? You don't have to try and kid me with your sense of duty. It's the best excuse you've ever had for playing cowboys and Indians, since you were young enough not to need any excuse. Don't you mind me. What with Red Cross sales of work, and the parish jam centre, and knitting for the Forces, I'm not doing so bad myself."

"I thought it was me that was joining up," said Jim meekly. "Seems you're running it all right between you without any help from me." But still, for all his pleasure in them, for all his abject happiness at being with them again, it was as if he talked to them brightly and glibly across a dark abyss. He dared not look down into it, but still he was aware of it at every step, a thronging void separating him from his own, a populous desolation of memories.

His mother pressed his arm. "Don't talk that way, Jim. We know better than that, if we do talk a lot of foolishness."

He said quickly: "Here, don't turn serious on me. I like you the other way. I'm going to sit around for a fortnight and listen to you two pull each other's legs, see, and I'm going to enjoy it, so don't go and spoil my fun." He threw back his head, and looked at the blue sky flecked with dazzling white, and the demure lace curtains in every parlour window of the little red-brick houses, and the veronica-bushes in the front gardens, and took every detail to his heart. "Gosh, this is grand! You don't know what it's like to be back."

"You really like it?" asked his father eagerly.

"Like it? What do you think? Do you mean one of these is ours?"

It was, and they halted him before it anxiously, both together apologising for its uniformity with the rest, its towniness, its raw ripe pinkness. For his part, if he could not go back to the cottage in Morwen Hoe, with the sunflowers leaning over the wall, he saw nothing wrong with this. It had pleasant wide windows, and a green front door, and two mezereon-bushes in glorious flower in the garden, rosy-purple spires of bloom with a sweetness like summer itself. Delia would like a little house like that, he thought, so shiny-respectable, in a residential road where she could outshine all the women with her beauty and vigour, and yet disarm them all with her fearless friendliness. She would like that almost better than a cottage in Sheel, and if it made her happy he would like it, too. The fever of his longing for her seemed to make his heart molten in him. "To-morrow," he thought, "I'll go to Morwen Hoe. To-morrow I'll see her."

"There's the key," said his mother. "Go on inside. I wouldn't wonder if there isn't a friend of yours waiting to see you."

He knew who that would be. He could hear her already, as he approached the door, whimpering and scratching inside, frantic with joy. He opened the door and swooped into the tiny hall, and she was in his arms, embracing him slavishly, writhing, whipping her slim tail like mad, licking his face, his neck, his hands, every part of him she could reach, quivering in an agony of love.

"Sue! Susie, my honey-girl! Gently, you mad thing! Here, let's have a look at your silly face again." But she went on with her dervish-dance, crazed with joy, until she had him seated in one of the shabby leather arm-chairs in the front room, lying back upon the worn cushions; and then, suddenly satisfied, she lay down with her chin across his toes and held him there, so that even if she slept he could not get away from her again. Her large, luminous eyes fastened upon his face. She was utterly content.

"You'll have to have a look round the house," said his mother, trotting busily back and forth as she laid the table for tea. "See what you think of it. You'd be surprised the way Sue settled in. Just put her basket in the corner there, and gave her her ball to play with in the backyard, and you'd have thought she'd been raised here, the speed she took to it. I wouldn't say so to your dad, but it isn't what I'd have picked if I'd had my way. Parlour type, they call it. Give me a cottage every time, with a nice kitchen to sit in. You wait till you see that bit of a box I have to do my cooking in. Kitchenette, indeed! Still, the bedrooms are proper nice, I will say that. And after all, there's a war on. Lucky we were to get it, and I'm an ungrateful old woman to grumble about little things when lads like you are putting up with so much and never saying a word."

Jim smiled, remembering how they, too, had grumbled about the little things, and how the greater evils had found them silent. It was not of the bomb she complained, only of the cramped kitchenette. He found in this something strange and reassuring, something which bound him to her in a union not subject to separation, however wide the abyss might yawn between them. If only he could stop himself from thinking, he would be all right; but memory kept putting strong sinuous fingers into his vitals, and wrenching him into the old hideous pain. All very well for him to come out of it whole; and with all his body and mind he embraced and thanked God for this wonderful ease; but that was no longer enough. What had André done that he should die with his hard-planned freedom almost in sight? Or Miriam, that the things which made life worth living should be stripped from her one by one? Or young Brian, who had hardly even begun to live? Or the children. . . ? No, he could not any longer thank God and be still. He was wronged with all their wrongs, pierced with all their wounds. There was no separate peace. He felt it then more than ever, sharp against the happiness, the kindness and relief of being home, heightening he light and deepening the darkness.

She saw trouble in his face; she had seen it there ever since he had come back; but she told herself that it was only the shadow of the past which had not yet slipped wholly from his

257

spirit. She said, turning back from the kitchen door with the tea-caddy in her hand: "You're all right, Jim? You haven't got anything to worry about now. We'll have to see what we can do to plump you up again, this fortnight. It worries me to see you looking so thin and poor. Remember—I know you've been through an awful time—but it doesn't do to look behind you these days. You're home, now. All you've got to do now is rest, and enjoy yourself, and get your appetite back, and forget all about everything else. That's orders, mind!"

It was what he had told himself, over and over. He grinned back at her across the hearth, and the shadow withdrew itself suddenly for a moment, and she saw her son again, scarred but the same.

"Yes, sir!" he said meekly.

"That's a good lad! You'll see the difference we'll make in you. Seven days of my cooking and Midshire air, and good long nights in your own bed, will soon put the flesh back on your bones."

"Don't you worry!" he said. "I'm going to eat you out of house and home."

She would worry, of course. They were made that way. She would worry about how he got his wounds, and what sort of people he had known while he was away from her, and how he felt towards the enemy. But she wouldn't ask him any questions; she was not a demonstrative woman; she knew better than that.

Their tongues, curiously unpractised after so long a separation, were soon loosened over tea. He got all the news of the village, from births and deaths to the full story of the great Home Guard exercise, in which Sergeant Benison, assisted by the rest of the Morwen Hoe platoon, had successfully invaded Sheel. Little imperceptible cords of familiarity wound about him, drawing him back to his own. Only afterwards, in the end of the evening, when the twilight gathered over Caldington like a lavender veil, did the world expand again to contain all the alien things he had found to be in it.

He had meant to go along with his father to one of the locals, and have a pint and maybe a game of darts, but they had talked so long and so hard that it was closing time before they knew; so he took Sue for a last run, instead, out of town by the bridge over the railway, and across the meadows and back by the level crossing. He wanted quietness and air and the night; and they wanted to talk him over between them, as he very well knew, to say: "Did you notice this?" and "He'll soon get over that!" and "What are we going to do about the other?" He could hardly hope to fall back into his old setting right away without a few adjustments. They would not, he thought, find it strange that he could not bring himself to talk about Tommy just yet; but what would they make of it that he had not once asked after Delia? He had asked her, before he went away, to see them now and then, and had told them casually that he was engaged to her; but he had never taken her home. There had been so little time. Perhaps they hadn't fully realised how bent he was on having her, and therefore took it for granted that the flood of events had washed her clean out of his mind. Well, that was one thing he would get straightened out this time, once for all. To-morrow morning he would go away quietly to Morwen Hoe, and get her, and bring her back with him. She'd come. She'd do anything for him. Hadn't he seen it in her face, that day when she saw him off by train as his leave ended? Hadn't he seen the awe in her so-confident blue eyes at the size of the feeling she had for him, and the strangeness? She'd done a lot for him already, if she only knew it, just by virtue of the clear way he remembered her; and what would not her brave body do for him, for his battered flesh and his wincing mind?

He walked out across the meadows in the deepening dusk, with Sue flashing like a slim dark arrow ahead of him. The sky was lofty and very clear, the soft pearl glimmer of the earliest stars limpid in the zenith, and Venus diamond-white above the last westward flash of the afterglow. The wind had died with the day; even the crests of the trees were motionless. The most profound silence distilled from the cool of the air like dew, hushing his steps in the grass, and his breath within his lips. In the fields of the Sheel Valley, going down from the Norman church, he had known such a peace once, before the war began.

Then suddenly out of the east a murmuring arose, distantly familiar, like music heard and recognised even through sleep. From the dim outskirts of the town searchlights unfolded themselves like the petals of a great primrose-coloured flower, and smoothed the stars away out of the polished lapis lazuli sky; and the silence seemed to lean down to the earth and dissolve into it like water as the thrumming crescendo of sound soared overhead, and the bombers passed by.

Jim stood still in the crown of the field, feeling the old quivering awareness go through his flesh like a chilling stream. He saw the night close again over the wake of the enemy, and heard the silence rise upright and shake out its draperies over the wound the sound of their flight had made. The trees, motionless and secure, were unaware of any stress; the hills did not cower, nor the stars, momentarily lost in light, veil themselves. He looked, and saw that in all that immensity of night only he, only man, was impermanent and afraid.

3

It was past one o'clock when he put his shoulder against the swing door of the "Clay Pigeon" next day, and walked into the bar. The room was full of workmen snatching a pint and a gossip and a game between shifts, and finishing, those of them who lived too far away to go home for lunch, their midday sandwiches. Some of them he knew, but more were strange to him. Even in six months the village was changed. He had seen his old home, a mound of raw new rubble in the wreckage of its garden, even its neighbour cottages split and ripped open by blast, and for ever uninhabitable. He should have known that nothing could survive unchanged. In the bar there were certainly faces he knew, though none of his oldest friends were there; and Joe was in and out from the snuggery in his baize apron, and Mrs. Joe, with her ample bosom propped upon the bar, was swopping stories—bomb stories, invasion stories, at any rate something momentous—with a middle-aged commercial traveller on his way into Caldington. But neither of them noticed him; and the barmaid, who turned impudent, attractive eyes upon him as he came to the bar, and cocked a round and dimpled chin, was not Delia. Six inches shorter, a primrose blonde with too much lipstick, and buxom shoulders, for that red-gold, blossoming goddess he had hoped to see.

She had two young soldiers already buzzing round her honey, burly youngsters in brand-new battle-dress, very professional, and innocent, and assured; but she spared a smile for the stranger, appraising him at a glance as she invited him, with that engaging tilt of her head, to name his fancy. He wasn't her fancy, exactly. Tall and straight enough, if he'd had any flesh on his bones; but he was in civvies, which in itself was damnation, and his face was yellowish-pale from weathering and sickness, and he had two queer white naked stripes in his close-cropped hair. She had never seen wounds, and did not recognise these for the work of machine-gun bullets. She knew only that they were ugly. She liked the two boys in uniform best.

"Any draught Bass?" asked Jim. He couldn't just march up to the bar and say: "Where's Delia?" though that was all that mattered in the world.

"No, sorry, it's right out. Got some nice old beer, though— or bitter, if you like it?"

"Pint of old, please!" And when she brought it, though she would have given him only the flash of her eyes and made off back to her embryo soldiers again, he made shift to keep her. How had he begun it with Delia? It was so long ago he could hardly remember. This time he pushed back the change she was skimming towards him, and smiled at her with his marred face, and said: "Will you do me a favour? Have something with me. Bad luck to have the first one by myself when I'm just home."

The girl was kind. She shook her head, but because she would not drink with him she felt bound to linger for a few minutes and talk. "Sorry, but I don't, not when I'm at work. Not very much ever, really. You live around here, do you? I don't remember ever seeing you in before, but there's so many I could easily have forgotten."

"I haven't been here for six months or so now."

"Oh," she said, "I haven't been here so long myself, not nearly. It isn't quite six weeks, even."

"What became of the girl who used to be here?" asked Jim, amazed at the unshaken level of his own voice.

"Who, the one with the red hair? She left. It was in her place I took the job on. You may meet her in the village any time—she's still living here." She looked back over her shoulder at the two boys, and signalled with a smile that she would come back to them gladly when she decently could. "She lives in that little rough-cast cottage back of the Sunday School," she added blithely, her mind very far from Delia Hall. "Roselea, they call it."

"I see," said Jim. Thanks! Thanks very much!" And he carried his beer to the quietest corner and finished it there, leaving her to slip back to her infant cavaliers with a last brilliant, withdrawing smile, as little interested in him as he was in her.

It was all right, after all. There'd been no need for that stab of horrid doubt at the sight of a stranger behind the bar. Delia was still in Morwen Hoe, even if she had changed jobs and moved to new lodgings. He wasn't particularly surprised at that, for she'd never really hit it off with the straight-laced old Perry woman; and the nice little spinster at Roselea would be the easiest person in the world to get on with, thinking and expecting, as she did, the best of everybody. But why had she left the "Clay Pigeon"? He'd always known she was too good for that sort of life, but that was a thing which had never worried Delia. She'd been happy, he could swear, surrounded with friends and admirers. Why had she given it up? What had happened six weeks ago, to make her withdraw herself from the place she had made so securely her own.

Then it came to him that for roughly so long had he been officially listed as missing, believed killed. No one had spoken to him of that time, no one at home ever would. Nothing which could call to mind old stresses and deprivations would ever be said; but if it had been hell for him and his parents, hadn't it been as bad for Delia? Was that why she could no longer bear to face the sympathy of friends and the cheerfulness of strangers, here in the "Clay Pigeon"? The thought of her in retreat, her confident eyes grown wary, her armour on, made him tremble. No word had passed between them since he was lost from his unit, first because there was no possible means of communication, and latterly because he had been so ill that he could not yet lift any duty, however dear, however vital. He had desired desperately to end his own purgatory, but he had extended hers. He was ashamed. The nurses had told him he had done well to live at all, and that but for the appalling need for beds he would never have been discharged so soon; but he forgot all that now. He remembered only that he had somehow, in the way of his nature and his moral sickness, lost sight of her distresses in his own. Easy enough to assume that his mother would have passed on any and all news of him during this last period when he was rediscovered living. Would she? Had she? Supposing Delia still believed him to be dead? Was it enough to have hurried to her like this on his first day of freedom, when he had not even sent her a single line to reassure her that he lived? How was a man to realise that he could be to his sweetheart as one dead six weeks, a mere richness in the French clay, under the feet of the conquerors? No one had pointed that out to him. No one had ever even said to him that he was officially missing. He had just come out of a darkness, slowly, and been greeted quietly, and treated as a sick man behaving after his kind. He had thought only: "I must get well. I must get strong, and go to her." Never: "I must let her know I'm all right, so that she needn't worry about me any more." He hadn't written to anyone. His mind was so stunned with the single wonder of being alive that trifles like letters did not exist for him as yet; and he had never, even in the old days, been much of a correspondent. But there was no excuse for him, none. A man ought to think of these things.

But it would be all right when they met. She would know how it had been with him. Nothing would have to be explained. She knew how his mind worked, how impossible it was that he should persuade his feeling for her into words. She would understand that he had lain still and dreamed of her, and done no more.

He finished his drink and went out quietly, and walked down through the village, wishing in his new and strange sensitivity to avoid notice rather than attract it; but he was several times recognised joyfully, so that his progress was punctuated with five-minute stops here and there for exclamation and enquiry. It was good to see his friends again, and to watch their faces light up at sight at him, and hear the warmth of their voices welcoming him home. Some of them had heard he was back, and counted on seeing him in the village sooner or later; some had had no news since late May, and could not persuade themselves he was real without handling him. All he wanted was to be left alone to reach Roselea by the quickest possible way, but it was ungracious to hurry away from such sincere kindness, and it was later than he had realised when he finally pushed open the white gate of the cottage garden. Suppose she had already finished dinner and gone back to her work, whatever it might be? Suppose he missed her? Certainly someone came hurrying along the diminutive hall when he rang the bell, but that would, of course, be old Miss Field.

But it was not Miss Field. The front door swung wide back to the very wall, as only the vigorous and candid open doors, and Delia stood looking at him across the threshold, Delia in a flowered chintz overall, stockingless, her arms pink and steaming, and her hair combed up into a tight top-knot of curls bursting ebullient from a green chiffon scarf, like a gold chrysanthemum opening. She was not made up at all, and her face was flushed and dewy and altogether lovely. The very sight of her went through his mind like a gust of Spring air scented with May, she looked so radiant.

He drew a deep breath, as if he could draw her into his being; and: "My oath, kid," he said, "you're just glorious."

Delia said nothing for the better part of a minute. Only she stood there with her hands spread either way against the wall, as she had halted in mid-flight at sight of him; she stood there with her fixed and flaring eyes upon his face, and her beautiful boisterous mouth dropped open, while all the colour ebbed from her face, and over her spontaneity there visibly settled a sort of frozen deliberation. "Jim!" she said, in a voice very thin and sharp and still, like brittle ice. "Oh, my God, this would have to happen!"

"What's the matter?" he asked in quick alarm, and made a step towards her into the house, but she as quickly stepped back from him. What's the matter with you? Can't I touch you now? What are you running away from?" But because of her eyes he did not follow her again.

She stared for a moment, her hand pressed against her mouth; and then she laughed, short and hard. "Yes, what? What have I got to complain about? I had it coming. I wish I knew what to do or say about it, but I don't, and that's the truth."

"Just for a start, why not ask me to come in? Whatever this is, we can't stand here and talk it over on the doorstep." He sounded to himself very reasonable and assured as he said it, but that wasn't how he felt. He was frightened. He couldn't understand why anything in the world should make her look at him like that, why she should step back from him when he made to touch her.

"Yes," she said, still in that thin, bitter voice, "I suppose you'd better come in. Not that you'll want or need to stay very long. Come into the parlour." And she turned and led the way, and for the length of the tiled hall, while her face was hidden, that lofty, long-stepping walk of hers caught him up again into the old joy in her; but when she faced him across the width of the parlour it was as if he looked at a different woman, older than Delia though like her, and sullen against some helplessness in herself where Delia had swooped grandly upon all circumstances and trodden them underfoot.

She closed the door, and leaned back against it. "Well, here we are! When you begin to want to shout you needn't even bother not to. Nobody else will hear you. There's no one else in the house."

"What's happened to Miss Field? Is she out?"

"Out? They didn't tell you much, did they? She's dead. What d'you suppose I'm doing here?"

"I thought you'd swopped lodgings, that's all. What's all this about?"

"It isn't so simple," she said. "Did they tell you anything at all? Did they tell you anything about me?"

"No," said Jim. "You're going to do that."

Her mouth jerked, the corners twisting in something between a grimace of pain and a laugh. "I suppose I am. That'll be nice for me, won't it? Well, it serves me right. I was determined to get something out of it; I've got no kick coming if I got more than I bargained for." She looked up suddenly, and caught the doubt and distress of his eyes; her hard smile quivered into warmth and gentleness. "It won't be any good saying I'm sorry, Jim, but I am, deep down sorry. I've been dreading this for over a week, ever since I heard you were back. This isn't the sort of welcome you expected."

"No," he said, "it isn't. So you did know I was back!"

"Oh, it gets around! What I can't understand is why you— why your mother——" She looked back at him as she remembered him, and frowned over the dizziness of change which had swept them so far out of their course. "Yes, I suppose it's all pretty simple, really. You didn't talk about me? To your mother, I mean? No, you wouldn't. You never did talk about anything more important than the football results. So she didn't say anything either. She was hoping you'd got over being fond of me, and gone on to something else. Then you wouldn't ever have bothered to find out about me. She didn't know you very well, did she? I could have told her you didn't let go as easy as all that."

"Stick to the point," said Jim. "What was there to find out —about you?"

Her voice rose wildly. "My God, man, do you have to be told in words of one syllable? Can't you see? What d'you think I'm doing in Roselea, with a week's washing on the line, and suds up to my elbows? Look at me! Do I look as if I was visiting? Look! Do you know a wedding ring when you see one?"

She lifted her left hand, and held it before his eyes; still crumpled and pink from the washing, and smelling of soap, the fingers rigidly spread, the new gold ring shining on her marriage finger. "That's what there was to find out. That's what she hoped she wouldn't have to tell you. That's what I hoped to God she or somebody would tell you, and keep you away from here." She paused; she was trembling, with impatience as well as wretchedness, goaded by his silence, frightened by the fixity of his stare. Why didn't he say something? Why didn't he shout at her, even hit her if he wanted to? She wouldn't have blamed him; and anyhow it would have been better than just standing there like stone, with his head drawn back as if she'd spat in his face, and his eyes staring at her hand like a rabbit at a snake. She couldn't look at him any longer. She swept her hand across her forehead, pushing back the green scarf, so that the moist gold curls fell down upon her neck and over her eyes, making a sweet-scented shadow across her face. "You were dead," she said in a dull, level voice. "They said so."

Jim asked: "Who is it?" Even his voice frightened her, it was so quiet and so heavy with effort.

"Sam Reddin."

He drew a hard breath, as if he had meant to laugh, and could not. "My God," he said, "you don't mean me to get conceited, do you?"

Her shoulders lifted. "I know you never liked him. But I did. And he was always around me."

"Yes—he would be! *Liked* him? Is that all it needs with you? Was that all it was for me?"

"You were dead," she said violently.

"When was it?"

"We've been married a month to-morrow."

"You didn't wait long, did you? Three weeks? It couldn't have been any longer."

"I hadn't heard from you since the beginning of May," she said simply. "When they said you were missing, believed killed, they were only saying what I knew already—or thought I knew. I know you can't see it my way. I don't expect you to. It wasn't me you wanted, it was somebody out of a fairy tale, somebody who'd go on being true to you all her life, even after you were dead. Well, it's too bad, that's all. I'm not that kind. I'm a woman; I want a home, and a husband I can live with, not a beautiful memory. You were gone, and Sam wanted me; and he was doing well, too, he could afford to keep a wife and family. And the house was going, and hundreds after it; I had to make up my mind quick. I'm sorry it's turned out this way, but if it happened all over again I should do the same."

"Still," said Jim, his insatiable stare never wavering from her face, "I should have thought it was rather too soon to be comfortable. In a village people talk so. They must have got quite a lot of fun out of that bit of gossip. Was it worth it?

Even to be settled for life?—with a nice safe husband making a good thing out of the war?"

Delia threw up her head suddenly, shaking back the rich shadows of her hair from a face blanched with unexpected anger. "Listen, you can call me all the dirty names you like, if it helps you any. I know how you feel. But since when did I do things or not do things to stop the neighbours' mouths? If I'd been ashamed of marrying him, I'd have thrown up the idea altogether, not postponed it for six months to make it look more decent. Surely you know me well enough for that?"

"Know you?" he said. "Much I ever knew of you!" It seemed to him that he had never really seen her until this moment. If she could do this to him, what had happened to the Delia he had once believed in, the golden creature who had met him at the gate on Christmas Eve, the one who had recoiled from Sam Reddin's clumsy kiss with the shining indignation of a Diana? What had happened to his cottage, and the roses, and those evenings by his own hearth in the world after the war? The whole structure of his life was crumpled in that flushed left hand of hers, and she was trying to tell him that she was honest and brave at least out of all the things he had believed her to be. Having stripped him and herself of all other illusions, how could she hope to keep him deceived in this last particular? She was no worse than the rest; the damage was that he had thought her better; but she would never now be able to cover her transparency again from him. He saw with desolate clearness how she had argued it out with her own conscience. There's a war on. Bombs have fallen already, and more will fall. Time's short. Better to make sure of Sam Reddin while he's still in the mood. The other one's gone, and a lot of the men you know are disappearing. You don't want to go on pulling beer for ever, or maybe get raked into some sort of war work you'll hate like poison. Hardly anyone will think anything about it. Hardly anyone knows you had Jim Benison's ring. He wouldn't talk about it, and you didn't. Even those who saw you about with him last winter won't think anything of it—they've seen you about with others since then. That was how it had gone; she didn't realise it herself, but he knew, by some clairvoyance of shock, just how she had reasoned herself into Roselea, and him into a limbo at the back of her mind.

"You're not even straight!" he said marvelling. "Look, Delia, will you tell me something? How long did you wear my ring after I went overseas? A week?"

Her moment of anger had ebbed uncertainly away. She had said that she was not ashamed, but she could not look at him full. "You're not fair to me," she said sullenly. "I wore it until May, and I swear that's the truth. Oh, Jim, I tell you I'm sorry, but it's done, and can't be undone."

"So you wore it till May! On your right hand, wasn't it? Wasn't it?"

If she had stood up and cursed him he could have borne it; but she put her hands over her face suddenly and began to cry, and that he could not bear. He turned away from her, and groped his way to the door through a void grey darkness, all his hurt, all his anger gathered into a single overwhelming desire to get away from her. And she, who should have been glad to see him go, launched herself after him with a despairing cry, and hanging upon his arm with all her weight tried to hold him back. Her hair, sweet and fine as silk, brushed his face. She panted against his cheek: "Oh, Jim, you can't go away like this. Don't hate me! Please don't! I couldn't help myself. It's bad for a barmaid to wear an engagement ring. I had it on a chain round my neck, but it meant the same to me, I swear it did. It was only afterwards, when they said you were dead—— If it hadn't been for that I wouldn't ever have looked at Sam, you must know I wouldn't. It was you I wanted, Jim, always you—nobody but you!"

He had stopped at the urging of her hands, because to persist would have been worse than all; but the face he turned on her was as chill as stone, with the bitter hint of a smile dragging at his mouth. He took her by the wrist and lifted her touch from him, not gently. She began to cry again, unbecomingly, without restraint.

"What's the matter with you?" he said indifferently. "You can't have it both ways. You wanted a husband you could live with. Well, you've got him. What more do you want?"

He left her there sobbing into her hands in a fury of anger and frustration and spite; for she wanted him. That was true, if all the rest was a lie. Sam Reddin was all right while Jim Benison was dead or out of sight, but not for a moment longer, it seemed; the best thing he could do for her or himself was to get out of sight again and stay out. It hadn't taken her long to find comfort for his departure before, and it need not take her long now. In a week she would have put him by.

He closed the garden gate after him, and walked back along the road by which he had come, with the sunshine upon his face.

and a strange, aimless coldness in his mind. Everything had changed, though everything looked the same. He did not know where he was going. There was nowhere he wanted to go, but he had to keep moving until the numbness passed and he was able to think again. He had no purpose, no impulsion at all. About him there was only a blankness, unpeopled by any companion. He had friends, yes; but he could not live solely for a casual contact or so over a pint in a pub. He wanted to get away even from himself, but that is a thing you can never do.

He went back to the "Clay Pigeon". There was nowhere else to go; no train home for over an hour, and nowhere he could hide himself except in the most populated place. This time Clye was in the snug, and Fred Blossom, and Joe and one or two more, all willing and anxious to buy him drinks. After the first three or four drinks the coldness at last receded, and left him in a blank physical comfort. That helped. The sharp clarity with which he saw her face, for ever upturned to him, became softened, the lines blurred, and the blue of her eyes receded into a mist. He knew he was getting drunk. It seemed to him an infinitely intelligent thing to do.

4

There wasn't time to do the job properly. He knew that. He could only hope to dull the razor edges of reality, and remove the world to a hazy distance where he could contemplate it without being blinded. There was no possibility of drinking himself into a coma before they closed, and in any case he had to get himself home somehow. He'd never yet left that job for someone else, and he wasn't going to start now. But at least he could withdraw himself into a warmed and indifferent state in which betrayal and loss and humiliation would matter less. Clye was yarning away nineteen to the dozen, so that all he had to do was put in the right monosyllable at intervals. He needn't even listen to what was said, if he didn't want to. So, at least, he thought for the first ten minutes or so, while they were still exclaiming and reminiscing, so voluble themselves that his silence passed unremarked; but in a little while the wrappings of talk, and beer, and hazy comfort began to wear thin, and his senses came into resentful play again. It was damned unfair. When he wanted to think clearly he couldn't, and when he wanted only to close his mind and lock it like a disused room

he couldn't stop thinking; thinking of Sam Reddin who had
made hay in his fields; thinking of Delia who had looked at
him, on parting, with that awed look of a snared demi-goddess,
and had yet put his ring out of sight for fear it should cramp
her style with the more racy customers; thinking of these well-
meaning, limited people who sat in saloon-bars winning and
losing campaigns over the table as lightly as they won and lost
games of dominoes, while A Company broke itself in bloody
pieces along the frontiers of France, and the brave were shot
down before the eyes of children for a bar of the "Marseillaise".

They were still at it. He supposed it had gone on all the
time, while he was away, this map-making across the snuggery
table, this smug rearranging of the past and settlement of the
future. He hated them all at that moment, not because they
theorised, but because even now it was a kind of game to them,
this thing which was life and death. They should have known
it by now, surely, after Dunkirk, after personal loss and the
shock of defeat, one little island standing alone against a con-
tinent, with a moat just twenty-one miles wide between them.
Nobody wanted them to be scared or discouraged; but they
could at least open their eyes like responsible creatures and take
a look at the facts. It did not at first occur to him that they
conceived they had done so. That had been his trouble
once. Hadn't he persisted to Miriam that he knew what he was
facing?

"There's plenty of folks in this country now," said Joe,
stubbing down the tobacco in the bowl of his pipe, "who thinks
we're beat. Only last week there was a bloke in here, some big pot
or other from Caldington, saying that you'd only got to look at
the figures of the case to see England hadn't got a dog's chance,
and had much better get what terms she could, before the position got worse. 'No need to venture into the higher strategy,'
he says, 'it's pure mathematics.' Lucky for him it was early in
the evening, and there was none o' my Home Guard lads in
the bar. Not that he got away with it, mind you. I'm a peaceful sort o' chap, but there's a limit. 'After the way we've been
let down right and left,' I says, 'by the Dutch, and the Belgians,
and the Poles, and the French, seems to me it's a good thing
to be on our own at last. We know where we stand now.
Nobody else can let us down now.' "

"There's something in that," agreed Clye thoughtfully.
"They all went down like ninepins, when you come to think
of it. How long did Poland last? About three weeks, wasn't it?

And Holland was gone in five days, and Belgium didn't stick up much longer. And then France—— Well, there's only us now. Sure enough, nobody can open up our flanks, now. That was a dirty bit of work Leopold did, if you like!"

Dirty? What right had they to talk that way, they who hadn't seen the villages behind the Dyle, and the broken Flemish soldiers coming back through the lines, sleeping as they walked? If anybody could afford to rise up and curse, it was the battalions who had suffered by that disintegration; but he doubted if they would ever speak. And as for betrayals of country by country, that wasn't the whole trouble. Everywhere there had been a crazy reluctance to examine responsibility, and a flat refusal to lift it. There was no realism. They took the facts, and held them carefully so that only that facet showed which bore out their crazy theories. Anything to save the trouble and pain of thinking.

"After all," said Joe comfortably, "there's nothing new in us starting with a bad reverse. We did the same last time, at Mons. I'll never forget that walk back, not as long as I live. Here was us, d'you see—just contacting the Huns about here——" And he was off again, drawing more maps of last war's fighting retreat; they must all be alike to him.

"Have another, Jim?" said Fred Blossom, emptying his pint.

"This one's mine. Time I got one in, anyhow."

"Oh, well—it ought to be our call to-day—your first time back from France, and all that, you know."

The commercial traveller, who was sitting at a corner table eating some sandwiches Mrs. Joe had made him, looked up with new interest. "Oh, were you at Dunkirk? Must have been a hell of an experience, that."

"Very likely," said Jim. "I wasn't there. I made the trip since Dunkirk."

"Oh? How was that?"

"In a boat, from a little place south of Boulogne."

"Makes it sound easy, doesn't he?" said the traveller, good-humouredly. "You don't talk much, do you?"

"No, I don't. Not unless I've got something to say."

"Very wise, too." He lifted his tankard cheerily. "Skin off your nose!"

Even the beer wasn't what it should have been, though, or Jim wouldn't have been caring by now what they said or how they looked at things, even if he was still capable of hearing.

"What I want to know," said Clye, "is what happens next. Think they will try and invade?"

Joe came back from St. Quentin with aplomb, before anyone else could appropriate his role of general adviser. "Invade? Certain sure they will. They'd be fools not to."

"Must look like a heaven-sent opportunity to them, I suppose. Think they'll get anywhere?"

"Will they, my foot! I've fought Germans before. They won't stand up to a concentrated defence like we've got in these islands now. Look at the numbers of armed men there must be here—more than there's ever been in such a small place in the whole of history, I should think. And there's the Navy and the Air Force to reckon with before they can ever make a landing. No,—the Germans never had no relish for Britishers in close fighting—not unless the weight was on their side about twenty to one."

Jim wanted to get up then and say that it was a lie, but it didn't seem to matter enough. He knew how the Germans could fight. Why not admit it, they fought with as little regard for danger as their opponents, and a more single, more coherent purpose. It was people like Joe who had sent the kids out to fight convinced of their invincibility, instead of teaching them how to be invincible.

"They didn't do so bad against Britishers in Flanders," said Clye, the one realist among them.

"That was different. Look at the position our allies put us in. There was the Belgian collapse on our left flank, and the French break-through at Sedan down on our right. What chance did our lads have? Granted they were newish at the job, and never had much practice, but still it never came to a showdown. Now in 1914——"

In 1914! Did he think there was any parallel, or was it that he didn't realise the world had moved at all in the last twenty-six years?

"Mind you," said the traveller weightily, leaning forward from his corner to tap an emphasising finger into the middle of their table, "it wasn't all so marvellous with our own performance, by some accounts. You hear tales. I was told by our man who works the Dover district that a lot of young fellows came back from Dunkirk minus their rifles—*minus* their rifles, mark you—but with their pockets and their packs full of French cigarettes and tobacco. That's a fact, mind. Our man had it from a tradesman in business at Deal, and he had it from an

272

R.N.V.R. man who was helping with the disembarkation. So you can take that as solid fact."

"I dunno," said Fred, "there may have been a few. After all, wherever you get thirty thousand or so young men together you're bound to get a mixed bag. I wouldn't judge one way or another from one tale. Anyhow, seems to me they had no chance at all in Belgium once the French let the Nazis through in the east. I never did like the French. Something shifty about 'em—unreliable."

"Well, if they let us down," said Clye, pushing away his empty tankard, "all I can say is they're paying for it pretty hard now, poor devils."

"Not as hard as you might suppose," said the traveller, mysteriously. "You don't want to swallow all those atrocity stories you always get in war-time, especially from occupied countries. Make fifty per cent cut for propaganda, and you may be somewhere near the truth. Oh, we use propaganda ourselves, you know—every bit as much as the Nazis do. Naturally nobody wants their country over-run; it means shortage of all supplies, of course, because they have to support the occupying force; it means comparative poverty, for a period at least, because of inflation; and it means oppressive restrictions for security's sake. But that's all in the nature of things. But the fancy frills—all those shootings and maimings and massacres—forget it! Now I happen to know——" The finger prodded again, tapping the table for a moment to ensure that he had all their attention. He tapped for a fraction of a second too long.

Jim's chair shrieked backward across the tiles of the floor. He heaved forward and crashed his fist down upon the table with a force that made the glasses leap and shiver. "That lets me out!" he said, breathing hard between his teeth. "That finishes it. I can just about stand having the Poles and the Belgians and the French blamed for what happened to us. I can sit and listen to you tell one another how unbeatable the British are, and how feeble everyone else is, and still keep my mouth shut. I can even bear it when you decide between you that if there was a weakness in the English case it was in us—us who did the fighting. I can stand a lot. But when it comes to sitting here while you come to the conclusion Hitler's bloody well doing France a favour by tearing it to pieces, and all the natives who complain of him are just plain liars—well, that's the finish. I pass!"

He knew he'd made a mess of it. He was too drunk to keep
quiet as his past custom was, and let them have it their own
way; and not drunk enough to keep quiet because he was past
caring. He had to talk, he who never talked; he simply
couldn't keep his mouth shut. But he wasn't doing it right. It
carries more weight if you say what you have to say calmly,
instead of spitting the words out like a man strangling with
anger and grief. The trouble was that he was too drunk to do
it that way. For the moment he had so blinded himself that
he could see them only as so many formless white faces in a
red haze, but he knew by the appalled silence how they were
staring at him, with astonished eyes and mouths fallen slack.
None of them tried to interrupt him.

"You none of you know what you're talking about," he said,
swaying forward on his spread hands. "That's been the trouble
from the start with this country, yes, and all the others for that
matter. If we'd taken the trouble to find out what was really
going on there needn't have been any war. If we'd even learned
quickly we needn't have come back from Brussels with our tails
between our legs. But no—it was too much trouble to find out,
and too uncomfortable to be in the know. It was easier to sit
by the fire and make it up as we went along, the way you're
doing now. That's why we're in this infernal mess. 1914! This
is 1940, not 1914! If you think there's no difference you're
bloody crazy. You and your sneers at the Poles! They fought
as long as we did, with a frontier as flat as your hand, and next
to no weapons—yes, and certain from the start they hadn't a
dog's chance of survival, but that didn't stop 'em. And what
right have you got to run the Belgians down? Do you know
what they went through? Do you know what sort of show you'd
have made in their shoes? Then shut your mouths till you do.

"And as for you——" He saw the traveller's face clearly
for a moment, ludicrously offended, too staggered for speech.
"You know all about the way the Nazis run their occupation,
do you? You happen to know! You've been there, I suppose?
You've seen 'em for yourself, the way they go to work? Well,
if you haven't, I have. I've seen the way they treated the
French after they conquered 'em. I've been in a village where
they shot the schoolmaster dead in front of a class-room full of
kids because he played the 'Marseillaise'. I've been in a house
in the same village when they went through it systematically
and stole every single thing that was worth taking. They shot
dogs just for fun, and when I got away there was a man under

arrest for hiding his wireless set when they were rounding 'em up. And I've seen the way they fight, too. Don't kid yourselves, they do fight. I don't like the way they do it, but they can fight all right. It's about the dirtiest, bloodiest process I've ever seen, but it works. You think they're round about half as black as they're painted? Listen to a few of the things I've seen 'em do! *Seen* 'em! Not heard of a chap who knows another chap who says he's seen 'em. I've seen kids coming out of a Flemish school machine-gunned and dive-bombed—nothing else on the road they could be aiming at, mind you. I've seen 'em come back and make another run to get the one they missed. Every day we saw refugees dive-bombed—that was the commonplace in Belgium, they did it to block the roads for us. But nothing blocked the roads for them. I've seen their tanks machine-gun the road ahead packed with old people and women and kids, and then dive along it full speed. I've seen one of those main roads after they'd been over it—even what bits of the road were visible you couldn't walk on without being sick. Oh, yes, it's all propaganda! We do it, as well as the other side. What about the wounded they drove over—deliberately? I saw the tracks, remember, but I suppose that was just something I dreamed? What about the convent school they bombed to pieces south of Tournai? What about the woman I saw them hunt along a road near the French border, and kill? She couldn't run very well, she was seven months gone with child. How do you account for her? I suppose I imagined her, or read of her somewhere? Because it's all propaganda, you know. Things like that don't happen. Don't you realise it's only because you live on an island that they aren't happening here? You and your theories and us and our guns couldn't have stopped 'em at Boulogne. The sea did that for us. But for God's sake get it into your heads that we're in this with the unlucky devils who haven't got any sea between them and the Germans. You happen to know? I wish you did. I wish you had to remember a few of the things I've seen. I wish you had to live with the things I've got to live with——"

It was not the queer, steady staring of their eyes, suddenly clear through the dissolving mist of his passion, that snapped his voice off there. It was not the quality of their regard, inquisitive and distressed and sympathetic, concerned for him rather than offended for themselves. All those careful, opaque, humouring glances converging on him, pitying him, openly saying: "Poor chap! They get like that from shock. He isn't long out of hospital." But these he did not see. He saw only the things he had to live with. He, not these. He couldn't hand them on, he couldn't share them. Never again could he make the attempt, drunk or sober. Out of the darkness they returned, all those pitiful ghosts he had tried to banish, and refuged in his mind. There was no Delia now to keep them from the door, no dreams of the future to shoulder them out. He had conjured them to enlighten a company of the uninitiated, but it was upon him they came crowding and crying. Only he saw them; only he had to live with them. How could he have believed he could show them to other people, make for them visible bodies of words when they were beyond all words? No, they belonged to him. He felt them pressing into him, indissolubly linking themselves with his spirit, feeding upon his substance. He had to live with them. He was haunted.

No one said anything. It was all infernally embarrassing. They couldn't just sail right off the subject and start talking about the weather, it was too obvious; and no one could think of anything else sufficiently soothing. They didn't want to excite him any further. Poor old Jim, who'd have thought he'd have taken it as badly as all that? He must have been desperately ill to end up in such a state of quivering hysteria. They were very much relieved when he drew back from the table like a spring recoiling, and turned and walked out of the place. No one followed him. He was steady enough on his pins, and they didn't think he'd like it if he found someone trailing him.

Jim walked out from the porch of the "Clay Pigeon" very firmly, very carefully and away down the road, past the school, along the lane by the rear wall of the churchyard, towards Sheel Magna and the railway station. He met people he should have known, and recognised none of them. The sun was warm on his uncovered head and scarred neck, but he did not feel it. He did not see the red campions under the hedges, nor the tangled rose-briars articulate with buds, nor the little whirls of dust that rose before him from the cart-ruts and danced in the breeze. He did not notice the girl who came walking briskly out of the back gate of the vicarage garden, until he had cannoned into her and knocked the books from under her arm. Then, starting out of his trance, with a muttered apology, he stooped to pick up the books, but the girl took him by the shoulders suddenly in small, brown hands, and held him so, and: "Jim!" she said, "Oh, Jim!"

There was so much joy in it that he was brought up short, as if by a half-familiar tune suddenly heard again and found to be more beautiful than he had thought it. And here it was only young Imogen Threlfall, the very same goblin he had left behind at Christmas, though he felt as if a century or so had rolled over them both since then. She was a little thinner, perhaps, a little paler, and for once she wore a hat and stockings; but the only other change in her was in the way she greeted him. She must have heard, like the rest of those who knew him, that he was dead or prisoner; but who would have thought she could feel so badly about it? She held on to him hard with her sharp, thin little fingers, shaking him gently to reassure herself he was solid; and her face, which she had to tilt far back to look up at him, was shining with a sort of astonished triumph, a child's delight at a gift and a woman's delight in a conquest rolled into one.

"Oh, Jim, you *are* a ghost! Oh, I can't believe it! It's too good to be true." But by the glow of her eyes, dark as pansies, she could and did believe it, she had believed it obstinately all along, against the evidence, against the possibilities.

"It's true, all right," he said slowly smiling down at her. "Easy on that left arm, kid, it's still a bit tender. Oh, not as bad as all that! It was a clean break, it healed like mad. It's just a bit funny to the touch, that's all."

"Oh, Jim, it's nice to see you again! I thought—they said—— Are you really all right?"

"Yes, I'm really all right. A bit chipped here and there, but still in working order. Didn't they tell you I was back?"

"But I haven't seen anybody. I'm not living in Caldington now, you know. I'm working in London. Oh, but of course you didn't know," she said with a queer little sighing laugh. "It's been so long."

Jim picked up her books, and tucked them under his arm. "Coming my way? If you're catching the train back to Caldington you can talk all the way, but I think we ought to keep moving."

"Oh, yes, there's so much to say." She put her hand within his arm, her touch feather-light because of his warning. They stepped out together along the lane, he shortening his step to time with hers. Under the brim of her linen hat he could just see the curve of her cheek, and the thick dark lashes brushing it.

"So you're working in London now? How's that? I thought you were going to settle down in Caldington for the duration."

"Well, I did intend to, but after Dad went I wanted to get right away, so I got this job in London as an ambulance attendant, because of my First Aid. It's full-time, you know. I get home now and again. I've only got three days this time, but I wanted to come over and see Mrs. Ridley. You know she's lost her boy?"

"Yes," said Jim. "I know." He still could not speak of that loss.

"He was a great kid, Brian."

"Yes," said Jim, "Brian was all right."

"She's always been very kind to me. I felt I had to come. Not that it does any good, really, but you know how it is. She wrote to me after we heard about Dad." She felt the question he hesitated to ask, and looked up at him suddenly with her deep blue glance. "Didn't you hear? But, of course, you couldn't. He was killed at Dunkirk."

"I see," said Jim slowly. "I'm sorry, kid."

"You can't afford to be sorry," she said firmly. "It's happening to everybody. You don't like to make a lot of fuss about your own bits of trouble, when there's so many others. Besides, since they started bombing I've seen some of the others —the ones that aren't killed. I'd rather be dead, myself. At least," she added carefully, "I honestly believe I would. I've thought about it a good deal, but you can't be sure about these things." A big sigh lifted and shook her like the rise of a wave. "Not that all the thinking will make any difference. You just have to take what comes."

Well, that was her secret, at any rate. She'd taken it, straight between the eyes. However she might be able to reason about it now, she'd been hit all right. He knew enough of her to be sure of that. It was clear to him, too, that she had found in herself, when the moment came, an inexhaustible fund of this strange kind of strength, as elemental and unconsidering as the persistence of a tree upon westerly cliffs where the gales batter it. As often as she was felled she would recover herself and go on, because that was the way she was made, without conscious heroism, without romantic satisfaction, simply responding to the impulse of her nature. As a kid she'd had the root of it in her. When she'd tumbled, and broken her knees, she hadn't been

278

too proud to cry, but her tears had been brief and practical; she hadn't frowned away sympathy and praise, but only negatived them with that faintly derisive, unwavering stare of hers, which pierced clean through all exaggerations and excesses. Patronising grown-ups, willing at first glance to gush over her dimpled face and dark curls, had recoiled from that blue stare with half-superstitious uneasiness. She had not been popular with them, nor tolerant of them. More like a boy than a girl, they had found her. So she was, now as then; this very stubbornness of honesty which found all the inoffensive little shams of humanity suspect was a masculine quality, even if the uncomfortable clairvoyance resulting from it was a woman's peculiar strength. She was a queer kid. She always had been a queer kid, one you couldn't pet, even when she was hurt. He knew how she felt. He had been pretty badly hurt himself.

"Yes," he said, "that's about it." You have to take what comes and let go what goes. It's simple enough. But though his voice was carefully cool, he resettled her arm in his so that their fingers interlaced and clung; and something, some last fold of darkness, was lifted from him, because he was not alone. Queer he'd not felt that with anyone else. Sympathy was nothing; fellow feeling was not enough, nor bereavement, nor injury. There had to be this patient, pauseless, unquestioning acceptance of the burden of the world. An acceptance very far from blind, and entirely deliberate. Bomb or no bomb, Home Guard or no Home Guard, he hadn't felt that his parents were in this war; but he knew that the war belonged to Imogen.

"You'll have heard about Tommy Goolden," he said.

"Yes, I heard. Not much—just that he was killed." And she didn't ask any questions, or even feel like asking any; that was why he wanted to tell her. That, and perhaps a little of this urge to talk came quite simply from the fact that he wasn't as sober as he would have liked; not so far from it, not far enough now to dull the edges of perception, even, but still his control was marred.

"It isn't as if he'd copped it fighting," he said. "If he had I wouldn't mind so much. You expect men to get killed in a war. You're prepared for it. But when you've gone through hell with a bloke like I had with him, and then some dirty German murderer comes down on you when you're past doing him any harm, and shoots the living daylights out of your pal just from sheer lightness of heart—no, you can't put it by you so easily then. Not when you're grovelling in three inches of water in a disabled boat, and you hear the devils coming back to finish you, and you can't do anything about it—no, nor when you have to sit by your pal and hold on to him while he dies, and you can't do anything about that, either. We knew we might get blown to pieces in action, but we didn't know it would be worth while to shoot up three miserable little unarmed men in a fishing boat in the middle of the Channel, where they couldn't raise a hand to help themselves. You live and learn. I tell you, kid, I've learned plenty."

"But you did fight," said Imogen, in the small, cool, hard voice which reminded him somehow of that stage in the world's pre-historic past when the molten matter of earth shrank and congealed into rock. Just so had the granite crust covered the fires within, and the granite chill closed over the primeval heat at the earth's heart. Imogen would not shout nor burn again. She had been whirled at speed through that period of transition when the contours of character cool and harden into shape. It should have taken years; she had lived through it in six months. It was that way with those who had been caught in the current. Once you lost your feet in the flow of that river you were changed, you became an Ishmael for whom there was no rest this side of victory. The others, those who paddled about unsuspectingly in the edge of the torrent, they were not changed. Hadn't he seen them? Hadn't he tried to tell them what the abyss was like, and hadn't they looked at him pityingly for it, as at one who had lost his balance and his sense of proportion from too much suffering? But how had young Imogen been drawn into the darkness with the initiates? Could the mere loss of a father, safely out of her sight and knowledge, do this to her? "Anyhow, you did fight," she said.

"Yes, we fought. That made it seem worse than ever. After all he'd lived through, all the hand-to-hand battles on the Dyle, and the business on the ridge when all the rest of the company went west, and after that pneumonia, and the Gestapo hunting us—and all to end up like that, when we were all but in sight of England. Don't tell me how we fought!"

"The ones I've seen didn't even have that much satisfaction," said Imogen. "They were never in a position to hit back at all. Your bad time in the boat—it's like that all the time with them. All the time they're exposed and helpless, and just have to stick it out as best they can. That isn't anything new to me."

Shaken beyond measure, he said: "Yes—I never thought of

that. You must have seen it, too. Here, they don't know the war's even begun, much less what sort of a war it is, but *you* must have seen the things it does. You've been in London all the while they've been bombing—and in an ambulance there isn't much you don't see——'' It was horrible to him that she should know so intimately what he dared hardly remember; and yet again his own loneliness was diminished, because someone else was sleepless in the dark.

"No," said Imogen clearly, "there isn't much you don't see. I've seen more than I ever knew I would, and gone on working after it. There wasn't anything else to do, you see, and some-body had to get on with the work. We had one of the other ambulances from my station hit in the street once; there were four casualties in it when the bomb hit it, and the attendant. We were first there. All the time we were trying to get the attendant out of the mess I was thinking: 'This could have been me.' She was alive, too. There were splinters of metal driven right into her, and her face was—it was—almost crushed—but she kept on living for nearly twenty-four hours after that. You wouldn't think it possible, would you? And one of the people she'd had aboard was a little boy. He—he kept screaming—he was only seven——'' Her voice did not break, but only faded and ceased, as if she had come to the end of the usefulness of speech.

He said: "Yes. Yes—I see—I'm not telling you anything you don't know." And he looked down at the steady, consider ing profile of her face, and wondered if this was the same Imogen he had known; but in his heart he was in no doubt of it, for the change in her was bewildering only because of the speed with which it had been accomplished. And was not he trans-muted?

"I don't know about that," said Imogen sombrely. "It's different for you. Mine's bad; but after all, the people who're killed here in raids die among their own folks, with nothing but kindness and concern round them, however horrible the pain may be. But the ones you've seen in France—not just the ones who were bombed, but those who had to live among the Ger-mans afterwards—that's different, that's worse. To have to be hurt and hated, too—to be surrounded, by cruelty, and sus-picion, and violence, and malice—that's much worse. The one," she said strangely, frowning in the effort to find the just phrase, "is a crime against the body, but the other is a crime against the mind and the soul as well."

How did she know so much? She'd never been there, never seen the humiliation of man, or the spoiling of cities, or the exploitation of power for sadistic pleasure. How did she know what he had learned with so much amazement and dismay?

"You're a queer kid," he said involuntarily.

"Am I?" She looked up with a wry little smile. "You always thought so, didn't you? It used to make me mad that I didn't even count as a person with you—just a queer kid."

"That's changed, anyhow," said Jim, not troubling to deny that it had been true.

"Yes. You're changed, too, you know."

Yes, he knew. Miriam had said it to him, and in her mouth it had been a strange sadness; but Imogen said it with a wondering, warm interest, as if she hoped much from the development she witnessed in him.

"Only this looks the same," she said, and with her small sunburned hands sketched upon the air the contours of the Midshire hills before them, and the green and silver Sheel threading its way through the meadows. They had reached the curve of the lane, and the first outlying cottages of Sheel Magna sat among flowering hedges of honeysuckle and wild rose on their right hand, and on their left, at the foot of the winding slope, was the railway station, fast asleep between the lane and the river sallows. There were aeroplanes in the sky overhead, circling in the eye of the sun; and far up the valley the smoke of a train blew back in a thin straight pencil-line between the hills; but these disappeared into the drowsy, shining afternoon as motes of dust into the sea, leaving the magical tranquillity unscarred. The Sheel valley had outlived a great many wars and illimitable sorrows, and the pattern of its patchwork of fields, green and fawn and gold and darker green, silver of willows and amber and jade of hazels, sunlight of gorse and sapphire of scabious, had not been withered nor changed. It seemed a long while since he had seen it, much longer than the six months he knew it to be; and something in him ached as he looked at what had been his world, as if the heart of him would have gone back if it could, and struck its roots deep into this enchanted earth, and never again relinquished that hold. But he knew it was rather the aching of the stump of a limb, beyond restoration, and without cure until time saw fit to put an end to it by numbing all sensation. No one who knew what he knew could ever come back and resign himself to this quiet heaven until the war was over, though his heart was sick for it. He looked at Imogen as they went down the hill, and he knew that there was another exile.

"And this is only the beginning of it," he said suddenly.

"I suppose so. It's bound to be a long business, now."

"You sound so calm about it," said Jim, marvelling that she could tell over without a word of bitterness the count of her stolen years; for he knew that she saw it as he did, as a long and arduous banishment.

"What's the use of making a fuss? That won't alter it. I've got to put up with it, I may as well do it gracefully." Her fingers pressed his arm. "Look, the train's coming in. I thought we were dawdling along a bit too hopefully. Let's run! Can you run?"

"Can I run! You saucy little imp, I'll show you if I can run." And he caught her by the hand as she withdrew her arm from his, and towed her along the lane at a fierce speed, though his side ached at the sudden strain, and his head was queerly light. He felt that she could have shaken him off and passed him had she wished, but instead she maintained her place just at his elbow, laughing as she ran, and it was good to hear her laugh, even if that, too, was in some measure changed. Their feet rang upon the sun-gilded bricks of the platform just as the train came in, and they climbed into an empty third-class compartment and sat down in opposite corners to recover their breath. The laughter was over. Walking together down a lane, you can look ahead into the sunny sky and talk without considering each other, but sitting face to face in a narrow railway carriage you cannot choose but study each other stare for stare.

In her pale face, somewhat flushed now from running, a richer, darker colour began to gleam and hide and gleam again, and the blue of her eyes was dark and deep as the blue of the midnight sky between the stars. He felt her glance pass slowly, slowly over the wrinkled white furrows in his hair, and the hollow lines of his cheeks, and linger long upon the drawn scar across his neck, which was still russet-red and very unsightly. She drew a long, quiet breath, not of horror, for she had seen worse things by far than these, but of gratitude that he had lived to show them, and she to see.

"How long have you got?" she asked abruptly. "I mean, before you report at the depôt again?"

"Fourteen days."

"It isn't nearly long enough. You won't be fit."

"No, I expect I'll get another seven on top, but I may not.

283

They'll give me a soft job for a month or two, I expect, playing around the depôt."

"And then?"

"Then off again somewhere. Most likely buried alive somewhere with a new battalion scratched up from the raw kids just coming on military age. Some muddy camp miles from anywhere for the duration."

"But they'll want you for something better than that, you people who've been in the front line already. I bet you'll be off abroad again as soon as you're really fit to go."

"Abroad!" said Jim bitterly. "Where is there to send us? We're pushed out of Belgium and France, and we're pushed out of Norway. Where is there for us to go?"

"Maybe we'll soon be back in France. You don't know. They may be planning another landing before the summer's out." She saw how he smiled, remembering the steel fist which had closed upon Boissy-en-Fougères, utterly efficient and pitiless, not soon to be unclenched. "Or there's Egypt—or Abyssinia —they're fighting there, according to the papers."

"I don't know," he said, shaking his head, "I don't know. I don't want to get shipped off east, miles away from the war. This is where the war is now, here in England, and you and your people are deeper in it than I'm ever likely to be. And yet I don't want to stay here. It's too near home, it reminds me too much." No, anything but that—to stay in Midshire, and come home now and again for a week-end, and see his father playing at soldiers up and down the Sheel Valley, and Delia—Delia Reddin—walking out on her husband's arm, with the sunlight brave on her bright hair, and the blue of the sky in her conquering eyes—no, that was more than he could bear. If they didn't move him off pretty soon he'd ask for a transfer; he'd even tell them why he wanted to go. The chaplain— though in general he despised chaplains—might pull a wire or so for him. They were unexpectedly human about these personal issues.

The eyes of Imogen, steadfast upon him, drew his eyes. "You haven't missed much," she said, and it was one of the fiery utterances of the goblin who had teased him over the churchyard wall, falling strangely from the lips of the new Imogen. Nor had she any right, in the old incarnation or the new, to know so much of what went on in his mind that she could answer the flash of a thought so aptly or so angrily.

'You think not?" he said, fiercely quiet.

"I'm *sure* not," she said sturdily, "but I'm sorry I said it. I didn't mean to. Is that—where you've been to-day?" He did not answer, but she knew. "All right, I'm not asking any questions. It's nothing to do with me. Only—well, I knew how you felt about her; a lot of people don't seem to have realised, and she didn't wear your ring often enough for them to get the idea, so it wasn't the scandal it might have been. But *I* could have *killed* her," said Imogen vehemently, and abruptly turned her face to the window, and stared out blindly at the sorrely slopes of the cutting ambling by, and the rabbits sitting up gravely in the mouths of their burrows.

She was going back to London in a day or so, and he wouldn't see her again; and besides, she was caught into the same trammels with him, lonely in the same desolation. With life becoming so uncertain a thing, there was no time to be angry with her, no time to quarrel, no time even to stand by and let her shed furtive tears in the opposite corner if he could do anything to dry them. He reached over and took hold of her hands. "You silly kid! Here, look at me. I'm all right. I'm not tearing myself in pieces over her or anyone, and neither would you if you had any sense. That's just one of the things that happen, and you needn't be scared I shan't get over it, because human nature isn't given that way. You can get over anything. So stop smudging the windows, and put some more powder on your nose, quick, before we get into Caldington."

Imogen came out of her cloud, half-reassured, and half-cajoled against her judgment. She shook herself, and somewhat reluctantly smiled at him. "All right—I won't slander her any more—she's a paragon."

"She is not, and you know it. She's an ordinary, pretty, not very clever girl with both eyes on the main chance," he said, feeling for the words Imogen might have used of her, instead of giving utterance to what he himself felt. And indeed, what did he feel? Imogen at her fiercest, partisan to the back-bone, could not have hated and miscalled Delia as he had done; why, then could he not put her out of his mind? He supposed it all took time. You can't stop loving a person all in a moment, just because something happens to show you she's no good. It isn't as easy as that.

"So you do see her like that?" said Imogen, startled.

"She didn't give herself much chance to stay on any pedestal, did she? No, don't you worry about me, kid. It's liable to rankle for a bit, but I shall get over it all right. There are other

285

girls in the world, after all, and presently I'll be able to see 'em. In the meantime—well, there's plenty of jobs to be getting on with. I shan't have time to brood."

He thought, in the dark void of his mind, how black, how monstrous a lie it was; but she would believe it, and it would please her, since she seemed to care that he should not be un-happy. He was glad he'd seen her, though so briefly; he would always remember her with gratitude because she understood what had happened to him. It the darkness among the unrelent-ing ghosts, in that insatiable pain, he would never again be quite alone. Distance did not matter. He would not forget.

The train slowed into Caldington, and he leaned out and turned the handle of the door. "I'm going to walk up to your Uncle Jack's with you, kid, if you're not sick of my company by now. And—look, when do you go back to London? You won't leave without saying good-bye, will you?"

He turned to give her his hand then, and wondered what he had said or done to work such a magic upon her; for she was smiling with an unguarded joy such as he had never seen in her face before, and her eyes seemed to fill all the shadowy space of the doorway with their quiet shining.

More Historical Fiction from Headline:

THE BROTHERS
OF GWYNEDD
QUARTET

EDITH PARGETER
WHO ALSO WRITES AS ELLIS PETERS

'A richly textured tapestry of medieval Wales'
Sunday Telegraph

The story of Llewelyn, first true Prince of Wales, is the history
of medieval Wales in dramatic and epic form.

Llewelyn's burning vision is of one Wales, united against the
threat of the English. But before he can achieve his dream, he
must first tackle enemies nearer home. All three of his
brothers hamper his efforts to create an independent state. The
best-loved of the three, David, brought up throughout his
childhood at the English court, restless, charming, torn
between two loyalties, is fated to be his brother's undoing.
Despite the support of his beloved wife Eleanor, Llewelyn finds
himself trapped in a situation where the only solution is his
own downfall and a tragic death . . .

Edith Pargeter writes:
'I have previously written historical novels in which Llewelyn
the Great and Owen Glendower appeared, and it struck me as a
great pity that virtually nothing had been written about the
second Llewelyn, who came between the two, and seems to me
a greater and more attractive personality than either, and a
fitting national hero.'

Here, for the first time in one volume, is the entire saga of
The Brothers of Gwynedd, including:
Sunrise in the West
The Dragon at Noonday
The Hounds of Sunset
Afterglow and Nightfall

'Strong in atmosphere and plot, grim and yet hopeful . . .
carved in weathered stone rather than in the sands of current
fashion' *Daily Telegraph*

HISTORICAL FICTION   0 7472 3267 9   £6.95

More Crime Fiction from Headline:

ELLIS PETERS

The author of the bestselling *Brother Cadfael* novels

DEATH TO THE LANDLORDS

'Another of her enjoyable India-based stories. Miss
Peters writes extremely well, and her vivid, loving
descriptions of the Indian scene are a delight'
Daily Telegraph

Landlords the world over are not the most popular
people, and there is little mourning when the
greedy, ruthless Mahendralal Bakhle is blown up in
his boat on the beautiful Periyar Lake. Suspicion
falls on the boat-boy who died with him, but
Dominic Felse, one of a party of young tourists
accidentally involved in the fatality, is not
convinced of the boy's guilt. And when they move
on it seems that the terror is still pursuing them.

Violence and death erupt yet again in the home of a
very different landowner, where Dominic and his
friends are guests, and follow them relentlessly
south to the very tip of India, where Dominic and
the Swami Premanathanand, a man of peace,
unravel a deadly Indian rope trick of hatred
and murder.

FICTION/CRIME   0 7472 3122 2   £2.99

ELLIS PETERS

The author of the bestselling *Brother Cadfael* novels

MOURNING RAGA

AN INDIAN WHODUNNIT

As a favour to his girlfriend Tossa's beautiful but erratic filmstar mother, Dominic Felse agrees to escort a teenage heiress back to her father in India. But travelling with the spoilt, precocious Anjli is no sinecure – and the task of delivering her to her family proves even less easy.

Dominic and Tossa find themselves embroiled in a mystery that swiftly and shockingly becomes a murder investigation. For behind the colourful, smiling mask of India that the tourist sees is another country – remote, mysterious – and often shatteringly brutal...

'Strongly plotted story of kidnapping and murder in a well-observed Delhi. Exciting and humane.'
H. R. F. Keating, The Times

FICTION/CRIME   0 7472 3121 4   £2.50

More Compelling Fiction from Headline:

CHRISTINE THOMAS

Bridie O'Neill is just sixteen years old when her beloved
mother dies, leaving her in charge of the family. Mad
with drink and grief, her father shamefully abuses his
eldest daughter, who flees her Irish home for safety in
England. Helped by her parish priest she finds refuge as
housemaid to Francis Holmes, a kindly widower doctor
who fights disease and poverty in London's East End.

The glowing red curls and sweet ways of his Irish maid
touch Francis's heart and gradually their relationship
deepens into more than that of master and servant. But
just as security and contentment seem assured, the
shadows of Bridie's past return to haunt her and she is
forced to be self reliant once more. The slums of Plaistow
in the 1920s are no easy place for a woman alone and
Bridie chooses an unconventional way to support herself
and her small son – as a money lender. Gradually she
becomes a familiar figure in the mean streets, her money
belt strapped tightly around her waist, and is much
respected for her kindly firmness and honest dealings.
And at last, love, too, comes Bridie's way from a rather
unexpected quarter . . .

Full of authentic detail of East End life in the early days
of the twentieth century, and introducing a spirited and
appealing heroine, BRIDIE is sure to please all fans of
Beryl Kingston and Lena Kennedy.

FICTION/GENERAL   0 7472 3246 6   £3.50

DAUGHTER OF LIR

D I A N A
N O R M A N

author of TERRIBLE BEAUTY

Although she's been raised in the richest, most sophisticated convent in twelfth-century France, Finola is Irish, and because of that the Pope sends her to take charge of the powerful Abbey of Kildare.

But her French upbringing is in opposition to the complex, political power struggle of the clans around her, and one prince especially becomes her enemy – Dermot of Leinster. Within months she is an outcast – to be rid of her, Dermot has had her raped, and she has been publicly humiliated by her Church.

All she has left is the desire for revenge. With the help of an English knight, she finds her way to her birthplace in western Ireland where an academy of warrior women teaches her to fight. In the process she gains friends and a love of her country; though Ireland is in danger of invasion by the Normans.

By building her own network of spies Finola opposes Dermot, the Normans and the machinations of King Henry II's spymaster. But one of the lords she's fighting is the man she loves . . .

"A fast-paced read." *Best Magazine*
"Rich and entertaining." *The Times*
"A ripping historical yarn with much authentic detail."
                                          Publishers Weekly

FICTION/HISTORICAL   0 7472 3282 2   £3.99

A selection of bestsellers from Headline

FICTION

SUCCESSION	Andrew MacAllan	£4.50 ☐
DECLARED DEAD	John Francome &	
	James MacGregor	£3.50 ☐
WINNERS	Penelope Karageorge	£3.99 ☐
BRIDIE	Christine Thomas	£3.50 ☐
THE BROTHERS OF		
GWYNEDD QUARTET	Edith Pargeter	£6.95 ☐
DAUGHTER OF LIR	Diana Norman	£3.99 ☐

NON-FICTION

IT'S ONLY A MOVIE, INGRID	Alexander Walker	£4.99 ☐
THE NEW MURDERERS'	J H H Gaute &	
WHO'S WHO	Robin Odell	£4.99 ☐

SCIENCE FICTION AND FANTASY

SLAVES OF THE VOLCANO		
GOD		
Cineverse Cycle Book 1	Craig Shaw Gardner	£2.99 ☐
THE ARGONAUT AFFAIR		
Time Wars VII	Simon Hawke	£2.99 ☐
THE CRYSTAL SWORD	Adrienne	
	Martine-Barnes	£3.99 ☐
DRUID'S BLOOD	Esther Friesner	£3.50 ☐

All Headline books are available at your local bookshop or newsagent, or can be ordered direct from the publisher. Just tick the titles you want and fill in the form below. Prices and availability subject to change without notice.

Headline Book Publishing PLC, Cash Sales Department, PO Box 11, Falmouth, Cornwall, TR10 9EN, England.

Please enclose a cheque or postal order to the value of the cover price and allow the following for postage and packing:
UK: 60p for the first book, 25p for the second book and 15p for each additional book ordered up to a maximum charge of £1.90
BFPO: 60p for the first book, 25p for the second book and 15p per copy for the next seven books, thereafter 9p per book
OVERSEAS & EIRE: £1.25 for the first book, 75p for the second book and 28p for each subsequent book.

Name ....

Address ....

....

....